Winter Longing

Far From Home: A Scottish Time-Travel Romance, Volume 8

Rebecca Ruger

Published by Rebecca Ruger, 2024.

This is a work of fiction. Names, character, places, and incidents
are either a product of the author's imagination
are used fictitiously, and any resemblance to actual persons,
living or dead, events,
or locales is entirely coincidental.
Some creative license may have been taken
with exact dates and locations
to better serve the plot and pacing of the novel.

ISBN: 9798304417259
Winter Longing
All Rights Reserved.
Copyright © 2024 Rebecca Ruger
Written by Rebecca Ruger

All rights reserved. No part of this publication may be reproduced,
distributed or transmitted in any form or by any means,
or stored in a database or retrieval system,
without the prior written permission of the publisher.
Disclaimer: The material in this book is for mature audiences only
and may contain graphic content.
It is intended only for those aged 18 and older.

Chapter One

Buffalo, NY
2024

Cole ducked his head against the driving wind and crossed the street, thankful that the wind was not yet—or again—accompanied by snow. Ahead stood the Swan Street Diner, which was fronted by an old train car and boasted a long counter with red leather stools. Seating was limited, with five booths of the same red leather made just for two and only a handful more larger booths and tables, each of which would comfortably fit four. It was Aunt Rosie's favorite place for breakfast so even though snow was expected, and he'd offered to drive out of the city for their weekly breakfast, she'd opted to drive into Buffalo.

"If I can't drive in Buffalo snow by now, at sixty-one years old," she'd texted him yesterday, "I got no business driving at all."

Aunt Rosie was basically the only family Cole had left in Buffalo. His parents were both gone, he had no siblings, and he wasn't married. So it was just her—and she took that role seriously. Every week, no matter what, they had breakfast together after his shift at the firehouse. Fortunately, Aunt Rosie had retired early, so she could work around his consistent but unusual shift schedule. He worked a 24-hour shift on Day One of the week, which was Tuesday this week, followed by 24 hours off, then another 24-hour shift on Day Three—Thursday this week. After that, he'd get five days off before the cycle repeated. Since it was Friday, he was already done for the week, even though he'd only worked two days. But regardless of when his week ended, he and Aunt Rosie always met for breakfast after his second shift.

The wind tugged at the door of the diner as he opened it, but Cole's grip held firm. He stomped his boots on the black commercial rug just inside the entrance, knocking off snow that had fallen two days earlier. Running a hand through his hair, he tried to tame the mess the wind had made of it.

As he passed the counter, he gave a quick nod and half-smile to Kirsten, the long-time server who stared wide-eyed while she absently refilled salt and peppers. Cole's smile faded as soon as he moved out of her line of sight.

Kirsten had gushed over him, embarrassingly loud, when that ridiculous calendar came out a few months ago, causing Cole to instantly regret his participation. Buffalo's shirtless fireman calendar wasn't a new concept, but this was his first year in it. Combine that with adorable puppies from the rescue of the charity being supported—one of which he'd have adopted if his schedule wasn't so crazy—and it became the talk of the city for weeks. He'd been July's image, and thanks to his MVP status from the Buffalo Bandits' championship lacrosse season, his photo had made the rounds on TV and social media more than anyone else's.

He wasn't entirely comfortable with the attention. Not the constant ogling, at least. He'd be lying if he said his ego hadn't swelled a bit at first, but the novelty had worn off fast. Now, whenever women started fawning over him or if they simply stared overlong—*talking about you, Kirsten*—it was just awkward. And the guys at the firehouse, even those who'd taken part in the charity calendar themselves, would not let him forget it.

Aunt Rosie had already arrived—no surprise there. She had her back to him, but her smile was instant and wide as he showed himself, kissing her cheek before sliding into the booth across from her.

"There you are," she said. "Did you skate unnoticed by what's-her-name behind the counter or did she eat you alive again? That girl needs a man—not you, of course; she's not your type—but a man for sure."

Cole smiled. He loved his mother's sister. Aunt Rosie was practical, no-nonsense, and called it like she saw it. She always said what she meant and meant what she said. She didn't whine, rarely complained about people, and was never—ever—without a smile. And she had plenty of opinions about everything and everyone. Curiously, Cole never felt like she was judging anyone. Instead, it was more like she saw the solution to whatever their problem was—if only they'd had asked her or listened to her.

"Sally Shriner's walking like she's got one leg shorter than the other. Should've went to Dr. Philips for the hip replacement like I told her and not that butcher on the West Side."

"Pete Shaughnessy—remember him from high school? He married Tamara Barkley last weekend. Of course they don't call them shotgun weddings anymore, but that's what it was. I told his mother she would trap him, didn't I?"

"Father Rob says hello and goodbye. He's being transferred up to some church in Lewiston, so there goes that, the only priest I ever liked at Saint Barbara's and they're putting him out to pasture because he made some comment—totally blown out of proportion, mind you—about Connie Blecker's boobs. What? Like you never noticed them? C'mon, they're visible from the space shuttle for crying out loud."

Rosie was nothing if not entertaining. She knew everybody, from all different parts of Western New York and from all walks of life, and could have—Cole's mother had often said about her sister—'talked Christ off the cross.' She knew more than half the guys at the firehouse, having taught elementary school in the city for thirty years.

Coffee was already waiting for Cole, courtesy of Rosie.

"We'll have the usual, right Cole?" She said when Kirsten ambled over, cheeks ablaze while her gaze fixed almost too purposefully on Rosie. "The veggie benny for me and he'll have the regular eggs benedict. Side of bacon and a side order of pancakes for him, also." Rosie put her hand to the side of her mouth and said, in what Cole's mom used to call her 'sober Irish whisper', "He'd order himself but sometimes the Tourette's twitch is out of hand and clamping his lips really saves him tons of mortification."

Cole did clamp his lips, but only to keep from laughing. From the day Kirsten had begun her fangirling, Rosie had introduced a new disease, condition, or disorder each week, intending, she'd said, to dissuade the server from her crush.

A sneak peak at Kirsten before she skipped away with the menus showed her eyeing Cole with what looked like adoring pity.

Rosie shrugged. "Who knows? Maybe she's a glutton who loves a good project."

"Might be," Cole said, shaking his head and grinning. "And you've made me quite the project—Tourette syndrome now? An actual condition? On top of all the fictional ones you've invented for me?"

"Well, hell's bells. I thought for sure the mention of a chronic case of IBS would have turned her off for good. I couldn't think of anything else that wouldn't have killed you by now." Rosie leaned forward and giggled like a woman much younger. "She probably googled the shit out of Aphylactic Myelitis a few weeks back—I was certainly proud of that one."

"And Syndrome Xytoplasia," Cole reminded her, the only other fake ailment his aunt had used whose name he could remember.

"That was a good one, too" Rosie decided, beaming with pride.

"I'm surprised I can still work," he teased.

"Ah, but you're a trooper, not about to let a little rare genetic disease get you down."

"You're nuts, you know that?"

"Not yet, but I probably should lay off the sci-fi books for a while."

Cole and Aunt Rosie sipped their coffee and talked about the impending snow, they dissected the Buffalo Bills' game from last Sunday, and Cole updated Rosie on Jenna Volkosh, the wife of a firefighter who'd been struck by a vehicle several weeks ago and was still recovering, all before their breakfasts were served.

Rosie then launched into a predictable recitation of her schedule for the week, which had her going morning, noon, and night, mostly with church activities, lunch dates, and her regular volunteer duties at different churches, two libraries, one school, and the Friends of the Night soup kitchen. Retirement hadn't slowed her down. She had a sweatshirt that said, *Stop Me Before I Volunteer Again*. It basically summed up her life: service to others.

She'd never had children, and her husband was gone now more than twenty years. Marty Patronik had one day been painting their house when he stepped off the ladder, called into the house he was running out for cigarettes, and drove off, never to return. While Rosie had been devastated at first, numbed by pain and confusion, when six months later she'd received divorce papers from an attorney's office in Nevada, she'd gotten over it. "Took him long enough," she'd begun to joke then. "I don't know how many maps and glossy brochures of resorts on the other side of the country I'd left in his car before he got the hint."

All in all, she was exceptional. And honest to God, though Cole sometimes thought the hand he'd drawn in life sucked, that he lost his mom so young and then his dad when he'd just turned eighteen, that he had no siblings, and yeah, that he sometimes even at almost thirty years old felt like an orphan, he was grateful all the time to have Rosie in his life. If he was only to have this one person, she was perfect, filling every role admirably, generously, and most of all, happily.

"And what ever happened with that date with...ah—what was her name?" she asked when they were nearly done with their breakfasts. "The dental hygienist?"

"Sarah," Cole supplied and grimaced.

"I assume since I haven't heard anything," Rosie said as she pushed her plate off to the side, "that she didn't light your fire." She winked at him.

Cole smirked. "No, she did not. No fire at all to speak of." Ah, and there had been such promise. Sarah was gorgeous, smart, and initially seemed really fun. But about fifteen minutes into dinner, she'd pulled out her phone and barely put it down the rest of the night. By the end of dinner Cole had felt like he'd spent the evening with the top of her head.

"I had better conversations with the waiter," Cole said, half-amused, still half-pissed about her rudeness.

"Idiot," Rosie concluded with a roll of her eyes. "No worries. And no rush. You'll find her. She's out there, the perfect girl for you. You'll know it when you meet her."

Cole shrugged dismissively at his aunt's words. He wasn't desperate for a wife, not like some of his friends who had gotten married young and were already raising kids and navigating marriage, family, and jobs. But he knew, in a quiet corner of his mind, that he wanted a family someday.

The thing was, with his lacrosse career, timing had never felt right. The last few years with the Bandits had been a whirlwind—championship seasons, his MVP award, and the high of playing at his best—but lacrosse wasn't like football or baseball. It didn't come with a massive salary or great prospects of career longevity. He wasn't delusional. He knew the younger guys coming up behind him were faster, hungrier, and ready to take his spot when he started to slow down. And thirty was creeping up on him fast. He'd always told himself he'd focus on a relationship after the season ended, after the next big game, or when his contract was up. He liked the idea of a wife, a partner, kids, even. But he knew there was no urgency at the moment—or at least he didn't feel that way. And yet, while he didn't want to rush into anything just because his friends were settling down, he also didn't want to wake up one day and find out he was too late.

But then, the bottom line, to which Rosie had just alluded: he simply hadn't found anyone that he wanted to make a priority in his life right now.

Just as Cole took another sip of coffee, the diner's door swung open with a gust of cold wind, and a familiar voice boomed through the small space.

"Cole!" Was shouted across the diner, in the same drawn-out manner the fans did at the Bandits' game when Cole scored or made a great play. "Knew I'd find you here, dude," said Hank "Tank" Morrison as he strode toward the table, his grin easy, natural. Without hesitation, he plopped down onto the end of the booth seat next to Cole's aunt, uninvited, and helped himself to a few leftover home fries from Rosie's plate. "Morning, Rosie," Hank said with a wink, unabashedly popping the home fries into his mouth. "As beautiful as ever." He flashed a charming grin, the kind that made everyone forgive his brashness.

It wasn't unusual for one or more of the guys from the firehouse to join them for breakfast. In fact, it was rare that Cole and his aunt were able to dine alone. Aunt Rosie knew and loved all the guys and they her. If Cole was forced to cover a shift and miss their breakfast date, Aunt Rosie would invariably stop by the house with a tray of cookies, packages of bagels and cream cheese, or sometimes an entire casserole, enough to feed the whole crew.

"Hank," Rosie greeted her former pupil with a chuckle. "I swear you sniff out leftovers. Help yourself," she said belatedly, though there was hardly any chastisement in her tone.

"Sharing is caring," Hank replied as he did indeed help himself, picking up the fork Rosie had used and digging into the mound of fried potatoes with peppers and onions.

Hank was built like a tank—his nickname fit him well. Broad shoulders, thick arms that strained the fabric of his Buffalo Fire Department hoodie, and a beard that made him look like he could handle anything life threw at him, from raging fires to bar fights.

"Cole, I'm serious about the Scotland thing," Hank said around the food in his mouth. "Come with me."

Rosie frowned at her nephew. "What Scotland thing?"

Tank turned his head, facing Rosie, his beard scraping his shoulder. "Doreen's gone. Kaput. *Finito*. But we had plans for a trip to Scotland—her idea, by the way—and I'm stuck with everything. It's all paid for. Flights, hotels, tours—everything. Doreen bailed, and I've been bugging this knucklehead to go with me." He turned his attention to Cole. "C'mon, man. I'm not doing Scotland by myself."

Cole shook his head, deflecting with, "He only asked me because I'm the only guy he knows with a current passport." More seriously, he refused Tank again. "I can't, man. I told you; I've got the tile guy coming to redo the bathroom floor next week. We've got Steve's stag this weekend and I'm back to work next Wednesday." He also wasn't a big fan of last minute, big plans.

Hank groaned dramatically and grabbed a napkin from the table to swipe at an imaginary tear. "Come on, dude. Don't leave me hanging. We'll hit the Highlands, drink some whisky, forget about snow and everything Buffalo for a whole week. Craig said he'd cover your shifts—you've got vacation days, I know. Jesus, if anyone needs a vacation, it's you." He shot Rosie a wink. "Am I right, or am I right?"

Rosie laughed softly and tilted her head at her nephew. "Hank is right, actually. You should take a break. I can be at your house when the tile guy comes."

Cole glanced down at his coffee, trying to think of other reasons he couldn't go. The idea of heading to Scotland had its appeal, sure, but he wasn't exactly eager to jump on a plane and head halfway across the world at the drop of a hat. Then again, it wasn't like he had anything really keeping him here, nothing that couldn't be missed or rescheduled, or apparently, taken care of by his aunt.

Hank, clearly sensing the hesitation, leaned in closer. "Worst case, we hit some pubs, see some castles, and have ourselves a wee good time," he said, employing at the end what turned out to be a terrible Scottish accent. "Back in time for Thanksgiving."

Rosie aided and abetted Tank, adding her own encouragement. "When would you have an opportunity like this again? Do it. Go. And don't whine to me if you don't and then regret it."

Reluctantly conceding, Cole nodded, hoping he wouldn't regret it. Tank could be a lot to handle—he always ran on full throttle, was loud, brash, and assertive, and never did anything halfway. Whether it was fighting fires, hitting the gym, or tossing back beers, Tank operated like life was a competition, and Cole didn't know if traveling with him would be an adventure or a headache.

"I guess I'm going to Scotland," Cole said, the smile he forced being larger than what he felt.

Hank grinned wide and stole one last fry from Rosie's plate. "'Atta boy!"

Chapter Two

Cole had learned quickly that going on vacation with Tank was both a headache *and* an adventure—luckily, more of the latter than the former. Tank's boundless energy seemed to ignite around six in the morning and didn't extinguish until long after midnight. By day four, Cole, several years Tank's junior, was struggling to keep pace.

Scotland was fabulous, proving to be a feast for the senses, a great mix of history, natural beauty, warm hospitality, and whiskey nearly at every corner. They'd started their trip in Edinburgh, where they explored the cobbled streets of the Royal Mile, the imposing majesty of Edinburgh Castle, and Mary King's Close in Old Town, a labyrinth of passageways, vaulted chambers, and old tenement houses that dated back to the 1600's. Reputed to be haunted, the close lay entirely underground, its tenement buildings remarkably intact, with doors, shuttered windows, gutters, and even rooms still visible. Tank had insisted on a night tour, a spooky affair filled with tales of restless spirits that had left Cole rolling his eyes and Tank grinning like a kid.

From there, they'd rented a car and driven north through the scenic hills of Perthshire, stopping at Stirling Castle for a dose of William Wallace history. Tank had a knack for befriending strangers, and by the time they'd reached the castle's great hall, he was sharing a dram of whisky with an overly enthusiastic local guide. Cole had caught some of their conversation, which Cole himself had heard on the plane, regarding Tank's high school's production of a musical version of Braveheart, in which Tank himself had played the lead.

"You sang? In a musical?" Cole had needed clarification when he'd first heard this. "*You* did?"

Tank had shrugged in the seat next to Cole on the international flight. "Dude, it was twenty years ago—yeah, I sang. By the way, all the hottest chicks were in the drama club. But seriously, it was awful—I mean, *I* was great, but the play was brutal."

"Please tell me there's video of this somewhere." Cole had pleaded. "In some old metal file cabinet in the basement of your high school."

"Colorado next, if you want to get your hands on that," Tank had teased, referring to the four years he'd spent as a teenager in Colorado when his mother and father had split and he and his mom had briefly moved out west.

Their journey had continued into the Highlands, where the scenery became even more dramatic. Yesterday, they'd spent hours near Loch Ness. While Tank had discussed with their guide the probability of the fabled monster Nessie being real, Cole had been more interested in the tranquil beauty of the loch and the ancient ruins of Urquhart Castle perched along its shores.

Now, on day four, they found themselves near Loch Linnhe, the towering slopes of Ben Nevis looming ahead. Tank, ever the adrenaline junkie, had declared it hiking day.

"We can't come all this way and not see the view from the top," Tank had said in an effort to cajole Cole.

Cole was game for many things, all the tours Tank had previously booked and plenty of sightseeing, but wondered if he should draw the line on hiking. While he appreciated the rugged beauty of Scotland, he wasn't convinced that trudging up the UK's tallest peak after three days of nonstop adventure was the best idea. He and Tank were both healthy males, but they weren't hikers. Yeah, he'd done short climbs around Buffalo at Chestnut Ridge and Letchworth parks, but those were a far cry from what Tank had in mind.

Still, Tank's zeal was hard to resist—and they were right here—so that Cole found himself suppressing a groan and lacing up his hiking boots, consoling himself with the hope that the hike would be short, uneventful, and a good dinner with a nice glass of whiskey would be his reward later.

Adjusting the straps on the small backpack he'd purchased and filled with water, a multitool, a flashlight, an extra pair of socks, and an entire box of energy bars, Cole glanced up the trail that snaked toward the peak of Ben Nevis. The morning sun was deceptively warm, but the chill became obvious as they slowly reached higher elevations.

Tank was a few paces ahead, arms spread wide as if embracing the mountains.

"This is what it's all about, man," Tank said, his voice carrying over the stillness of the trail. "Fresh air, nature at its purest, and a challenge to remind you you're alive."

"That reminder came this morning at 6 am," Cole called up to Tank, "when you scared the shit out of me, bouncing on the bed like a five-year-old."

"You snoozed through two alarms, dude!" Tank shot back, spinning around to walk backward with a cocky grin.

"For good reason," Cole defended, adjusting the winter hat he'd purchased at the same time he'd bought the backpack. "We closed that pub last night." They hadn't gotten back to their hotel until almost 2 a.m., and Cole had struggled the entire trip, and more so last night, to sleep with Tank's snoring being loud enough to shake the rafters.

"Gotta make the most of every hour, my man. When are you ever going to get back to Scotland?"

It was a good point, or it might have been, except that Cole was really impressed with Scotland, and had already decided it would definitely be a place he'd like to visit again. They were cramming a lot into each day, but there was so much more to see.

"This is soul-repair," Tank pronounced, his voice carrying easily over the wind.

Cole couldn't argue with that. There was some benefit to traveling with Tank. While Cole tended to overanalyze everything— *until all the spontaneity was sucked out,* as Tank had pointed out several times over the years—Tank was the kind of guy who turned every moment into an adventure. And sure, Tank's relentless energy could be exhausting, but Cole couldn't deny that he was glad he'd been talked into coming.

As they crested a ridge, Tank paused to admire the view. The mountains rolled out in endless layers of white-capped green and gray, the sky stretching impossibly wide above them.

"Worth it, huh?" Tank said, pointing toward the horizon.

Cole nodded, breathless from both the climb and the scenery, but hardly able not to appreciate the vista presented to them. "Yeah. That's quite a view."

They continued up the trail, the conversation meandering from the landscape to Tank's latest business venture—a juice bar he wanted to open in Buffalo.

"I'm telling you, it's gonna be huge," Tank said, gesturing animatedly. "Cold-pressed, organic, all that good stuff. It's what the world needs right now."

"Uh-huh," Cole replied, his smile amused. "And when exactly did you become a health guru?" Cold-pressed, organic juices weren't in the same arena as fries, chicken wings, or Tank's favorite—and Buffalo's own—beef on weck. Certainly, it shouldn't be mentioned in the same breath as beer and whiskey, Tank's other favorites.

Tank laughed. "You've got your little side gig, MVP. I can have plans as well."

"You sure can," was all Cole said, unconvinced that anything would ever come of it. Last spring, Tank had been all gung-ho about opening an ax-throwing bar, from which he'd quickly been dissuaded when the cost of insurance was projected to be more than the monthly lease on the property he'd had in mind. Before that, Tank had talked nonstop about buying a used cube van and turning it into a mobile pet grooming business, though he hadn't a minute's worth of experience with either pets or their grooming. During Covid, curious about places he was unable to visit, Tank had bought half a dozen drones, determined to start a drone photography business. He'd crashed four of them before scrapping those plans.

"Actually, the juice bar was Doreen's idea," Tank admitted, "but she'll never do anything with it. And I still think it's a great investment. There's only one other one in all—"

Tank went suddenly silent as a strange wind rose from behind them, cutting his words short. It wasn't a typical gust but felt instantly unnatural, carrying with it a faint, otherworldly hum that Cole felt more than heard. It prickled at his skin, like static electricity crawling along his arms and neck.

Cole stopped dead in his tracks and exchanged a sharp glance with Tank, whose usual lively expression had dimmed into wary confusion.

"Wind's been coming straight at us all day," Cole muttered, his eyes narrowing as he scanned the darkened peaks surrounding them. "Why's it blowing backward now?"

Tank didn't answer immediately. His lips pressed into a tight line as his gaze swept the trail they'd just climbed.

The air had shifted, growing heavier with each passing second, pressing down on them. It wasn't just heavy—it felt alive, charged, like the moments before a thunderstorm, but magnified a hundredfold.

"You feel that?" Cole asked, his voice low and tight.

Tank met his gaze again, his frown deepening. "Yeah," he admitted, his usual confidence replaced with something closer to unease. "What the hell is—"

The words died in his throat as something rippled through the air. Cole felt it first—a faint vibration beneath his boots, like the earth itself had taken a shallow breath.

Then, Tank blurred. Not gradually, not subtly, but as if someone had dropped a gauzy material between them. His form wavered, distorting in and out of focus, while the world around them seemed to ripple, like heat waves rising off sunbaked asphalt.

"Tank?" Cole's voice cracked, the single syllable betraying the fear clawing its way up his throat.

Tank was only a few feet away, close enough that Cole could have reached out to grab his arm, except now, it felt impossible.

An invisible barrier seemed to rise between them, a thin, vibrating wall of pressure that pushed back against every instinct Cole had to lunge forward.

The air buzzed, filling his ears with a low, eerie drone. Cole's stomach twisted as the feeling intensified, his pulse hammering in his temples. The mountains around them seemed to grow darker, ominously so.

"Tank!" Cole tried again, louder this time, but the word seemed to dissolve in the dense, oppressive air.

Tank turned his head toward him, his blurred features contorted in confusion and alarm. "Cole—" he started, but his voice warped, stretching and distorting, sounding like he was underwater. His figure flickered, one second solid, the next translucent, as if he were being pulled apart by unseen hands.

A thin, hair-raising breeze whipped past Cole, carrying with it a faint metallic tang that made his stomach churn even more.

This wasn't normal. This wasn't nature.

Something wasn't right.

Panic gripped Cole as his vision wavered. He tried to move, to reach for Tank, but his limbs felt weighted, unresponsive. The last thing he saw before the world went black was Tank's distorted figure reaching toward him.

And then—nothing.

***

Cole awoke to a biting cold that seemed to cut through his clothing and sink directly into his bones. Snow covered him in a thin, icy layer, dampening his jacket and soaking into his jeans. His breath misted in the frigid air, the sharp inhalation burning his lungs. He groaned as he tried to sit up, his muscles stiff and unresponsive, as though he'd been lying there for hours. Disoriented, he blinked against the dim light of dusk—or was it dawn? He wasn't sure.

The world around him was eerily silent, save for the occasional whisper of wind. Sitting up now, he paused and tried to orient himself.

He squinted, his heart thudding against his ribs as the realization struck him: the ground beneath him was covered in snow. Not just a dusting or a patch here and there, but a thick layer, at least half a foot deep. How? When they'd started their hike, the mountains had been bare except for snowy caps on the highest peaks and a few wind-swept pockets.

What the hell had happened?

"Tank?" he croaked, his voice raspy and weak. No answer. He twisted his head, scanning his surroundings. His gloves were missing, leaving his fingers red and burning from the cold. "Tank!" he called again, stronger this time which resulted in a bout of coughing, but no response came.

He coughed again, louder, and struggled to get to his feet, his hands plunging into the snow as he braced himself.

He turned his head, his pulse quickening as he took in his surroundings. The winding trail they'd been climbing was gone. In its place was a dense grove of trees, their branches burdened with snow. Shadows crept along the forest floor, and the faint light above cast the entire scene in a surreal, bluish hue. The ground was without any marks, save for his own imprint. No trail. No footprints. No sign of life.

A gnawing fear ate at him. Where was Tank? He couldn't fathom his friend leaving him behind. Tank was the type to drag him over his shoulder if need be, not the type to disappear without a word.

Cole forced himself to stand, his legs trembling under the strain. His boots crunched in the snow as he took a few unsteady steps. He tried to steady his breathing, but his chest tightened with rising panic. He called for Tank again, louder this time, his voice echoing uselessly into the void.

Nothing. No response.

The sun—or what little light there was—was fading fast. Shadows crept across the landscape, stealing what little warmth the day had provided. Cole's training flashed through his mind: *Hypothermia doesn't just make you cold; it clouds your judgment, slows your movements. Keep moving, keep your blood circulating, stay sharp.* But where would he go? He spun in place, searching for any sign of civilization. No lights in the distance, no smoke trails from a chimney, no sound of cars or planes—nothing but an unrelenting wilderness.

Where the hell was the mountain?

He forced himself forward, each step an effort against the biting wind.

His thoughts raced as his body slowed. Did Tank go for help?

Had there been an earthquake?

Did Scotland even have earthquakes?

Could he have hit his head?

His pulse spiked at the thought of more sinister possibilities. What if Tank had been injured—or worse?

As he trudged through the snow, the cold settled deeper into his limbs. His fingers were numb, his lips dry and cracked. After about an hour of walking aimlessly, Cole realized with growing alarm that he'd left his backpack behind. But then he didn't remember seeing it at all after he'd woken up, and he did recall searching the immediate area. Maybe it was still on the mountain, where he and Tank had first noticed the change in the air, before he'd blacked out?

Another puzzle, that. Why had he passed out? He couldn't make sense of anything, not one damn thing. It was beyond maddening.

Presently, however, finding warmth, shelter of some sorts, needed to be his first priority. He would freeze out here in the elements. He tugged his coat tighter around him and lowered his hat over his ears, but it was no use; his body was losing heat faster than he could retain it. He clenched and unclenched his fists, stomped his feet, even jogged for a little bit, tried anything to keep his blood flowing while another hour passed.

Just when despair threatened to overwhelm him, he saw it: a dark opening in the side of a small hill. A cave. It wasn't ideal, but it was shelter, and right now, it was his only option. Stumbling toward it, he ducked inside and collapsed against the rough stone wall. The air was stale and damp but marginally warmer than outside.

Cole's breaths came fast and shallow as he assessed his situation. He knew the risks of staying here, but he also knew the risks of wandering aimlessly through the cold. *Stay put,* his training said. *Make yourself easy to find.* But the gnawing fear that no one was looking for him at all made him second-guess everything.

He pulled his knees to his chest, trying to conserve what little heat he had left. The darkness pressed in on him, amplifying his thoughts. The surrealness of the situation was almost too much to process. One moment, he'd been hiking with Tank, grinning over Tank's desire to be a businessman. Now, he was freezing in the middle of nowhere, no Tank, no explanation, no idea what to do next.

As exhaustion tugged at him, Cole fought to stay awake. He had to survive. He had to figure this out.

For the first time in a long while, he felt something dangerously close to panic.

And as he closed his eyes against the cold and the dark, he couldn't shake the feeling that something just wasn't right, that he was missing some crucial piece of the puzzle surrounding his circumstances.

Chapter Three

Torr Cinnteag
The Highlands
1302

She feared that the unusually frigid autumn was only a portent of a brutal winter to come.

Ailsa tipped her face skyward, closing her eyes as fine, cold flakes settled against her cheeks. The first snow of the season was gentle, each flake kissing her skin with a delicate peck before melting away. For a moment, the quiet world around her felt as still as a held breath. She opened her eyes slowly, watching the flurries fall around her, hoping the snowfall remained as soft and picturesque all day.

The Sinclairs of Torr Cinnteag could not withstand a harsh winter.

The rolling hills surrounding the keep had long since shed summer's warmth and were now bare and windswept, with patches of frost clinging stubbornly to the earth every day. The landscape had prematurely faded to dull grays and browns, a sorry prelude to a possibly mean winter. In a year that should have allowed them peace and comfort, with the uneasy truce struck between the English and Scots, it seemed the land and nature itself had decided to defy them. Cold rains had ruined much of their harvest, and what little they'd managed to salvage wouldn't last through any long, miserable winter season.

Already, they were rationing what little grain they had, and men, women, and children grew thinner with each passing day. If this snow hardened into a winter as merciless as the seers and signs predicted, Ailsa wondered how many of them would still be here come spring.

Not intending to court useless worry, Ailsa pulled her cloak more snugly against her neck and turned, her gaze surveying the landscape surrounding Torr Cinnteag, while she waited for her maid, Anwen, to catch up.

As it often did, her gaze settle first on the Sinclair keep, which stood breathtakingly atop a rugged promontory overlooking the wild beauty of Cuil Bay at Loch Linnhe below. Thick walls worn by wind and rain appeared a steely gray under the overcast sky, their rough stone blending into the surrounding cliffs that cascaded down toward the water. Despite the forbidding look of the keep from afar, there was a natural beauty to the rugged landscape, where the stony outcrop met the expanse of the loch. Ailsa never tired of the view.

Beyond the keep, pockets of Sinclair farmland dotted the hillsides sectioned off by simple stone barriers. The fields lay empty, harvested months ago and quiet now, waiting for renewed life in spring. The bay itself, though often turbulent in winter, today lay almost still beneath the light snowfall. Small boats were moored along the shoreline and might see more frequent use as fishing became more necessary.

Beyond the keep to the south lay an ancient pine forest, its branches dusted with early snow, forming a natural windbreak for Torr Cinnteag.

Anwen Lamont climbed up the rise in the path toward Ailsa, toward the northern village.

Though she looked much younger, Anwen was more than twice Ailsa's age, and had been first her nurse and later her maid, but always her confidante and friend, though truthfully a very bossy one. She was broad-shouldered and sturdy, built in a way that suggested an unyielding hardiness—which was not the case at all—yet her appearance was softened by an effortless smile and a lively, expressive face. Her cheeks were perpetually rosy, contrasting beautifully with her otherwise flawless skin. She was tall, nearly of a height with Tavis Sinclair, Ailsa's brother and laird of Torr Cinnteag, and sported a gap between her front teeth that was ever on display as Anwen was rarely without the appearance of a smile. In quiet contemplation or even in moments of angst or fear, Anwen appeared to be grinning. "Tis simply how my face is fashioned," she's said once to a young Ailsa when questioned about her constant, peculiar expression.

Anwen breathed heavily now, puffs of white air dancing and dissipating in front of her face.

"I dinna ken what the hurry is," she groused, blowing a wisp of her brown hair off her forehead. She stopped at Ailsa's side, possibly pleased for the reprieve and glanced down at the northern village, where dozens of sleepy cottages sat silently under the gentle fall of snow. "He'll get nae better nae worse ere we get there, sure enough," she said, referring to Mallaig, the aged and frail farmer to whom they were bringing bread and mutton stew. "Does my bones nae guid, though, I'll tell ye that, as much as ye have me out of doors with...this," she said, holding out her hand to catch a few flakes of snow.

"But look, Anwen," Ailsa, said, directing her gaze behind her. "Is it nae striking, the way the clouds seem to hover right over the keep? And how through the snow ye can still see the blue of the loch?"

Anwen turned but was unimpressed. And though it appeared that she smiled, she said, "Could've seen as much from half the windows in the keep. Mayhap in a chamber with a fire."

Ailsa grinned, even as she knew Anwen was more than half serious. "And we'll get there. We've the altar cloths to finish, which is certainly best done near a fire."

"God bless ye, lass. Aye, near a fire."

They walked on, tucking their chins into their chests as the snow continued to fall. Mallaig's cottage was the first they came upon, being closest to the keep and more run-down than any other, owing to Mallaig's infirmity—which, by Anwen's way of thinking had gone on long enough; "Be dead already, he should be," she'd said not long ago, "if he's nae going to bother living."

While Ailsa didn't exactly subscribe to Anwen's callous view, she did agree with her maid on another complaint she had against the old man: Mallaig sometimes took advantage of his ailment, which was not quite specific enough to be named so that it was generally accounted as aging frailness.

At the worn-down cottage, its exterior walls cracked and peeling, Anwen took the lead, giving a brisk knock before pushing the door open without waiting for an answer.

The cottage door creaked loudly, revealing Mallaig hunched in his usual chair, near enough to the hearth that his wiry, white hair almost blended with the haze of smoke curling from the fire. Deep lines creased his face, giving him a permanently displeased look, though his blue eyes shone bright with pleasure at the company. A moth-eaten plaid was draped over his frail frame, hiding almost everything but his long, knobby fingers, which held the plaid together at his narrow chest.

As they stepped inside, Ailsa held up the small basket she'd brought, lined with cloth to keep the warmth in, revealing a loaf of fresh bread and a crock of mutton stew. "Guid day, Mallaig. We've brought ye a bit of bread and—"

"Mutton again?" Mallaig interrupted, disappointment evident in his tone as he leaned forward in his chair, eyeing the basket's contents skeptically as Ailsa bent and laid it at his feet. "What I really need is a joint of venison. Easier on the teeth, aye?"

Ailsa opened her mouth to reply, but Anwen cut in. "Aye, ye'd need a fine stag, then, wouldn't ye? But we've got bread and stew, just the thing to warm ye," she said. "Bread's fresh-baked, and soft enough for a bairn, so I ken it'll do ye fine."

Mallaig sighed theatrically, then looked purposefully at Ailsa, his expression as doleful as it was hopeful. "If only ye'd a drop of ale, or at least some mulled wine for the chill," he suggested.

Ailsa smiled politely at him. "Maybe next time, Mallaig, when—"

"Nae next time," Anwen cut her off, crossing her arms over her ample chest. "Warm enough, ye are. Sitting closer to that fire than ye do your bed, and ye ken the ale's for healthy men that work to keep the clan fed." She nodded sharply to underscore her remark. "Try the stew first," she said to Mallaig as Ailsa put the crock in his hands. "We'll see if it doesna set ye straight."

Mallaig gave another small sigh and gingerly took the stew, spooning a bit with a skeptical look.

"Warmer still ye'll be when we return," Anwen predicted. "We'll bring yer peat and stoke yer fire and fine as mulled wine ye'll be—though ye'll still have none of that."

With food in hand, Mallaig now paid scant attention to the women so that Anwen tugged at Ailsa's arm and inclined her head toward the door.

"My own fire awaits me," she reminded Ailsa. "Let's get his peat and get back to the keep."

Ailsa nodded and leaving Mallaig to his stew, lifted the empty basket, following Anwen to the door. They started toward the peat stacks on the far side of the village, where they were kept near the edge of the bog for easy access. The snow had settled into a steady, fine mist, the flakes now dusting their cloaks as they made their way down the narrow, winding path outside the village.

Anwen chirped the entire time, as she did almost daily, about Mallaig. "A man scarcely past fifty—nae much older than me—needing two women to fetch his food and fuel. Have ye ever heard such a thing?" she muttered, clearly annoyed. "No pride left at all, that one. If I were to sit idle as he does, I'd shame myself to the bone."

Accustomed to Anwen's tirades, Ailsa nodded and murmured sounds of assent before attempting to defend the man. "Perhaps he truly is as frail, as incapacitated as he seems," she offered, though even she had her doubts about Mallaig's supposed malady.

"Frailty, is it?" Anwen scoffed, stomping a bit heavier with her agitation. "More like laziness. I've got a mind that he'd move quick enough if we did bring ale or wine, and dinna set it in his hand but just out of reach." She shook her head, her cheeks ruddy with the cold and her usual lively expression hardening into one of indignation. "He'd rise out of the chair then, ye mark my words."

As they reached the peat stacks, Anwen dug in with practiced hands, loading thick, dense clods into the basket Ailsa held, each heavy enough to burn long and steady. "There's enough to see him through the night and more. And if the old goat complains, I'll be bringing him barn cats next time, nae peat, though they'd probably bring him more warmth than he deserves."

Ailsa hid another smile, trying to keep her voice neutral. "I've said, Anwen, many times, have I nae, that you dinna need to accompany me to Mallaig's cottage? I ken the chore annoys ye."

Anwen laughed outright. "And leave ye to be taken advantage of? Nae. He'd have ye spoon-feeding him and supplying him with the bluidy wine and next ye ken, ye'd be ploughing his runrig and keeping house with him. Och, and yer brother should set him straight. Hear it from the laird and aye, Mallaig'd be singing a different tune..."

On and on she went, grousing now about Ailsa's brother, Tavis, who in Anwen's mind, contributed also to Mallaig's laziness by not putting his foot down.

"I dinna get it," Anwen went on. "Hard as stone is the laird, suspicious by nature of everyone and everything, and yet he's nae better than ye, coddling Mallaig as ye do."

As Ailsa and Anwen made their way back toward Mallaig's cottage, the familiar path wound quietly through the snowy landscape, edged by the sparse trees of the Little Forest, a stand of pines and bare, knotted oaks flanking the trail. The snow fell thicker here, muting sound and casting a haze across the view ahead. Ailsa pulled her cloak tightly against the chill, only half listening as Anwen droned on.

A slow flash of movement caught Ailsa's attention, lifting her gaze from the ground.

There, where the trees met the path, a figure materialized out of the soft white haze of snow. At first, she thought it must be one of the Sinclair soldiers, but as he stepped onto the lane, Ailsa's breath caught in her throat, realizing this was a person unknown to her. She'd lived her entire life at Torr Cinnteag, had never stepped foot off Sinclair land, and she knew every person of the demesne. But not this man.

This man was taller than any man she'd ever known, her own brother included, was broad-shouldered, his clothes dark against the snow, and he moved with a heaviness, a deliberate stride that spoke of either exhaustion or wariness. He was no Sinclair—that much was clear by the unfamiliar cut of his garments and the odd footwear worn. His face was shadowed but there was something about his movement, his very singular presence against the wintery backdrop, that seized her attention so profoundly.

Snow swirled around him, and the sudden cawing of a crow split the silence, the bird's dark shape swooping low near the man. The man's face came into focus as he pushed back the hood of his unusual cloak, revealing a strong jaw, square and unshaven. Dark and tousled hair clung to his forehead, the front of it dampened by the snow, giving him an untamed aura, heightening a rawness in his appearance that was neither refined nor delicate, but arresting all the same. His gaze seemed to settle with some decisiveness on Ailsa, the blue of his eyes glaring against the muted winter landscape. Though his features were unfamiliar, the weariness and the depth in his gaze struck her as curiously intimate, as if she were not just seeing this stranger for the first time.

No sword hung at his hip. He carried no weapon, not so far as Ailsa could see, carried nothing at all though his hands were fisted with what seemed like urgency at his side.

Anwen, belatedly realizing the man's presence, drew up beside her, clutching Ailsa's arm with a gasp. "Who... who do ye think that is?" she whispered, her usual bluster softened to a murmur.

Ailsa didn't answer, her gaze locked with the stranger's. She felt her heartbeat quicken with an inexplicable thrill while at the same time a very reasonable apprehension gripped her. This man looked as though he'd walked through hell itself, his expression harsh and yet desperate, and in stark contrast with the softness of fresh snow collecting on his broad shoulders.

She couldn't tear her eyes away from him. Even as she grasped the danger of his presence and the vulnerability of their position, removed yet from the core of the village and quite a distance from the keep and the house guards, Ailsa's lips parted in wonder, and she didn't move. Couldn't move.

"Why does he stare so at ye?" Anwen asked. "Do ye ken him?"

Ailsa shook her head, unblinking, but did not answer Anwen. She had no answer, or rather couldn't think, not with his gaze devouring her so. She was aware only of him, and of the powerful pull that kept her frozen in place.

The blue of his eyes was startling, his gaze unyielding, as though he were trying to reconcile what he saw with what he'd known—or expected. She knew nothing of this man, nothing but the way he looked at her, oddly as if she were both his salvation and his undoing. The weight of it left her breathless, and her hand unconsciously rose to her collar, her fingers grazing the soft fur lining of her cloak.

"To the right," Anwen said urgently, nudging Ailsa in that direction. "We'll cut through the barley fields. Straight to the keep. Sound the alarm. *Jesu*, but he's 'bout to slay ye with that gaze."

And then the man spoke.

Anwen stiffened and yipped a squeak of fright.

"Hello," called the man, holding up his hands in a non-threatening manner.

"Mother Mary save us," breathed Anwen, her grip tightening on Ailsa's arm. "What manner of speech is that?" She nearly spat, her voice hushed but sharp, each word laced with accusation.

A foreigner, Ailsa concluded with less hostility than Anwen. Neither his deep voice nor the unfamiliar word or language startled her. Though unusual in cadence and tone, the low pitch of his voice did not jar her but rather rolled through her, as would a warm current through icy water.

"Guid day, sir," Ailsa said, finally finding her own voice. Recalling her role as the laird's sister, she straightened her shoulders and called out, "Ye've come onto Sinclair land, sir. State yer purpose or turn yerself around."

"Christ, you're real," was the man's curious response in what was decidedly an English tongue. "Thank God. I'm..." He paused and shrugged his wide shoulders, lifting his hand helplessly.

"On yer way, is what ye are," Anwen insisted. "Off with ye, ere the guards come."

Ailsa shook her head. "Nae, he needs our help," she said quietly to her maid, quite sure of her guess.

"Needs to make hisself scarce," Anwen argued, "before yer brother finds him at Torr Cinnteag."

The man sighed, holding up his hands in a non-threatening manner as he heard Anwen's statement. "I'm not a threat to anyone. I just need some...direction." He grimaced, as if in pain or just now coming to some realization. "Maybe a hospital."

"We can offer ye victuals and point ye south," Ailsa offered in a firm voice, "but nae more than that."

"Lass," Anwen hissed a warning, yanking again at Ailsa's cloak. "The laird'll have yer—"

Anwen stopped speaking and both women gasped now as the man, large and seemingly invincible, slumped to the ground. He'd only just nodded his acceptance of Ailsa's offer when he bared his teeth, as if fighting back the inevitable, before his blue eyes rolled back in his head and he dropped like a heavy rock, his legs buckling. He pitched forward onto his chest, his cheek smacking against the cold ground.

Ailsa didn't think but ran to him, ignoring Anwen's high-pitched warning to stay away. She slid to her knees at his side and tried to turn him over, needing every ounce of strength to do so.

"*Jesu*, he's as big as a horse," she grumbled, finally managing to shift his dead weight so that he was on his back.

With that done, she sat back, hesitant now to touch him, wondering if the stranger had just expired right before their eyes.

"Is he dead?" Anwen wondered the same thing, hovering over Ailsa's shoulder.

"I..." she began, lifting her hand to touch him, pulling it back twice before she finally committed to making contact with him. She laid her hand against the soft fabric of his cloak. Beneath her fingers, beneath the smooth, cold material, his chest was rock hard. Staring at his unmoving face, Ailsa pressed down, waiting to feel the beat of his heart.

Beyond the swift beating of her own heart, it took her a moment to recognize signs of life in his. An unexpected burst of relief escaped her, breathed as a sigh, when she felt the slow but regular thud against her palm.

"He lives," she said excitedly. But what to do for him?

She glanced over her shoulder. "Anwen, return to the keep and fetch a cart and a few men to lift him," she instructed, lightly slapping at Anwen's hand when the maid's eyes widened with shock. "Dinna be like that. We canna leave him here. He is alive now but willna be for long if we simply abandon him." She thought it prudent to advise, "Dinna say a word about him being English. He'll be nae threat, nae in his condition. Anwen, promise me."

"But lass, we canna—"

"We can and we will," Ailsa demanded. "Simple human decency will see him made well. Let Tavis decide then what's to be done with him, when he learns he's English."

"Playing with fire, ye are," Anwen cautioned.

"And it will be my difficulty to manage with Tavis, but nae now. Go! Hurry, Anwen. Say only that we found him like this."

"I willna be—"

"Ye will," Ailsa ground out between her teeth, knowing precious moments were being wasted. "Now, Anwen. Go!"

'Twas rare that she employed so strict a tone with her maid, but it was occasionally needed to remind Anwen that Ailsa expected to be obeyed.

Ailsa watched Anwen only for a moment as she stomped away before turning her attention back to the unconscious man.

She stared at him for quite a while as he slept, serenely unconscious of all the curiosity and concern in the watchful face bent over his.

She thought he might be possessed of bronzed skin but that it was pale now, disposed to his illness or his current frailty, which she determined distractedly was more authentic than Mallaig's.

Believing herself useless at that moment, for doing nothing for his comfort, Ailsa picked up his closer hand, where it had fallen onto the snow-covered ground. His hand was large, nearly twice the size of her own, but so cold. She began to chafe his flesh between her warmer palms, first one hand and then reaching across his broad body to collect the other, warming it in the same fashion.

Though she shivered with the cold herself, she next removed her cloak and bundled it into a pillow shape, sliding it under his head to distance him from the cold earth.

Exposure to the elements, she prayed, was all that ailed him, and not anything far more serious. There was no visible wound or injury to the man, not that she could see.

Again and again, her gaze strayed to his face, ignoring the unusual garb and boots he wore.

Her brother and laird of the Sinclairs, Tavis, was deemed by many a tittering female to be a handsome man. Will Tulloch, whom Ailsa had been smitten with for quite some time when he'd visited from Clan MacGillewie a few years back, had a face worthy of a woman's appreciation. Even Swanny, Torr Cinnteag's robust farrier, had drawn admiring gazes before he'd chosen the smith's daughter, Clara, to wed.

This man, though, put each of those men to shame with his beauty, Ailsa judged. How extraordinary he was—unconsciousness aside—with so noble a face. She wasn't sure how he managed to appear so vital and virile in his present lifeless state, but she found she couldn't take her eyes off him. Still, though, questions abounded about him, who he was, where he'd come from, how he managed to find himself on the very remote Sinclair land.

While she maintained a hold on his left hand, he stirred, causing her to pause her efforts to warm him.

Though his eyes remained closed, his lips moved and soft sounds emerged.

Ailsa bent over him, turning her ear toward his face.

"Don't let me die," he murmured weakly. "I need to get home."

His weakness was evidently great but the desperation in his feeble words was palpable.

"Shh," she soothed, reaching out a hand, laying her palm against his pale forehead. "All will be well."

"Rosie," he murmured.

Chapter Four

More than thirty minutes passed before Ailsa recognized sounds of people approaching. The cart's wheels creaked and groaned a bit, disturbing the somber quiet of the cold winter day. Glancing down the lane, Ailsa realized that not only a few of the castle guards had come, but at least ten of them, including the captain of the army, Dersey Sinclair.

Ailsa groaned internally. Dersey would be worse than Anwen, would likely insist same as the maid had, that whoever the man was, he wasn't their problem. Ailsa would bet her last coin Dersey would command the cart be used to deliver the man to some place outside Torr Cinnteag, far away from the Sinclairs.

She hopped to her feet and faced the party that approached, prepared to have to fight to have her way even as she knew she wouldn't be able to explain why she felt so strongly that she needed to help this man.

Dersey's frown was wild with confusion, darkening even further his habitual disagreeable expression.

"Step back, lass," he said, unaccountably drawing his sword.

"Sweet heavens, Dersey," Ailsa protested. "Disarm yerself. The man is nae conscious and thus nae threat—"

"And nae to be brought to the keep," Dersey finished gruffly. "'Tis nae a lame duck, nae a fawn with a broken leg or some wretched hog ye'll nae let us slaughter. 'Tis a man—an Englishman at that!"

Ailsa turned her glare upon Anwen, who'd accompanied the men and the cart. The maid had at least enough sense to shrivel under Ailsa's furious glare for revealing the man's nationality.

"We dinna ken that he's English," Ailsa said to Dersey, which was strictly the truth even as she had guessed he was. "And nae matter his origins, he finds himself at our mercy and we Sinclairs do nae reject—"

"Aye, aye, aye," Dersey grumbled dismissively, waving a hand to silence what would have been her appeal to see the man cared for. "He's English and hence, meant for the gaol. If he lives, he'll have ye to thank as he rots beneath the keep." The captain then waved his hand at the idling soldiers, beckoning them closer. "C'mon, then. Get him up and onto the cart. We dinna want his carcass stinkin' up the lane."

The soldiers dragged their feet. Lyle and Peile arrived first at the man's side. Lyle frowned down at the man's strange shoes before lifting his leg and then waiting on the others to grab a limb. When Peile positioned himself near the man's upper body, meaning to take hold of his arms, Lyle decided that position was more favorable and callously dropped the man's long leg from waist height, moving to stand beside Peile.

"Good heavens," Ailsa cried. "Stop that! How can ye be so callous?" A much younger Ailsa would have shoed them all away, announcing she'd see to the chore herself—she'd been taught a lesson or two in her youth about her own stubbornness and the limits of her strength. She was older and wiser now, and rather than taking over to see it done as humanely as she'd have liked, she smacked her hands on her hips and used blatant threats instead. "Recall, lads, if ye will, that I do have some sway over the kitchen staff. Unless ye want to eat boiled straw and fried dirt cakes—again—ye will imagine this man is someone kent and admired, and ye will handle him accordingly."

Dersey turned a baffled glower her way, possibly wondering why she cared.

But the Sinclair soldiers responded appropriately—Ailsa did not make idle threats, each one of them knew, reminded of the last time they'd ignored her instructions and of the poor meals they'd been served for almost a week until her brother had returned from the south. They lined up around the unconscious man and with greater care gathered his limbs, carrying him over to the waiting cart. When their heave to swing him into the cart just missed banging his head against the wooden bed, Peile swung a frantic gaze to Ailsa, fearful that she'd noticed.

"'Tis fine," she allowed, since they had not struck the man's head. "Make haste, please," she said, collecting her cloak before she scrambled up into the cart herself, taking up a defensive position at the side of the vulnerable man. When Anwen approached, obviously meaning to ride as well, Ailsa bristled at her, recalling her treachery, revealing the man's Englishness. "Ye'll have to walk, I fear," she said in a rare moment of pettiness. "Nae room for even one more. Mayhap bring that forgotten peat to Mallaig now."

Anwen gasped at what was obviously meant to be a retribution, but she did not argue.

Dersey mounted his big red destrier and frowned down at Ailsa. "Ye yerself can take it up with yer brother, lass, whatever this sudden love of the English is to ye."

Ailsa made a face at the captain but wasn't wholly immune to fright. Her brother had no love for either strangers or the English specifically, and was known to be volatile, often reacting excessively. Tavis might lock her in the gaol as well for daring to bring this stranger into their home.

One problem at a time, she reminded herself, her gaze moving back and forth from the stranger's face to the path ahead and the keep as it came into view within a few minutes.

Torr Cinnteag itself was a tall, square tower, built with thick dark gray stone, nearly blending into the surrounding cliffs, and streaked with moss, weathered from more than a hundred years of exposure to the rains and winds that blew across the deep loch. They crossed a stone bridge which spanned a natural gorge, creating a choke point for anyone approaching the fortress, making it nearly impregnable by direct assault. Just beyond the bridge stood the gatehouse, fortified with a heavy, iron-bound gate, flanked by two towers where the castle guards stood watch. Just inside the gate were the stables, housing the laird's horses and those of his officers, and beyond that, adjacent to the main keep, sat the chapel, where Father Gilbert said daily prayers. The stone chapel was simple but solid, with a carved wooden cross and many Gaelic inscriptions merging Christian faith with ancient symbols of protection favored by the Sinclairs.

Ailsa sent a longing gaze toward the chapel, a bit of eager relief flooding her when, as if on cue, Father Gilbert emerged from the arched doorway, his psalter curled in his hand and tucked against his chest.

She didn't want the Englishman sent straight to the dungeon, as her brother or Dersey would no doubt insist. But she knew, too, that no guest room in the keep would be allowed for him. The chapel, however—more specifically, the chambers at the back where Father Gilbert lived—offered a solution. In earlier times, when the Sinclair lands had been more populated, those rooms had housed other religious figures to tend the flock. Now, they were rarely used, quiet and sheltered, and, Ailsa imagined, perfectly suitable for a weary, and surely harmless, traveler.

"Father Gilbert," she called out, waving her hand to summon the priest as the cart came to a stop near the doors to the keep and the main hall.

"Now dinna be disturbing the cleric with yer nonsense," Dersey grumbled loudly as he dismounted.

"A person in need of attention is nae nonsense," Ailsa chastised the captain. She scooted out from the cart's bed, landing on two feet, her cloak bundled in her grasp and not on her person though the cold was beginning to seep through to her bones. "Father Gilbert," she addressed the priest again as he neared.

The priest approached, his brow furrowed, his sharp eyes moving from Ailsa to the unconscious man sprawled in the cart. Originally from England, Gilbert had once studied at the University of Paris before returning to serve as rector in Nether Wallop, Hampshire. Despite his intelligence and dedication, again and again he'd been denied appointments because he'd been born illegitimate. Decades ago, he had met Ailsa's grandfather at York Minster, during the enthronement of the archbishop on Christmas Day, 1279, and the two had struck up an enduring friendship. When Maraug Sinclair had offered Father Gilbert the role of rector at Torr Cinnteag ten years after their first meeting, the young priest had accepted, eager for a place where his birth would not be held against him.

Though Father Gilbert and Dersey were of a similar age, they could hardly have looked more different. Dersey, with his long, gray-streaked beard and gravelly voice, had a permanent air of irritation. His hair, what little remained, lay thin and unruly atop his head, adding to his rough appearance. Father Gilbert, by contrast, was always impeccably groomed. His clean-shaven face and the neat black hair framing it lent him a certain solemnness, further emphasized by his calm demeanor and thoughtful gaze. Where Dersey's voice was loud and more often than not edged with impatience, Father Gilbert's tone was ever soft, measured, and soothing—meant for counsel, not commands.

Ailsa spoke quickly, hoping to cut off Dersey before he could make any damning statements about the stranger. "Anwen and I found this poor man on the road. He collapsed nae long after, but nae before pleading for our help." She moved closer to Father Gilbert, clutching the sleeve of his woolen tunic in a gesture of desperation. "Dersey insists he should be taken straightaway to the gaol, but Father Gilbert, that's as good as a death sentence for a man who's likely committed nae crime. Though it appears he might be English, he seems lost more than dangerous. Ye won't let him suffer for that, will ye?" She paused, her gaze searching his face. "The chapel chambers, the empty ones, would be far better suited for an innocent man, aye? Ye'll see to him, won't ye?" she asked, trusting him to take on the role of caretaker as he so often did in Torr Cinnteag, where they lacked a formal healer.

"Your brother and I travel to Torwechwhy tomorrow, lass," Father Gilbert reminded her gently, "where we hope to make progress in the peace talks with the MacLaes."

Sweet Mother Mary, how could she have forgotten? She had been dreading these talks, knowing they would likely include some discussion of marriage—namely hers, to the younger MacLae son, Alastair.

Behind her, Dersey grumbled. "The laird willna go for it, nae that it's the priest's decision to make," he muttered.

Ailsa turned, shushing him sharply. "It's nae your decision either, Dersey."

The captain scowled, but Father Gilbert merely raised a hand to restore calm. "Fear not, lass," he said, his voice gentle. "Our departure does not mean we abandon all goodwill. Naturally, the man should be housed in the rectory. Margaret and Mary from the household can tend to him—but not you, Ailsa," he added pointedly. "Your brother will object as it is, but he can be placated knowing you'll have no contact with the stranger. English, you say?"

Ailsa nodded, feeling the weight of defeat settle. "We believe so, from the few words he spoke."

Father Gilbert nodded thoughtfully. "All the more reason, then, to keep your distance. And perhaps," he added, his gaze shifting meaningfully to Dersey, "the captain and the laird might be further appeased by stationing a few guards around the chapel. A simple precaution."

Managing to contain the heavy sigh of disappointment that wanted to come, Ailsa nodded again, conceding to Father Gilbert's suggestion. At least the man would receive some care, even if it did not directly involve her. "If you will supervise the transport of the man to the rectory, I will summon Margaret and Mary to attend him."

"I will," Father Gilbert assured her.

"And I'll be alerting yer brother of the situation," Dersey advised at the same time.

The urge to stick out her tongue at the captain was strong but Ailsa resisted. "Ye do that, Dersey," she snapped. Her skirts twirled around her as she spun and marched toward the keep.

***

Cole woke to the unsettling sensation of being poked and prodded. Blinking against a dim, flickering light, he registered two young women standing over him, both intently focused on his arms and shoulders. They were dressed in old-fashioned, modest clothing that reminded him of the Amish he'd seen back home—high-necked dresses, thick wool aprons, and linen caps covering their hair. One girl, likely no more than sixteen, had a round, freckled face, while the other looked older, maybe in her early twenties, with a dull expression on her long face.

Neither of them, he noted with a flash of disappointment, was the striking woman he'd encountered earlier in the snow.

As the girls continued their inspection of him, muttering to each other, Cole snapped out of his groggy confusion. He jerked his arm away when the older one reached out to touch him.

"What the hell? Who are you?" His words came out sharper than intended, and both girls froze, wide-eyed as he sat up.

It was then that he realized that he was in a bed made up with heavy furs and that he was shirtless, his bare chest exposed to the chilly air in the stone-walled room. Frowning, he lifted the fur blankets, discovering that he'd been stripped down to his boxer briefs. Horrified, he spotted his clothes draped over the arm of the younger girl—his jeans, shirt and sweater, and coat clutched tightly to her chest.

Cole extended his hand, alarmed now by how weak he felt. "My clothes," he demanded angrily, wondering why they'd felt the need to undress him.

At his barked command, the girls backed toward the door, the younger one glancing nervously at her companion, who tugged at her sleeve to hurry her along. Within seconds, they were gone, leaving Cole alone and pissed, painfully aware of how vulnerable he was, practically naked in a strange room.

As the door closed with a faint thud, Cole let out an exasperated breath, glancing around the small, dim chamber. It was more of a cell, with rough stone walls and barely any furniture—the narrow cot under him, a small wooden table and stool, and a heavy iron candlestick on a ledge in the wall.

He saw no vents, no radiator, no source of heat at all beyond the furs draped over him and a small fireplace, where coals burned but no flames blazed. The only hint of the outside world came from a sliver of a window high up in the wall, just wide enough to let in a thin stream of cold air. The opening had no glass, and through it, he could see that daylight was gone, as there was only the grayness of an evening sky visible.

"Great," he muttered to himself, slumping back against the thin pillows, feeling an unwelcome wave of dizziness. His mouth was dry, and his head ached—symptoms he knew probably meant he was dehydrated. He strained to remember how many days he'd been out there, separated from Tank. At least two, he thought, though it was hard to tell. He hadn't eaten or drunk anything substantial since then, save for a few freezing gulps of stream water.

Minutes passed, stretching into what felt like an eternity in the cold, quiet room. For a while, he watched the candle slowly burn down, noting how much shorter it had become. He wondered if it might be possible to track the passing hours by watching its progress, but he had no sense of how much time an inch of melted wax might represent—was it an hour? More than that?

He was just beginning to nod off, despite the cold discomfort and unnerving weakness, when the door creaked open again. He tensed instinctively, eyes darting toward the movement.

He wasn't sure how he knew, certainly when the figure remained in the shadow of the open door, the hall beyond pitch black, that this was the woman he'd met earlier, the gorgeous one with the unforgettable face.

She crept carefully into the room, now cast in the warm, flickering light of the lone candle, hardly more than a shadowy figure. Earlier—today still?—he'd been almost instantly captivated by her, how ethereal she'd seemed, so vibrant with life and color against the backdrop of white snow everywhere. A wild mane of dark hair had blown round her face, dramatic against the pale skin dusted generously with freckles and her soft, full, pink-red lips. Her nose had been pink as well, an effect of the cold, but it had been her eyes that had truly struck him—clear and piercing, a startling bright blue that had somehow reached him across the snowy distance. Now, in the candlelight, that blue vividness was subdued, softened to a glimmer beneath her long lashes. What had been bright and intense by daylight was now tempered, her gaze shaded by curiosity and a guarded caution, where earlier there had been more an unfiltered interest.

Feeling an unexpected surge of hope at the sight of her, though he didn't fully understand why, Cole slowly sat up as she cautiously stepped further into the room, leaving the door open.

Like this afternoon, and like those two girls who'd swiped his clothes, she was dressed in a long gown, one that fell all the way to the floor. He wasn't exactly an expert on fabrics—or women's fashion, for that matter—but he could tell her clothes were finer than the others. The fabric looked heavier and more tailored, with a subtle pattern woven into it that he thought might be some kind of plaid or tartan, and her sleeves flared in a way that struck him as... old-fashioned? Definitely not something he'd ever seen outside of a period drama on a movie screen.

The other girls had worn simpler, rougher-looking clothes, like work uniforms in an Amish community or something you'd see at a Renaissance fair, with plain aprons over basic linen dresses. But this one... her dress seemed more elaborate, like it was designed to be worn by someone important.

"I should nae have come," she said, her voice hardly more than a whisper. "But I wanted to see for myself that ye...how ye fared."

"Who are you?" It was his most pressing concern, afraid she might disappear, leaving him to kick himself for not knowing her name or how to find her again if something even stranger happened that what already had.

She stopped, several feet away from the foot of the bed. The candle was now behind her, putting her face in shadows.

"I am Ailsa."

"Elsa?" He repeated, struggling to understand her thick accent.

She nodded, but repeated her name, pronouncing it just a little bit differently, so that it sounded like *Al-sa*.

"I'm Cole," he introduced himself. "Cole Carter. Did you bring me here?" He asked.

She shook her head. Her dark hair, which earlier had been whipped about by the wind, was tamed now, pulled away from her face in a subdued knot, not a strand out of place. As gorgeous as she was right now, a golden vision, Cole decided he almost preferred that earlier, outdoor Ailsa, and that wild and windswept look.

"I did nae—I arranged it, of course, but I could nae lift ye. The guards did so, conveying ye from the Little Forest to the chapel." She pointed over her shoulder, where presumably, the chapel was.

No, she wouldn't have been able to move him. She was petite, possibly five-three at the most, and slim. At six-three and weighing 220, he was at least a foot taller than her, and he would guess more than a hundred pounds heavier.

"Did you say guards?" She had her own personal security?

"Aye, the castle guards."

Only a few answers had come his way, but he was not enlightened at all, only more puzzled.

He rubbed his hand over his forehead and then through his hair. "I guess I'm more confused than I thought. Castle, chapel, guards—what is this place? Where am I?"

The first part of her response was incomprehensible to him spoken in a rush, words jumbling together. But he did catch fragments and bits of it. "Your brother, I got that. He didn't want me brought here—you got into a bit of trouble." Cole shook his head, feeling simple and stupid. "I'm sorry, I'm really struggling to understand your accent. I don't know what a *laird* is, or that other—are you saying *torsion*?"

"Torr Cinnteag," she repeated, slowly this time.

"And what is Torr Cinnteag?"

"This is Torr Cinnteag," she responded, the hint of a smile curving her mouth as she opened her arms to include all the room. "And beyond—the castle, the village, the farms, the land.

My brother is laird...um, chief of everything that is Torr Cinnteag."

All right, they were getting somewhere. Her brother was a big shot, maybe the mayor or whatever Scotland's equivalent was.

"And what? He doesn't like outsiders? Helping people? That he gave you shit—sorry, gave you grief for bringing me here?"

She shrugged and downplayed his concern. "'Tis done."

"You didn't happen to see another man, did you?" He asked hopefully. "About my size? With darker hair, tattoos, kind of looks like he belongs in a biker gang? He was wearing a bright red sweatshirt and navy coat."

"Ye were alone," said the beauty. "And the guards have nae found another within the boundaries of Torr Cinnteag."

"Within the boundaries? Okay, so how big is this...town? City?"

"Aye, Torr Cinnteag. Sinclair land. Thousands of acres, it is. Ye were nae alone? Lost yer friend as well as yer way?"

"Honestly, I haven't seen him in more than a day. We were separated when... on the mountain."

"Ye were separated from Rosie as well?"

"Rosie?" His brows knit, wondering how this woman would know of Rosie.

"Yer wife? Or lover?"

His frown deepened before he made a face that might have been interpreted as, *Ew*. "Rosie? What? No, why would you—?"

"Ye cried for her, wept her name."

Mildly offended, Cole challenged, "Okay, I'm sure I didn't cry. I didn't weep for anyone. Rosie is my aunt," he explained. "I mean, yeah, I'm a little worried about her. I know she'll fly into a panic when she doesn't hear from me. What did they do with my phone?"

"Phone?"

"My cell phone. Is there wi-fi here?"

Her blank look was eerie, and nearly made the hair rise on the back of his neck. "My phone was in my pocket. I couldn't get reception out there the last few days...where is my phone?" He asked, a bit of panic encroaching.

"I dinna ken *phone*." She moved to the small table across the room, drawing Cole's gaze. "Here is what was recovered from your person—"

"That's my phone," he said, holding out his hand as he recognized it. And then, stricken with frustration over his own behavior, as if he couldn't move, as if she should bring it to him, he frowned and threw back the covers, swinging his feet over onto the floor. He stood quickly, a little desperate to get to the lifeline of his phone. But he'd moved too quickly and was instantly lightheaded, wobbling on his feet. At the same moment he realized how weak and unsteady he was, he was also reminded that he was wearing only his boxer briefs.

"Shit," he said, falling back onto the bed, planting his feet on the cold floor beneath him. He took a deep breath, trying to salvage his equilibrium—and his modesty, flipping a corner of the fur over his lap.

A quick glance at Ailsa revealed her lips slowly parting as her wide-eyed gaze was fixed on the fur. Oddly enough, at the moment she reminded him of that actress who'd been paired with Orlando Bloom in the pirate movie—what was her name? She'd also starred in *Pride and Prejudice*. Cole only remembered the title of that one because he'd watched it back in high school as a favor to the girl he was dating (brownie points, he'd been trying to score). He'd approached it with more than a little prejudice, and—if he was honest—pride, considering himself too macho to watch what he deemed was a chick flick. However, he specifically recalled the actress for being easy on the eyes, making the whole thing surprisingly bearable.

Cautiously, Ailsa stepped forward, biting her lower lip, holding out his phone to him, holding it gingerly with two fingers as if afraid it might bite.

The light inside the room was certainly dim but he could have sworn a blush crept up her cheeks as she seemed to studiously avoid eye contact with him, her blue eyes fixed on his chest.

Keeping his gaze locked on her face, Cole blindly reached for the device, his fingers brushing hers as the exchange was made. Ailsa swallowed and took two steps backward.

Cole cleared his throat. "Is there wi-fi?"

She lifted her eyes to his. "As I dinna ken what that is, I fear there is nae."

"An internet signal?" He asked, having believed that wi-fi was a universal term.

Again, to his great consternation, her expression said she had no idea what he was talking about.

Cole sighed, realizing it didn't matter. Either the battery in his phone was dead or it had been snow-covered and now broken, but it wouldn't turn on.

He lifted his troubled gaze from his useless phone to the woman, noting once more first how gorgeous she was, and then how she was dressed. What the hell? Between this cold, dreary room and the lack of heat, the way the few people he'd met were dressed and the lack of internet, or even knowledge of it...if he didn't know better he might have guessed he had stumbled upon an ancient clan of Scots' people who disavowed modern conveniences. Either that or he'd somehow found himself in another century.

One idea was as improbable as the other.

"I will have Margaret return with a tray," Ailsa offered, backing away more until she was near the door. "Like as nae, ye need to eat to regain yer strength."

He nodded absently, a million more questions swirling in his head.

"Ailsa," he called as she went to the door.

She turned and arched one dark brow.

"Please don't..." *leave me,* he wanted to say, but was reluctant to sound so pathetic. "You'll come back, right?"

She smiled and Cole's frustration over his lingering confusion briefly dissipated.

Christ, she was gorgeous.

"Aye, sir. I will return."

Chapter Five

As promised by the remarkable Ailsa—who he could not stop thinking about—the woman named Margaret returned, this time accompanied by a silent and stoic man, assumed to be one of those castle guards Ailsa had mentioned—also remarkable for carrying a sword and dressed just as peculiarly as everyone else he'd met. Margaret delivered a tray of bread and cheese, the latter unlike any variety he was familiar with, being soft but then kind of chewy and sharp in flavor.

They did not linger, and Cole's clothes had not been returned to him, despite his request—he was angry that he hadn't thought to ask the same of Ailsa, who thus far had been the friendliest and the most reasonable. As he ate, he let his mind wander, puzzling over what Torr Cinnteag could be and what could have happened to him. He didn't remember hitting his head, but somehow, here he was...in some remote commune? A feudal reenactment village? A cult? He had no idea, but something felt very off.

Hours passed and though he wore only his underwear, the fur blanket was surprisingly warm, which kept him in bed for much of his wakeful time. Strengthened by the little bit of food offered and the bitter ale, Cole stood and checked the door, finding it unlocked. Because he had no clothes, he only cracked it open, but did not leave the room. Outside the door revealed only a narrow corridor swallowed in blackness. He investigated the bed, curious about how it seemed to sag so much, and found that it was constructed only of ropes strung taut across sturdy rails. There was no boxspring, and the mattress, such as it was, seemed to be nothing but a giant pillowcase filled with feathers and straw. It wasn't uncomfortable, but Cole imagined it would be if one spent more than one night on it.

Though he had no precise idea of time, the darkness and the stillness outside the window suggested sometime after midnight. With little else to do, he tried to sleep.

He was woken up next to the door banging open, which roused him instantly, same as the alarm inside the firehouse would when a call came in.

Cole shot up to a sitting position, heart hammering, as a towering figure filled the doorway, a wild, fur-clad character straight out of *Game of Thrones*, or an ancient Highland warrior as depicted in more than one statue encountered in his travels across Scotland over the last week.

The man was built like a bear, broad-shouldered and barrel-chested, with a heavy, weather-beaten face partially hidden beneath a dark, unruly beard. Layers of furs draped across his shoulders and chest, looking as if they'd been skinned and stitched together by hand, the pelts still rough, the edges ragged. His boots, massive and rough-hewn, laced up over thick calves, and looked decidedly homemade, crisscrossed with leather ties that seemed almost primitive. A thick belt at his waist held a long, vicious-looking dagger, and incredibly, a long sword was attached to his hip. There was an air of absolute command in his stance, as if he had authority over everyone and everything in the room. Even as the man's piercing blue eyes suggested he might be Ailsa's brother, everything about him spoke of another time.

Cole couldn't shake the feeling—one he'd steadfastly resisted for the last twenty-four hours—that he was living inside some medieval fantasy, and the longer he traded stares with this imposing stranger, the more he started to fear that wasn't far from the truth.

Visited by this impressive man and feeling particularly vulnerable—essentially tucked in bed and wearing only his underwear—Cole's most pressing concern was, *what the hell was going on*?

While the man continued to study him studiously, Cole heard himself blurt out, "Christ, what year are you living in?"

The man's response, delivered in a thick voice and accent, was a scathing, "English, are ye?"

Believing that the animosity against England was mostly a thing of the past to a great part of the population, Cole resisted rolling his eyes. But he did correct the man. "American. I'm a Yankee," he added sarcastically, wondering if the label would be as distasteful to this guy as "English" seemed to be. After all, he'd come across places in the world where *Yankee* wasn't exactly a compliment.

"How did ye come to be at Torr Cinnteag?" The man asked, coming to stand at the foot of the bed, his thick, caterpillar brows lowering to a glower.

"I was lost, separated from my friend," Cole answered, confused by the sense he got—from Ailsa as well—that his trespassing was a huge crime.

The man fired more questions at him, one after another. Knowing he'd done nothing wrong, that he'd truly been lost and nearly desperate for the cold, Cole kept his answers short.

"Yer name?"

"Cole Carter."

"Do ye spy or scout for an army or lord?"

"What? No."

"To whom do ye owe yer allegiance?"

"My allegiance?"

The scowl deepened. "Do ye bear allegiance to either an enemy clan or to the English king?"

"No," Cole answered, bewildered by what seemed evidence of a medieval mindset.

"Why do ye travel with nae weapon? And lacking proper attire?"

"I don't...generally carry weapons—"

"Ye are a man of God?"

"I'm a Catholic, if that's what you mean. What's with the inquisition?"

Ignoring Cole's curiosity, the man pressed on. "Do ye bring illness? Disease?"

"I do not," Cole ground out, annoyed now, but not in much of a position to do anything about it—he was nearly naked, and this guy had a sword, and Cole had a crazy suspicion it was not only decorative.

"Do ye fight?"

"What do ye mean?"

"Do ye fight?" The man repeated, a larger hint of irritation darkening his tone. "Ye're a braw man. Do ye use the sword? The bow? A hammer? Or do ye rely on yer fists?"

Christ, had he stumbled into some kind of underground Scottish fight club? Did something like that even exist? His head swam with strange possibilities. Were people being "rescued" in the wilderness here only to be thrown into some archaic trial by combat? More and more, he began to wonder if he were only hallucinating from dehydration or the cold. None of this made any sense—why would anyone expect him to know how to wield a sword or a bow? He was barely hanging on to a vague thread of logic that this was some elaborate dream, but a voice at the back of his mind whispered that this was real.

"I'm not looking for a fight, man. I was lost and dangerously cold, and...and admittedly, I'm eerily confused—"

"Ye frighten easily?"

Cole snarled at the man. "I don't. I'm pissed about what you're doing here, obviously trying to intimidate me, but I'm not afraid. I haven't done anything wrong, I have no bad intentions, so unless you're some cult leader trying to test me or meaning to detain me, I'd appreciate it if I could have my clothes back, and I'll be on my way."

He needed to get out of here. Something was definitely wrong with everyone he'd met here at Torr Cinnteag. A bunch of freaks, taking his clothes and wanting him to fight—well, not everyone. He couldn't bring himself to lump Ailsa in with the rest. Ailsa was no freak.

"Yer clothes will be returned, though they serve little purpose. Nae guid here o'er the winter," said the man, with an arrogance that was starting to annoy Cole. "Yer boots remain, and I'll want ye to speak with the tanner about their construction. Ye appear earnest," he decided, and then qualified, "or mayhap a fool. Time will tell, aye?"

Cole scowled darkly at the man. *What the hell did that mean?* "Seriously, man. I just want to get going. If I could just have my—"

"Ye've seen, have ye nae? Ye canna survive the forest, nae the mountains, nae at this time of year."

Cole huffed his annoyance. "Well, I can't stay here until spring. Doesn't anyone drive into...town? Or some bigger city?

Where is Torr Cinnteag? We hadn't gone that far from Fort William."

"We, ye say?"

"Yes. I was with a friend. Hank Morrison." He was unwilling to express any weakness, but his concern for Tank overrode his own pride. "I'm worried about him. He was out there with me when...when we got lost."

The man eyed him suspiciously, almost as if he were trying to decide if Cole were making this up, or more broadly, if he should trust anything Cole said.

Cole returned his stare, fury rising for being suspected of...of anything. Jesus, was this how they treated Americans in this part of Scotland?

"More snow comes, and if there is a man out there," he said, inclining his head toward the door, "he's likely lost to the elements by now."

More annoyed by the guy's imperious manner, and his dismissive attitude toward Cole's rights and the prospect of Tank's survival, Cole tried to turn the tables and began to question him.

"And who are you?" He asked, a bit of arrogance infused in his tone, as if the man were beneath him. It was a tough sell—again, sitting in his underwear, unable to stand.

A slow and deliberate smirk materialized on the man's weathered face, as if he were amused by Cole's attempt to shift the tide of their exchange. Squaring his shoulders, which made him appear larger, more formidable, the man finally introduced himself. "Tavis Sinclair, I am. Mormaer of Torr Cinnteag, laird of all the Sinclairs, beholden to nae man but the king of Scotland, whoever shall wear the crown, and to God above. And ye," he said pointedly, his seemingly natural frown easing, "are nae the first stray my tender-hearted sister has brought to us."

Not sure what he should make of that statement, or the reason it might have been mentioned, Cole did not respond before the door opened, and another man, similarly dressed in fur-covered woolen garments, tall boots, and wearing a sword at his hip, entered the room.

The man eyed Cole suspiciously as he approached Tavis, whispering something in his ear, to which Tavis bent and listened. His features sharpened into hard lines as the man spoke at his ear. When the man finished speaking, Tavis gave a single, decisive nod before casting a brief, appraising look at Cole.

"Ye'll stay here, under watch, until we're certain what to make of ye and yer vague tale."

My tale? Cole thought, his own displeasure matching Tavis Sinclair's.

Before Cole could respond, Tavis gave a low command to the man who'd entered, and with one last enigmatic look, he strode toward the door. The second man threw a hard, silent glance in Cole's direction, which Cole supposed was meant to scare him, before he followed Tavis from the room, pulling the door closed behind him.

This place is insane, Cole thought as he ran a hand through his hair, exhaling. If he didn't figure out what was happening soon, he was liable to lose his mind—or worse, end up as some pawn in whatever strange game these people seemed to be playing.

Cole considered again the strange change in the atmosphere, when everything changed, and how nothing was as it seemed, or as expected since then. Shit, *had* he traveled back in time? Had he somehow, miraculously, stumbled through a worm hole?

Christ, listen to yourself.

This was real life, not some sci-fi book or movie. This wasn't some elaborate virtual reality experience, and he sure as hell wasn't dreaming. Every moment here was too vivid, too jarringly real. But if this wasn't the past, or a hallucination, or some kind of medieval cult...then what was it?

He shook his head, frustration gnawing at him as he tried to make sense of the endless, strange details that surrounded him. The clothes, the swords, the archaic way they spoke—everything seemed to be something that might have been found on a history channel special or in an epic Hollywood movie.

Cole took a deep breath, trying to tamp down the rising panic.

What the hell was happening?

***

Ailsa rarely felt compelled to see her brother off when he left Torr Cinnteag, but this morning she made a point of being present. The courtyard was crowded with men preparing to leave, as Tavis was to be accompanied by several units of the Sinclair army. Busy barking out orders to his men, Ailsa hoped he didn't leave her with any commands, specifically that she not visit the weary traveler she'd brought home and who presently kept a chamber in the back of the chapel. If Tavis expressly forbade her, she would have no choice but to obey. But if he neglected to do so, she might just have an excuse to pay Cole Carter another visit.

Though she appreciated her brother's intentions, his overprotectiveness was an ever-present burden, one that often frustrated her. Today, with him leaving to meet the MacLaes—likely to negotiate her marriage, she was painfully aware—Ailsa couldn't help but wonder: if Tavis succeeded in seeing her wed, what would he do with all the time he now spent worrying over her? How would he bear not having complete control over her actions, her choices, her daily life?

She sighed softly as she made her way through the throng of men and horses toward her brother, her thoughts straying toward and staying with Cole Carter. Recently, her brother's plans to secure a match for her had filled her with growing apprehension but she found that her concern over this matter had paled considerably in the last twenty-four hours, being overshadowed by thoughts of Cole Carter.

She sidestepped the swish of a horse's tail as she passed and supposed one—any living, breathing female—would be hard-pressed to prevent her thoughts from straying toward Cole Carter. Repeatedly.

The man was unlike nay she had ever met. Foreignness aside, he was the most incredible man—person, mayhap—she'd ever encountered. She found it impossible to tear her gaze from him. Fancifully, she'd equated his voice to be similar to the feel of velvet skimming over naked flesh. The brilliant blue of his eyes was beyond striking. And though in all her twenty-one years she'd never had her head turned by a man's figure—and living in proximity of an army of several hundred, she'd seen many—she'd been rendered frozen and speechless at the sight of Cole Carter's bare chest yesterday.

In a moment of lingering awe, she'd said to Anwen that the man was decadent. She'd used that word. *Decadent.*

Her statement, which she'd instantly regretted, had sent Anwen into a near apoplectic shock. The maid's eyes had widened dramatically, her mouth had hung open to the count of ten, and she'd stammered a string of unintelligible words before chastising Ailsa soundly and coherently, threatening to tell Father Gilbert of her sin of lust.

Ailsa had hardly been chastised but had insisted firmly that it was simply a matter of appreciation of natural beauty.

After that, she'd taken hasty leave of Anwen, leaving the maid alone with her visible skepticism.

Tavis had his back to her as she approached, checking his horse's gear and fastening the flap of his saddlebag.

"Tav," she called softly. Her use of the familiar nickname earned her his attention immediately. He turned, his expression softening as his gaze settled on her.

"Ye dinna usually see me off," he remarked, his tone warm but slightly suspicious.

"I wanted to this time," she replied, stepping closer. "Please be careful."

Tavis's brow furrowed slightly, the ghost of a smile tugging at his lips. "I'll nae face any danger with the MacLaes," he assured her. "Their mormaer passed last summer, and the son who's taken his place is a reasonable man."

"That may be so, but danger is everywhere and are ye nae the one who proclaims that to me?" Ailsa countered. "The safest place for ye is here, at home."

"I'm nae much use to ye or anyone else if I stay here all my life," he said with a wry smile, but his tone turned serious as he continued. He narrowed his gaze at her, studying her. "Ye ken I might well return with the promise of a betrothal—ye to Alastair MacLae?"

"I ken," she acknowledged, aiming for indifference. "I understand my role, brother." She abhorred it, but she knew she had little choice in the matter.

"I'll nae betroth ye, nae wed ye to a monster of any kind, nae to a man unworthy of ye."

Ailsa hesitated, his words settling uncomfortably in her chest. The problem with Tavis's vow was that she wasn't sure he truly understood her—not as a person, not as his sister, not as someone with hopes and fears of her own. How could he possibly decide what she was worthy of, when he seemed to view her more as a chess piece than a flesh-and-blood woman?

Another, separate concern was that Tavis's idea of what constituted *a monster* was far different from Ailsa's.

The fact that he was intent on engaging her to Alastair MacLae said either that Tavis didn't know her at all, or worse, that he simply didn't care, and that he valued an alliance with the MacLaes more than her safety or her dignity. Alastair MacLae, it was no secret, was a man with predatory eyes, a man whispered about even in the kitchens and halls of the Sinclair keep. Ailsa had heard the hair-raising stories: of women cornered in dark hallways and kitchens, forced into silence through threats or worse. There was talk of one young maid who had vanished from his household altogether, her absence chalked up to family matters no one could seem to verify. And there were others—maids who'd been summoned to his chambers and returned pale and hollow-eyed, unwilling to speak of what had happened but clearly changed by it.

Presently, Ailsa forced a smile and reached for his forearm, patting it gently. "Just come back safely," she said, her voice steady.

He nodded, his expression softening further. "Aye, and so I will."

As Tavis mounted his horse, Ailsa stepped back, wrapping her arms around herself.

The Sinclair banners fluttered in the cold morning breeze as the party began to move.

She didn't wait long after her brother and the dozens of soldiers had cleared the gate before she turned and went toward the chapel, undeniably, childishly giddy with eagerness to see Cole Carter again.

***

The floorboards were cold beneath his bare feet as Cole paced the small room, one hand holding the fur blanket around his shoulders, the other raking through his hair. Morning light spilled through the narrow window, its brightness doing nothing to banish the chill in the air or the confusion gripping him.

His thoughts chased each other in circles, none offering answers. He still had no idea what kind of place this was, where he'd wound up, and his worry over Tank was growing by the minute.

He stopped, pausing near the window to listen to the unfamiliar sounds. Outside, he could hear faint voices carried on the wind and the occasional clatter of hooves, the latter seeming to grow distant.

A knock at the door startled him, spinning him around. He turned, tightening the blanket around him. "Yeah," he called, his voice raspier than he'd intended.

The door opened slowly, revealing Ailsa. Her gaze swept over him—barefoot, disheveled, and wrapped in the fur like a makeshift toga—and she arched a delicate brow.

"Good morning," she said, a slight smile softening the wariness he thought he saw in her gaze.

"Morning," he muttered, adjusting the blanket with a flicker of self-consciousness. Realizing that the fur draped over his shoulders left his legs—and far worse, his crotch—exposed, he decided it might be wiser to prioritize modesty. With a quick motion, he let the fur slide down, rewrapping it securely around his waist, much like a towel after a shower.

"I thought I might check on ye," she continued, stepping farther into the room and letting the door close behind her. "Ye seemed...adrift, yesterday. Are ye feeling better?"

He hesitated, the weight of his bewilderment pressing against the fragile dam holding back his panic. Was he feeling better? Not even remotely. But he couldn't bring himself to say that aloud, not yet. "Better," he lied, forcing a faint smile.

She didn't look convinced, but she nodded. "Good. And are ye warm enough?" She glanced around the small room. "Och, I said to Margaret to return your clothes. She has nae?"

"She has not."

"Ye are hungry as well, nae doubt?" She asked and then bit her lip, awaiting his response, suddenly more shy.

"Yeah, I am, but Ailsa..." he paused, something of greater concern than his hunger itching at him. It would sound ridiculous, but he couldn't *not* ask—he needed to know. "Ailsa," he began again, his voice tighter than he intended, "I have to ask you something—and it's going to sound ridiculous, but..."

She waited, her expression softening, arching a brow. "Aye."

He hesitated, rubbing a hand over his face. His pulse hammered. He met her cautious blue-eyed gaze and simply spoke the words. "What year is it?"

Her brow furrowed in confusion. "Year? 'Tis thirteen hundred and two. Why would ye—?"

Cole didn't hear the rest. Her words hit him like a blow, and his legs buckled. He staggered back over to the cot and sat, his breath coming in short, ragged gasps. Panic clawed at his chest, and he gripped the fur at his waist with one hand and the edge of the bed with the other, his fingers rigid and curled, trying to anchor himself.

"Sir?" Ailsa moved and was at his side in an instant. Her voice was tinged with concern. "Are ye unwell?"

He waved her off weakly, squeezing his eyes shut. "No—yes—I don't know. Just...give me a second."

The air in the small room felt impossibly thick, the walls pressing in. He fought to stave off the rising tide of panic, the sting of tears threatening to betray him. God, he hadn't cried in years, and now—now of all times—he couldn't lose it.

"Sir?" she probed gently, kneeling before him.

Cole lifted his gaze to her, wondering what his expression looked like that caused a small gasp from her.

"1302?" He repeated. "You're not lying to me? You're not joking?"

Ailsa shook her head, and a few strands of her hair slipped from beneath her hood, falling across the rich fabric of her cloak. Cole's attention was riveted by her, specifically her cloak.

The fabric was heavy, coarse but well-woven, and faintly textured in a way that was entirely unfamiliar. It lacked the smooth perfection of modern textiles, seeming handmade, with small irregularities at close inspection. The stitching, too—rough, uneven, but clearly done with care—looked like it belonged in a museum exhibit, not around her body. The fur lining the collar and possibly the interior, looked imperfect—real—not like the faux fur that was familiar to the twenty-first century.

Absently, he reached out, hesitated, then let his fingers brush lightly at the wool at her shoulder.

Ailsa's brow furrowed in confusion and it seemed she held her breath, but she didn't stop him. He dropped his hand, staring at the fur wrapped around his own waist. It was supple but raw, the kind of hide more likely to come from a pelt cured by hand than anything mass-produced.

The panic surged again, mingled with a reluctant, dawning realization. Nothing around him belonged to the world he knew.

His throat tightened. "What the hell?" he murmured, his voice barely audible.

He scowled fiercely and rubbed both hands over his face, his fingers digging hard into his flesh and eyes.

He stayed like that for a long moment. Even when he stopped trying to rub disbelief from himself, he sat with his hands over his face, trying to make sense of it.

"What troubles ye?" Ailsa asked quietly after at least a full minute had passed. "Perhaps if ye speak of it, I can help."

Despite himself, Cole barked out a laugh. He dropped his hands, one of them returning to the fur, meaning to keep that in place. He met Ailsa's compassionate gaze.

How the hell could she possibly help?

He laughed again. "Here's the kicker—yeah, I'd love to run this by someone, but...Christ, there's no way in hel—er, sorry, no way on earth you would ever believe me."

Ailsa responded without hesitation. "But if ye say something true, why should I nae believe ye?"

He stared at her, dumbfounded.

And then laughed some more. "It's that easy? Okay. Fine. Here it goes. And this is the truth—I'm from another time. I mean, I was born in the year 1995, and somehow, impossibly, I've been brought back in time to...now."

She stared at him, for a moment looking like he no doubt had a moment ago, utterly confounded.

And then she flashed a nervous but still gorgeous smile and rose from her haunches. "I understand now," she said mildly. "Ye've said that to show me how naïve I am to imagine that people tell the truth at all times. I only meant that ye dinna personally strike me as one who told fibs. I am nae entirely gullible, though."

Wilted by defeat for a moment, Cole allowed his shoulders to slump. He did, however, announce that he'd proven his point. "There, I have told the truth, and you have found it impossible to believe so how am I...?" He stopped and blew out a frustrated breath. "I don't even know what questions to ask, what discussion to have, who to talk to about this."

Ailsa returned his stare and bit her lip again. "I find Father Gilbert's counsel to be most effective. Aye, he's critical and does nae spare one's emotions, but he counsels wisely, listening with a benevolent ear and advising most cleverly."

"You think I should speak to a priest about this very strange..." he paused, waving his hand, searching for the right word, "*unholy* thing that I've somehow done."

Cole had never been overly religious, but whatever had happened to him didn't feel like something God would have had a hand in. In fact, it felt like the exact opposite—unnatural, maybe indeed unholy. Time wasn't meant to bend or break, wasn't meant to send people spinning backward through the centuries. There was something off about the whole thing, something that made him feel like he was messing with forces beyond what any human should touch. If there was a divine plan, surely it didn't involve throwing a man into the past like a rag doll.

Cole considered the impossibly beautiful Ailsa and the very evident doubt of her expression.

"You don't believe me," he guessed.

Tilting her head to one side, she asked, "Believe ye? About yer...predicament?"

"Yes, my time-traveling predicament."

"I..." she began with great hesitation. Evidently, she would attempt to spare his feelings, and refused to outright say she thought he was nuts, or that he lied.

"You said I only needed to speak the truth, and you would believe me and here you are, in the same conversation, expressing an offensive disbelief." He hadn't intended to speak so sharply, but the weight of his bewilderment and the edge of rising panic bled into his tone. While he was captivated by her, his own predicament did override any interest in Ailsa. He didn't want to alienate her—he needed her help.

"Ailsa, is there any way I can get my clothes back? The big guy—he said his name was Tavis—"

"My brother," she supplied.

"Yeah, well, he said he would return them but he hasn't"—huge BS, by the way, taking his clothes away from him, over which Cole was really pissed about, but he wasn't going to argue that with Ailsa—"and I need...well, I can't stay here in my underwear. I need to leave. I need to find Tank."

"But ye are nae well enough—"

"I am," Cole insisted. "I'm fine. I was definitely rundown by cold, hunger, and exhaustion, but I'm fine now. I thank you for what you've done for me, but I need to find my friend."

"Ye...ye will need my help with that as well, I believe."

"Yeah," Cole conceded, never having felt so helpless as he did at this moment. "Yeah, I do."

Chapter Six

There was no denying the thrill of freedom Ailsa knew whenever Tavis left Torr Cinnteag. With her brother gone, there was a precious quiet in the air, the weight of his watchful gaze lifted, allowing her to feel unencumbered, almost light. She relished it—the chance to wander as she wished, to linger over the small tasks and visit with those in and around the keep without him worrying over her every move.

And yet, invariably, as the hours ticked by, certainly if he were gone for any length of time, days or weeks, a pervasive disquiet would inevitably set in. Without Tavis's constant presence, Torr Cinnteag somehow felt...exposed, as if something vital was missing from its stone walls. His absence cast a shadow, not because she depended on him to feel safe but because his presence was such an integral part of what *made* the keep feel safe. And though his vigilance sometimes bordered on stifling, she understood the strength behind it, the command he brought to their home.

Today, however, she was nearly giddy with her brother's absence. If Tavis were here, she would never be allowed to assist Cole with any search for his friend. But, in order to help Cole, she would have to abide by certain rules. Tavis would fuss when he found out—little ever escaped him at Torr Cinnteag, thanks to his ever-watchful soldiers, whose clacking tongues and keener ears might rival a flock of sharp-eyed ravens, and Anwen, her maid, who never failed to report to Tavis things she deemed worthy of his consideration. Nothing stayed hidden for long, and no tidbit of news or rumor went unreported. Ailsa knew her best chance to escape her brother's censure was to arrange the particulars of the rescue to Tavis's liking. She would need her maid present and a suitable number of guards to accompany them. Tavis would lock her in her chamber if she ever dared to venture outside of Torr Cinnteag by herself—and with a man who was a stranger to them and who was so much a mystery.

It took her twenty minutes to track down Cole Carter's clothes. Curiously, she found them in the rectory's larder. Supposing that Margaret or Mary might have considered his clothing strange, and possibly soiled from his journey, either of the cautious maids might have been the one to hang them about the larder to air out. Ailsa suspected this might have had something to do with a vague belief that the garments might have been imbued with foreign energy or bad luck—both Margaret and Mary subscribed to such foolishness—and had hoped the coolness of the larder might have cleansed them properly. His shoes were there as well, sitting innocuously on the packed-earth floor just inside the door.

Ailsa wrapped up everything tidily and returned to the chamber he occupied. Meaning to allow the undressed Cole Carter to maintain his pride, she rapped at the door and announced she would leave the bundled clothes and his boots just outside the door.

"Come to the courtyard when ye are ready," she called through the door.

With that done, she set off to find Anwen and Dersey and make further arrangements for the day.

Fifteen minutes later, Ailsa arrived in the courtyard, accompanied by a protesting Anwen.

"Enough to be done indoors where it's warm," Anwen was squawking in Ailsa's ear, "and here ye are, wanting to traipse around the countryside looking for a man ye dinna ken—as if the cap'n could nae manage the search hisself."

Ailsa did not respond to Anwen's grousing, knowing that the maid would complain also in the middle of summer, arguing that the sun was too strong, or that flowers attracted bees, or that no sane person would be traipsing about in such heat. To Anwen, any weather was an inconvenience, and any task outside her usual routines was cause for concern.

"And what's more, it's nae just that we're wastin' the day, but a full party we need to keep after ye, makin' sure ye're safe! And for what? A stranger—"

"A person who might be in danger," Ailsa interrupted gently. "A person in need is one worth helping. Is it nae our duty, as decent folk, to see to those who may be lost or in danger?"

Anwen harrumphed and asked, "Aye, ye're nae one to let one in need go wanting, but would this have anythin' to do with currying favor with the *decadent* man?"

It didn't, not really. But God, how Ailsa wished she'd never described her feelings about the look of Cole Carter to her maid. Ignoring Anwen's question, she asked instead, "Were it one of our own, would we nae be pleased for any kind stranger who helped them?"

Anwen sighed dramatically but fell silent, though Ailsa could feel her maid's disapproving gaze at her back as they continued through the courtyard.

Dersey hadn't been any easier to convince, the old captain grumbling in much the same manner as Anwen—what a pair! Ailsa's argument that it was the decent thing to do hadn't carried so much weight as when she'd said she would simply arrange the effort herself and go without him.

But Dersey was among those gathering in the courtyard, he and half a dozen men as she'd requested. Horses were ushered out from the stables, their hooves kicking up small clouds of dirt and snow as they were led to waiting soldiers.

Ailsa weaved her way through the throng of men and horses, moving toward the chapel at the south side on the courtyard, and the rectory behind it. She donned her gloves as she went, having grabbed those along with her heavier, hooded mantle and her sturdier, warmer boots. She didn't get very far before she spied Cole Carter emerging from the small door of the rectory that opened into the bailey.

He did not see her immediately. He'd just stepped outside and stood in profile, dressed now as he had been when first she'd seen him yesterday, just before he collapsed. Ailsa stared with some bewilderment at his clothing. The material of his close-fitting cloak was bright and unlike any fabric she'd ever known, seeming too thin to be of any protection against the cold. Because she'd seen the items hanging in the larder, she knew there were several tunics, having delivered three items with sleeves. She'd judged the several thin layers odd, and utterly inappropriate for the harsh Highland climate, where layers were thicker and more functional. And yet, he did not now appear to be cold. Compared to the footwear she was accustomed to seeing, Cole Carter's boots, tied with multi-colored laces and having unusual smooth and shiny soles, wrought a curious frown from Ailsa, who wondered if they were made by artisans rather than craftsmen, or invented entirely by magic. Being both intrigued and perplexed by the unfamiliar shapes, textures, and the questionable functionality of his clothing, Ailsa interpreted his appearance as something mysterious, which naturally compelled her to consider his own implausible explanation, that he'd come from another time.

Though she continued toward the chapel, her steps had slowed considerably at the sight of him.

Cole Carter took in the courtyard scene with slow, sweeping glances, his expression shifting as the scene unfolded before him. Ailsa noted the subtle creasing of his brow, the way his gaze lingered on the fur-clad and helmeted men and restless horses as though he were trying to comprehend their presence in front of him. His mouth opened slightly, suggesting the need to question what he saw, but it closed again, and he remained silent.

But then he spotted her, and Ailsa's heart flipped quietly as his expression lightened immediately, showing what she gauged as relief as he began to walk toward her with a purposeful stride as he closed the gap.

Ailsa recognized straightaway the almost mesmerizing contrast in his movement compared to those around him. Hale and hearty now, he moved with a confident, unhurried stride, his frame loose and ready. She noted the powerful build of his shoulders and his thighs in his strange, snug breeches, and at the same time saw that he lacked the stiff, burdened posture of men used to bearing the weight of armor. He walked with a casualness that was as foreign as it was captivating, his stride easy and fluid, yet perfectly controlled.

As Cole approached Ailsa, the relief she thought she'd noticed seemed to evaporate. He cast swift glances around the courtyard again and then over Ailsa's shoulder, where Anwen followed. His jaw tightened, and his lips pressed into a thin line.

He did not stop at a polite distance but came very close to her, causing Ailsa's pulse to race.

He leaned close and kept his voice low. "This really is...1302?" he asked, with just enough caution to imply he was aware of the strangeness of the question. Taking a step back, he met her gaze. His eyes held hers, full of uncertainty but also a faint flicker of hope that she'd understand what he was grappling with.

Caught off-guard by what seemed a genuine bewilderment, Ailsa nodded wordlessly, and glanced around the courtyard, wondering what might seem strange to him. What did his world—some unimaginable *future*—look like? Born in 1995, he'd told her, which seemed as distant and mysterious to her as anything on the edge of a dream. Just as he gazed at the familiar sights of the bailey with an air of disbelief, she felt her own curiosity spark at the thought of this strange, far-off century, where all she knew and trusted would likely not be found.

As quickly as these thoughts came, she shook them off, silently chiding herself for even allowing the smallest flicker of belief in his wildly improbable tale. The idea of a man from another time—born nearly seven hundred years into some distant, unthinkable future—was nothing but an absurd fancy, she reminded herself sternly. In all likelihood, his recent illness, wrought by exposure to the harsh elements, had left him muddled, susceptible to fevered imaginings.

"But all will be well," she assured him with as much sincerity as she could muster. "Dersey and the lads have assembled now and the search for yer friend will commence."

Dersey had wrangled half a dozen lads, among them a few who were hopelessly enthralled with Ailsa. Rory, Colin, and

Cian regularly vied for her attention with transparent eagerness. She did not encourage their interest, but she wasn't above making good use of it if it suited her purposes.

The lad, Somerled, was present as well in the bailey, seated atop a borrowed palfrey. He showed no particular interest in Ailsa, the stranger in their midst, or the mission, but hummed a low tune, swishing his blade through the air above his head, more amused by his clever slashes than anything else.

"This beats drills, at least," he said to no one in particular.

Anwen snorted. "Aye, if ye're looking to avoid useful work," she said tartly, her sharp tongue cutting through the morning's chill. Unlike Ailsa, she didn't spare Cole even a flicker of admiration. If anything, her narrow eyes seemed to weigh him as one might a three-legged goat, considering him more troublesome than he might be worth.

Another soldier, Domhnall, kept his gaze fixed on Cole, the watchful suspicion in his dark eyes an unmistakable contrast to the others. While he said nothing, his posture betrayed an unwarranted dislike of Cole Carter, as though waiting for the stranger to confirm his opinion. Domhnall could be troublesome, and she hoped he would cause her no grief today.

Ailsa moved toward the chestnut mare that had been brought for her. She placed her foot in the stirrup and swung into the saddle with ease, the spirited horse tossing her head as if she, like Anwen, protested the idea of a long winter ride. Ailsa arranged the long folds of her mantle to cover her hose-clad legs, exposed by her position astride. Beside her, Anwen mounted a gentle, sturdy palfrey, her grip on the reins firm, her expression tight with displeasure.

Cole remained afoot, studying the lively horse brought to him by the stable lad. He looked at it skeptically, his attention divided between the saddle and the animal's shifting hooves. He hesitated, glancing up at Ailsa. "I can't ride a horse—or rather, I never have."

Ailsa blinked, momentarily speechless. Never had she known a man, not infirm or otherwise disabled, who was unable to ride. A flicker of doubt coursed through her, wondering if he jested, but his blue-eyed gaze seemed sincere.

Just then, Dersey approached, his discontented frown deep, suggesting he'd overheard Cole's outlandish confession.

"What's this?" Dersey's gruff voice carried, his gaze shifting from Cole to Ailsa with obvious impatience.

Dragging her incredulous gaze from Cole, Ailsa hastily introduced them, having forgotten until now that they'd not properly met. "Dersey, this is Cole Carter, the man ye brought from the forest yesterday."

Cole covered the space between him and the mounted Dersey, reaching up his hand. "Pleasure to meet you," he said, his voice firm.

Dersey stared at Cole's extended hand as if afraid it might produce a weapon from thin air, scowling as he circled his fingers around the hilt of his sword.

Without a word Cole took a step backward, lowering his ignored hand. While Ailsa was embarrassed by Dersey's mute hostility, Cole seemed unphased, more captivated by Dersey's weathered face and imposing stature, his eyes bright with interest rather than intimidation.

"Anyway, thanks for what you did," Cole said and turned his back to Dersey, effectively—and haughtily, Ailsa thought with a hint of a smile—dismissing the older man.

"Ailsa, I appreciate this, I really do," Cole said, drawing her full attention, in part for how easily her name came to his lips, "but I don't think this will work. I can't ride a horse, and I wouldn't expect you or these men to walk with me. I don't mind going out on my own. If you can just point me in the right direction, either where you found me or where I might have come from...?"

"Canna ride a horse, he says," came Anwen's voice behind Ailsa, her tone derisive.

Ailsa's fingers tightened on the reins of her own mount, unprepared for the unexpected pang that came with the thought of him leaving. She couldn't fully explain it, but something in her balked at the idea of letting him search alone. If he found his friend, she had the unsettling notion they might not return to Torr Cinnteag—and that idea filled her with a strange, wordless disquiet.

"Nae, 'tis dangerous to go off on foot, and alone," she determined. "Ye'll ride double. We're safer on horseback, sir."

She turned and stared expectantly at the men waiting to accompany them, annoyed to find that each of them had found something suddenly fascinating to inspect on the ground or in the distance, deliberately avoiding her gaze and clearly uninterested in offering a ride to Cole Carter. Though Cian faced her, wearing a wince that suggested he was not keen at all with the idea of sharing the saddle with Cole Carter, Rory and Colin kept their gazes averted.

While even Anwen frowned with displeasure over the obvious slight, Ailsa rolled her eyes with frustration, and faced Cole again, directing her mare to sidle next to him. "Climb up. Ye can ride with me." She removed her foot from the stirrup so that he might use it to mount.

"Och, Sweet Mary," Anwen squeaked in dismay.

Domhnall spoke up as well, his tone curt. "He will nae!"

Dersey groused vehemently, "We can spare the horse—he'll have to learn to ride as we go."

"The laird would nae take kindly to—*Jesu*, lass," added Cian, aghast at the very idea.

They'd each spoken in their own Scots' language, but Ailsa wouldn't have imagined that Cole Carter didn't understand their objections based on their harsh tones.

She addressed Cian specifically, in English, ignoring the others. "If ye fear ye canna protect me from a lone male who is scarcely recovered from his weakness..." she began with feigned innocence.

At her side, Cole objected to her characterization. "I'm not weak," he insisted, mildly offended.

Ailsa shot him a disgruntled look, willing to sacrifice his pride to make her case.

When no one offered any other objection, and after a cautious glance at Dersey, Cole shoved his foot into the stirrup and grabbed hold of the pommel in front of her, hauling himself up behind Ailsa. He landed with a bit of a bounce and Ailsa scooched forward in the saddle, hoping there was enough room for him. Even as she imagined she should have expected it, she stiffened when Cole's hands landed on her hips, his fingers curling lightly into the fabric of not only her mantle but the léine beneath it.

Ignoring the fact that her cheeks were no doubt flushed once again with a furious blush, Ailsa turned what she hoped was an innocent gaze onto Dersey. "Shall we?" she asked.

The captain's lips were thinned so dramatically they were lost entirely inside his beard. "Be the death of me, ye will," he muttered. But he moved forward, taking the lead of the small party as they moved out through the gates of Torr Cinnteag.

Anwen, a proficient but awkward rider, fell into step beside Ailsa and Cole and made no secret of her inspection of him.

"Ye speak English well enough, Anwen," Ailsa reminded her. "If ye've a question for him, ask him."

"Nae query have I at this time," replied Anwen imperiously, as if to impart that she would reserve judgment.

"We'll start where we found Sir Cole yesterday," Ailsa called out to Dersey, "and work from there to the south."

"Aye, I ken what I'm about," was called back.

"He's not too keen on this mission," Cole guessed, his voice close to Ailsa's ear.

She swallowed against the tumult raised by the warmth of his breath tickling her flesh and hair. "In truth, he harbors a natural and relentless aversion to strangers."

"Your brother seemed to share a similar dislike."

"Tis nae to be taken to heart, sir, as in this—"

"Just Cole. I'm not...well, there's no need for the *sir*."

Ailsa thought quickly enough that this was likely true. A knight, deserving the *sir*, would have great experience on horseback. "Very well. But please dinna take offense to their lack of a warm welcome. 'Tis rare that strangers find their way to Torr

Cinnteag, and then even more uncommon that they dinna bring trouble with them."

"As I told your brother and if I recall correctly, as I said to you when I first saw you, I don't mean any harm. I'm not dangerous."

Oh, but he was, of course, but not in the way he implied or as Tavis and Dersey, and possibly Anwen and some of the Sinclair soldiers, feared.

Changing the subject, Ailsa inquired, "But what were ye and yer friend—"

She lost her voice and her thoughts as Cole extended his hand from her side, wrapping it around her middle. As he did so, he tightened his grip briefly, adjusting his position until her back was pressed against his chest. While staring straight ahead, Ailsa's eyes widened and her body became rigid.

"Sorry," he offered almost immediately. "I felt like I was about to tumble off the horse's rear end. This is better."

Ailsa swallowed, holding her breath. She wasn't at all certain this was *better.*

"My friend's name is Tank," Cole said then, as if he'd not created so much tumult within her by wedging himself so familiarly against her. "That's his nickname, anyway. Hank Morrison, known as Tank."

Ailsa cleared her throat. "Very well, and what were ye and Tank doing that ye were separated and so far inside Sinclair land?"

She felt him glance around, as if gauging who their audience might be. He lowered his voice, and again his breath wafted warmly against her ear. "We're simply tourists, visiting Scotland.

We were out on a hike—Tank wanted to climb that mountain. But...something happened, everything got really weird."

"What do ye mean?"

"The air was funny—I don't know, like just different, but it wasn't too heavy or too light. I can't describe it, but suddenly, though I could see Tank—he was standing just a few feet away—he sounded like he was under water. Or in a barrel, really far away. It was hard to hear him. It makes no sense, I know. And then I lost my...I blacked out. And when I woke—it must have been hours later—I couldn't find him anywhere. I wasn't in the same place, wasn't up on the mountain anymore. But nothing was familiar, and there were no tracks. Tank was just...gone, like he vanished into thin air. I spent half the day looking for him, and then as it got dark, I was trying to find the road we'd come in on, or any road. I wanted to get emergency services out here, a search party, but I never found any signs of...civilization. Nothing. You were the first person I saw in more than twenty-four hours."

While he'd spoken, Ailsa had glanced frequently at Anwen, deciding that she was trying to eavesdrop but could not. Cole kept his voice low and with his face so close to her head, she believed the sour look Anwen wore said only that she couldn't hear anything being said.

"I don't know how much longer I'd have survived out there if I hadn't run into you," Cole continued. "So yeah, I'm really worried about Tank."

"We'll find him, I'm sure," Ailsa said, but she wasn't sure at all. The countryside around Torr Cinnteag was unforgiving, brutal and inhospitable. As much as Cole seemed ill-prepared for it, she wasn't sure his friend would be much better able to survive it.

Cole was quiet for a few minutes before he spoke again. "Ailsa, some of these soldiers look pretty young. And you're telling me it's 1302, and they're wearing swords pretty comfortably. Should I assume those swords aren't just for show? That they've killed people? Even though a few of them don't look old enough to vote?"

Ailsa glanced around at their escort, at Colin who was possibly already ten and seven. And Rory and Somerled, who might be a year or two older than that. They were the youngest, but certainly old enough to have slain another as needed.

"Aye. Mayhap without a war, they'd nae have killed another already," she said, shrugging, "but possibly, they're alive today because they did."

"War?"

Ailsa frowned over the simple question. "Aye, the war."

"There's a war going on? Sorry, I preferred science and math to history in school. I don't remember half of what we learned about world events in this time."

"We are at war with England, sir—er, Cole," she said, a wee bit prickly, part of her assuming that he only feigned ignorance to further his pretense. Pretending ignorance about such a costly and devastating war was simply beyond the pale. Ailsa's lips tightened, her temper flaring at the audacity of his question. The war—the war that had torn the land apart, that had claimed so many lives—was something no one in these parts could ignore, and she didn't care at all for how nonchalantly he asked about it. Nonetheless, she was forced to qualify her answer. "At the moment, however, there is a truce. That is the only reason my brother is in residence. He'd been gone for more than two years until last February."

"Jesus," Cole breathed, a bit of wonder tainting the sound. "And these guys here—even these kids—they fought as well?"

"Aye. At Falkirk and Stirling Bridge—"

"Okay, those I've heard of," he said with some excitement, seemingly happy to recognize something. "Well, admittedly, only since Tank and I had come to Scotland, but we did visit the Stirling memorial."

"From where did you come?"

"From home. New York."

"York?" She bristled. "Ye said ye were nae English."

"I'm not." He paused and blew out a breath, one of frustration "New York is in America. Although, I guess it's another couple hundred years before that's discovered."

Ailsa laughed unexpectedly, which she supposed was done to conceal her confusion. "Discovered? What was discovered?"

"America, another country. You know what, let's not get into that now. That's another discussion for another day."

Sensing he was becoming agitated, Ailsa remained quiet for a while.

The search took the group along the rugged path between the hills and the edge of the forest, their horses picking their way over rocks and uneven terrain. The snow, having stopped falling the day before, had begun to settle, but the trail Cole had left had already been trampled by the bustle of the Sinclair army's departure earlier that morning. They had little to follow but the remnants of disturbed earth and crushed grass, barely enough to discern any signs of direction. The landscape stretched before them—rolling hills, patches of heather, and the occasional stand of birch trees whose bare branches creaked in the cold wind.

They traveled for several miles, crossing a small stream and ascending a wooded rise, from where the valley below unfolded in shades of gray and brown. A few birds flitted through the trees, their calls sharp against the stillness of the morning. As they pushed further, the trees gave way to open moorland, where the ground was boggy and treacherous. There were no signs of Cole's trail here or any others, only the occasional print of critters and larger beasts.

At length, they had to consider that their search presently was fruitless and that the further away from the keep they went, the more they were exposed to danger.

As it was, Domhnall and Colin had been arguing about just that—continuing or halting the search—for the last few minutes. Domhnall wanted to give up while Colin suggested generously that they could at least carry on the few more miles to the larger crags.

"Ye two bicker like old hounds tied to the same post," Anwen pronounced about their discussion.

When Dersey finally called a halt to the search, Ailsa felt a reluctant sense of agreement. It was clear they had come as far as they could. Had they found even the faintest trace of the man called Tank, there might have been reason to press on, to scour the land for any other sign of him, however small. But with no trail, no indication of Cole's friend at all, the effort was really nothing more than a frustrating, hopeless endeavor.

"I am sorry, sir," she said quietly to Cole as she turned the horse around as did the others, "that we could nae find your friend."

"Me too. I don't suppose it would be possible to search again tomorrow?"

Ailsa winced, knowing it would indeed be difficult to cajole both Anwen and Dersey a second time. “I’ll see what I can do,” she promised him.

Chapter Seven

He hadn't really expected to find Tank. Though it unsettled him, Cole wasn't weighed down by any gut-wrenching fear that his friend was in actual danger. Part of him wondered if the way Tank's voice and his image had blurred and grown distant suggested that Tank hadn't been zapped through time with Cole. More than believing Tank was here in the 14th century with him, lost in the harsh winter terrain, Cole imagined that Tank had been left standing on that mountain in the twenty-first century, scratching his head and wondering where the hell Cole had gone.

Tank would have likely made it back to town safely, was Cole's guess. Maybe he'd already alerted the authorities, flagged down a mountain recovery team to search for a missing hiker—Cole had seen the signs and pamphlets scattered around the hiking store about the recovery services for lost climbers. The thought of those resources being spent on him, only to end up in a futile search, made him feel guilty. How could they know he'd slipped through time itself, seven hundred years into the past?

Despite his determination to focus on the search, Cole found it almost impossible to ignore his proximity to Ailsa, his arm wrapped loosely around her waist. The steady rhythm of the horse's movements brought him closer with each jolt and dip, and he became aware of details he hadn't fully noticed before: the warmth of her back against his chest, the slender strength of her frame, and the way her hair, loose strands escaping her hood, brushed against him. He almost regretted putting his arm around her earlier. He should have taken his chances, should have kept as much distance between them as possible, even if it would have meant he did eventually fall off the horse

It was cold enough that his breath clouded in the air, but he hadn't once been bothered by the temperature. And while she seemed entirely at ease, her focus sharp on the landscape ahead, Cole wondered if Ailsa was aware of his physical presence and touch in the same distracting way he was.

He respected her skill with the horse—there was an ease about her riding and managing the horse that seemed second nature to her, communicating effortlessly with the animal with only subtle shifts and nudges rather than sharp commands and physical strength. His own lack of experience felt almost laughable by comparison, but with everything else he was dealing with, that hardly seemed to matter.

Still, even as he told himself to concentrate on staying upright and in the saddle, to keep his eyes peeled for any sign of Tank or evidence that he'd come to the past, Cole couldn't ignore Ailsa's steady warmth against him, the faint, earthy scent of her hair, and most improbably, the simple, disarming realization that he trusted her.

After several hours of searching, they'd turned around and returned.

Torr Cinnteag came into view.

Cole had his first real, complete view of the castle, its walls and towers looming up from the landscape as a startling scene of rugged permanence. The stone walls were imposing, not the weathered ruins he'd visited back in the twenty-first century, but fully intact and alive with activity. From the torches lit at the gate to the guards pacing along the wall-walk, Torr Cinnteag was unmistakably a castle in its prime. The stone looked newer, sharper at the edges, and though covered in moss in places, it lacked that eroded look he had seen since coming to Scotland. A clang of metal resounded from behind the gates, followed by some order barked in another language, and the growing wind brought to Cole the scent of woodsmoke and pine, marking the fortress as fully in use, not some abandoned relic.

With each detail acknowledged, the reality of his situation struck deeper. This wasn't a scene from a movie, with set pieces arranged to look authentic. Nor was it some elaborate historical dream. In all their search today across hills and woodlands, he hadn't seen one sign of the modern world—not a paved road, not a single power line, not the faintest hum of machinery or any trace of the twenty-first century. No plane crossed the clear winter sky, and no artificial light shone anywhere.

Ahead, the massive wooden gates swung open and they rode through into the courtyard, where men and women dressed in wool and fur idled in conversation, while others were busy with chores. One man chopped wood just inside the gate. There was nothing here but the raw simplicity of medieval life, and Cole couldn't ignore the jarring fact: this was another time, another world altogether, one where the only thing out of place was him.

The group halted in the courtyard just as a light snow began to fall straight down, and the men began to dismount. Cole, unsure whether he or Ailsa should go first, hesitated, and Ailsa answered his unspoken question by swinging down with practiced ease. He realized, a second too late, that he hadn't been watching closely enough to learn anything useful about getting off a horse. It seemed simple enough... maybe just swing a leg over and slide down?

"Do ye need help?" Ailsa kindly asked, unintentionally heightening his embarrassment.

"I do not," he assured her, with more bravado than certainty. Trying to be subtle, he shifted his weight and managed to swing one leg over, but the horse shifted slightly, throwing him off balance. With a half-stumble, he landed, somehow managing to save himself from face-planting, so much less gracefully than intended. He straightened quickly and cleared his throat, brusquely brushing off his jacket. "No, no. I'm good. Just...getting my sea legs."

Ailsa raised a quizzical brow at him, while a hint of amusement curved her gorgeous lips.

Sea legs? Seriously? I'm an idiot.

He glanced around, his gaze straying toward the small chapel, where the room was that he'd been given.

"I, uh, I guess I'll call it a day," he said awkwardly, considering the darkening winter sky.

Ailsa removed her hood, lowering it down to her shoulders. Absently, she pulled the length of her hair forward over her breast, one hand smoothing down the length of it while she used her other hand to point behind her at the castle.

"'Tis nearly time for supper," she said, while snow landed and melted on her hair. "Mayhap ye'd rather enjoy yer meal in the hall than alone in the rectory?"

An invitation to dinner? He wasn't about to turn that down. "Sure, I'm starving." He realized right away how that sounded—like he hadn't been well-fed. The truth was, the portions so far had been pretty light compared to what he was used to, but still, he felt like a bit of a jerk for implying anything lacking in their hospitality. He added quickly, "I mean, I'm always hungry," with a smile, hoping to brush off more awkwardness.

Ailsa seemed to make nothing of his remark, returning his smile before turning and walking toward the castle, saying, "This way."

Cole followed, not at all reluctant to spend more time with her, and not only because the room in which he'd been staying was pretty dreary and depressing, and he feared the evening would drag on relentlessly with only his own company.

The main door of the castle opened directly into a dim, cavernous space where flickering torchlight danced along thick stone walls, revealing their coarse texture and faint patches of aged mortar. The vaulted ceiling was impressively high, and criss-crossed with wooden beams, reminding him of Aunt Rosie's church. He paused when something shifted and crunched beneath his feet. Glancing down, he saw that the stone floor was covered in what looked like straw and other dried plants, giving the grand room a very rustic, hayloft vibe. He guessed it might be used to add or hold warmth, and maybe to prevent slipperiness. This version of carpeting had a very earthy, kind of herbal scent, and he wondered if that served a purpose as well.

He continued forward but did not catch up with Ailsa, given pause by the sheer size and aesthetic of the room. Tall, narrow windows stood high on the interior wall, some of them covered with animal skins. Torches hung in regular intervals along the wall but still the huge room was dimly lit, the light shifting as did the flames. One windowless wall was covered in a hodge-podge of tapestries, flags, and weapons, adding color and what he supposed was meant to signify the Sinclair lineage and might. Being that the only heating source was a central hearth, a massive structure of stacked, rounded stones, he wondered if the animal hides and tapestries also lent a hand at insulating the room.

Rows of long wooden tables stretched across the hall, scarred by heavy use over many years, and lined with sturdy benches. The grand scale and arrangement of the tables reminded Cole of a college cafeteria, albeit far more solemn and charged with centuries of history, but the overall atmosphere of the nearly vacant room left him with an impression of both grandeur and simplicity.

A handful of maids moved through the space, one of whom he recognized as the same woman who had offered him bread and—strangely enough—beer first thing this morning. She gave him a brief glance as she passed, busying herself with setting the tables. The air smelled faintly of roasting meat and smoky firewood, with the underlying scent of something plant-like, perhaps from the straw and whatnot scattered on the floor.

Ailsa paused beside him, her eyes briefly following his as he took in the hall. "I'll just be a moment to change," she said. At his nod, she walked away, lifting the hem of her long cloak and her gown, possibly with a two-fold intent, to neither allow her clothes to drag in the straw and possibly get dirty, nor to disturb the floor covering itself.

With her departure, Cole suddenly became more aware of his surroundings and felt more conspicuously out of place. He shifted from foot to foot, and shoved his hands in his front pockets, trying to appear casual as he observed the room. Gradually, people began to trickle in: soldiers came in first, their boots echoing crisply across the stones near the doorway before being hushed by the scattering of straw, a strange but oddly practical rug beneath their feet. Then came others, bundled against the cold in worn but sturdy clothing, looking for all the world like the medieval peasants he'd only ever seen depicted in historical paintings and movies. Cole found himself watching with an odd sense of awe, seeing people from another world he couldn't quite believe were real.

The awe he felt quickly morphed into another sense, one that nearly put him at ease, the ordinariness of their expressions. As the hall filled, he watched people wearing the same familiar emotions he'd see on any street corner in the 21st century. Some entered laughing together, others looking relieved to be indoors, brushing snow off their shoulders and stamping their feet to shake the cold. One boy, no older than four or five, tugged at his mother's skirts, his small voice rising insistently for her attention as she juggled two younger children, trying her best to quiet him while casting an apologetic glance at the woman at her side. A wiry, middle-aged man entered, wearing the weary look of one who'd been working hard all day, his walk sluggish, shoulders slumped, eyes heavy, yet relieved to be somewhere warm and familiar. A few people glanced curiously at Cole, giving him sidelong looks as they entered, one woman nudging a friend and pointing him out. Others looked away quickly, trying not to stare, but unable to resist another look at the stranger in their midst. More children came, darting inside, racing ahead of their parents or bumping into others before casting glances that suggested they expected a reprimand.

Watching silently, Cole mused that despite the differences in clothes, lifestyle, and setting, human nature appeared unchanged by the vast gulf of centuries between them.

Ailsa appeared then, returning through a different door than which she'd left minutes ago. Her long cloak was gone, and her hair was no longer loose, but had been quickly braided and knotted at the back of her head, highlighting the shape of her jaw and neck.

Cole's breath caught a bit as he took in her full appearance, unhidden by the heavy cloak. Ailsa wore a simple but elegant gown that fell in soft, natural folds to the floor, the dark wool fabric colored like rust really bringing out the blue of her eyes. Her sleeves were long and close-fitting, extending almost to her knuckles, but slit at the forearm to reveal a pale layer beneath, which matched the linen at her collar and cuffs, with a sewn-on design of leaves and flowers.

A wide belt cinched around her waist, adorned with a tone-on-tone embroidery that was detailed intricately enough to suggest it had been done by someone with great skill. It drew attention to the natural curves of her figure, and the way the gown skimmed down her body seemed designed to flow with each movement. She looked regal, but not in a way that felt forced or overdone—more like she belonged naturally in this setting, radiating a quiet elegance that set her above anyone else in the room. She looked both every bit the medieval woman and somehow timeless—like she could be just as captivating at a modern dinner party as she was in this ancient hall.

He told himself not to stare, and yet he couldn't *not* look as Ailsa approached. Without the barrier of her loose hair or hood, her face was infinitely more striking. Her jawline was delicate but defined, her cheekbones high and smooth, adding a natural grace to her expression that seemed perfectly suited to the ancient stone around them. There was a touch of color on her cheeks that he recognized as a blush, and despite her clear confidence earlier today and here in her own world, Cole had a feeling that she was just as aware of him as he was of her.

Her eyes met his, and for a brief moment, she looked almost self-conscious, though she quickly masked it, her lips lifting in the faintest, polite smile. His heartbeat sped up, and his return smile felt as natural as it did unexpected. His pulse thrummed, surprised by how easily her presence calmed him and captivated him. He wasn't sure if she noticed, but it definitely felt as if he'd known her for longer than only a few hours or days.

Ailsa's smile softened, and she gestured to the end of the hall where a long, solid table stood raised on a low platform. "Come and sit with me, Cole. A valiant search for yer friend deserves a proper seat."

Cole felt a mix of gratitude and apprehension, even as he wasn't sure his effort in the search could be construed as valiant. A spot at the head table seemed a little too formal, but the thought of sitting with Ailsa, close enough to watch the flicker of firelight across her face, compelled him to accept her invitation. As they reached the main table, however, the high-pitched voice of another echoed across the hall.

"Och, so the *stranger* sits at the head table now?" chirped that other woman often seen with Ailsa, her tone dripping with what seemed like playful yet pointed disapproval. She passed in front of the table, casting a dubious look Cole's way and then fixing her gaze on Ailsa, one eyebrow lifted in unmistakable challenge.

"Pay Anwen nae mind," Ailsa said, indicating the chair that Cole should occupy.

He made to sit but recalled his manners and shifted a bit, pulling out the chair in which Ailsa would sit.

"*Merci*," Ailsa murmured as she sat.

"You speak French as well?" Cole questioned, having not even a smattering of a second language in his repertoire.

"*Un petit peu*," she replied before returning to English. "Father Gilbert speaks many languages, and he's been teaching me—French, English, Latin—since I was a bairn. In the last few years, our laird decided that it would be useful for his soldiers to know some English—just enough for those who might find themselves face to face with Englishmen in the war. Most have a rudimentary knowledge while others,"—she shrugged, smiling faintly— "well, not everyone takes to languages as easily as others."

Cole watched as Dersey, along with two other soldiers, took their seats at the opposite end of the head table. The rest of the chairs, including one richly adorned chair next to Ailsa—presumably her brother's—remained unoccupied. Dersey made no effort to hide his disapproval, sending Cole pointed glares down the length of the table. Supposing that Ailsa likely outranked him and understanding that if she wished for his company at the head table, there wasn't much Dersey could say about it, Cole let the man's obvious contempt roll off him.

Ailsa nodded to a woman standing at the end of the table, maybe only waiting on Ailsa's cue. The server immediately stepped forward, filling Ailsa's goblet with wine before moving on to the other guests at the table. Soon after, as people took their seats, the room bustled again, this time with a bevy of servers moving around, between tables, laying out platters of food.

Cole glanced down and then along the table, curious about the lack of utensils.

Unsure of the protocol and not wanting to misstep—still many sets of eyes were trained on him—he leaned toward Ailsa, inquiring, "Do they bring out the silverware?"

"Silverware?" She questioned, her brows knitting.

"Um, forks, knives, spoons," he clarified.

She cast her gaze to his hip between them, her brow remaining drawn. "Ye lost yer eating knife?"

Pretty sure she wasn't talking about his multitool, which did have a small spork and a selection of different knives, he shrugged and murmured, "I guess so."

She caught the eye of one young kid carrying bread, giving him a simple but direct nod, requesting an additional loaf be brought to their table along with an extra knife—but oddly, not a fork or spoon. However, no words were wasted, and the kid scurried off without a hint of hesitation.

He contemplated the way Ailsa managed the servants and couldn't help but liken her to a princess—maybe that wasn't the right word, but as some rich person directing their servants. She was kind, polite, didn't seem overly bossy, but it was evident she'd been born to the higher class, the ones who gave orders rather than received them.

Ailsa faced Cole again. "Would ye prefer a trencher or a plate?"

"I have no idea what the difference is," he admitted, "so I'll have what you're having."

In front of Ailsa looked to be the heel of a loaf of bread, flattened and wide, and he guessed that was a trencher, to be used as a plate.

A moment later, Ailsa summoned the next server to happen by, a young girl this time. She said something in her own language, ending it with a nod and smile, at which the girl nodded in agreement and scampered quickly away.

"Mildred will bring another trencher," Ailsa informed him. "'Tis customary for us to share a trencher, and in some circumstances, that I should feed ye," she said—straight-faced despite Cole's widening eyes. "But my brother considers the practice unseemly and does nae allow it."

Cole thought he might agree with her brother on this point. That sounded very awkward, certainly in the mixed and watchful company of the dining room. A few covert glances out into the hall showed that the skinny gaze of the woman, Anwen, was steady on him.

The extra trencher arrived. Cole tapped his fingers on it, sorry to find that it was rock hard. He'd assumed that whatever the dish with the meat and gravy was, it would be perfect for soaking into a soft, warm bread plate, something to mop up the rich sauce at the end of the meal. This thing, though, dry and solid, might have better served as a doorstop than anything meant to accompany food. He gave it another disappointed poke, wondering how anyone could manage to eat such a thing without chipping a tooth.

Ailsa was watching, he realized, meeting her puzzled gaze.

"Sorry," he murmured. "I thought it would be...different."

A ghost of a smile curved her pretty lips before she picked up her own knife and began cutting into a roasted bird—chicken?—delicate but sure-handed.

The food itself was a mystery to Cole. He could only guess at each dish's identity based on appearance: meat stews, hard bread, cheeses, and vegetables he couldn't name crowded the table, none of it anything like what he was used to. His stomach rumbled, but he hesitated, unsure how to approach it. Everything seemed to be served in large cuts, and the arrangement was completely foreign to him.

"What's this?" he asked, pointing to a small dish directly in front of them, something yellowish-orange and lumpy.

"Turnips, cooked in butter and honey," she said simply, though her tone suggested she was more amused by his confusion than anything else.

"Turnips," he repeated. "I've only ever seen turnips at Thanksgiving dinner at Aunt Rosie's table." And he'd never liked them, considering them too bitter.

He took his cue from Ailsa and everyone else dining in front of him, all of whom used only their knives and their hands to eat, and did the same. And he found that he was pleasantly surprised by the food. The meat was tender and savory, the cheeses not what he was used to but very tasty, creamier, and the turnips were hardly bitter at all. The bread was dense and kind of dry, but it had great flavor.

Still, the entire setting was surreal. As soon as he began to feel satisfied for the food hitting his stomach, he peppered Ailsa with questions, reminding her he knew nothing about the year 1302.

"So who pays for all of this? The food, the staff...this whole...operation?" He gestured vaguely at the hall, trying to make sense of it all. "Seems like an awful lot for just one place."

Ailsa paused as she sliced another piece of meat, considering his question carefully. "It's all part of the laird's responsibility," she said after a moment. "Tavis manages the lands and the people here, he and Torr Cinnteag's steward and bailiff. All these resources come from the land, the animals, and what we grow or trade." She continued, explaining how the complex web of feudal obligations worked—the people worked the land, paying part of their earnings in kind or in coin, and the laird, in turn, provided protection and resources in exchange.

Cole nodded, though his confusion hadn't entirely dissipated. "And the... people? Are you all related? All Sinclairs?"

"The Sinclairs, of course, are a large family," she replied, "but the ties are nae just of kinship. We have many allies, and some have become like family over the years. Some people live here by choice, some by obligation, but we all share the same cause—keeping the land safe and prosperous."

It was curious, how she didn't always or exactly meet his gaze even when she faced him and spoke directly to him.

Still, Cole liked leaning close to her, liked the scent of her, appreciated how perfect her skin was, no filter needed. He really liked her voice, which was neither throaty nor too high-pitched, was delicate but not too soft, just perfect for her. Her lashes sometimes fluttered when their gazes met, a subtle sign of hesitation, or maybe something else. There was something in the way her posture subtly shifted whenever he was near, a slight tension in her shoulders that spoke volumes. She wasn't exactly avoiding him, but she certainly wasn't as at ease with him as she appeared to be with everyone else. More than once, sitting so close, sharing the meal, their hands had brushed against each other's, brief and accidental. Ailsa had yanked hers back much quicker than Cole had.

He thought she might be interested in him. He guessed she wasn't terribly young, but her poise and confidence—how she commanded people and managed tasks—suggested she was capable, even tough. Yet right now and often during the search today, there was a certain shyness that softened her. It made him wonder if maybe she hadn't had much experience with dating. Perhaps that was why she seemed so visibly nervous when he was close—her fingers fidgeting with the hem of her sleeve, her cheeks occasionally flushing red here and there. It was a peculiar thing, to be both attracted to someone and yet so uncertain in their presence. It all seemed... well, medieval—so different from the boldness he was used to, where women didn't shy away but took the lead. Where he was from, women were more forthright, they'd ask a guy out, even initiate a kiss and more. Because of his role in the Buffalo Bandits and even that silly calendar, he'd experienced his share of being pursued, mostly without any attempt at subtlety.

On the other hand, Ailsa seemed very at ease in her role as—what? Lady of? Mistress of?—the castle.

He said as much to Ailsa. "You are very comfortable here, with this life."

That hadn't come out right; it sounded as if he were judging her, maybe wondering how she could be.

Quickly, he added, "I mean, you seem happy here, a perfect fit inside a castle."

Still, she must have considered his remarks strange. She tilted her head at him, her smile more confused than placating.

"My mam, when she lived, was a model of grace and responsibility," she said. "She was warm and loving, indeed, but never failed to remind me of my place in the world—my duty to my kin. She'd say, 'Ailsa, you are nae just a Sinclair by name, ye must prove it in every choice you make.'"

"What does that mean?" Cole asked. "What, specifically, is your duty?"

"I must never forget the importance of alliances in our world, or that the Sinclair's survival depends on the strength of our connections. In other words, I must marry well to preserve our family."

"You mean...like an arranged marriage?" He wasn't sure how he knew the term, but he did.

"Aye."

"And you're okay with that?"

"We, all of us here, have roles to fulfill. Mine is nae any kinder nae any meaner, than any other."

Cole's instinct was to challenge that, but he did not. This was another time, another world entirely from his own, where personal freedoms were something many never knew. In his world, people made their own choices, set their own futures. But here, where he was beginning to understand that loyalty to family and clan was everything, Ailsa's acceptance of her brother's decision made a painful kind of sense. She had no choice, not really. What he supposed was her meek acceptance wasn't weakness, but the only path she had ever known.

"But if you had your choice?" He approached in a different manner. "What would you do?"

"I would never leave Torr Cinnteag, that much I ken."

"Not even to travel? To see all the rest of the world?"

"I have nae traveled, surely nae as broadly or as far as you have," she said, grinning a bit, which advised she spoke cheekily of years and not miles, "but I canna believe there is any place so beautiful as the Highlands, nor so warm and familiar as Torr Cinnteag."

"It's certainly different than from where I'm from."

"And what is that like?"

He hesitated, wondering how much he should or wanted to reveal to Ailsa, having some reliable suspicion that she still didn't believe he was from another time. However, he enjoyed her conversation, and she'd been very open with him. He figured he had nothing to lose.

"Well, for starters," he said, lowering his voice after a cautious glance around to be sure no one was listening, "there have been a lot of advancements in basically, every area of life. So there's modern roads, big highways, and we have vehicles that drive on them—vehicles being cars, automobiles, that are...I guess I would describe it as a mechanicalized horse, if you will. But it moves even faster than the swiftest horse, so that what takes hours here, to get from one point to another, takes us only a fraction of that time. But okay, let's see, what do I like about where I live? Buffalo has...I'm not sure, maybe a quarter million people. Erie County as a whole has probably a million people, give or take."

Ailsa's eyes widened. "A million people," she mused in whispered awe. "How do they survive? Who feeds them? Where do they live?"

"Everything is different now," he paused, wincing, reluctant to use the phrase that came to mind but unable to conceive of an alternative, "er... in the future. People build their own homes. They work at jobs outside of their home. They earn regular wages. By the way, we live in a democracy—we don't have a king."

Once again, her eyes widened. She opened her mouth but apparently couldn't imagine the next question to ask.

Cole grinned. "We have a president, voted on by the people. Oh boy," he said, grinning, shaking his head. "Ailsa, this could turn out to be an entire history course on the birth of a nation and the American government. Probably best saved for another time."

She nodded, even as she seemed to struggle with what little he'd divulged so far. "Very well. Then back to your home. Yer life. Tell me about it. What about yer family?" She paused, lifting her fingers to her lips, an expression of sorrow dampening her features. "Oh...yer family must be so worried about ye."

"Aside from my aunt—Aunt Rosie, I think I mentioned her already—I don't have any other close family. My mother passed when I was in second grade." He shrugged. "My father died of lung cancer about ten years ago."

"Ye lament the loss of yer mother more than yer father," she guessed.

Stunned by her astuteness, wondering how she'd arrived at her guess, Cole questioned it.

And now Ailsa shrugged. "Yer voice changed, seemed graver when ye mentioned yer mother's passing."

That did not surprise him, so much as the fact that she noticed it. "My mother was...she was great, smart and funny, and all about family. My father, on the other hand, was...not any of those things." But he didn't want to get into that, drudging up all the unkind history of his relationship with his father. "All right, so I live in my own house. I drive to work in a car. I—"

"What is yer work? Ye are a craftsman?"

"A craftsman?"

"Ye are nae a knight, told me nae to call ye *sir*. Ye dinna ride and carry nae sword, so ye are nae a common soldier. Ye are nae of the clergy, I dinna believe. But ye are more... refined than a framer. Ye might be a craftsman."

"Actually, I'm a fireman," he said.

"A fireman?"

"Yep. In...well, in my time, we have fire...I guess you might call them fire brigades?" He ventured, but her expression hinted that was not the case. "A fireman's job is to respond to a variety of emergencies, including fires, medical matters, hazardous material issues, and road traffic incidents. We also get calls for search and rescue for people trapped or injured. It's not just putting out fires, though that's a big part of it—we do a lot of first aid, saving lives, and community education, with the goal of preventing disasters before they happen."

She listened carefully, but he couldn't read her polite expression, didn't know whether she comprehended anything he'd said. So then, he didn't think he should bother getting into his *other* job, with the Bandits. How would he ever explain the purpose of that, let alone the specifics of professional sports?

Catching a glare from Anwen while he consumed more of the food covering his trencher, he thought to ask Ailsa, "So, is Anwen your...sister?"

Ailsa showed surprise at his guess.

"Anwen is my maid."

"Oh. Shit, really?" At Ailsa's show of greater surprise, he explained. "I only mean, she's kind of bossy with you, kind of like an older sister might be."

"She was my nurse first and then my tutor, essentially, meaning she spent all my young life fostering me, plenty of time to ascend to her commanding role."

Cole considered her, measuring her tone and inflection, coming to a decision. "You love her, but she annoys you. You resent that she still treats you like a child, even though you are clearly an adult."

"Ye are nae far off in yer assessment. She is guid-hearted, but she laments the loss of control she has over me." She leaned in toward him, whispering even lower, "She runs with every tale—every imagined indiscretion or wrong—to my brother, and I swear sometimes I just want to....to pinch her. Hard."

Cole chuckled at this, having expected that she would threaten something a little more dangerous, maybe a slap or a dismissal. Pinch her? Not punch her?

Being from seven hundred years in the future, unsure how long he might stay, and fully aware that this could in no way be considered a date—despite the private conversation they'd enjoyed throughout the meal—Cole was sure of only one thing: if this had been a first date, he'd definitely be wanting a second.

Chapter Eight

Cole woke to a thin strip of light streaming in through the narrow, frosty window of the small rectory bedroom. The cold had crept in despite the heavy woolen blankets and furs piled on top of him, and though it wasn't bright white, he thought he saw his breath above him as he stared at the timber ceiling. A surge of disappointment swept through him, and he sat up and rubbed his eyes. Last night he'd fallen asleep hoping that he'd wake up back in his own bed at home, or even at the hotel in Scotland, finding that the last few days had been some long and fantastic dream. But the stone walls, the simple wooden furniture, and the smell of the woodsmoke told him otherwise. This was still...wherever here was. He still hadn't sorted that out. Or made peace with it.

He swung his legs out of bed and fumbled for his clothes, the same ones he'd been wearing since he got here, the only clothes he had. The jeans felt stiff, and his shirt carried a faint scent of greasy food and the hall's smoky torches and fire. Last night, having no other choice, he'd turned his boxer briefs inside out. What he wouldn't give for a washer, or a change of clothes. He might need to figure that out soon, though he didn't know how on earth he'd manage it here.

Ailsa would know, he guessed.

Pulling on his clothes, he found himself lingering over thoughts of her, recalling snippets of the conversation with Ailsa over supper. Though she seemed a true part of this world, she had something almost modern in her spirit, a quickness and wit that fascinated him. Cole was fairly certain she'd tried as much as he had to hide the curiosity, and he'd found himself captivated by her small, amused smiles and the way she'd catch herself glancing his way when she thought he wasn't looking. His confusion and anxiety over his situation was huge, but he couldn't deny how much he enjoyed being around her. She was intelligent, a little fiery, but guarded, as if she'd already learned to be careful with the people in her life.

Sighing at the thought of another day spent in a place and time that was so implausible and unfamiliar, Cole grabbed his coat and made his way through the narrow and low-ceiling hallway, stepping into the winter chill outside. He hoped that Ailsa might have worked something out to go out on another search for Tank, but didn't know how to find her if she didn't come to get him. Certainly, he didn't feel comfortable enough to simply walk into the castle looking for her. Or, what? Knock at the door and ask to see her?

Cole sighed, shoving his hands deeper into his coat pockets as he made his way outside. If he stayed idle too long, his thoughts would keep circling back to the bizarre reality of where—or *when*—he was. His thoughts were still tangled enough that he knew he'd better do something useful today until or unless he did run into Ailsa; he needed busy work. Back home he was better able to manage any concerns or uneasiness, usually with a hard run that left his lungs burning or a heavy session at the gym to clear his mind. When life on the field got intense or after a long, grueling shift at the firehouse, he'd always had an outlet. And on the worst days, he'd throw himself into a home project—something he could start and finish with his own two hands to remind himself he was capable, in control.

But here, none of those escapes were available. There was no punching bag, no gym, no projects to tackle. The best he could do now was to find something physical, something that would burn up the tension threatening to gnaw at him.

Almost immediately, he noticed a small group of men standing by the outer wall. He approached the group bent over the corner of the castle, trying to figure out what they were doing. The discussion among the five men was not in English so Cole could only guess what they were about, but when he was close enough, he saw that the base of the castle was in need of repair, some of the stone having fallen away. His approach drew the attention of the group, turning one pair of eyes after another, several of them filled with cool suspicion or outright hostility, the least of which was seen on the young guy he recognized from yesterday's search party group, Davey, who greeted him with a head nod and not half the wariness of the others.

"What's going on?" Cole asked, inclining his head toward the corner of the castle. "Aside from the obvious, that the castle is crumbling."

Davey shrugged. "Mayhap heavy rain has re-shaped the ground," he said by way of explanation, "or the frost, the ice, has shifted all of it."

"And you guys are supposed to fix it?" He asked, sending his gaze up along the great height of the wall.

"Aye," replied Davey. "But Dersey dinna say how. We were now discussing mayhap ramming some larger stones into place there."

Cole winced. He was no engineer, but he guessed that wasn't going to work. "I think you might have to dig out all that sagging ground and replace that with more stone." With his hands in his pockets, he shrugged as well, admitting, "But that's just a guess, though I think it might prove more stable in the long run."

Davey twisted his mouth in conjecture and consulted the guys with him, repeating what Cole had said, and then speaking in their language, possibly repeating it again for their benefit. A few of them nodded, even as none of them seemed to be pleased with the extra work. Seems they'd have been happy to take the easy route, simply adding more stone to the vulnerable base.

"If you have a shovel, I'll give you a hand digging it out," Cole offered. At the blank look of Davey and the others, Cole made shoveling motions with his hands. "Shovel? Dig? Spade?"

"Aye, spade," Davey said, catching on, while at least one other nodded his understanding as well.

Fifteen minutes later, Cole bent over the smooth-handled spade, stabbing the ground repeatedly to loosen the packed earth. The section of the wall they were reinforcing showed clear signs of erosion, and his task was to remove the area where the ground had washed away. He'd called a halt a few minutes earlier when he realized the others with shovels were digging far too wide a section, risking more unnecessary work than progress.

"Hold up," Cole had said, stepping into the middle of the activity. Drawing on his experience as one of the older players on the lacrosse team, he slipped naturally into the role of directing and correcting. Using the tip of his spade, he marked two rough lines in the ground. "We don't need to take out that much. Just this section here." He pointed between the lines. "Dig inward until you hit the stone, then we'll pack in another layer of rocks before we cover it all with this dirt we're pulling out."

It might all be guesswork, but it seemed a solid enough plan.

The two digging men exchanged uncertain glances, but when Davey translated the plan—delivered with the same easy authority of someone who knew how to manage people as Cole had—they seemed to relax.

Even with the adjusted, smaller section, the work was grueling. The ground was a stubborn mix of clay and dense earth, threaded with shards of slate and chunks of stone. Every strike of the spade jarred his arms, and the cold bit into his hands. Sweat began to gather beneath his coat despite the frigid air, and the steady rhythm of digging was punctuated by grunts of effort and the occasional muttered curse.

It took nearly half an hour to prepare the trench. While Cole and the other two men labored to dig, Davey and the remaining workers fetched the heavy stones they'd need to reinforce the wall.

By the time they'd finished clearing the trench, Cole straightened up with a groan, pressing a hand to his lower back. He wasn't sure whether it was pride or exhaustion that kept him from complaining out loud, but either way, the work felt satisfying. There was something deeply rewarding about using his hands to solve a problem, even one as foreign to him as shoring up a medieval castle wall.

He turned when he heard the sound of horses approaching, expecting that Davey had made use of a wagon and animals to move the stones. At the same moment he understood the noise was too loud to be only one or two horses pulling a wagon, he heard the gate being opened and turned to see a large group of riders coming into the yard.

Resting a hand on the handle of his spade, his gaze went to the open passage, watching as a group of mounted riders began filing in, their armor and cloaks stirring in the cold breeze. At the head of the procession rode Tavis Sinclair, his posture straight and commanding in the saddle. Behind him, a lean, older man in a dark robe followed—his presence almost austere compared to the armed men surrounding him. Cole realized this must be the priest Ailsa had mentioned, Father Gilbert, though he had little time to dwell on it.

His attention was riveted to someone else—Tank.

There he was, astride a powerful bay horse. Cole's breath caught in stunned disbelief. His friend looked haggard but whole, his familiar broad-shouldered, canvas-clad frame a strange but welcome sight amidst the sea of medieval warriors. Tank's face, however, told a story all its own. A livid bruise darkened one cheekbone, and his lip was split and swollen, stark red against his pale skin. At that moment, Tank lifted his hand and scratched at his nose, and Cole saw that his knuckles were scraped raw, as if he'd been in a fight.

Not realizing that he was frozen with shock, Cole watched as Tank dismounted—much more suavely than Cole had, by the way, except there was a stiffness to the way he moved that suggested he'd taken more than a few hits in whatever fight had made him black and blue.

"Tank?" Cole murmured, the word audible only to himself, hardly able to conceive what appeared to be true: Tank was here in the same impossibly foreign time and place, looking like he'd fought his way through hell. Shaking himself free of his shock, Cole tossed aside the spade and climbed out of the trench. "Tank!" He called.

Tank froze and searched the now crowded yard, lost briefly to sight by the number of men and horses between them.

"Cole?"

"Yeah," Cole laughed, his mood and desperation vastly improved. Impatiently, he pushed men and horses out of his way and finally had a clear path to Tank, peripherally aware of all the watchful gazes, including that of Tavis Sinclair. He didn't care, though, was so thrilled to find Tank alive.

Tank's eyes widened and his expression became silently animated. Bruises forgotten, Tank opened his mouth in a huge smile and rushed forward to meet Cole. They embraced heartily, clapping each other on the back, talking at the same time.

"Christ, dude," said Tank with obvious relief, "I thought you were either dead or left behind."

"Jesus," Cole exclaimed. "I was worried sick."

Cheek to cheek, Tank whispered, "What the fuck is going on?"

"Sadly," Cole replied, "probably just what you're imagining."

"Shit. Really?"

"Maybe. I don't know." After one more squeeze, the men separated. "Who did this to you?" Cole asked.

Tank scoffed and threw his thumb over his shoulder, where Tavis Sinclair and many of his army stood watching.

"These fine gentlemen," Tank answered and then smiled devilishly. "Took more than four to subdue me."

Because Tank hadn't been killed, and because he himself hadn't been harmed as of yet in any manner, Cole felt bold enough to address Tavis, who had just dismounted almost twenty feet away. "This is my friend that I'd told you about. You felt the need to rough him up like this?"

Unaffected by the censure of Cole's tone, Tavis shrugged. "He should nae have refused our efforts to assist him."

Tank harrumphed once more, though Cole was surprised by how good-natured it sounded. "C'mon, Sinclair. Be honest. You're heavy-handed with your *efforts*. Came with a bit more menace than you're making it sound." To Cole, he added, "I thought they were trying to kidnap me or something."

A fleeting glance around the gathered and watchful soldiers showed a few faces looked similar to Tank's, bruised and swollen. Yep, he'd put up a good fight.

"But all good now?" Cole asked quietly of Tank.

Tank waved off Cole's concern. "All good." He searched the crowd and pointed to a young kid who looked as pale as death and was burrowed in more than one heavy fur. "That pimple-faced brat went under, horse and all, into this huge crevice beneath the snow. Good thing I was there, or they'd still be peering down into the abyss, wondering how to get the kid out of there. Anyway, so Mr. Sinclair here understands I'm neither an idiot nor meaning any trouble." He faced Tavis again and moved his finger between himself and Cole. "We save lives, that's what we do. We don't leave a guy behind."

"We are appreciative of yer selfless efforts, sir," Tavis acknowledged stonily. "And that is why ye live yet and have been allowed to be reunited with yer friend."

"What a guy," Tavis said drolly under his breath. He then glanced around again. "So what is this?" He asked Cole. "Aside from the obvious."

Unable to help himself, Cole laughed. "Sadly, it is just that: the obvious. A medieval castle."

Out of the corner of his mouth, without moving his lips, Tank said, "Dude, we need to talk about this—"

"Not here," Cole advised.

"No, somewhere private," Tank Agreed. "This is crazy."

The door to the keep swung open, drawing Cole's attention as Ailsa stepped out into the yard. She wore no cloak or wrap despite the chill, her posture straight and purposeful, but her gaze was what caught his attention. It swept over the gathered faces, lingering briefly on her brother with what Cole assumed was relief at seeing him returned safely. Tavis acknowledged her with a nod as he swept by her, pausing only briefly to say something quietly to Ailsa.

She did not follow her brother into the keep. Instead, her eyes continued round the crowded yard, this time landing on him. Cole's breath hitched at the deliberate way her gaze found his, like she'd been looking for him. The small, almost shy smile that curved her lips didn't fade, and for a moment, it seemed like they were the only two people in the bustling yard. He couldn't stop the answering grin that tugged at his own mouth, his heart giving a quick, unexpected thud in his chest.

"Christ, who is that?" Tank whispered in awe at his side.

Cole's smile froze, as awed by her as if seeing her for the first time, same as Tank.

"Be careful. That's Tavis's sister, Ailsa, aka off-limits."

"Hmph, a full-time job for him, I'm guessing."

"Undoubtedly."

To both his surprise and delight, Ailsa stepped away from the castle, walking toward them, her gaze skimming over Tank, dressed similarly to Cole.

"Yer friend, I presume," she guessed as she neared.

"It is," Cole said. "Apparently, your brother found him in his travels." He did want that private conversation with Tank, about how it had come about, where Tavis had found him, but it could wait. "Hank Morrison, this is Ailsa Sinclair, sister to the laird, Tavis Sinclair."

Tank's usual air of unshakable confidence faltered as he extended his hand, his movements slightly less smooth than usual. "Jesus," he breathed, likely in response to Ailsa's beauty. "I mean, a real pleasure, Miss Sinclair," he said, his voice tinged with an uncharacteristic hesitancy that reminded Cole of a bashful teenager rather than a battle-hardened Marine and veteran firefighter. His words almost seemed to carry an 'aw shucks' tone.

Cole blinked. Tank—*aw shucks?* The man who could walk through chaos like it was just another Tuesday and charm anyone in the room had suddenly been rendered nearly tongue-tied. Cole smirked, filing this away for later ribbing. Clearly, even the indomitable Hank Morrison wasn't immune to a pretty face.

"The pleasure is mine, sir," Ailsa returned, her tone gracious but tinged with curiosity. Her gaze lingered on Tank for a moment, polite but assessing. "Cole was quite worried about ye. In another half an hour, we'd have gone out on our second search for ye had ye nae been delivered to us. Welcome to Torr Cinnteag."

Tank nodded, his usual composure starting to return, the smile evolving being that practiced one Cole had seen used countless times with countless women. "Thank you, Miss Sinclair. Appreciate the hospitality."

Coming almost immediately on the heels of his surprise over Tank's mildly flustered manner, Cole couldn't ignore the odd twist of unease that warred with his true happiness at having Tank here with him. Tank was Tank—charming, confident, and, well, notoriously good with women. And Ailsa? Ailsa was...different.

Cole had only known her for a day, but he already felt a pull toward her, something more than just admiration for her stunning beauty or her kindness toward him. He felt oddly protective of her, and he found himself hoping—no, silently *willing*—his friend to keep it respectful. He knew Tank meant no harm—he'd never cheated on Doreen, but he was single again. But Ailsa didn't belong in the same category as the women Tank usually flirted with during their nights out back home. She was...more. More real, more innocent, more sincere. And the idea of Tank seeing her as anything less made Cole's jaw tighten.

Even as the thought crossed his mind, Cole felt a pang of guilt. He had no claim to Ailsa, no right to feel protective or territorial. Still, he couldn't shake it. He wanted Tank to see what he saw—Ailsa's quiet strength, her easy grace—and respect it, not ruin it with any of his usual antics.

Ailsa surprised him by bringing up—very directly— the secret Cole had shared with her, his suspicions that he wasn't in Kansas anymore.

As the courtyard emptied, Ailsa leaned forward a smidge toward Tank and lowered her voice. "Do you also believe ye've traveled through time, sir?"

Tank stiffened, the question seeming to hit him like a blow. Very slowly, he asked, "What did you just say?"

"I asked if ye believe ye've traveled through time," Ailsa repeated, "as Cole does."

Tank looked at Cole, his jaw tightening. "What the hell?"

Cole sighed, the weight of his own confusion pressing down on him. "I didn't tell her—well, I asked her the year. I needed to understand—"

"And I told him it was marked as 1302 presently," Ailsa supplied helpfully, seemingly unperturbed by Tank's sudden edginess.

"Thirteen hundred and two?" Tank repeated, his voice low and disbelieving.

"Apparently," Cole said, when Tank seemed to look at him for confirmation. He was very familiar with Tank's confusion, which he still grappled with himself. "It makes no sense, obviously, but... look around, it's also the only thing that *does* makes sense."

Tank's face hardened, a flicker of anger and disbelief crossing his features. "You just believed her?"

Now Cole frowned, defensively of Ailsa, for Tank having just suggested that she lied. "Do you have a better explanation? Look around—at the castle, the people, the clothes. This isn't...this isn't right. It's not *our* time."

Tank shook his head slowly, running a hand over his bearded jaw. "No. No, it's not possible. Time travel? Come on, man. That's—"

"Crazy?" Cole finished for him. "Yeah, I know. You think I wanted to believe it? You think I don't still wake up hoping this is some screwed-up dream? But don't tell me you haven't considered it, certainly not if you've spent even just a little bit of time with Tavis's army. On horses. Carrying swords."

Tank's silence stretched for a long moment, his hands flexing into fists at his sides. When he finally spoke, his voice was quieter but no less strained. "I don't know what is... what happened, but yeah, I recognized that something was different." He looked at Ailsa and seemed to measure her character with a hard gaze. "You're not lying about what year it is?"

Ailsa shook her head, her expression softened by what Cole believed was sympathy for Tank's sudden misery. Very gently, she said, "Ye are both troubled by this. But does the truth nae lie before ye? What ye see and feel—does it nae convince ye?"

"I don't know what to think. But yeah, I considered it. But...but if this is real..." His voice trailed off, his words heavy with uncertainty.

Cole exhaled, his own confusion resurfacing. "If it's real, Tank, then what? What do we do?"

A gasp from Ailsa drew their attention, but her gaze was focused beyond them, abruptly turning Cole and Tank around, ready to confront a threat.

There stood the solemn man Cole had noticed earlier, the one he thought might be the priest Ailsa had mentioned.

"Shit," he muttered, widening the man's already startled gaze, leaving Cole to assume the man might have overheard their quiet conversation.

"Ailsa, lass," the man said calmly, his speech ten times more English than either Cole's or Tank's. "Come to me."

Away from Cole and Tank, Cole guessed he meant.

"Father Gilbert," Ailsa protested, "these men are nae dangerous. They are—"

"Deranged, would be my guess," said the mild-mannered man. "A danger in itself."

Cole took offense. "We're not crazy," he insisted heatedly. "We're...just lost. And just as confused as you."

"Who's this guy?" Tank wanted to know, adopting an intimidating pose, the kind one assumed in a bar late at night when some drunk got out of hand. He straightened, lengthening his body to its full height, half a foot taller than the priest, and brought his thick hands together in front of him, cocking his head. Cole almost expected Tank to crack his knuckles in a sinister manner. It was all for show, of course. The priest and Tank had just traveled together with Tavis, so they must have met.

Ailsa stepped between the three men. "Father Gilbert, ye have nae been properly introduced. This is the man we found two days ago, Cole Carter," she said, speaking quickly as if to ward off a coming fight. "He is returned to guid health and pleased to be reunited with his friend, Hank Morrison."

The man didn't so much as blink, though he did pass what Cole considered a sanctimonious gaze over both him and Tank. "And they are not deranged, though both believe they have come from another time?" He asked, not bothering to hide his doubtfulness.

Cole responded, trying to keep his temper in check. He didn't like the guy's self-righteous attitude. "Yeah, I know it sounds crazy. But it's true. I was born in 1995 and Tank—" he glanced at him, not quite sure what year he was born, unable to do quick math right now.

"1990," Tank supplied.

The priest said nothing so that Cole felt compelled to explain what happened, and this time, Tank helped him out with the telling.

"We were hiking—" Cole began.

"It was right back there, where you guys found me yesterday," Tank added.

"Everything seemed fine, normal," Cole continued.

"Until it wasn't," Tank picked up the story. He questioned Cole, "Did you feel that, too? The way the air changed?"

"Yes!" Cole answered promptly, pleased to have this corroborated, having begun to wonder if he'd imagined it. "It was weird and then you seemed really far away, or like you were moving away—"

"Exactly," Tank concurred. "Same. We were only a few feet apart, but it was like I was seeing you through binoculars. And then...nothing. I woke up, covered in snow, not exactly where we'd been, though I could see the mountain."

"Yes. Same. I wonder how close we were, and if I simply went looking in the wrong direction?"

"I thought I'd die from exposure," Tank said. "It's fuc—pardon, Father—it's freezing out there overnight."

Cole nodded, having endured the same, though apparently one less overnight than Tank. "Jesus, man, I'm so happy you made it, that they found you."

Tank grinned and nodded. "Dude, I've never been so confused or so certain of my own death before that."

Cole understood completely.

As one, they turned to the priest to gauge his reaction.

"Nineteen hundred?" He questioned softly. "'Tis unnatural."

Cole seized on this as well. "Exactly. That's what I said to Ailsa."

He was treated to a fairly dark glower from the priest, and had the impression the man did not like how easily her name rolled off his lips, how familiar it made them seem.

Ailsa inserted herself again into the conversation, clearing her throat first. "I might suggest—Father Gilbert, do ye agree?—that we nae say anything of this to Tavis." She glanced at Tank. "Or...is it too late?"

Tank shook his head. "No. He asked a lot of questions—you were there, you know," he said to Father Gilbert. "I told him I was an American. I assume now he appeared to think I was lying since America isn't even...discovered yet."

Cole watched the priest while Tank answered, trying to discern his attitude. "You don't believe us?" He guessed, and wasn't surprised. He'd be riddled with skepticism if their positions were reversed.

Father Gilbert didn't immediately respond, his eyes flicking to Ailsa, who was looking at him with a mixture of concern and hope.

The priest took a deep breath, clearly weighing his words carefully.

"Believe you?" he echoed, his voice thick with skepticism. "That is a hard thing to do, young man." His gaze hardened slightly. "I have spent my life in service to God, not to whims or fantasies. Traveling through time... is a fantastical thing to claim."

"But why would we lie?" Tank asked, his voice rough, challenging.

Father Gilbert didn't look at Tank immediately, his eyes fixed on the ground for a moment, as if pondering. "Lying... no. But what you speak of—what you claim—it does not fit into any truths that I know. It is not natural." He paused, his voice softening, "And yet, Scotland is a land full of strange happenings and tales—some may say cursed, others enchanted. But even so..." He sighed and met Cole's eyes. "There was a rumor, not long past, of a woman who married a northern laird. Word spread of her... dealings with demons, witches, and her ties to another time." The priest shook his head as if to dismiss the thoughts, but the unease remained in his voice. "I thought it madness, then. But now..."

He trailed off, glancing over to Ailsa, as if to gauge her reaction.

"I'm not a fool," Father Gilbert continued, his voice taking on a more cautious tone. "I have seen enough in my years to know that there are things—unexplainable things—that can happen in this land. Whether you believe in them or not, there are mysteries here, and to dismiss them outright would be foolish. But that does not mean I believe everything I hear." He folded his hands together, eyes narrowing. "However...."

Cole leaned forward, pressing, "However?"

Father Gilbert hesitated, his fingers tightening around each other. "If your story is true, then you are in grave danger. The laird—Tavis—would not entertain such madness. He might rather guess you are spies or agents of the English. And if not that, he might decide you are cursed and bring ruin to this keep."

Cole felt a cold weight settle in his stomach. "So what do we do?"

Father Gilbert's lips pressed into a thin line. "You say nothing of this...time-traveling nonsense. If you must offer an explanation, you tell him you are from Spain. Far enough away to explain your strange ways and mannerisms, but not so far as to draw suspicion."

"Spain?" Tank muttered, exchanging a look with Cole.

"Yes, Spain," Father Gilbert said firmly. "It is the safest, most plausible option. And if you are wise, you will keep your heads down and draw as little attention as possible."

Cole nodded slowly, the priest's words sinking in. "We'll be careful. You won't even know we're here. And you'll keep our secret?"

Father Gilbert hesitated again, his gaze piercing. "For now. But mark my words—if I suspect you mean harm to this place or these people, I will not hesitate to act."

Cole exchanged a glance with Tank, and the two men nodded slowly. They were still caught in a web of confusion, and apparently one of danger, but the priest's warning made sense.

Father Gilbert turned to leave but hesitated, his eyes narrowing as they locked onto Ailsa. "And you, lass, are no fool. You know your brother's nature. His protectiveness over you burns hotter than any fire in any hearth. If he sees you lingering too often in the company of strangers—these strangers—he will take notice. And when he does, it will not end with mere questions. It will bring scrutiny they evidently can ill afford."

Ailsa opened her mouth to respond, but he held up a hand to stop her. "Do not mistake my meaning. I do not doubt your intentions, only your foresight. If you care for their safety—and your own—you must tread carefully, meaning you must distance yourself."

Cole shifted uncomfortably but said nothing, sensing the truth in the priest's warning. Ailsa's lips pressed into a thin line, her chin lifting slightly in defiance, but she didn't argue.

Satisfied that his words had sunk in, Father Gilbert straightened and pulled his cloak tighter around him. "Come along, lass."

Again, Ailsa looked as if she wanted to argue, but eventually bowed to the priest's command, sending a half-smile to Cole and Tank before she followed Father Gilbert into the keep.

Cole turned and met Tank's wide eyes.

"We have to get out of here," Cole concluded.

"Yep," Tank agreed. "Preferably, before we get killed."

Chapter Nine

Not knowing what else to do after Father Gilbert and Ailsa left, and with the courtyard nearly empty, Cole led Tank to the small room he'd been given at the back of the chapel. Tank followed, his broad shoulders brushing the edges of the narrow hallway as they walked. But as they passed the open door to the chapel itself, Tank stopped short, his jaw slack as he stared into the dimly lit interior.

"Unreal," Tank muttered, his voice low and reverent.

Cole glanced back, recognizing the same awe he'd felt when he'd first peeked inside. The chapel, though simple, was steeped in an otherworldly atmosphere that brought home the extraordinary concept of being in another time.

The interior was constructed of rough-hewn stone, the walls cool and damp to the touch, their uneven surfaces bearing the marks of crude tools. Wooden beams stretched across the ceiling, darkened by years of smoke from the iron sconces that held flickering candles. The chamber smelled of wax, damp earth, and faint traces of incense, lending the space a weighty, spiritual feel.

At the far end, an altar stood, draped in a coarse woolen cloth embroidered with a simple cross. Above it, a tall but narrow stained glass window let in a thin stream of winter light, casting a pale glow over the rough-hewn crucifix affixed beneath the window. Benches made of unpolished wood lined the nave, their surfaces worn smooth by countless worshippers over the years.

Tank shook his head, his usual unshakable demeanor replaced by something close to wonder. "Feels ancient," he said as he backed out of the chapel.

Inside Cole's borrowed room, while Tank now took in these sparse surroundings, Cole asked for a full accounting of what had happened to him. Sensing his friend needed warmth as much as he needed to talk, Cole bent at the fireplace, stoking the fire and adding another clump of peat. "I'm listening," he said, straightening as the flames leaped higher.

Tank joined him at the hearth, extending his hands toward the growing warmth. For a moment, he stared blindly into the fire, the flickering light casting sharp shadows on his face. "Like I said, I woke up—had to have been out for a while 'cause I was covered in snow—and started looking for you," he began, his voice low. "Problem was, nothing looked familiar. I didn't pay enough attention to my surroundings at first, so I had no clue which way I was going." He flexed his fingers toward the heat, a frown tugging at his lips. "I realized pretty quick I'd been walking in circles. After that, sorry to say, dude, finding shelter became priority number one. I holed up in a cave for two nights. Spent all day searching—for you, for food, for anything. Came up empty." Tank shook his head and shrugged at the same time. "Then I heard them. Weirdest damn noise—didn't even recognize it at first. Turns out it was a group of riders, galloping like bats out of hell. I didn't know what the hell was going on. Naturally, I ran the other way. But I was weak—too weak to outrun them." He paused, his jaw tightening, the memory clearly unsettling. "When they caught up, they pulled swords—freaking swords. I had no idea what kind of medieval crap I'd stumbled into, but I knew I wasn't going down easy. I fought back—what else could I do? Then everything changed when that kid got hurt, and I helped him. But it's all good—well, me and them are good since I helped rescue that kid. But otherwise...everything else..."

Cole nodded, shoving his hands into the pockets of his jeans. Briefly, he relayed his own tale, how he'd wandered near the castle and was discovered by Ailsa and another woman, but then had passed out. He advised what little had transpired since then, and then asked of Tank, "When did you start to suspect you...?"

"That I wasn't in the twenty-first century?" Tank finished for him, his tone calm but tinged with unease. "Not right away, not when Sinclair and his army found me. But it didn't take long after that. Just...everything. The way they dressed, the way they talked. The fact that they rode horses and carried swords instead of driving trucks and packing rifles. And the stuff they talked about—wars, feuds, kings..." He trailed off, shaking his head. "It didn't add up. Got me wondering." Tank turned slowly, his eyes sweeping over the room. "But, Jesus..." he murmured.

"What?"

"I can't—that is, I never..." He swung round a baffled frown toward Cole. "Would you ever have imagined?"

Frustration and confusion twisted inside Cole. He felt like they were missing something obvious, some logical explanation that hadn't presented itself yet. "But it *can't* be possible," he insisted, desperation creeping into his voice.

And then, reminiscent of a happy scientist discovering something thought not to exist, Tank exclaimed in a whisper filled with awe, "It is, though. We're here, living it, so it must be."

Cole stared at him, concerned about Tank's state of mind, what seemed now a dawning appreciation for what they'd accidentally, unknowingly done.

They discussed the possibility and probability for another entire minute, Tank willing to embrace it as real, while Cole fought with every fiber of his being to have it explained more realistically.

But then Cole recalled what he'd been doing at the moment Tank had ridden through the gates.

"Oh, shit," Cole said suddenly. "I forgot—I was helping some guys repair the castle wall. You good here? I might guess a maid will come with food—they did when I first came, or rather when I woke up." He glanced toward the slim window, which showed that it was still light outside, but graying a bit. "Actually, it might almost be time for dinner, which they have inside the castle."

"I'm weak as shit," Tank admitted, "but I can't just sit around. He harrumphed a short but amused chuckle. "Castle repairs, huh? Who'd have thunk?"

"Kept my mind occupied," Cole advised, justifying his own actions.

"That'll do," Tank reasoned. "Let's go."

The two men returned to the castle wall as the late afternoon light began to fade. Half the stones for the repairs were already in place, stacked and mortared inside the crevice that had been dug out. Tank, imbued with natural authority and not one to watch idly if he thought something could or should be done better, questioned the use of mortar, wondering if it would freeze rather than dry properly. Otherwise, still weak from days without proper food, Tank only casually directed the effort, leaving the heavy lifting to Cole, Davey, and the others.

"Good placement, but that gap's going to need more mortar," Tank instructed, pacing along the higher ground. He gestured toward a spot where two stones didn't quite meet.

Cole nodded and stretched out his hand for the wooden bucket filled with mortar, and got to work on the area.

The entire job was completed less than thirty minutes later, and Tank offered his hand to pull Cole from the ditch while two of the Sinclair men filled and packed what remained of the ground they'd removed.

A young maid approached, her brown skirts brushing the ground before she stopped a few paces away, drawing Cole and Tank's attention. She gave a polite curtsy before speaking, her hesitant English very thickly accented.

"Sirs," she began, her gaze flicking nervously between the two strangers, "the laird requests your company at the head table for tonight's meal."

While Cole and Tank exchanged a silent communication that seemed to question the reason behind this, the maid added, "He awaits ye now."

Cole quickly recovered, nodding at her. "Thanks. We'll, uh, clean up and head that way."

The girl gave another quick curtsy before turning and retreating back toward the castle.

"Probably wants to keep us where he can see us," Tank said.

"Yep," Cole agreed.

They returned to the room at the back of the rectory and set about making themselves presentable. A ewer of water sat beside the basin on a low wooden stand, delivered earlier that morning by a servant, same as yesterday. The water was cold by now, but neither man was in a position to complain. Cole splashed the frigid liquid onto his face, shaking off the chill as he used a rough cloth to scrub away the grime of the day's labor. "Medieval luxury at its best," he muttered, running damp fingers through his hair to smooth it down.

Tank chuckled faintly, but his movements were sluggish as he took the basin next. "Beats freezing in a cave," he admitted.

Cole glanced down and swiped at a bit of mud and dirt on his jacket. "I'd rather not go to dinner looking like I was just dragged through a sewer."

From behind the cloth as he washed his face, Tank said, "I just spent twenty-four hours with an army on horseback and I can assure you, there was little evidence of high grooming standards."

Cole grinned, accepting this was probably true, and the two men made their way to the hall. From the chapel to the door to the castle was seventy-five steps, Cole counted, just long enough—and cold enough—that he wished he'd had a towel to dry his face. The dampness on his cheeks seemed to amplify the cold, making it feel as though shards of ice were pricking his skin.

Once more, the hall was dimly lit by flickering torches along the walls and a few braziers that struggled to push back the growing shadows of the evening.

But it was not exactly dinnertime, Cole realized, as only Tavis and three of his soldiers occupied the hall presently.

"Shit," Cole cursed quietly without moving his lips.

Tank had the same ominous feeling. "Hmph. Interrogation first, it seems, and then supper."

"Might be," Cole agreed as they moved cautiously forward.

At the dais, Tavis Sinclair sat flanked by three of his officers, their painted liberally with curiosity and mistrust as they observed the newcomers. The laird's sharp gaze followed Tank and Cole as they crossed the hall.

"Come," Tavis called, his voice firm and commanding. When they reached the dais, Tavis leaned back in his chair, his piercing eyes narrowing as he studied them. "Strange men," he said finally, his voice low but laced with suspicion. "Ye arrive, both of ye, with nae clear explanation. Ye dress, speak, and carry yourselves like nae men I've ever kent."

Neither Cole nor Tank moved. Cole spoke first. "As I've said, and as it seems Tank has proven, we mean no harm. We were simply...lost."

"And we appreciate your hospitality, Sinclair," Tank added. "As soon as we're able, or as the weather permits, we'll be on our way."

Considering their unusual circumstances, Cole wasn't sure that was exactly true, or possible.

On their way? To where?

"But where were ye going? Ye hide something, I trow. I dinna ken what it is, but I ken ye are hiding something. What brought ye into my demesne?"

Cole's mind briefly went blank, wondering what a safe answer might be. But what did he know about good excuses for trespassing in medieval Scotland?

"Looking for work," Tank surprised him by answering. "The war has taken everything from us—our home, our family, even the land we worked. We've nothing to return to and no money to our name. We hoped to find honest work up north, rebuilding, repairing—whatever needs doing."

Cole resisted the urge to turn and gape at Tank, even as he suddenly wondered who his friend was right now. A quick-thinking inventor of tales, it turned out.

Holding Tavis's gaze steadily, Tank continued. "If we've overstepped by being on your land, we meant no disrespect. We were only hoping to survive, to find a way forward."

Tavis raised a hand, suggesting he didn't want to hear any more. He studied both men a moment longer before saying in a low and slow voice, "Ken this: ye are being watched. Guards have been posted round the rectory. If ye step out of line—if ye so much as breathe wrong—ye will be imprisoned. Or worse."

"Understood," Tank replied promptly. "But have no fear, Sinclair. You won't have any trouble from either of us."

Cole decided he didn't care for Tavis Sinclair. He seemed too much in love with his power, as if he reveled in intimidation. Maybe it was simply part of his medieval lord's mentality, but Cole didn't like it. On the other hand, he could appreciate that he and Tank must be suspicious characters to any or all people they'd met.

Though he appeared still skeptical of them, Tavis sat up and indicated the chairs on either side of him. "Ye will dine here tonight but mind your place. Do naught to draw more eyes than ye already have."

Cole and Tank exchanged brief glances, and Cole thought that like him, Tank was trying to keep unease from showing in his expression.

"You got it, chief," Tank said agreeably before he and Cole rounded the table from the same side, approaching Tavis. Tank went behind Tavis, taking the chair to the laird's left.

Cole was prevented from sitting directly on Tavis's right by the hand swept over the arm of the chair there.

"'Tis where my sister presides," he announced regally, pointing to the next chair. "Ye sit there."

Cole had no problem with that, being removed from too close a proximity to Tavis, and then knowing that he would be able to enjoy Ailsa's company this evening.

Cole had just resigned himself to the awkwardness of sitting at the head table when the hall began to fill with people arriving for the evening meal, their chatter and footsteps breaking the tense atmosphere. He noted something he hadn't last evening, that people came not only from the main door to the hall, but from other passageways inside the keep.

Admittedly, he only noticed this because Ailsa was one of them, coming from an arched doorway to the right of the main table. She was followed by that other woman, Anwen, who was a curious person as she wore an expression that looked like she was constantly smiling, but her manner—at least so far that Cole had noticed—was neither welcoming nor particularly friendly. Cole watched as the robust Anwen cast her gaze over Tank as she walked past, wearing for a moment a new and different expression as she curled her lip in what looked like strong disfavor.

Little did he dwell on it, though, the maid and her silent disapproval, his gaze settling instead on Ailsa, who had changed for dinner as she'd done yesterday. He was as certain now as he'd been earlier, as he'd been yesterday and in every moment he'd spent in Ailsa's company since he'd met her, that he'd never encountered a woman more beautiful. Her long dark auburn hair, loose and soft, fell around her shoulders and framed her face perfectly. She had those striking blue eyes—bright, clear, and impossible to ignore—that seemed to catch the light just right. She moved with an easy kind of grace, her skirts swishing faintly as she walked toward the table, and for a moment, Cole forgot where—and when—he was. She wasn't just beautiful—though she was that, unquestionably—but she carried herself so confidently, so calm and steady, like she knew exactly who she was and didn't need to prove anything to anyone.

When her eyes flicked his way, he felt his chest tighten. He wasn't one to be easily impressed, but Ailsa had a way of holding his attention without even trying.

Strange, how so much of his awkward discomfort evaporated the moment she sat down next to him. He felt an undeniable lift in his spirits, and when she offered him a small smile as a greeting, he found himself returning it automatically.

"Good evening," he said.

"And to ye," she replied. With a quick glance at her brother seated at her left, finding him occupied speaking with one of his soldiers who'd come to stand in front of the table, she leaned incrementally closer toward Cole and said softly, "I apologize for having abandoned ye earlier. I kent it better to appease Father Gilbert by acceding to his wishes that I...maintain a distance from ye." She straightened but quickly leaned closer again and added, almost as an afterthought, "And yer friend, of course."

"No need to apologize," he assured her. "I get it, the priest's misgivings. Better safe than sorry."

This made Ailsa turn her face rather swiftly toward him, her brows raised. "Will ye give me cause to be sorry, Cole Carter?"

The question hung in the air, layered and open to interpretation. Her intent wasn't entirely clear, but the way her lips parted slightly, and the way her gaze lingered, told Cole enough. It was a challenge—a cautious probing of his intentions.

"I won't," he said firmly. "Not if I can help it. And not ever intentionally."

As Ailsa straightened, giving her attention to the room, Cole found himself lingering on her words. *Will ye give me cause to be sorry, Cole Carter?* The question echoed in his mind, not just for its odd phrasing but for the subtle weight behind it. It hadn't felt like an accusation or even a warning, and yet....

It was as though she'd acknowledged something unspoken between them. Could she feel it too? The powerful awareness of her had been there since the first moment he'd met her—her presence both soft and commanding, her gaze piercing yet guarded. There was no denying it now; he'd been and was drawn to her. But did she feel the same pull, the same magnetic undercurrent that made him notice every shift of her expression, every flicker of emotion in her eyes?

Cole's chest tightened as a wave of reality crashed over him. What was he doing? What was he *thinking*? He had no business imagining or examining a supposed connection with her—or anyone here, for that matter. He was a man out of time, separated from his world by centuries, maybe forever. Every second he spent here only reminded him of how much he wanted to go back to the life he knew: his job, his home, the people he'd left behind.

This... connection with Ailsa, or whatever it was, meant nothing. It was a bad idea to let it grow. He had to keep his focus on finding a way home, not on the way Ailsa's smile had stirred something he hadn't felt in a long, long time, or the quiet grace with which she moved, or the way her voice seemed to wrap around his name like she owned it. Those were dangerous distractions, and he couldn't afford them.

Ailsa's voice broke through the din of his puzzled reverie as servants began placing platters of food along the table. As she had the night before, Ailsa quietly identified each dish to Cole. "Roast venison," she murmured, gesturing toward a platter garnished with chunks of meat covered in buttery herbs. "And there—spiced parsnips and onions," she said, pointing toward another dish—unnecessarily, as Cole could easily identify the familiar vegetable. "They're a favorite of the laird's." When another dish arrived, looking like a rich, golden-crusted pie, Ailsa's face brightened with unmistakable delight. "Ah, bridies," she said with some excitement. "Stuffed with minced meat and spices. These are my favorite."

He smiled at her enthusiasm. Though he was hungry, and the savory scent of roasted meat made his mouth water, he found himself more intrigued by Ailsa than the food.

"You must try one," she urged, pulling the platter forward after Tavis Sinclair had helped himself.

Ailsa served him, generously giving him a much larger portion than she spooned onto her plate.

"Thank you."

She graciously continued to fill his plate, and he hadn't the heart to tell her he didn't particularly care for venison. He knew he'd eat every bite, so as not to cause her any embarrassment, but he definitely wished she'd not been so generous with that serving.

When his plate was filled, Ailsa slid her hand onto the table between them. With a subtle motion, she pulled her hand back, leaving behind a small silver knife. "An eating knife for yer own," she said softly, and with her other hand, she revealed another knife—the one she'd used the previous night.

Cole blinked, caught off guard by the gesture. Overcome by her thoughtfulness, and still a bit surprised by the absence of forks or spoons, he managed a warm smile. "Thank you, Ailsa. That's... really kind of you."

It struck him then how rare it was for someone to do something so simple, yet so considerate. Aside from his Aunt Rosie, he couldn't remember the last time someone had thought of what he might need and offered it freely.

Having a sense that Tank was well occupied with both Tavis and Dersey on his far side, Cole allowed himself to enjoy dinner with Ailsa once more. However, and possibly her brother's presence had something to do with it or maybe the priest's warning, but she made fewer overtures, fewer attempts at conversation, seeming to want to be a part of her brother's conversation with Tank.

Though disappointing, it was fine with Cole, as it was not his intention at all to bring focus onto himself, or worse, to rile either Tavis's suspicions or anger. He wasn't sure if his presence and Tanks had warranted the additional guards in the hall tonight or if the half dozen armed soldiers standing directly in front of the table, their backs to those seated, were simply Tavis's bodyguards, and only routinely stationed to protect the laird.

At one point Tank's voice cut through the ambient noise, "So," he said, "what exactly is going on with this war?"

A hush seemed to fall over the head table and all heads swiveled toward him.

Tavis arched a brow, Ailsa glanced sideways at Cole, and Father Gilbert paused, his spoon halfway to his mouth.

"The war," Tavis repeated slowly, his voice laced with incredulity. "Are ye telling me ye dinna ken the state of the country? Of war? Or, God's bluid, the price paid for it?"

Tank cleared his throat, a sheepish grin tugging at the corners of his mouth. "We...er, we come from a very small village. Hardly ever gets news."

Dersey, seated next to Cole, leaned forward and sent a sharp gaze to Tank. "A village that kens naught of England's invasion? Or of the decimation brought to us?"

"And before that," Tank added quickly, "we were in Spain. That's where we're from."

Cole resisted the urge to groan. *Really? Okay, so he wasn't meant for the stage, that was certain.*

Tavis looked neither amused nor appeased. "Spain, is it? A curious path that led ye here."

Tank shrugged, piling more bread onto his plate. "Long story."

Dersey shook his head, muttering something under his breath before addressing Tank again. "Long story or nae, ye're here now, and ye'd do well to listen." With his eating knife held in a tight grip, his tone was both sharp and somber. "This war has torn the Highlands apart, this house against that house, thousands of ours killed or captured. Crops burned, villages razed. I've seen bairns left to die in the snow, their mothers hanged above them. The English march through the south like a plague."

Tavis nodded grimly. "Dersey speaks true. The Sassenachs ken nae mercy. They've slaughtered families, destroyed homes. Those who resist are branded traitors. But Wallace and others fight on, rallying men, even after Stirling Bridge. He doesnae yield, and neither do we."

Ailsa's voice was quieter but carried no less weight. "The Sinclairs have suffered, too. We've given all we can to support the cause—men, food, coin. It's never enough." Her gaze seemed to drift, her expression softening.

Tank's easy demeanor faltered, the weight of their words settling on him like a physical blow. "I didn't realize..." He trailed off, uncharacteristically subdued.

Cole decided to jump in, hoping to redirect the focus. "What about your army?" he asked, looking at Tavis. "How do you keep fighting when everything's been taken from you?"

Tavis took a long sip of his ale before answering. "With grit, lad. And with the knowledge that surrender is worse than death. Three hundred men we've given to the war. Three hundred, just me and mine. The truce could nae have come at a better time, but 'twill nae stay—they never do. We'll be dying again come the spring."

Father Gilbert nodded. "The English offer naught but chains to those who submit. Freedom is worth any price."

The discussion continued, with the priest, Dersey, and occasionally Tavis and Ailsa contributing to paint a vivid picture of the relentless toll the war had taken over the years. They spoke of fields left fallow and villages emptied, the brutal losses at singular battles that took the lives of thousands of Scotsmen, and the constant specter of hunger during harsh winters. Stories of betrayal and shifting loyalties wove through their words, along with somber accounts of lives shattered by the conflict.

Eventually, conversation drifted to other subjects, and again broke off into smaller private discussions.

Being lucky enough to be seated next to Ailsa was only a small comfort to Cole. The weight of curious stares pressed on him, and he felt as though every move he made was under scrutiny. The low hum of conversation around the hall only heightened his unease, wondering if he and possibly Tank were the subject of some conversations. As the meal continued, he caught more and more glances, some speculative, others openly hostile, and his discomfort grew. He sat back in his chair and looked over at Tavis, a bit unnerved to find the formidable laird's gaze already fixed on him.

Tavis Sinclair stared unabashedly at him, his gaze sharp and unrelenting. And though there was no hostility in his expression—no scowl or furrowed brow—the sheer intensity of his eyes was enough to make Cole's stomach tighten. While he supposed the guy was simply taking his measure, this seemed more an interrogation than merely a glance.

A flicker of something unspoken passed between them, and for the first time since arriving, Cole felt the chill of vulnerability, as if he and Tank might actually be in danger here at Torr Cinnteag. Still, he met Tavis's gaze head on, refusing to show vulnerability or to appear guilty of whatever Tavis might suspect of him.

Possibly, Ailsa caught wind of the wordless exchange. She sat back as well, creating a barrier between Cole and her brother. She spoke for a few minutes to her brother before turning and giving her attention to Cole.

"Ye are uneasy suddenly," Ailsa said quietly, her voice just loud enough to reach him over the din.

He gave her a sidelong look, hesitating before responding. "Is it that obvious?"

She smiled faintly, a flicker of warmth lighting her eyes. "Aye. Ye shift like a man expecting an ambush."

That hit closer to the mark than she might have guessed. Cole looked out over the crowded hall and again found plenty of people staring at him. The Red Wedding episode from *Game of Thrones* crept into his mind. His jaw tightened.

Ailsa tilted her head, studying him. "What is it?" she asked, her blue eyes alive with concern.

Cole decided to ask outright. He leaned closer to her, keeping his voice low. "Is this some kind of trick? This... supper? To gain our confidence, put us at ease, and then—" He hesitated, but pushed on, "—kill us?" He didn't know why, but he knew she wouldn't lie to him. Ailsa would tell him the truth. At the very least, he would see it in her eyes, he was certain.

Ailsa blinked at him, clearly taken aback. For a moment, she seemed stunned into silence. Then, her expression shifted. Shock turned to confusion, confusion to offense, and then to something colder. The veins in her neck pulsed as her jaw tightened.

"We do nae practice deceit, sir," she said, her voice sharp enough to cut. "If my brother wanted ye dead, ye would be so. Certainly, he would nae be breaking bread with ye."

Cole winced at the whispered hiss of her tone, wishing he'd kept his mouth shut. "I didn't mean—"

But Ailsa didn't let him finish. She straightened her back, her expression unreadable. Whatever warmth she'd shown before was gone, replaced by a cool detachment. She turned her attention to her plate, and though she responded when spoken to, it was only in clipped, polite phrases.

He wanted desperately to take back his question, even as in his mind, it felt justified. His entire world was upside-down, nothing was as it should be, and he honestly didn't know who or what to trust.

One last quip of, “Ailsa, I am sorry. It’s only my second day in this century,” fell on deaf ears as well.

By the time Father Gilbert arrived to escort him and Tank back to the rectory, Cole felt like an idiot. He replayed the conversation with Ailsa in his head, cringing at his own words.

Chapter Ten

Frost clung to the ground in delicate white patterns as Cole and Tank exited the rectory the next morning, and their breath fogged the air as they scanned their surroundings. It was busier than Cole had expected at this early hour, the enclosed yard crowded with several dozen men and just as many horses.

Tank stretched, letting out a low groan. "Felt good to sleep in a real bed," he said, rubbing his neck. "But damn, I wonder if I'll ever be warm again."

"The no-heat, no-plumbing thing is a definite strike against the fourteenth century," Cole agreed.

"You got that right," Tank said, giving a good shudder as he burrowed into the collar and hood of his coat.

Cole smirked. "At least Father Gilbert had another room to share, or you and I'd have been sharing one of those too-small beds."

Tank chuckled. "I was profuse in my thanks to the good priest for just that reason. He's intense, right? But a good guy overall."

They hadn't gone far when Ailsa stepped outside at the door to the castle, a woven, cloth-covered basket hanging from her arm. Her hood was down, and the morning light caught the loose strands of her dark hair. With her was Anwen, the plump, smiling maid with the bad temper. Cole thought Ailsa might just now be trying to make Anwen laugh or promote a good mood. Ailsa wore a mischievous grin, saying something to Anwen as she playfully nudged her shoulder into Anwen's arm. Her eyes twinkled with playful warmth even as Anwen huffed in mock annoyance as Ailsa whispered something and lightly bumped her arm again.

Cole couldn't hear what Ailsa was saying, but the animated way her lips moved and the teasing tilt of her head suggested she was fully committed to her task. Anwen finally gave in, a short, sharp laugh escaping her, though she quickly masked it with a roll of her eyes and a muttered comment that made Ailsa grin even wider.

Then Ailsa looked up as she crossed the yard and caught sight of Cole and her smile faded.

For that he was deeply sorry.

Rather than only waving across the short distance, Cole stepped in her path.

"Good morning," Cole said, forcing a casual tone.

Tank, having followed, echoed him with an easy grin, asking, "And where are you two fine ladies off to today?"

"We go to Mallaig's cottage," she said, gesturing to the basket. "He's infirm and depends on our generosity."

Anwen scoffed at this, but said nothing, busy as she was once again studying Tank, her gaze sharp and critical, as if silently measuring him against some unreachable standard. Her expression clearly conveyed that he didn't quite measure up to whatever ideal she had in mind.

Cole ignored the maid and addressed Ailsa. "Need an escort?" The words came out more eagerly than he'd intended, but he covered it with a casual smile.

Ailsa's grip tightened on the basket but she did not hesitate to refuse him. "Nae, thank ye." Her voice was polite but clipped. "I believe ye're expected elsewhere this morning."

Cole frowned. "Elsewhere?"

She gave a nod over his shoulder. "At the training field. Tavis will be expecting ye."

Training? Cole turned and spotted Tavis among the crowd of soldiers and horses. The laird of Torr Cinnteag was a commanding figure, towering over his men with the kind of presence that made him impossible to ignore. He stood like a natural leader—broad-shouldered, powerful, and every inch the embodiment of a medieval ruler. Tavis wore his "crown" in the form of layers of fur-lined garments and heavy, jeweled embellishments that accentuated both his physical and his authoritative stature. While the other soldiers around him were dressed simply, in rough wool and leather—looking every inch the medieval grunts that they undoubtedly were— Tavis's attire seemed to have been designed not just for protection against the cold but to project an image of grandeur and authority. His movements were deliberate and controlled, the way he carried himself—a man used to being obeyed—adding to the almost regal aura he exuded. Even without a literal crown, Tavis Sinclair looked every bit a king.

When Cole turned back to Ailsa, she and Anwen were already gone, her hand tucked into the maid's elbow as the two walked out through the gate.

He sighed, shoving his hands into his pockets. "I think she's mad at me."

Tank didn't hold back his snort of laughter. "Ya think? What'd ya do?"

A tinge of embarrassment colored his words as he repeated to Tank what he'd said, what he'd asked her last night at supper.

Now Tank laughed outright, loud and long, causing Cole to roll his eyes.

"Good news for me, though," Tank said when he reined in his mirth. "Here I thought that between the two of us, I would be the idiot." He clapped Cole on the shoulder in good humor and turned him around toward the gathering army. "At least we've got something to do today."

Cole grunted in agreement, but his thoughts lingered on Ailsa. Something about her coolness toward him stung more than it should have. Purposefully, he shook it off as they looked at Tavis and his men preparing to head out to train.

"Might as well get to it," Tank said.

Cole's brow knitted. "Get to what?"

"The training," Tank answered.

"Us? Training?" Cole asked, his tone sharper than he intended.

Tank shrugged.

"You can't think that either they seriously want us to join them or that we have any business doing so," Cole remarked, partly as a question.

Tank turned to him, his expression uncharacteristically serious. "Why not? What? Are we just supposed to sit around and wait for some magic portal to take us home? I think we should embrace this," Tank said with conviction. "This is exceptional. What's happened to us—it's like something out of a fantasy novel. Why would we waste the chance to live it up?"

Cole raised an eyebrow, wary of where this was headed. "Live it up? Tank, we're stuck in the fourteenth century. There's nothing to live up to except disease, war, and maybe dying young." He thought they should focus their efforts on something of greater importance. "What about getting back home? To our time?"

"And how do you expect to do that?"

Frustrated by his own lack of ideas, Cole returned gruffly. "I don't know, but I think we should be thinking about it. There must be someone we can talk to, someone who—" he stopped, super annoyed when Tank began to laugh. "What?"

Tank waved his hand, as if to downplay the humor he'd somehow found in their circumstance. "All right. Say it happened in the reverse, that someone was brought to our time from now, or from any other time. And they want to talk to someone about getting home." He pointed at Cole and raised his brows. "They ask you specifically, who should I talk to about this? Who you gonna send them to? Who should they talk to?"

"Well, hell, I don't know."

"Exactly. Who is there to discuss this with? Are their time-traveling gods or wizards around? No, I'm guessing not. Listen, dude, just go with it. There's nothing to do about it. We have to live with it."

Unable to comprehend Tank's attitude, Cole tried another approach. "Don't you care about the people back home? They're probably worried sick about us—Rosie especially, your brother," he added, knowing that like Cole, Tank's parents were deceased already, something they'd bonded over years ago. "They must be frantic."

Tank's expression softened, and he nodded. "Yeah, I feel bad for them. You know I love your aunt. And the longer we're gone, the worse it'll be for them, not knowing. Even the guys at the firehouse—shit, some of them are going to miss us," he said, his attempt at lightness. "But Cole, what can we do about it? Nothing. So why wallow? This is the opportunity of a lifetime."

Cole shook his head. "I'm not wallowing. I'm simply suggesting that we need a plan, that we should underline what our priorities are. You're acting like it's a vacation."

Tank stepped closer, his grin giving way to earnestness. "Think about it. Before now, time travel was just a story, right? Something in movies or books. But we're living it, Cole. We're living in history. I'm not wasting that."

Even though part of him almost envied Tank's excitement, Cole couldn't let go of his frustration.

Tank sighed, possibly understanding how deep Cole's exasperation went. "This didn't happen for no reason. It's too big for that. Maybe it's fate or some cosmic accident, but it's real. I say we make it count."

Cole snorted. "And what's your grand purpose in all this?"

Tank's grin returned, devilish and unrepentant, and waved his hand toward the soldiers as they began to march through the gate. "Shit, I'm gonna be a bloody warrior, man. I'm going to fight the good fight—help these people, stand up to the oppressors. It's every guy's dream. Back home, yeah, we're sometimes small-time local heroes, sure. But here? We can really make a difference."

"Tank, they fight to the death, you know" Cole said, unable to keep the sarcasm from his tone. "This isn't a game. You heard them last night—thousands die in these wars. You really think you're ready for that?"

Tank's grin dimmed, but his resolve didn't falter. "I've always thought dying in a fire would be a good way to go. Heroic. Selfless. Maybe I'd get a street in Buffalo named after me." He shrugged. "But these people—what they're facing—it's worse than any fire. And I can do something about it. *We* can do something about it."

Cole wanted to argue, to point out the absurdity of Tank's optimism. But his mind drifted to Ailsa. To the stories she'd shared about English raids, the burned villages and stolen families. He couldn't deny the truth in Tank's words.

Tank clapped him on the shoulder, his voice gentler now. "Look, man. You don't have to agree with me. But don't waste this. Whatever you decide, just don't waste it."

Cole stared at him, Tank's enthusiasm both inspiring and maddening. Maybe this was Tank's way of coping, of finding purpose in the impossible. Or maybe, Cole thought, Tank was onto something.

"This is nuts," he pronounced, even as he began to consider his friend's arguments.

"Might be," Tank drawled. "Still—c'mon, dude—this is the opportunity of a lifetime." He lifted his brows and surprised Cole by bringing Ailsa into his argument. "Nice and cozy, you and Sinclair's sister last night at dinner," he remarked. "You gonna shoot your shot there? Or is that nuts, too? Ten bucks says you get back home and regret forever the chance you didn't take with her." And in typical Tank fashion, he irreverently pushed further. "And by the way, if you're not going to do anything about that, I wouldn't mind taking a stab at her."

Cole growled internally and clenched his teeth. He didn't particularly care for Tank's phrasing. But then he also had to contend with his instinctive response to Tank's proposition, making something out of whatever lived and breathed between him and Ailsa, what had bloomed and blossomed with a nearly frightening speed over what was only a few days, but that soared to life whenever she was near. He scoffed at any idea that Tank had a chance with Ailsa. It wasn't necessarily arrogance, not anything that said he thought himself better than Tank; it was simply facts, how Ailsa responded to him, how she blushed and how she smiled, but more so with him than he'd noticed with Tank. Aside from her coolness this morning—brought on by his own idiocy—Ailsa's behavior around him wasn't so much different from his around hers. Apparently, awareness and infatuation with someone of the opposite sex hadn't changed much over the centuries. She was at times shy and nervous, and he felt like a teenager again, not exactly confident, a little out of his element, as if he'd never dated, kissed, and so much more with another woman before.

Responding to the severe reaction in Cole's countenance, Tank laughed again and held up his hands, palms forward, as if to impart that he was no threat. "'Nough said—or supposed by that face. So then let's go see what this training's about. Maybe you'll be able to rescue a damsel in distress or something, win the lady's favor, or whatever they call it."

"How hard can it be?" Cole wondered, finally relenting, even as the idea of picking up a sword and fighting in a medieval war—possibly having to kill another or be killed—felt like madness.

Still, watching the rest of the motley crew exit the yard through the gate, a wry grin tugged at his lips. They appeared more like seasoned farmers than any proficient military unit. He imagined their techniques would be primitive and unrefined, their movements surely lacking a modern-day fighter's finesse. Between Cole's athleticism and modern mind and Tank's military experience, Cole was certain these provincials had nothing on modern men.

Tavis rode his huge horse behind the last of the men and paused in front of Cole and Tank. Cole was certain he wore a smirk in his gaze if not in his expression.

"The field is open, sirs, and to there we go," Tavis said. The smirk increased a bit. "We're always in need of bodies to beat on."

"We're coming, Sinclair," Tank said, happily picking up the figurative gauntlet thrown by the laird. "I'm ready to show you a thing or two about what a Marine can do."

Tavis was amused by Tank's swagger even as he couldn't possibly understand Tank's reference. "We are always delighted to be entertained."

Tank chuckled good-naturedly, thrilled with the challenge, and he and Cole fell into step behind Tavis.

"We'll show 'em a thing or two," Tank said to Cole. "Maybe that's the big 'why'—why we were brought or sent here, to give these guys a leg up in the fighting."

Willing to adopt Tank's mindset—somewhat—wondering if his reasoning might have some merit, Cole knew a bit of—well, not enthusiasm, but he was game for the moment. "Let's do this."

***

"In truth, it is their staggering ineptness that makes me distrust them so much less."

Ailsa's brother's words reached her, but her attention remained fixed on the scene unfolding down the hill. Cole was sparring against one of Tavis's soldiers, a strong, wiry lad who moved with practiced precision.

Cole was failing miserably.

He swung wide with a clumsy thrust, his movements lacking any real coordination or understanding of the fight. She winced as the soldier ducked, rolled, and came up behind Cole in one smooth motion. With a swift strike, the lad knocked Cole's legs out from under him with his wooden sword, which was all that was allowed on the practice field.

Cole went down hard onto his knees, his hands landing in the cold mud, and for a moment, she thought he might not get up. The soldier pulled back, waiting for him to recover.

"If spies they be," Tavis continued mildly, "or if their intent was to bring harm to the Sinclairs, they are indeed the most hopeless pair of villains I've ever seen."

Ailsa's eyes remained on Cole, watching him stagger to his knees, and she grimaced for him.

Her brother's words about spies and villains were a mockery, but there was truth in the observation. Despite her displeasure with the stunning—offensive, actually—fear that Cole had voiced at supper the previous night, she hadn't been able to dissuade herself from her want to appease her curiosity over how he performed on the training field. To that end, she'd dragged Anwen along with her from Mallaig's cottage, both of them traipsing across the half-mile path to the glen filled with two hundred brave and capable Sinclair soldiers.

And Cole Carter and Hank Morrison.

In truth, she had expected Cole to be more than he was. Broad and strong he was, yes, taller and larger than any Sinclair man including the laird, and possessing a natural grace that suggested he might make a formidable fighter. But it was clear now that whatever potential she'd seen in him was buried beneath an utter lack of training.

Cole's swing was wild, his stance too open. He had no concept of footwork or defense. The soldier, Domhnall, by contrast, was in control, fluid and quick. And yet, each time Cole was knocked down, he struggled to his feet again, his face twisted in frustration, but never staying down for long. Hank was similar, though he seemed to be learning at a quicker pace than Cole. Each time they fell, they rose, dusted themselves off, and went at it again, determined but, for the moment, hopelessly out of their depth.

However, she felt a reluctant admiration for their perseverance, even if their lack of skill made it hard to see any real promise in their abilities.

From behind her, Anwen's voice rang out drolly, cutting through Ailsa's thoughts. "If hitting the mud is the goal, the man's a prodigy."

Ignoring her maid, Ailsa looked over at her brother, whose ponderous scowl was gone now, replaced with a look of amusement. He leaned slightly toward her, his thumbs still tucked into his belt.

"I'll advise they might remain as they are," he mused, "naught but laborers who apparently have never met a fight in all their lives."

Ailsa shifted slightly, wincing once more at the sight of Cole yet again hitting the ground. She had to admit it: *he wasn't what she had expected.* Still, though he wasn't skilled, there was something in the way he kept rising, unwilling to admit defeat. She wondered if he might have more potential in him than was immediately apparent out there sparring with a now crowing Domhnall.

She was pleased in the next moment when a laughing Dersey intervened, pausing the mock fight to make recommendations to Cole, who listened carefully and watched Dersey's strong hands as he gestured accordingly. At least Dersey's intervention allowed Cole a moment to catch his breath.

Shortly after, Cole finally landed a strike with his wooden sword, a wild, uncoordinated hit that somehow connected with Domhnall's side. A small victory, but her stomach fluttered in spite of herself. She resisted the urge to cheer, schooling her face into calm neutrality when Tavis cast a curious glance her way.

A moment later, Cole was knocked down once more.

Behind her, Anwen's voice was tinged with morose pleasure. "Sure, and he's got the falling down part all sewn up."

Her curiosity satisfied and hardly able to stomach much more of the beating Cole Carter was receiving, Ailsa bid a curt farewell to her brother before she turned and began the trek back toward the keep, her skirts brushing against the frosty grass.

Anwen, of course, wasn't far behind.

"Dinna look so decadent now, does he?" her maid quipped, her voice tinged with smugness.

"He and his friend look like men willing to try and to learn," Ailsa said pertly, marching purposefully several paces in front of Anwen. "He looks like someone who dinna give up or give in." She said no more than that, unwilling to advise Anwen fully of her fascination with Cole Carter by defending him further.

Ailsa didn't see Cole Carter again until supper. When he arrived in the hall, his previously athletic stride was tempered by a stiffness that betrayed his soreness. He moved carefully, easing into the chair next to Ailsa at the Sinclair family's table, his jaw tightening briefly as he sat. Despite a lingering hurt from last night, she couldn't help but feel a pang of sympathy for him. The brutal training session earlier had left its mark, and perhaps now she understood why he'd been so vocal about his fear of being killed. With his lack of proficiency, an ambush would have been a death sentence.

She liked him, though, she couldn't help herself. When he wasn't being an eejit, he was charming, undeniably so, with a lop-sided grin that seemed to pull her out of her own head whenever he directed it her way. And handsome—impossibly handsome, really. His smile had the power to make her heart skip, though she cursed herself for being so affected by something as simple as the curve of his lips.

Trust, however, was another matter entirely. His story still seemed too fantastical, too implausible. Her heart and body clamored for her to believe him, to trust him, but her head whispered caution.

Their conversation during the meal was subdued at first, but when he caught her watching him as he winced while cutting his meat, he gave her a sheepish grin.

"Ye look dreadful," she remarked lightly, her tone carrying more concern than judgment.

"Thanks," he quipped, his smile softening into something self-deprecating. "The training was...humbling."

Ailsa grimaced and dared to mention, "I understand ye are expected to return tomorrow."

Cole groaned quietly, but then chuckled briefly. "Oh, I know," he said, plopping a piece of lamb into his mouth.

Ailsa watched him chew, noting the way his jaw shifted as he worked the bite of lamb, a strength visible even in such a mundane act. A faint shadow of stubble lined his jaw, the darker flecks catching the light of the hall's fire. His brow furrowed slightly, as though even the effort of eating required his concentration after such a grueling day.

It struck her as peculiar—how so simple and necessary a thing could seem so compelling. Every detail was sharper now, her focus narrowed so acutely on him. She couldn't look away, her gaze lingering on the strong lines of his face, softened by fatigue that couldn't quite dim the rich blue of his eyes.

"You're staring," Cole murmured suddenly as he met her gaze, his voice low, though it held no accusation—only teasing curiosity.

Ailsa startled slightly, heat rushing to her cheeks. "I was nae" she protested, far too quickly.

He smiled again, this time with a knowing slant, his brow arching just so. "Is the bruising that bad?"

As he didn't have even one bruise on his face, she thought he'd only asked that to give her an out, a way to excuse her blatant staring. As if to suggest there was, perhaps, a perfectly reasonable explanation for her attention. It was unexpectedly kind of him, in a disarming sort of way.

Flustered, she shook her head and turned her attention back to her plate, though her cheeks burned and her pulse buzzed with the memory of his grin. That unguarded expression was dangerous, she decided, more potent than his words, his charm, or even his laugh.

"Tomorrow's training is actually the least of my problems right now," he said after a moment. "I'm fully prepared to embarrass myself for the rest of the week, learning as I go, but your brother—sadist that he is—said earlier that next week, Tank and I should progress to learning to fight on horseback. I'm not sure how I can fight while I'm busy trying not to fall off the horse."

Fairly certain that the "sadist" remark was meant in jest, Ailsa found herself both amused and sympathetic. She remembered his earlier admission that he didn't know how to ride and grimaced inwardly at the thought of how poorly that training might go.

She had no words of encouragement to offer—there was little point in pretending optimism where none existed—so she opted for levity instead. Her lips twitched into a faint smile. "Possibly, if you fall with enough frequency, no aggressor will be able to land any strike against you."

To Ailsa's surprise, Cole laughed outright, the rich sound drawing curious glances from those seated nearby. If he noticed—or cared—about the attention, it didn't show. His blue eyes sparkled with mirth, and the broad smile lighting his face made him seem, for a fleeting moment, much more carefree. The sound of his laughter did glorious things to her insides, being silken and warm, a balm she hadn't known she needed.

Ailsa was transfixed, her earlier misgivings momentarily forgotten. The unguarded happiness on his face as he laughed struck something deep within her. It was absurd, really, how handsome he was, and charming he could be when he allowed himself to relax.

Before she thought better of it, Ailsa heard herself say to him, "I could teach ye. To ride, that is."

Her offer lingered in the air between them, his smile softening into something quieter, almost thoughtful. His gaze settled on her face, studying her in a way that made her breath catch. Then, slowly, his eyes flickered to her lips, with an intensity that made her pulse quicken.

"You would do that?"

She nodded and suggested in a whisper, "Meet me in the stables tomorrow. After training."

Cole grinned, a spark of mischief returning to his eyes. "If I haven't succumbed to my injuries by then."

She was fairly certain she could feel her brother's suspicious regard on her back, but Ailsa ignored it, focusing instead on the strange, undeniable pull she felt toward Cole Carter—despite all the warnings her mind continued to give her.

Chapter Eleven

Humble pie was not very sweet.

He'd been so certain that the fourteenth-century Sinclairs, with their primitive looks and rudimentary gear, would be so far beneath him as far as finesse and skill went. He'd been ready to show off, to impress with slick movements, his athleticism honed on the Bandit's playing field, his strength enhanced by years of fighting fires and regularly hitting the gym.

What the hell was wrong with him that he'd underestimated the soldiers so badly? He'd been so arrogant.

As he walked away from the training field today—or more aptly, limped, staggered, and shuffled—he felt like an ass for having judged the book by its cover. True, he'd been more prepared today, but damn, those guys were fierce. And strong. And merciless. How quickly he'd learned that the men of Torr Cinnteag had honed their craft over half a decade of bloody conflict and a lifetime of manual labor, their battle tactics as lethal as they were primitive. Cole had quickly learned that the brutal simplicity of medieval combat was more terrifying and effective than any modern mindset or workout could have prepared him for.

And yet, while he was indeed humbled, he wasn't necessarily embarrassed by his own poor showing. He looked at it as a challenge. It needed some hard work and dedication, of which he was never afraid, and Cole was bound and determined to prove both his worth and his competence.

He needed not only to improve with the use of the sword, but he needed to understand how better to wield both sword and shield, as he was being trained. He wasn't yet comfortable with his entire forearm being locked into the back of the shield, and thought too often that hefting the wooden piece on his arm sometimes threw off his balance. It felt clumsy, like an unwieldy appendage, and more than once, he thought he might want, at times, to grip the sword with both hands for better control—but the shield made that impossible. This, then, was also still a work in progress.

Here's hoping riding a horse is easier than wielding a sword, he thought wearily, heading back to the castle yard and the stables where he was looking forward to meeting Ailsa.

As he walked through the gate, with returning soldiers in front and behind him, he was struck not for the first time by how these people dealt with the cold—or rather, how they seemed so unbothered by it. He lived in Buffalo, NY, which was not exactly the frozen tundra but knew its share of frigid weather, but it couldn't hold a candle to the constant, biting, unrelenting chill of the Highlands. In Buffalo, the cold came with layers of modern convenience—thermal coats, insulated gloves, and the promise of indoor heating at the end of the day. Here, the wind seemed sharper, knifing through his winter layers and cutting straight to the bone, as if the mountains and wind themselves conspired to keep weak people away. The Highlanders, however, seemed immune. They didn't just endure the cold; they wore it like a second skin, unflinching and indifferent to the kind of weather that would have grounded half of Buffalo under emergency conditions. For Cole, the icy air felt like a personal insult, as if the land itself was mocking him as fragile.

He washed his muddied hands in a trough near the stables as others did, the icy water stinging his scraped, bruised, and chapped hands. And while he dried his hands on the sweatshirt beneath his coat, he scanned the interior of the stables, looking for Ailsa. She wasn't there but as he approached the opening, a young kid, about ten years old, bound to his feet from where he'd been sitting in a pile of hay, and came forward, looking as if he'd been waiting for Cole.

"I take ye to lady," the boy said in very stilted English.

"Ailsa? Where is she?"

The young kid responded in the Scottish language so that Cole wondered if Ailsa had simply taught him that one sentence. Cole nodded to show that he understood, and the kid nodded as well and then turned and led the way from the stables, scurrying like a little sewer rat, forcing Cole into a jog to keep up with him.

The boy led Cole down a gentle slope outside the gates, where snow crunched softly beneath their feet. Beyond the bridge, they turned left, off the main path and headed into a stand of trees. The boy darted swiftly around firs and birch trees, his small feet hardly making any noise at all. The wooded vale was quiet, save for the faint rustle of the wind through bare branches. Up ahead a clearing presented itself and Cole spotted Ailsa waiting there. She sat astride a sleek, reddish-brown horse with a white blaze down its face. The horse's ears flicked forward, its breath puffing in visible clouds. Ailsa's cheeks were rosy from the cold, and her eyes widened slightly when she noticed the kid and Cole approaching. Her back was straight, her posture poised, and her lips parted slightly before curving into a polite smile.

"Ye made it," she said, her voice light but uncertain. She slid gracefully from the horse's back, her movements fluid. Her cloak swirled around her legs, and she remained near the horse, her hand lingering on the mare's neck. "I kent it best to begin away from too many eyes."

Cole shot a glance back at the boy, who lingered a moment before darting off toward the keep, leaving them alone. "I appreciate the privacy," Cole said, grinning faintly as he stepped forward, eyeing the horse. "I'd rather not have any witnesses," he quipped, hoping this proved less difficult than wielding a sword.

"Ye've truly never ridden?" Ailsa asked, studying him carefully.

"No—unless carousels count," Cole replied, his tone dry.

Ailsa blinked, her brow furrowing at the unfamiliar word, but she chose not to ask. Instead, she stepped forward, apparently meaning to get straight to business. "We'll start with the basics," she said. "This is Ceara." She stroked the mare's neck affectionately. "She's gentle but strong-willed. Respect her, and she'll respect ye."

Cole reached out cautiously to pat the horse's side, surprised by the solid warmth of its coat. Ceara's ears swiveled toward him, and Ailsa smiled faintly. "She's watching ye. Horses are perceptive creatures."

"Yeah, I'd heard that," Cole acknowledged, though he couldn't remember from where.

"First," Ailsa began, her tone softening as she shifted into instruction, "ye need to approach a horse confidently but calmly. Nae sudden movements. Let her get used to yer presence." She encouraged Cole to come closer, having him stand by Ceara's shoulder and stroke her neck.

His hand brushed against hers accidentally as he reached out to pat the horse. Ailsa pulled her hand back quickly, her cheeks gaining some color.

"This is the bridle," Ailsa said after clearing her throat. She pointed to the leather straps fitted around the horse's head. "The bit—this piece here—rests in her mouth, just behind her teeth. It lets ye guide her with the reins."

She ran her gloved hand along the bridle with an ease that spoke of years spent in the saddle, her touch deft and sure. Cole's breath caught as an errant thought blindsided him—a vivid image of Ailsa's hand tracing over him with that same confident familiarity. Somehow he managed to keep his eyes from widening, though the sheer audacity of the thought left him stunned. *Holy hell.* He clenched his fists, willing the heat in his face to subside, but the idea lingered, unsettling and intoxicating in equal measure. Where the hell had that come from?

Unaware of his present distraction, Ailsa continued. "The saddle is where ye'll sit, of course, but the girth here"—she gestured to the wide strap beneath the mare's belly—"keeps it secure. Ye dinna want it slipping off mid-ride." She glanced up, meeting Cole's eyes briefly, her lips curving into the smallest of smiles. "'Tis hard to recover from the jeering ye'd take if that were to happen."

Cole grunted a laugh. "Yeah, there's been enough damage to my pride already, with the shellacking their giving me on the training field."

Her smile grew slightly wider, but Cole could not say if it was filled with sympathy or amusement. Either way, the subtle curve of her lips stirred something unexpected. He shifted his weight, forcing his focus back to the horse.

His pride wasn't a fragile thing, and never had been. By the time he hit the fifth grade, picked last for every team, he'd learned not to let anyone's opinion define him. Being underestimated didn't bother him; it only made him more determined to prove himself, to work harder until the results spoke for themselves. Yet here, with Ailsa, something felt different. It mattered what she thought of him, he understood. He wanted her to see him as capable, as someone who could rise to a challenge, no matter how foreign this world was to him. That desire unnerved him almost as much as her smile.

"Mounting comes next." Ailsa pointed to the stirrup, then demonstrated, swinging up onto Ceara's back with an enviable grace. She dismounted quickly and gestured for Cole to try. "Use the stirrup for leverage, swing your leg over, and settle into the saddle."

Cole hesitated, eying the horse warily. "You make it sound so easy."

"It is easy. If ye're nae made of jelly."

"Great vote of confidence," he muttered, planting his foot in the stirrup. His first attempt ended with him floundering awkwardly, half-draped over the saddle. He heard Ailsa stifle a laugh behind him.

"Try again," she said, her voice firmer now. "This time, put more strength into the jump."

Cole's second attempt was better, though far from elegant. He landed heavily in the saddle, startling Ceara, who sidestepped. Ailsa steadied the horse with a quick word and a firm hand on the bridle.

"That was nae so bad," she said, her lips quirking as she glanced up at him.

"High praise," Cole replied, gripping the reins tightly as he adjusted to the unfamiliar sensation of being alone on the horse's back, hoping the beast didn't bolt.

Next, Ailsa advised him how to hold the reins properly. "Firm but gentle. You're nae trying to pull her head off."

"Got it. Firm but gentle," Cole echoed, suiting words to action, loosening his grip a bit. "Now what?"

"We'll walk," Ailsa said simply, taking the reins to lead Ceara in a slow circle around the clearing. "Ye need to learn how to sit properly, balance, and use yer legs to guide her. Everything else builds from there."

Cole nodded, the cold momentarily forgotten as he focused intently on her instructions and keeping his seat as the horse walked. As he'd come to notice, Ailsa's initial shyness seemed to dissolve with time, her confidence growing steadily the longer they were together. Same as with dinner together or other meetings when her early reserve gradually gave way to a quiet ease, her words flowing more freely as their conversation unfolded, the pattern repeated now, and he found himself fascinated by the shift, drawn to the way her self-assuredness emerged in his company.

After a few laps with Ailsa walking beside him, keeping a steadying hand on the mare's bridle, she stepped back, letting Cole circle the horse around on his own.

"Use the reins to turn her gently," she said, her tone calm but watchful. "A slight pull to the side, just enough for her to feel it in her mouth."

Cole nodded, adjusting his grip on the leather reins. He tugged lightly to the right, and the mare responded with surprising obedience, turning in a smooth arc. Ailsa gave a small nod of approval.

"Good," she said, her voice carrying a note of encouragement that made him sit a little straighter. "Aye, keep yer hands steady—dinna jerk them—and try it the other way."

He repeated the movement to the left, finding it easier now that he understood how little effort it required. She watched for a moment before commenting. "Ye have a natural sense for this, I ken."

A flicker of satisfaction was stirred by Ailsa's mild praise. He guided the mare around another circle, growing more confident as he went. The clearing was small and hence, so were the circles he made round Ailsa who stood in the middle, but he felt like this was tremendous progress already.

"Now," Ailsa called after he'd made a few more arcs, "let's see if ye can urge her to move a wee bit faster." She gestured to the mare's sides. "A light squeeze with your calves—just enough to let her know what ye want. Keep in mind she's nae a mind-reader. If she dinna respond, give her a nudge with your heels, but dinna dig in too hard lest ye desire to fly."

Cole winced at the suggestion that using too much force might see the mare bolt, possibly causing Cole to tumble end over end off her back. Gingerly, he pressed his legs lightly against the mare's sides. At first, nothing happened, and he tried again, giving a slightly stronger squeeze. The mare's ears flicked before she picked up her pace, transitioning into a brisk walk. Cole grinned despite himself, the sensation of movement beneath him both exhilarating and slightly unnerving.

"There," Ailsa said, her voice tinged with approval. "Now ye're riding."

He was, but not well. What little he'd ever seen of riding—in movies—had always shown the rider moving in time with the horse but he felt that he was simply being bobbed along without any control.

Ailsa must have noticed it was well. "Ye're bouncing too much because ye're fighting the horse's motion. Instead of sitting stiffly, move with her. Relax yer hips and let them follow her rhythm—she'll tell ye where to go if ye listen to her."

Cole frowned. "I can feel the rhythm," he said. "I just don't know how to get into it with her." As the words left his mouth, a vivid thought crept in—another rhythm he'd practiced over the last ten years or more, one he'd never had any trouble with. He clenched his jaw against the unexpected thought of sex, even as he wondered if the same principles might apply—follow her rhythm. His hands tightened on the reins for balance, though his discomfort wasn't about the horse anymore. He cast a glance at Ailsa, but she was oblivious, watching the mare and Cole's progress with a practiced eye.

Thankfully unaware of his lewd thoughts, Ailsa recommended, "Feel for it. When she walks, her back shifts side to side. Let your body sway with that, like ye're part of her. Sit straight but nae rigid. Your hips should be as loose hinges, nae locked bolts. Riding dinna mean ye sit and do nothing. As is she, ye are in constant motion, moving with her."

He shifted in the saddle, trying to relax his posture.

"Better," she encouraged. "Now, when she speeds up, the bounce will come naturally unless ye rise with her. Use yer legs to steady yerself, but dinna step hard, just slightly stand in the stirrups as she steps forward. It's called posting."

After a few minutes, Cole wondered if this was something that would come more with time and practice, or more easily to someone who'd started riding when they were young. He wasn't deterred though, just resigned that it wasn't going to be something he learned in one day.

After an hour, his ass was sore and his arms and neck stiff from holding the reins. But they kept at it.

He was amazed by Ailsa, who exhibited keen insight into what he was doing wrong and knew exactly the words to speak to correct him. She also seemed to be gifted with an endless amount of patience, which he thought wryly might come more easily when you were standing on solid ground, not being bounced around in a saddle like a sack of potatoes.

He never would have expected that riding a horse was so much work. The movies always made it look effortless but in reality, it required constant attention, physical effort, and a subtle partnership between rider and horse that demanded motion, balance, and focus. Ailsa had been right: one did not simply sit back and expect the horse to handle everything. He could only hope that this coordination would come more naturally with time.

The thought, however, gave him pause. Time. How much of it did he even have here? Would learning these skills turn out to be a waste if he were snatched back to the twenty-first century? Or worse, what if he weren't sent home but hurtled somewhere else entirely? The very idea made his stomach twist.

Possibly the most maddening part of his predicament was the sheer uncertainty of it all. No rules, no guidebook, no clear sense of what lay ahead. Would he stay here for the rest of his life, forging an existence in this brutal yet strangely captivating world? Was there something he should be doing—some action, some choice—that could return him home? But, if he tried, could things actually be made worse? What if tampering with whatever had brought him here flung him into some other time period, somewhere even more unfamiliar and hostile than medieval Scotland? The lack of answers gnawed at him, each possibility more unsettling than the last.

And then, unexpectedly, the lesson took a turn—one that both intrigued and unnerved him. Ailsa, realizing he wasn't quite getting the hang of the rhythm, paused in her instructions and suggested something that sent a jolt of awareness through him: she would ride with him.

"It might help," she said simply, her tone matter-of-fact, though a faint flush tinged her cheeks, "if ye could feel how I move with the horse. Ye'll learn quicker by example than words."

The suggestion made perfect sense—was practical, even—but Cole's stomach tightened at the thought. Suddenly he felt like a teenager, a high schooler being forced into close proximity with the teacher he had a secret crush on. He nodded, unsure if he even trusted his voice, and began slowing the horse under her guidance. The truth was, he probably shouldn't be touching Ailsa at all while they discussed something as elemental as the natural rhythms of bodies moving in tandem. Especially not when his own body seemed to have its own ideas about being close to hers.

He swallowed hard, the faint wariness in his chest overcome by an undeniable current of anticipation. He could hardly deny it anymore—he was seriously attracted to her. And now, with her poised to join him in the saddle, he was achingly aware of how easily admiration and appreciation were tipping into something more visceral.

"Here," she said, approaching the horse. She placed a hand on the saddle and gestured for him to adjust his position slightly to make room. "I'll take the reins and ride in front, and ye should try to emulate how I move."

He obeyed, shifting back in the saddle with an awkward jolt, his grip tightening briefly on the reins before handing them off to her. Ailsa climbed into the saddle in front of him, her usual grace only slightly hindered as she maneuvered her leg around him and the horse's neck. She settled into place, her small frame fitting neatly against his, and Cole found himself acutely aware of how soft and warm she felt, her body pressed lightly against his chest. They were seated close enough that he caught the faint scent of her hair—something earthy and clean, like pine needles and fresh air.

She reached around and found his hand with her gloved ones, guiding his hand to her sides.

"Relax," she murmured, her voice soft. "Hold my hips and I'll show ye how to move."

Her words, perfectly innocent, jolted him. Cole gritted his teeth, his muscles locking as his brain conjured a setting far removed from horseback riding. The rhythm she wanted him to master was all too familiar, too intimate, and he cursed his traitorous thoughts.

He tried to focus, tried to keep his grip steady and his attention on the task at hand, but it was no use. His heart was pounding, his body hyperaware of every small shift she made, and no amount of effort could suppress the image forming in his mind—a scene where "moving together" meant something entirely different.

This was going to be impossible, he decided fairly quickly.

As the horse began to move again, Cole forced himself to focus, though every nerve in his body was keenly aware of Ailsa's dangerous proximity.

"Up and down, rolling your hips," she instructed. "That's nice. Move with me."

He tried to ignore the way her words seemed to echo deeper than the lesson at hand, or how her movements—smooth and synchronized with the mare and now Cole—seemed to blur the line between instruction and something far more intimate. He exhaled slowly, fighting to steady himself.

This was just about learning to ride, he reminded himself. That was all. But no matter how hard he tried to convince himself, his body wasn't listening.

Cole wasn't sure he learned anything except that he and Ailsa moved well together, but they did this for almost ten minutes before Ailsa brought the horse to a stop and dismounted. He edged forward in the saddle, gripping the reins she handed back to him with a little too much force, keeping his hands low, between his legs. All the while, he prayed she hadn't noticed the undeniable evidence of just how fiercely he desired her.

Blissfully unaware—or so he desperately hoped—Ailsa tilted her head up to him, a radiant smile playing on her lips.

Or maybe she *was* aware? Her cheeks were flushed a brilliant red, her gaze skittering past his eyes and landing, unmistakably, on his mouth. His heart stumbled. And the growing evidence of his attraction was not at all subdued.

"Ye can manage it for yerself now?" she asked, her voice light, though she still wouldn't quite meet his eyes.

He smothered a groan. *I'll have to, if I want to survive being in your presence without losing my mind.* Aloud, he lied smoothly, "I think I got it."

And, surprisingly, maybe he did. When he nudged the mare into a light trot at Ailsa's prompting, circling the clearing in a wide arc, he realized he was finally beginning to move with the horse instead of against her. The rhythm Ailsa had tried so patiently to teach him felt less elusive now, as though his body had finally begun to understand what his brain couldn't grasp before. Surprising, indeed, since he hadn't been thinking much about the horse—or *that* rhythm—for the past ten minutes. No, his thoughts had been consumed by something, or rather *someone*, far more enticing.

***

And so the days passed, one after another, Cole falling into a routine in the fourteenth century. Each morning, he dragged himself out of bed, groaning and stiff from the accumulated strain of medieval sword training and horseback riding lessons. The aches and pains were relentless, a constant reminder that this was no quick session at the gym or a rough lacrosse practice. However, as he'd mentioned to Tank, Cole was certain that years of those modern-day routines were what made this grueling warrior regimen endurable. He might have been battered, but he wasn't broken. For now, he counted small victories: fewer missteps, stronger strikes, and longer stretches in the saddle without feeling like he was about to be unseated.

In the meantime, it did not escape Cole's attention that Ailsa never again offered to get in the saddle with him, and he had to wonder if that first day of riding, of talking about the rhythm of the horse while their bodies matched pace had affected her in the same way it had him. Whatever the reason, he was only glad that she hadn't repeated that method of instruction.

On the third day of riding lessons, Ailsa asked, "Is nae yer friend in need of instruction as well?"

"I don't know what Tank is doing," Cole said, and there was plenty of truth to that statement. *Embracing medieval life,* was one answer. Despite their similar circumstances, he'd spent little time with Tank the last few days. His friend was enamored with this age and its people and was constantly out and about, wanting to learn and see and know, immersing himself in the culture.

That was Tank in a nutshell. He made friends everywhere he went. Kids gravitated toward him. Adults welcomed him. He could just as easily strike up a conversation with a homeless person as he could politicians back home. And it was no different here, Tank seen talking for more than an hour with the old blacksmith in his smoky forge, charming servants in the kitchen, and making friends with several of the soldiers. Tank could find common ground with just about anyone.

Cole, on the other hand, didn't have the same ease with people. He was fine one-on-one or in familiar settings—comfortable at the firehouse, confident on the lacrosse field with his Bandits' teammates—but in unfamiliar situations or around new people, he didn't put himself out there. Crowds and small talk weren't his forte, and he'd never enjoyed being in the spotlight. He struggled with the press requirements of the Bandits, as the players were required to give interviews regularly during the season as part of their contract and according to league rules.

Now, here he was in a world where fitting in wasn't exactly optional. Tank seemed ready to adapt and thrive, but Cole wasn't sure where he stood or how much he wanted to integrate himself. If this place became his reality—if he *never* got back home—he'd have to adapt whether he liked it or not. And unless he decided to learn a trade, which wasn't entirely out of the question, he had little choice but to keep working at the skills Ailsa and others were teaching him: riding, fighting, and surviving as if he were actually a warrior from this time.

After about an hour of lessons, and by now, Cole felt he had a firm handle on the extreme basics, Ailsa advised she was needed back at the castle.

"It's candle making day," she explained when he stopped the horse near her.

She had a habit of approaching whenever he brought the horse to a halt, and laying her hand on the horse's neck, idly stroking, usually while she mentioned something he was doing wrong or could improve, or often some helpful tip. For some reason, Cole liked these moments, when she stood close, her face tipped up at him. As ever, her eyes were a startling blue outdoors in natural light. Today, as there was scarcely any wind, her hood had been lowered and her hair was loose, falling over her shoulders in soft waves. He wondered if the small distance created by him being mounted, or if the presence of the horse itself calmed her, but in these moments she never appeared shy or hesitant, always open and at ease.

"Isn't that what servants are for?" He asked, his mouth curving a bit.

"Aye, of course, but my hands are nae broken," she answered before shrugging and offering a saucy smile. "Alas, someone has to direct them."

"I would think Anwen would be better suited for that job," he ventured.

"And dinna doubt she is," was Ailsa's grinning reply. "But she takes pride in her elevated role as my maid. Supervising the servants is beneath her—or so she says—and she makes nae secret of her disdain for the more tedious work."

"As in, she wouldn't be caught dead getting her hands dirty?"

Another shrug preceded her response. "Aye, ye might say that."

"I'm curious, because she's usually hot on your trail," Cole commented. "So where does she think you are everyday when you're here with me?" Though he had no proof, he suspected that their daily lessons were not something Ailsa wanted widely known.

"'Tis nae my absence I explain," Ailsa confessed, utterly unrepentant. "Instead, I give her wee tasks to keep her occupied. Yesterday, I sent her hunting for my favorite pair of riding gloves—which, as ye ken, I was wearing when we met here." Her grin turned impish. "And today, I suggested that there might be some grand trouble brewing between Aimil, the dairymaid, and the lad she fancies, Eachann. I sighed, lamenting how I wished I could smooth things over but admitted, with great reluctance, that 'tis hardly my place to meddle." She lifted her hand dramatically to her forehead, palm out, and let out an exaggerated sigh. "If only there were someone who *could* intervene."

Cole let out a startled laugh, shaking his head. "Ailsa Sinclair! You're a troublemaker—a schemer!"

Her smile didn't falter in the slightest, a gleam of mischief in her eyes. "Nae, I'm a woman who treasures the occasional moment of peace, free of her maid's ceaseless harping."

Cole scratched his head as though perplexed, his lips twitching. "And here I was thinking you were helping me out of the goodness of your heart. You're just using me to escape your warden."

Ailsa tilted her chin, her smile widening. "Och, I'm verra glad to help ye, Cole Carter. Escaping Anwen is just an added bonus."

Cole gave her a mockingly thoughtful nod. "Well then, I'm happy to be of service."

When they parted company, both going in different directions, Cole believed he had a few more answers as to why Ailsa—stunning natural beauty aside—intrigued him so.

Ailsa's straightforwardness and lack of pretension made her feel refreshingly genuine—Cole was convinced that Ailsa had no idea how ridiculously gorgeous she was. Her practical knowledge of so many things modern people had no experience in—herbal medicine, managing a castle, candle-making, and being skilled as a rider. Her hands-on competence was both captivating and admirable. Though he had the sense that she was treated as a much less qualified woman by her brother and possibly everyone in this time period, Ailsa was independent in so many ways that was so different than modern women.

Unlike the casual, often self-deprecating charm he'd come to expect in modern women, Ailsa's demeanor was shaped by a world of formalities, lending her an air of timeless grace. She was elegant, poised, and almost regal in her movements and speech, yet her wit and playful mischief—like the wild goose chases she orchestrated for her maid—showed an entirely different, lively, relatable side of her.

As Cole turned these thoughts over in his mind, he began to believe that aside from the rather inconvenient fact that she lived seven hundred years in the past, Ailsa Sinclair was, to his way of thinking, damn near perfect.

Chapter Twelve

Cole ran the brush along the mare's flank, following the instructions Ailsa had repeated over the past few days, the routine care of the horse. In a nearby stall, Tank brushed down a bay gelding, his broad frame moving with a practiced ease. He'd just returned from a ride with a few of the Sinclair soldiers, who had shown him a bit more of Torr Cinnteag, parts of the thousands of acres claimed by the Sinclairs.

"Where'd you learn to ride?" Cole called across the otherwise empty stalls.

Moments after Ailsa had left Cole in the stables, having been summoned by a young girl from the kitchen immediately upon their return, Cole had witnessed Tank and his new buddies riding in through the gates. Though Cole had never once heard Tank say anything about riding a horse, Cole hadn't missed how at ease his friend was in the saddle.

"My aunt and uncle had a horse farm in East Aurora," Tank answered, naming a mostly rural suburb of Buffalo. "I haven't ridden in years, but I spent a lot of summers there when I was a kid. Kinda like riding a bike, apparently," Tank said, chuckling a bit. "It does come back to you." Tank's head disappeared as he ducked, presumably to brush the horse's legs. His voice, however, carried to Cole. "You're catching on, though. I saw you in the valley from the ridge above it, you and Ailsa. She your riding instructor?"

"She is," Cole replied, expecting to take some ribbing for having asked her and not one of the soldiers.

"She must be good," Tank said instead. "You almost look like you know what you're doing."

Cole grinned. "It is getting easier," he admitted, "or at least I'm getting more comfortable in the saddle." Indeed, today, he'd *given the mare her legs*—Ailsa's wording, and hadn't once felt like he was in danger of falling off as the horse galloped up and down the glen. He actually felt as if he'd been in control for most of that ride, great progress in his mind.

"I hadn't realized how much I missed it," Tank continued. "Who would, with cars and trucks, right? But damn, I like the feeling of it: riding, open air, man and beast"—he deepened his voice comically, grunting a bit—"primal male shit. Argh. Argh."

Cole's grin widened. "That started out so poetic," he remarked. "So you had a good ride?" Cole asked Tank without looking up.

"Not bad," Tank replied. "These guys know their way around a saddle, that's for sure. They've been teaching me a trick or two. I've still got lots to learn if I want to keep up." He gave the gelding a final pat before setting the brush aside. "There's a hunting party going out tomorrow. I think we're expected to join them. Basically, I think they want to test our mettle—"

Before the conversation could continue, Father Gilbert appeared at the entrance, his steady gaze sweeping over the two men before landing on Cole. The priest approached, his hands clasped in front of him as if he'd been considering his words carefully before speaking.

"Cole," he began, his tone gentle but firm, "a word, if I may?"

Tank stepped back, sensing the seriousness in the priest's demeanor but staying within earshot. Cole straightened, setting the brush on the stable wall. "Sure. What's on your mind?"

Father Gilbert's eyes flicked briefly around the stables. "I feel it is my duty to caution you. If what you've said about your origins is true, you may be...whisked away at a moment's notice—returned to your own time. Or you may not, but the uncertainty remains. And in either case, you must be mindful not to grow too close to Ailsa Sinclair."

Cole frowned. "Why's that?" He felt a strange knot tighten in his chest, even as he figured he knew what the answer would be: he wasn't acceptable.

Father Gilbert sighed. "There are practical reasons. Ailsa is to be promised in marriage to the MacLae son. Her brother, the laird, would never allow her to entertain the courtship of another. Their alliance is essential for peace."

The words hit harder than Cole expected. He rubbed the back of his neck, grappling with the idea of Ailsa marrying someone else. "I don't remember that I was courting Ailsa," he said evasively.

Father Gilbert raised his brows at Cole. "Are you not?"

"She's teaching me how to ride a damn horse," he said, a little heated now under the priest's critical stare. "This... MacLae son," Cole said, his voice tight, "is he a decent guy?"

Father Gilbert tilted his head, considering—either Cole's interest in the man or his answer. "I believe he will not be unkind. The laird would never allow his sister to be mistreated, though the marriage will be one of alliance, not love."

Tank stepped forward, breaking the tension. "If it's an alliance, it's not exactly about what *she* wants, huh? That's some medieval shit we got rid of over the centuries," he said lightly, though there was an edge to his tone.

Cole stared hard into the priest's dark eyes. "So she's...what? Off-limits? Can't even engage in a simple helpful tutoring?"

Tightly, Father Gilbert announced, "Ailsa Sinclair must remain above reproach. She is not to be seen in the company of any man without a chaperone, no matter the purpose. Her duty is to her family and to her future husband. Anything that could jeopardize that—any appearance of impropriety—must be avoided at all costs." He thinned his lips and added pointedly, "She must remain untouched."

The priest possibly mistook Cole's clenched-jaw silence as understanding. He nodded approvingly. "If tutoring is what you need, I can make arrangements for someone else to instruct you. 'Tis wise to avoid any entanglements that could lead to trouble for her—or for you."

Cole's jaw tightened. He didn't want to give up the lessons with Ailsa, but he knew the priest was right. He had little say with what went on here, at Torr Cinnteag, with Ailsa, or in the fourteenth century. "Fine," he said after a moment. "Can you set that up?"

"I shall," Father Gilbert said. "A wise decision, lad." With that, he nodded to both men and departed, leaving the two of them in the stables.

Tank waited until the priest was out of earshot before turning to Cole with a knowing smirk. "You're not exactly subtle, you know."

"What's that supposed to mean?" Cole shot back, defensive.

Tank leaned against the stable door, arms crossed. "It hasn't escaped me how you look at her—or how she looks at you, for that matter. Not saying you're doing anything wrong, but the priest has a point. If we ever figure out how to get back home, do you really want to leave things behind that make it harder?"

Cole didn't answer immediately, staring at the mare as he resumed brushing her down. "It's not like that," he muttered, though he knew damn well he was lying.

Tank chuckled softly. "Sure it's not. Just... think about it, okay? This isn't our world, man. And if we're sticking around, we're gonna have to deal with whatever rules they've got here."

Tank left the stables, leaving Cole alone with his now frustrated thoughts. He knew the priest was probably right but that didn't mean he liked it, not one bit. Then again, it was ridiculous to feel this way about Ailsa after only a week. They'd just met. He didn't even know how long he'd be here.

And yet, as much as he tried to push it aside, the thought of her marrying someone else gnawed at him in a way that set his teeth on edge.

***

God's teeth, but Cole Carter was going to be the death of her.

He needed to learn faster how to ride, before she lost her wits completely and outright begged him to kiss her, touch her—anything!—to relieve this torturous, sweet ache that his presence stirred within her. Every lesson spent at his side, every exchange of glances, every accidental brush of hands left her trembling with emotions she could hardly name.

She paced the narrow corridor of the family solar, her hands clenched at her sides. It was madness, wanting something so wholly impossible. And yet... did it have to be? Ailsa forced herself to stop, gripping the back of a carved wooden chair as if it might ground her scattered thoughts.

Her brother's voice from earlier today still echoed in her mind: *"When ye return from our sister's house, we'll begin the serious negotiations with the MacLaes. William MacLae has expressed his eagerness to move forward on behalf of his brother."*

An arranged marriage, a strategic alliance—her future laid out before her. No consideration for what she wanted, what she longed for. The idea of binding herself to Alastair MacLae, a man she barely knew and felt nothing for, suddenly turned her stomach. Never mind that the rumors swirling around her expected intended frightened her, that he was neither good nor kind, that by all accounts there was little to love... but her heart, it was already wandering elsewhere.

It did not escape her notice, the realization that before Cole Carter's arrival, she had accepted her fate with dignified resignation even as she'd been terribly anxious about it. She had always known this was her role. She'd grown up knowing that she had, essentially, one goal in life: she existed to secure a strategic marriage for the benefit of the Sinclairs. Her sister had done so years ago, and Ailsa had known she would follow. There had been no expectation of grand romance or heart-stirring passion—such notions were for ballads and peasants. Yet, she had believed she could find a measure of contentment, carving out her happiness as a dutiful wife and, hopefully one day, as a mother.

But now, that once-stoic resolve felt fragile, threatened by something—someone—that made her heart pound and her thoughts stray far from the life she had always assumed would be hers.

Ailsa released the chair and resumed her pacing.

Cole Carter was unlike any man she had ever known. His eyes alone, the way they lingered on her, seemed to ignite flames in corners of her soul she hadn't even realized existed. The sheer presence of him stirred a disquiet within her, thrilling and unnerving all at once, leaving her both breathless and unsteady. And...wanting.

Each moment with him seemed charged, brimming with unspoken promises and tantalizing possibility. He made her want to take risks, to challenge everything she'd been taught about what her life should be.

But what could she do? The answer, of course, was nothing. Duty demanded her compliance, and her brother would never allow her to entertain such a reckless notion as pursuing anything with Cole.

Ailsa flopped down into a chair, her chin in her hand, staring out the window at the loch below. She couldn't stop herself from wishing for the impossible. She wanted to know him—more, better, wholly. She wanted to find out what lay behind the calm reserve in his eyes, to unravel the mystery of his presence in her world.

She wanted, impossibly, irrevocably, only him.

Thus, she was taken aback and caused a great deal of pain and confusion with what Cole announced at supper that evening.

In truth, she was a bit surprised that her brother allowed Cole to continue to sit beside her at the meal. Though she was certain Tavis—and others—had a newfound appreciation for both Cole and Tank, or certainly less suspicious hostility since they'd joined the daily drills—Tavis's reminder this morning about her inevitable betrothal had come after he'd made a cryptic remark about Cole to her.

"I dinna quite understand the man's dedication to the training," Tavis had remarked, his tone casual with curiosity. Then, watching her closely through narrowed eyes, he'd added, "Mark my words, sister, he will nae stay long. Fighting isna in his blood; he'll find his way back to whatever place he calls home. And when he does, 'tis better he leaves with no bonds or ties to hold him here, nae person who might tempt him to remain where he dinna belong."

At times, she suspected that Tavis entrusted her entirely with upholding decorum, as though it were her sole responsibility to avoid any awkward or compromising situation. He seemed to believe she could be relied upon to act with propriety in all circumstances, leaving little need for his intervention or concern.

The great hall was lively this evening, the long trestle tables buzzing with conversation, clinking tankards, and the scrape of eating knives on pewter and wooden plates. Ailsa sat in her usual place at her brother's right hand, with Cole beside her. On the other side of Tavis, Tank was deep in conversation with a few soldiers, laughing at some jest that Ailsa hadn't caught.

Her brother had spent most of the meal discussing trade agreements, but her attention was elsewhere—specifically on the man at her side. Cole had been unusually quiet, the air of ease that had been built, tarnished, and then repaired over the past days absent tonight.

Her suspicions were confirmed when, after he'd emptied his plate, he turned to her, his expression oddly sheepish.

"Ailsa, I wanted to say...that is, I really appreciate your help with the riding," he began, his voice low enough to keep their exchange private, "but I think I'm good now." He cleared his throat and avoided meeting her gaze. "I don't think I need any more instruction."

Ailsa blinked, caught off guard. "Oh." Her smile wavered, and she quickly steadied it. "Well. That's...that's guid then. I'm glad to have been some help to ye."

She meant to sound gracious, but even to her own ears, the words felt hollow. She didn't mention what came first to mind, that Cole was far from ready to ride competently without further instruction; they hadn't even begun to practice jumps, let alone navigating uneven terrain or handling a horse in more complex situations.

Cole shifted uncomfortably, his gaze darting away, out among the trestle tables, then back to her.

"You were a great help, very much so," he added quickly, as if to soften the blow. "It's just—uh, I think I can handle it from here."

"Of course." She inclined her head, her face a mask of polite composure. But inside, her thoughts churned.

Across the hall, a sudden commotion drew their attention. Two soldiers had risen from their seats, shoving each other amidst a clatter of spilled tankards and overturned plates. The larger of the two had his hand on the other's tunic, his knuckles white as he hauled the man close, their faces inches apart.

The hall fell into a brief hush before erupting with laughter and cheers, a few people egging the pair on.

Tavis rose to his feet and slammed the side of his fist on the table. His voice boomed over the din. "Enough! Take it to the yard if ye must act like a pair of rutting stags. Nae here!"

The two soldiers hesitated, then grudgingly separated, muttering under their breaths as they righted the mess they'd made.

Ailsa barely paid them any mind. She glanced at Cole, who was watching the scene with mild interest. His jaw was tight, his shoulders tense—not from the scuffle, she realized, but from something else entirely.

The hall's noise swelled again as the scuffle was forgotten, but Ailsa couldn't shake the unease curling in her chest.

Why did it feel as though Cole wasn't just stepping away from the lessons—but from her?

For the rest of the meal, she made an effort to join in the conversation, to laugh at her brother's occasional quips and nod along with the talk of trade, war, and an upcoming purchase of horses he planned. But her heart wasn't in it, her thoughts circling back to the man beside her and the quiet, undeniable hurt his words had left behind.

***

Two days later, Ailsa was in the stables, her brow furrowed as she ran a soothing hand along her mare's flank. The poor creature's breathing was labored, her sides shuddering slightly with each inhale.

"Ah, my sweet girl, what ails ye?" she murmured, stroking the mare's soft coat. Ailsa's heart ached at the sight. The stablemaster's absence due to illness hadn't helped matters, and it seemed the care of the animals had suffered for it.

Her thoughts were interrupted by the sound of voices at the stable door. She didn't need to look up to recognize one of them—deep, smooth, and unmistakable.

Cole.

He stepped into the dimly lit space, his presence commanding even in his disheveled state. His dark hair was windswept from his ride, his broad shoulders filling the doorway as he laughed at something the lad beside him said.

And just like that, the hurt she'd been nursing for days resurfaced.

Ailsa busied herself with attention to her mare, though her thoughts became scattered. She had managed to avoid Cole all of yesterday, missing supper in the hall, having thrown herself into the distraction of the unfortunate incident at Harailt's croft. The man, a wiry farmer known more for his quiet efficiency than any outward cheer, had taken a nasty fall just before the supper hour, snapping his arm in a way that made both Ailsa and Anwen wince. Ailsa and her maid had quickly joined Father Gilbert on the journey to his home, laden with supplies and some ambition to be of service.

The scene had been chaotic. The croft was cluttered with the practical chaos of a working man's life—tools scattered across a rickety table, a half-mended fishing net in the corner, unwashed kitchen supplies littering the ground around the brazier in the middle of his cottage. While Ailsa assisted, whispering to the pale and sweating patient, Father Gilbert had set the bones with grim but efficient focus. When the worst of it was done, she and Anwen had set to tidying, rearranging furniture and making small adjustments to ensure the man could navigate his space more easily while his arm healed. They'd swept out the rushes, tidied the hearth, and before departing had made a promise to deliver a simmering pot of stew that evening.

That kind of purposeful labor had been rather timely, she'd thought later, allowing her to escape Cole's company in the hall, where she feared she'd not have been able to keep her wounded heart hidden.

But now, with no such distractions, her pulse quickened at the thought of a confrontation. Tucked into the third stall behind her wheezing mare, Ailsa remained completely still.

"Remember to keep yer knees under ye, nae in front of ye," the man with Cole said. "Sure and ye had guid progress today."

A sudden frown wrinkled Ailsa's brow and she stood up on her toes, peeking over the mare's broad back. She recognized the man with Cole as Roibeart, the elderly groom responsible for training the war horses.

"Thanks, Roibeart," Cole said, leading his horse into the stable.

"Ye ken how to rub her down?" Roibeart asked, remaining near the entry.

"I do, thanks. I appreciate your time."

Ailsa did not duck quickly enough and winced when Cole moved forward, his gaze sweeping the stables until it landed on her.

"Ailsa," he said, showing some surprise to find her here.

Guilty shock? she wondered.

She turned reluctantly as he stopped just outside the stall, her expression guarded. "Cole."

He hesitated, then, frowning over her mare's noticeable wheezing, and asked, "What's wrong with her?"

Ailsa sighed, her frustration momentarily eclipsed by concern for the animal. "She's been wheezing. I dinna ken what to do for her."

Cole frowned, stepping closer. "I can barely breathe in here myself. You think it's the straw or something? Maybe it needs to be changed more often?"

Ailsa shrugged, wanting him gone. "The straw is scarce in winter. We conserve it as best we can."

"Well, that's not ideal," Cole said, moving the mare he'd borrowed into the stall next to her. "I'm not saying I know anything about this stuff, horses and stables, but it seems like it might help if the stalls were cleaned out more often."

Ailsa tilted her head, considering his suggestion. It wasn't unreasonable.

With renewed purpose, she decided she needed to do two things: remove Ceara from the stables for a while to see if fresh air might relieve her symptoms, and confront Cole Carter about what she'd just overheard.

"Ye said ye dinna need help with the riding," she said, a wee bit more tartly than she'd wanted, laying the saddle blanket over Ceara's back while she kept her back to Cole. "But it was me ye wanted away from."

She felt more than saw Cole freeze in the next stall, with only the half wall between them.

"Ailsa, no. Jesus, don't think that—it's not like that at all. Actually, it's the complete opposite."

Ailsa snorted her disbelief. "Och, ye wanted more time with me and thus cancelled our standing lesson."

"Listen," Cole growled with his own frustration, "don't just assume things about me. There's a good reason why I couldn't continue with lessons from you."

"So it seems," she said, hoisting the saddle up onto the blanket. "But leave it alone, I'm nae interested in your reasoning."

God's bluid, but she hated that it sounded as if she were about to cry. How extraordinary! That she suffered so greatly by his casual defection!

"I said *couldn't*, which means it wasn't my choice," he argued, coming to stand in the opening of Ceara's stall while Ailsa secured the girth. "Ailsa, will you stop and listen to me?"

She felt his hand on her arm from behind and shook him off, her face contorting angrily.

"Go on, leave me be," she commanded imperiously.

Cole did not heed her. "Ailsa, Father Gilbert said it was a bad idea, that it would cause trouble," he said next.

With stirrups in hand, about to attach them, Ailsa whirled, surprised somehow to find him so close. Her chest heaved with indignation and pain, but she looked up at him, startled by his revelation. "What do ye mean? What did he say?"

Cole's shoulders lifted slightly in a shrug, but his eyes never left hers, holding her gaze with an intensity that matched her own. His jaw clenched in frustration.

"Father Gilbert said that you weren't supposed to be seen with a man without your maid around, or a chaperone. He said that you must remain untouched, above reproach for your marriage to that MacLae guy."

While Ailsa stared at him, her brain whirring with more frustration for what the priest had said and done, Cole added pointedly, "He sought me out specifically to deliver that message, so it didn't seem like a matter in which I had a choice."

As she digested this, she couldn't honestly say that it came as any great surprise to her. She'd kept the lessons hidden, had gone out of her way to not be discovered, tricking Anwen to be rid of her confining company, engaging the lad to bring Cole to her, far removed from the keep and watchful eyes. She'd known herself that it wouldn't have been well received.

Still, she harbored some annoyance that Cole wouldn't have simply mentioned Father Gilbert's interference—it would have saved her two days of fretting, wondering what she'd done to earn his disfavor.

"Ailsa," Cole said, his deep voice softened, "let's not pretend the priest is wrong. Spending time with you was—is—dangerous."

"Dangerous?"

"Ailsa, you have to marry someone else and...I don't want to cause any trouble for that plan."

"Cause trouble?"

"You're intent on dragging it out of me, fine," Cole growled, his displeasure evident in the tightness of his voice. "Yeah, trouble. As in what seems to follow me every time I'm near you, Ailsa. I'm sure you're not blind to the fact...I want to—" He cut himself off abruptly, his mouth twisting in frustration, as though fighting to contain the words he wanted to say.

Ailsa's cheeks flushed a deep shade of pink, and she felt a stirring inside her—something that quickly replaced her confusion with a mix of wonder and an unexpected thrill. She could hardly believe it, but a flicker of hope seemed to bloom within her, despite herself.

"What do ye want, Cole Carter?" she asked, her voice slipping into something softer, more inviting. She hadn't meant to make her words sound so... coaxing. But they came out that way, almost a purr, unintentional but unmistakable.

Cole's gaze flickered over her, his jaw tightening, as if he was struggling with something he wasn't ready to share. The air between them thickened, heavy with expectant tension, yet still somehow fragile.

Sweet Mother of God, was it possible? Did Cole Carter feel the same unspoken awareness, the same yearning hope that pulsed within her?

Suddenly breathless, Ailsa dropped her hand which held the stirrups and stepped forward.

Chapter Thirteen

"Dinna ye want to ken me?" Ailsa asked, her words uncertain, as if she wasn't quite sure herself. "Dinna ye want to spend time with me? Ye enjoy the moments we've shared. Mayhap... ye want more hours together." She faltered, her voice dipping as she shifted from foot to foot, a nervousness creeping into her posture.

Cole noticed her chest rise and fall more quickly now, her breath betraying her unrest.

He knew it was in his best interest to remain silent. *Don't engage.* Hell, he should turn and run.

"Ye do want more, actually," she decided boldly even as her voice was small and her fingers twitched and curled. "Ye want to kiss me—have ye nae imagined it?" She took a hesitant step closer, then another, as if testing the ground beneath her feet, or gauging his reaction.

"Ailsa..." Cole growled, his gaze sliding away, a heavy warning hanging in his tone.

Christ, she was going to get him killed if she kept this up.

But she was undeterred, her voice trembling slightly but still bold. "I ken I'm nae wrong. I... I want the same." Ailsa's step was tentative, but there was a resolve to it as she moved within his reach. Her eyes, bright but unsure, highlighted by the healthy flush in her cheeks, didn't leave his. "I've thought about kissing ye. I... I might have even instigated it, but..." She paused, and blinked nervously, "I've nae been kissed before."

Cole's eyes widened. How the hell was *that* possible?

An image of Tavis brandishing his sword came to mind, swiftly and effectively answering that question. Next, Father Gilbert's words echoed in his brain: *she is to remain untouched.*

A crime, that, to leave untouched so tempting, so exquisite a woman.

When in the next moment, she put her hand on his chest and used those blue eyes to great effect, glancing up at him with seeming innocence, an open invitation, Cole was sure he was being set up.

Yep. She's going to get me killed.

It might almost be worth it.

Snaking one arm around her waist, he pulled her against him, their bodies colliding in a heat that defied the frigid air. His mouth claimed hers, firmly, unrelenting, a kiss meant to show her just how dangerous it was to play with fire. Almost instantly, she went rigid in his embrace, and Cole tamped down the fire inside him. He brushed his lips over hers in a deliberate tease—first one corner of her soft, trembling mouth, then the other—before pressing firmly again, urging her to yield.

When her lips parted, he deepened the kiss, claiming her with a fervor he hadn't intended to unleash. His tongue slid against hers, seeking, tasting, conquering, and for a moment, he lost himself completely in the heady sweetness of her.

The lesson he'd meant to teach her—about the dangers of provoking him—was all but forgotten as his focus shifted to something else entirely, giving and taking pleasure. Her lips were warm, her taste intoxicating, and the soft, hesitant response she gave made his heart pound. She was inexperienced; he could feel it in the way she faltered at first, then grew bolder, mimicking his movements. Her tongue touched his tentatively, then traced and stroked in a way that sent a rush of heat coursing through him.

His blood roared, his senses sharp yet overwhelmed. The softness of her against him, the shy but growing confidence in her kiss, surpassed every expectation he hadn't even realized he held. When her hands slid up to his shoulders, her fingers curling into him as if she couldn't bear to let him go, the last shred of his restraint snapped.

His brain shouted at him to stop, to pull away, to save himself from the chaos she was bound to bring into his life. But his body, his heart—they wanted none of it. Instead, he tightened his hold on her, ignoring every rational instinct that told him this was a mistake.

Nothing—absolutely nothing before this moment—had ever felt so right.

It was a long, delicious moment before Cole regained his senses and forced himself to break away, shoving her back just enough to create space between them.

"Stop," he hissed thickly. It was unclear from where the strength came to push her away—God knew he didn't feel it in his body. "Christ, Ailsa, are you *trying* to get me killed?"

Her lips were red, wet and glistening, and her cheeks were flushed a deep crimson. When her blue eyes fluttered open, they held a dazed, almost dreamy expression, as though she were still lost in the moment.

"Ailsa, Father Gilbert is right—and here is proof," he barked out, prudently taking a step backward. "This is a bad idea—any time spent with you. Yeah, I might want more," he said—*damn, I do want more*, "but it's dangerous. To you, to me, to whatever Father Gilbert meant about needing peace between the Sinclairs and the MacLaes and your marriage managing that. I...Ailsa, I'm not even supposed to be here. I can't be the reason that this time or your life, or even the safety of the Sinclairs gets all messed up."

It was a moment before she responded at all. When she did, her voice was small, filled with as much hesitation as it was hope. "Mayhap ye *are* here for a reason."

"And what reason would that be? To kiss you and get myself killed when your brother finds out? To ruin whatever peace your clan hopes to gain? To die in this century instead of my own?" He shook his head, raking a hand through his hair. A thought struck him, sharp and unwelcome. "And what are you even saying, Ailsa? You don't really believe I'm from the future. I know that. You've been polite, but deep down, you think I'm lying—or crazy."

Her gaze fell, and she absently brushed a hand down the front of her gown. "I did," she admitted softly, almost inaudibly. "At first, I thought ye mad—or mayhap jesting. But now..." She lifted her face, meeting his eyes, with what looked to be newfound determination. "Now I dinna ken what to believe. Only that, whatever the truth is, ye feel real. As if ye're meant to be here. As if *we're* meant to be."

Her words struck him like a fist to the gut, the context, the very idea presented leaving him momentarily speechless. Because the worst part of it was—no. No! He didn't want to believe it. It was nuts. *Meant to be, my ass.* This was simple, raw, maddening physical attraction. Nothing more than her soft lips, her wide, questioning eyes, and her damnable innocence baiting him into losing his head.

Logic would not allow him to hitch his wagon to some absurd star filled with BS about romantic destiny.

"Christ, Ailsa," he muttered, his voice rough, barely above a whisper. "You have no idea what fire you're playing with."

Her face fell, her expression crumpling like paper crinkling when thrown into the flames. For a moment, it looked as though she might retreat entirely. But then she squared her shoulders, the fire in her blue eyes sparking again.

Needing to leave before he did something even more stupid, Cole pivoted on his heel, forgetting about the horse he'd returned, and strode angrily toward the stable doors. Part of him, skeptical modern-day man that he was, felt a flicker of doubt. Was she using him to escape her 14th-century marriage? No. Ailsa wasn't like that. She wasn't devious, wouldn't have planned such a manipulation. Would she?

"Cole, wait!" Ailsa's voice caught up to him, cracking slightly, desperation threading through it.

It gave him pause, his hand stilling on the wooden doorframe. He didn't turn, but he couldn't force himself to leave either.

"I... I'm leaving on the morrow," she said, her voice trembling, her accent softening. "I'll be gone for nearly a week, visiting my sister at Kilbrae."

Another punch to the gut, but he masked his reaction with a sharp inhale, letting the sting of cold air clear his thoughts. It was probably for the best. Still, his chest tightened at the thought of her leaving Torr Cinnteag.

He tapped his fingers on the hard wood of the door frame, considering the possibility that he might well be gone by the time she returned. He had no hint, nothing had happened to allow him to believe he would again be moved through time, back to the twenty-first century... but what if he was? And he never saw her again? The idea hit him with the force of a sledgehammer, but he swallowed it down, baring his teeth, refusing to look at her.

"Be safe, Ailsa," he called over his shoulder, his voice quieter now, burdened with something he refused to name. Without waiting for a reply, he stepped out into the biting wind.

***

This trip to her sister's should have been a reprieve—a chance to escape the mounting tension of the upcoming meeting with Alastair MacLae and the expected betrothal announcement. It had been planned for this time for exactly that purpose. Normally, these visits brought her solace. She loved the sweet laughter of her nieces, the easy flow of conversation with her sister—even though Orla sometimes proved even more annoyingly overbearing than Anwen and could occasionally be excessively critical of Ailsa. But she loved her sister and had never before dreaded journeying to visit her. Yet now, the thought of leaving filled her with an unfamiliar sense of dread.

What if Cole Carter wasn't here when she returned?

The question gnawed at her, a persistent ache she couldn't ignore. The thought struck her like a physical blow. Cole was a man out of time. What if the same strange force that had brought him to this age decided to whisk him away again? The notion was as terrifying as it was plausible. She could picture it all too vividly: returning to the castle, finding his room empty, and realizing he had vanished as suddenly as he had appeared.

Ailsa had pleaded with Tavis last night, trying every argument she could think of to delay the journey.

"Surely it can wait a few more days," she had insisted, only to meet the steady wall of her brother's unyielding will.

This morning, she'd tried a different approach, claiming illness as her excuse. "I can't manage a seven-hour carriage ride, Tavis," she said, adopting the most pitiful tone she could muster. "I'm quite sure I'm feverish."

He'd placed a warm, calloused hand against her forehead, his skeptical gaze pinning her. "You're as cool as a Highland morning," he said dryly.

"But I *was* feverish! Overnight," she protested, though even she heard how unconvincing she sounded.

Her attempts were futile. Tavis was immune to her feeble ploys and determined to send her on her way.

And so here she was, bundled into the carriage, the rhythmic clatter of wheels against the uneven road doing little to distract her from her rising anxiety.

She'd had no opportunity to see Cole Carter this morning. Either he was a man unaccustomed to early rising or he'd gone out of his way to avoid the bailey, as she and her party of a dozen men had been seen off by Tavis and a few others.

Anwen, opposite her on the other bench, was blessedly silent for once, allowing Ailsa to revisit every glorious second of Cole's kiss, which had lingered like a sweet echo, softly in the corners of her mind since yesterday afternoon. Even now, with only the memory to hold onto, she felt the warmth bloom inside her chest, spreading outward. She could almost feel the heat of him still, his hand firm at her waist, the intensity of his presence overwhelming in the best possible way.

Her heart fluttered at the recollection, and though she tried to steady herself, the delicate thrum of excitement would not settle. None of her imaginings had come close to reality. The way his lips had moved against hers, so commanding yet tender, was a sensation she'd never expected.

At length Ailsa moved aside the curtain and looked out the carriage window at the passing landscape, her thoughts drifting as her heartbeat quickened.

What if she never knew another kiss from him?

How would she feel if he actually *was* spirited away while she was gone?

Ailsa dropped the curtain into place and sank further into the upholstered seat, pressing her fingers to her temples as the answer surfaced with startling clarity. She would feel as if something extraordinary had been stolen from her—a fleeting, beautiful opportunity to connect with someone who intrigued her in a way no one else ever had.

***

"Three days, Ailsa. Three days you've been here, and I've yet to see ye truly *here*."

Orla's voice carried its usual sharpness as she adjusted the lace cuff on her sleeve with a disapproving tug.

"Ye might as well be a ghost, haunting this solar. What have ye? Has Torr Cinnteag suddenly become irresistible that ye dinna want to be here?"

Despite the cold winds howling through the narrow windows of the stone house, Orla's solar was pleasantly warm. Ailsa sat near the hearth, the fire crackling brightly in the corner, sending warm orange light dancing over the tapestries that adorned the walls. Her niece, Bébhinn, played quietly with a doll beside her, while her older sister Mairead hummed softly, as she worked on her embroidery. The room smelled faintly of cedarwood and herbs, and was a comfortable space, though one in which she had never truly felt at ease in. The furniture was old, heavy oak, worn with years of use, not softened by any cushion, and the low ceiling made the room feel more enclosed than she preferred.

It had been quiet, wonderfully so.

Ailsa blinked, momentarily caught off guard. Her fingers went still, abandoning their task of attempting to untangle several knots in the skeins of yarn. She swallowed and her eyes flicked to her youngest niece, a round-faced cherub of four winters, who was blissfully unaware of the sudden tension in the room. The child giggled as she stripped her linen doll of her wool dress, playfully tossing the miniature garment up into Ailsa's lap, oblivious to her aunt's sudden unease.

"Apologies, Orla, for my inattention," Ailsa replied too quickly, a touch of defensiveness creeping into her tone. Her gaze fell to her hands as they folded over the yarn in her lap, suddenly aware of the heat blooming in her cheeks beneath Orla's sharp scrutiny. "I had said to Tavis that I was nae feeling well and that perhaps I—"

"Ha!" Orla snorted, her laughter grating against the quiet atmosphere. She nudged her sewing basket aside, sitting up straighter, preparing to pry deeper. "Rubbish. I dinna believe that for a moment. Ye've barely spoken a word to anyone, and dinna ken I haven't noticed that ye stare...at naught. It's like watching Mairead," she said, gesturing with distaste toward her eldest daughter, who was in fact not so earnestly working on her embroidery but only staring at it. "What has ye in such a state, then? And pray dinna tell me this unsettling cloud is only anxiety about Alastair MacLae."

Ailsa flinched at the mention of her betrothed. Her sister's words hit too close to the truth, the weight of the betrothal hanging over her like a heavy shroud. "I dinna ken what you want me to say," Ailsa murmured evasively, folding her hands tightly in her lap. She avoided Orla's gaze as the sudden pressure of the conversation threatened to suffocate her. "Perhaps I just... miss the familiarity of home," Ailsa finished, though the half-lie sat uncomfortably on her tongue. It *was* partly true, but it wasn't the whole truth.

Anwen's disdainful snort from the corner of the chamber turned both sisters' heads around.

Ailsa's lips pressed together as she glared at her maid.

Orla eyed the smirking maid with speculation. "Ye might as well tell me, Anwen. We both ken I'll find out eventually."

"Nae for me to say, m'lady," Anwen pronounced.

Ailsa snarled silently at her maid's sudden reticence, after she'd purposefully revealed so much with only one scathing sound.

At that moment, Bébhinn climbed into Ailsa's lap, wanting help with dressing the doll she'd made naked. Pleased with the distraction, Ailsa turned the little girl around in her lap and with her arms around her, proceeded to dress the figure in the discarded clothing.

"A man is my guess," Orla said suddenly, startling Ailsa. "That's what ails ye."

Just as Ailsa raised her gaze, wondering how Orla had arrived at that conclusion, Anwen snidely provided, "Aye, Cole Carter, he is—a more unworthy soul I'm sure ye've never met, m'lady."

Ailsa closed her eyes, willing calm upon herself, even as she fleetingly fantasized about slow torture methods she might inflict upon the loose-lipped Anwen.

Ailsa sighed heavily, lifting her niece off her lap as she'd been scrambling to get down. The child toddled away, giggling as she noticed that she inadvertently dragged the unraveled yarn along with her.

Ignoring her daughter and the mess she'd made of Ailsa's tedious efforts, Orla's eyes glinted with a knowing spark. "Ah, now that makes sense. And who is he who's got ye all twisted up like a fisher's net—Cole Carter, ye say?" She smirked, clearly relishing the moment of revelation. When Ailsa said nothing, Orla turned her attention to Anwen. "Mooning, is she?"

Ailsa's chest tightened. The room seemed to shrink around her, and a rush of heat flooded her cheeks. She could feel her heart pounding in her throat, and before she could stop herself, she blurted, "I am nae mooning over Cole Carter."

The lie was spat out with indignation she had no right to feel, since it was in fact the truth.

Orla's loud laugh startled both Ailsa and the girls. Mairead looked up from her embroidery in mild surprise, and Bébhinn paused in her play, sensing the shift in the room's atmosphere.

"You're nae a guid liar, Ailsa," Orla chuckled, completely unbothered by her sister's discomfort. "Ye never were."

Anwen—who prior to this had rarely said anything unless directly spoken to in Orla's house, as she was more readily cowed by Orla's changeable temperament and sometimes curt manner—continued to betray Ailsa.

"Stranger he is, and there's something nae right about him."

Stunned, blindsided by the depth of Anwen's betrayal, Ailsa could muster no immediate response, not even the harsh rebuke Anwen so richly deserved right now. Having known Anwen all her life, having trusted her so implicitly for so long, she would never have anticipated such blatant disloyalty. Was it intentional malice? Jealousy? A misguided attempt to help?

Anwen simply raised an eyebrow and shrugged, the perpetual smile she wore seeming to mock Ailsa now. She said no more but what she had revealed hung in the air, and Orla seized upon it.

"What is nae right?" Orla demanded to know. "Who is this man?"

Directing her icy gaze to her maid, Ailsa instructed coolly, "Leave us."

Though Anwen blanched a bit at Ailsa's frosty tone, she dared to challenge the edict. "I said only what—"

"I said leave us!" Ailsa said, raising her voice as she so rarely had cause to do. Her lips quivered with her effort to refrain from sending Anwen on her way, on her own, away, forever, from Ailsa.

"She speaks of that which she dinna ken," she told her sister after a shocked Anwen had stood and huffed and stormed out the door.

But now it was out there—Cole's existence, his name, a suggestion that something existed between them. Ailsa knew her sister well enough to know she'd have not an iota of peace until her sister was satisfied she knew every last detail.

After releasing a bitter sigh of resignation, Ailsa explained as much as she knew—as much as she dared—about Cole Carter, without confiding in Orla about Cole's asserted origins, seven hundred years in the future. She described him as a lost traveler, not precisely a lie, and focused more on what he was *to her* rather than simply who or what he truly was.

"He's... nae like any other I've ever met," she murmured, her voice barely above a whisper. "He's different. Strange in some ways, aye, but—" she faltered, struggling to find the words. A faint smile curved her lips. "Sister, he's the most beautiful man I've ever encountered. Nae matter how I try, I canna stop thinking about him. I ken it's foolish, but..."

Orla's dry, humorless laugh interrupted her. "Foolish? Foolish? It's madness, Ailsa. Do ye forget the MacLae is coming? You're to be betrothed—announced, nae less—in a matter of days! And you're here dreaming on a stranger? God's bluid, has he ruined ye? Tell me you're nae so weak, so simple to have been—"

"It's nae like that," Ailsa protested weakly, though she could feel her cheeks flush even deeper, the memory of his kiss returning. "I ken my duty," she assured her sister. "But when I'm with him, I feel... alive in a way I never have before. Like I can breathe."

Orla's voice rose higher, her incredulity stark. "Alive? Breathe? Ailsa, marriage isna about that. It's about loyalty to the clan and securing alliances. When I married Iain, do ye ken I felt 'alive' or like I could 'breathe'? Nae! I did it because it was required, because it strengthened the Sinclairs. And ye dinna get to shirk your duty just because ye've stumbled across some handsome distraction."

Ailsa recoiled as though struck, her fingers tightening into fists in her lap. The bluntness of Orla's words stung, but she couldn't deny their truth. "I dinna say I meant to shirk anything," she muttered, trying to steady her voice.

"Ye dinna have to say it. Your face says it for ye," Orla retorted. Then, softer, she reached out and took Ailsa's hand, her grip strong, more forceful than reassuring. Her following words were quiet but still carried the weight of experience and the starch of authority. "I ken it's difficult. I ken what it is to dream of something else, something more or better. But dreams dinna protect the people we love. Duty does."

Ailsa swallowed hard, her throat tight. The truth of her sister's words was inescapable, pulling her back to the grim reality she couldn't escape. She looked down at their clasped hands, her own trembling slightly. "But how can I wed the MacLae if my heart is elsewhere?"

"What's in yer heart has nae bearing, sister." Orla's brow furrowed, but she didn't release Ailsa's hand. She squeezed it. "I'm sorry, luv, but life dinna always give us what we want."

Ailsa nodded, tears threatening behind her eyes. She understood the truth in her sister's words, but it didn't make the pain any easier to bear.

***

Ailsa did not speak to Anwen for the next three days, her first words coming as they departed Orla's house and climbed into the carriage. And then it was only to tersely instruct her maid to not speak to her for the entirety of the journey home.

Anwen, chastised to some degree by Ailsa's chilling silence of the last few days, dared to open her mouth to object.

Ailsa held up her gloved hand. "Nae a word from ye," she repeated with greater force.

Anwen didn't speak for the first hour of their journey, until, apparently, she could hold back no more. "What I did and said was done with only yer best interests at heart. He's nae guid and ye're nae meant for him but another. Begging trouble, is all yer doing, and I canna sit by nae more and only watch."

Having closed her eyes some time ago, but hardly able to sleep, knowing that unless Cole Carter had disappeared while she'd been gone from home, she would see him this day, Ailsa did not bother to open her eyes now, even as she responded coolly. "Unless ye mean to make the trek to Torr Cinnteag on foot, I suggest ye say nae one more word," Ailsa said, unmoved by her maid's stated justification. "'Tis your final warning."

Chapter Fourteen

The frigid air bit at Cole's face as he adjusted his grip on the reins. The horse beneath him, a large bay gelding named Dùghall, he'd been told, snorted and shifted as if impatient to move. Cole leaned forward, patting its neck.

"All right, big guy. Let's try this again," he muttered, more to himself than the horse.

Cole was aware that across the training field, Tavis watched with crossed arms, a faint smirk playing at his lips.

"Wagers have been placed, lad," the laird called out, "most saying ye fall again, thrice in one morning."

Cole shot him a dismissive glance, adjusting his posture in the saddle. "*Wagers placed, lad*," he mimicked to himself, employing a cartoonish voice to caricaturize the mighty laird.

It drove him nuts, the way Tavis called him *lad*. They were not only possibly the same exact age, but Cole was certain he might have a full inch and twenty pounds on the laird, but then that was only a guess since he'd yet to see Tavis without many layers of wool plaid and fur.

He really wished he'd managed to keep his riding lessons—and any semblance of progress—a secret. Roibeart, a solid guy—*salt of the earth,* Aunt Rosie might've said—had decided Cole was ready for jumps. Unfortunately, the only suitable fences were out in the training field.

This meant Cole had to endure the daily ordeal of pretending he didn't notice the constant scrutiny of never less than a hundred nosy, big-mouthed soldiers, who were all pretty good at judging and ridiculing.

He ignored them now, nudging Dùghall into a canter. The rhythm of the horse's gait thudded beneath him, and he focused on keeping his movements fluid, absorbing the motion rather than fighting it. He circled the field a few times before guiding Dùghall toward a low wooden barrier. His heart thudded as they approached the jump, as Tavis had not misspoken, and Cole had indeed fallen off the horse three times in the last half hour. At the last moment, he shifted his weight forward, and the horse sailed over the barrier with an ease that staggered Cole for how easy it seemed on that occasion.

"Hah!" he shouted as the horse landed cleanly, and to his relief, he stayed firmly in the saddle. He swung his gaze round to the watching Roibeart, who slowly clapped his hands, about as much congratulations as he was likely to receive from the quiet, unexcitable man.

Next, he looked to his left, where Tavis and his army were supposed to be training but were apparently otherwise occupied. betting against him if Tavis was to be believed. Feeling vindicated, Cole pumped his fist in the air. "Hah!" He called out again, louder this time.

"Dinna let it go to your head," Tavis shouted from thirty yards away. "Ye've still got the grace of a three-legged deer over jumps."

Cole curled his lip. *Screw you, Tavis.*

Buoyed by his first success, Cole circled back, preparing for another run at the waist-high barrier, confident he'd have his second success today

He did not.

As the horse sailed cleanly over the jump, Cole promptly went flying in the opposite direction, landing with a bone-rattling thud on the hard-packed earth. Pain shot through his body, and his head smacked against the ground with enough force to leave him dazed. Thank God for the helmet—a precaution he'd stubbornly insisted on, though he wasn't entirely convinced of its medieval efficacy. He'd been toying with the idea of padding the inside with something softer, but so far, he hadn't figured it out.

Groaning, he lay flat on his back, staring up at the sky, willing the earth to stop spinning. Somewhere in the distance, he heard Tavis and many others laughing.

He stayed as he was, only lifting his hand to give a thumbs up for Roibeart and just in case when the laughter died down on the other side of the field, anyone worried that he might actually be hurt since he didn't feel like moving right now.

He heard Roibeart give a low, familiar whistle, wrangling the horse that had dumped him.

Flat on his back, Cole stared at the clear blue sky, a rarity here—either in Scotland or in this century, he hadn't figured that out yet either—and thought again of Ailsa. He'd bet anything that her blue eyes would be even more stunning under sunlight like this.

He sighed, wishing she were here to share this little victory. Ailsa had been the one to teach him the basics, patient despite his clumsy beginnings. She had every reason to mock him back then, especially given how wary he'd been of the horse and for how slow had been his progress then. But no, she'd smiled at him—bright, generous, and full of pride—whenever he managed even the smallest accomplishment.

Cole tried to picture her reaction now. She'd have cheered his first successful jump, probably teasing him a little about his subsequent swagger. And then, of course, she'd have laughed as well at his spectacular crash. He grinned faintly, wishing for both her company and that smile of hers.

He wondered what she'd think of his present appearance, though. Father Gilbert had very kindly—surprisingly—gifted both Cole and Tank with a stack of folded clothes, with a pair of leather boots tucked beneath them. After presenting them with a complete set of medieval attire, right down to the underwear—*braies,* as Father Gilbert called them—the priest had gone further, arranging for their modern clothes to be laundered.

The stack of clothes smelled faintly of a sharp but clean soap, and of the outdoors, suggesting they'd been aired recently. The *braies* were loose linen shorts that tied at the waist, not entirely different from old-fashioned boxer shorts, but somehow very different indeed. Over these went woolen hose, which he tied at the knees with simple garters, the rough wool scratching slightly against his skin.

Next came the tunic, a long, knee-length garment of undyed wool, simple but well-made. It fit loosely over his torso, cinched at the waist by a sturdy leather belt with a plain iron buckle. Father Gilbert had even provided a linen undertunic, which he wore beneath for warmth, as well as a plain hooded cloak to shield him from the biting Scottish weather. The pants he'd been given—breeches, he'd heard them called several times by now—were much thicker but then more comfortable than jeans and fit him well. The ensemble was topped off with a pair of leather boots that laced up to his calves, surprisingly comfortable once he got used to the feeling of them.

At first, he thought he looked ridiculous, but pretty quickly he felt just the opposite, that he fit in so much better, and stood out so much less. Would Ailsa think he fit in better now? Would she look at him and see not a stranger thrust into her world, but someone who belonged?

Presently, he sighed and forced himself to sit up, grabbing the back of his thighs to make rising easier since his body continued to suffer bruises and aches, even after another full week of training.

He was missing Ailsa like crazy, but the week had not been wasted. Christ, he couldn't even keep track of everything he'd learned. A few things stood out, though. He'd mastered cleaning the horse's tack and now knew all about their feeding schedules—information he hadn't expected to find even remotely interesting. He could start a fire with flint and tinder now, and at his first success, he and Tank had reenacted the *Castaway* fire-making scene, dancing around and pounding their chests like triumphant cavemen.

He'd even picked up a bit of the language. Now, he could confidently say words like "water," "sword," "shield," "bread," and "fire." He'd also learned "God's blessing," a polite greeting that doubled as both hello and goodbye, making him feel slightly less out of place.

Most surprising of all, the soldiers they trained with had warmed up considerably. Hostility gave way to camaraderie. A few had even become downright friendly, going out of their way to speak English in his and Tank's company, even though it was clearly not their first language. Small gestures, but they went a long way in making Cole feel like he might finally be finding his footing here.

The most shocking realization of the past week was that as much as he wanted to go home—back to good ol' Buffalo, New

York, in 2024—he'd prayed every morning since Ailsa had left that today wouldn't be the day.

He *needed* to see her again. He wanted, desperately, to apologize. He still stood by his actions—stopping the kiss, stepping away when he had—but he regretted how he'd handled it. He could have been gentler, kinder. He should have been honest with her, told her that while he understood why kissing her—or anything else—was a bad idea, he didn't like it one bit either. He'd felt just as she had seemed to feel in that moment: bereft, as if something vital had been ripped away.

He hadn't wallowed, though. Not at all. There simply wasn't time.

He and Tank hadn't just absorbed information over the past week—they'd shared knowledge as well. While the Sinclair soldiers were undeniably skilled with swords and adept in hand-to-hand combat, it quickly became clear that many of them lacked stamina.

Tank had been the first to suggest introducing conditioning drills, but explaining the concept to Tavis had been a task in itself.

"What is this ye speak of?" Tavis had asked, brow furrowed as he watched Tank drop to the ground to demonstrate a push-up.

"Strength and stamina," Cole had explained, gesturing toward Tank. "Right now, your guys are tough and skilled, but they tire quickly."

Tavis had given a dubious snort. "We train to kill swiftly, nae to linger on the field."

Cole had held up a hand. "Fair, but what happens if you're facing an enemy who doesn't drop so quickly? Or you're forced to retreat uphill, in the rain, wearing armor?"

To convince Tavis of the benefits of conditioning, they'd had to put on a demonstration. Cole was pitted against the young soldier, Domhnall—the same kid who'd humbled him during his first day of training. Cole had been running since he was seventeen, so the outcome was never in doubt. He and Tank mapped out a five-mile course that looped through the practice field, circled the village perimeter, followed the low stone wall lining the brown and fallow fields, skirted the edge of the beach, and ended back at the field.

When they began, Domhnall took off like a shot, clearly mistaking the endurance race for a sprint. Cole paced himself, knowing the uneven terrain and lack of proper footwear would already test his limits. He returned in just under an hour, winded but far from spent.

Domhnall, however, stumbled back a full thirty minutes later, dragging his feet and gasping for air. By the end, he wasn't running but walking, his exhaustion plain for all to see.

The demonstration had made its point.

"Aye, but how do ye train for that?" Tavis, more resistant than skeptical then, had wanted to know.

Tank had laughed. "You run. Everyday. For miles."

The discussion had carried over to the dinner hour, with Cole advising that daily training should begin with warm-ups and running, which Tavis reluctantly agreed could be implemented.

He and Tank had also advocated as well for the use of helmets, which hardly any wore during training.

"Most the lads consider the helms to be cumbersome," Tavis had reasoned. "They limit vision."

"They also keep your brain inside your skull," Tank had quipped. "Can they stop an arrow?"

"Nae always," Tavis had answered.

"But sometimes?" Tank had pressed.

"Aye."

"Even without an arrow or blade," Cole had interjected, "a blow to the head can be crippling, or worse, fatal."

Dersey was there as well and frowned. "Crippling how? A knock to the skull is common enough. Most men recover well enough after a day or two, save for a bit of soreness."

"Not always," Cole countered. "You might not see any injury, but that doesn't mean there's no damage. Your brain can get shaken up inside, slamming against the skull. That's what we call a concussion, and it can lead to all kinds of problems—memory loss, confusion, headaches that never go away. Sometimes, if the injury's bad enough, a man might seem fine, but he could die later that night."

Tavis's expression darkened as he absorbed this. "Some time ago, a lad took a blow during a skirmish, seemed to come out of it right enough. But he passed before dawn, nae wound to show for it."

"That's exactly what I'm talking about," Cole said. "Even if they survive, repeated injuries can add up. Over time, a man might lose his wits—forget things, act strangely. I'll bet you've seen that too, right? Soldiers who've fought too long, taken too many blows to the head?"

Tavis's brow furrowed as if recalling specific men. "Aye," he said at last.

"That's traumatic brain injury," Cole explained, glancing at Tank, who nodded in agreement. "Helmets can't stop every injury, but they can make the difference between a man walking away and not walking at all."

Tavis fell silent, his gaze distant, before he narrowed a suspicious gaze at Cole. "Ye are nae a healer, nae a fighting man, but how do ye come by this knowledge?"

Cole scrambled for an answer. "Um, where we come from—Spain—there's a better understanding of this kind of thing."

Still, Tavis wasn't sold on the idea of forcing his men to wear helms at all times.

However, that changed two days later, but not because of any head injury.

The kid, Somerled, who was a huge trash talker—and all-around pain in the ass, both Cole and Tank agreed—had been flipped over Davey's back during their sparring, and dropped hard on his shoulder. He'd howled in pain, somehow managing to sit up, holding his arm. The onlookers froze, having no idea what to do for him, several wincing at Somerled's obvious pain.

Accustomed to running toward those in need, Tank and Cole had arrived just as Somerled announced he couldn't move his arm. Tank immediately took control, clearing the too-close crowd, while Cole began to strip the kid of everything above his waist, having to use his knife to cut away his tunic. It was then patently obvious that his shoulder was dislocated, the joint of it bulging forward, looking like a big goose-egg.

Cole had glanced at Tank, who'd named the injury.

"Saw this in Afghanistan," Tank had said, referencing his tour in 2011 with the Marines. "Quick fix," he'd pronounced over the kid's loud moaning.

With guidance from Tank, Cole had stabilized Somerled before Tank guided the joint back into place.

Somerled, pale but breathing easier, gave a shaky thumbs-up—another thing brought to the 14th century by Cole and Tank—announcing he could feel his arm again.

On the sidelines, a watchful Tavis had witnessed the whole thing, his jaw slightly slack, a rare expression of awe crossing his features.

Someone had commented about how quickly that had been resolved, while another had made some mention about how well Cole and Tank had worked together, with hardly any communication.

"Teamwork makes the dream work, baby," Tank had pronounced with a wide grin while Cole fashioned a sling from Somerled's sliced tunic.

That evening in the dining hall, Tavis was eager to revisit the helmet discussion, and Cole had some suspicion that their earlier actions with Somerled had earned them some credibility. It seemed that Tavis was now more open to hearing out their suggestions.

Cole was accustomed now to the general din of the great hall during the supper hour, and in truth looked forward each day to the communal meal. One evening he found himself seated beside Father Gilbert, the priest's austere robes standing out among the colorful tartans.

The meal had just begun when Father Gilbert turned to Cole with a curious look. "Ye strike me as a man of faith," the priest said, breaking a piece of bread. "Yet ye've said little of the church since ye arrived."

Cole hesitated, unsure how to frame the complexities of religion in his time for a man rooted in medieval Christianity. "I wouldn't say I'm deeply religious, but I do have faith," he began. "Where I come from, though, religion is more... personal. It's not as tied to the government or daily life as it is here."

Father Gilbert raised a brow. "Personal, ye say? That's a curious notion. How do ye keep order if the church is not at the center?"

"In my time, we separate church and state," Cole explained, leaning closer so their conversation wouldn't carry. "Religion is important to many, but laws and governance are meant to be neutral, not influenced by any particular belief system. People are free to worship—or not—however they choose."

The priest's brow furrowed as he digested this. "Neutral? Such a thing would be seen as chaos here. The church is the foundation of all: law, morality, education. Without its guidance, how do you ensure that men act justly?"

Cole paused, choosing his words carefully. "We have laws based on fairness and reason, not necessarily religion. People are taught ethics at home, in schools, and we trust that they'll act responsibly."

Father Gilbert stroked his chin, his expression one of both fascination and skepticism. "And what of their souls, lad? Who watches over them? Secular laws cannot save a man from damnation."

"No, they can't," Cole admitted. "But where I'm from, the idea is that faith is a choice. It's not forced. People decide for themselves what they believe, and that freedom means something."

The priest gave a soft chuckle, shaking his head. "Aye, I see the appeal of such freedom, but it's a dangerous path. A man untethered from divine guidance is like a ship without a rudder. He may find the shore, but he's just as likely to be dashed on the rocks."

The conversation shifted as Father Gilbert turned to more pressing matters. "Perhaps these dark times are when we need God the most, eh? His ways may be beyond our understanding, but faith can be a strong shield. In the unlikely event that a siege was laid against Torr Cinnteag, the laird fears he wouldn't be able to protect his people," Father Gilbert articulated. "But he has yet to understand that it is all in God's hands."

"And it all falls to him?" Cole asked, trying to steer the conversation away from a strictly theological debate. "The protection of Torr Cinnteag?"

Father Gilbert nodded. "Aye. It's his burden to bear, but it's shared by all who live here. The people look to their laird for protection, and he does what he must."

Cole leaned back, his appetite waning as he tried to imagine the weight of such responsibility. Aside from his job, during which he had a responsibility to save lives, he was responsible only for himself. "But the English wouldn't come this far north, would they?"

"Nae the English, perhaps," the priest conceded. "But armies aligned with them, aye. This past summer, the Comyns laid siege to Inverlochy, hoping to gain a foothold in the north."

The gravity of their situation settled over Cole like a heavy cloak. He'd seen the strength of Tavis's soldiers in training, but numbers didn't lie. They were vulnerable. And if Torr Cinnteag fell, what would happen to Ailsa and the people who called this place home?

Father Gilbert offered a faint smile, as if sensing Cole's unease. "Ye've the look of a man who would carry others' burdens. But dinna fret, lad. God works in ways we cannot understand, even in the darkest times."

Cole nodded thoughtfully, positing, "But he wouldn't have—or couldn't have—had a hand in what has happened to me and Tank."

"If what you say is true," the priest replied, "I would wager it was not an act wrought by the hand of God."

Cole considered him. The middle-aged priest seemed capable, was obviously spiritual, and was clearly intelligent. But Cole had to ask, "Aren't you curious? Even a little bit? About life in the future?"

Father Gilbert paused, his fingers lightly tracing the edge of his wine goblet. He regarded Cole for a long moment, his gaze thoughtful, before responding. "I must admit," he said slowly, "the idea of the future does pique my curiosity. But it's a curiosity tempered by skepticism." He smiled faintly, as if acknowledging the paradox. "The Lord made this world as it is, and I believe we are meant to live within the confines He has set. The idea of a different world, one so removed from our own, but alive at the same time, is difficult to reconcile. I wonder if it's not the work of the Devil himself, a temptation to distract us from the purpose we're meant to serve here and now." He shook his head, as if casting aside the thought. "But still... yes, there's a part of me that wonders. What will be, how will it all turn out? I suppose it's only natural."

Sensing the priest's reticence, Cole decided not to push him. He grinned. "Let me know if your curiosity ever wants those answers."

And though he kept himself occupied each day—indeed, seeking out tasks to occupy his mind—each night, without fail, he found himself lying in the narrow cot, thoughts of Ailsa ever-present. He longed for her return, wanting her return to be soon, to be now, wanting her to be here at Torr Cinnteag while he still was.

***

Cole and Tank stepped into the cold morning air, their boots quiet on snow-covered ground. Their breaths plumed in the chill as they exchanged a few words with Father Gilbert, who was getting about his morning at the same time, the three of them expressing surprise over the snow that had fallen overnight, amounting to about three or four inches.

Their attention was quickly diverted, however, by calls from the battlements for the gates to be opened. Seeing Father Gilbert's frown and knowing the gates were rarely opened without Tavis's orders, usually in time for the army's drills, Cole and Tank followed the priest as he approached the opening.

The sound of hooves echoed across the snow-covered earth. Two riders, their horses lathered with sweat, charged into the yard. The tartans they wore—green, blue, and brown—told Cole they were Sinclair men. The urgency of their arrival gave him pause.

"This...is not good," Father Gilbert muttered. "Those are scouts from the lass's party."

Cole's stomach tightened. *Where was Ailsa?*

The riders dismounted, their faces weary. One of them spoke urgently in Scots to another soldier before heading into the keep. Father Gilbert's expression darkened as he strode toward the keep.

Cole's concern deepened as the priest hurriedly lifted the hem of his long robes and jogged inside. Exchanging a worried glance, Cole and Tank followed without hesitation.

Inside, Tavis stood at the head of a long table, barking orders to a cluster of soldiers who sprang into action the moment the scouts entered. The taller of the two scouts wasted no time explaining, speaking hurriedly in Scots, his voice taut with fatigue and anxiety.

"They were separated," Father Gilbert translated, his voice low and hesitant. "They went ahead, scouting as they would, but when they returned...the party was gone."

Cole's heart lurched, the words slamming into him like a punch to the gut. "Gone?" His voice was louder than he intended.

The scout grimly continued, and the priest translated sparingly. "There was no sign of a struggle where they'd left them, he says. They searched but the snow made it impossible to track them—there were no tracks, he says."

"Gone," Cole repeated, barely able to wrap his mind around the word.

His blood felt like ice in his veins. Ailsa.

He stepped forward, announcing to Tavis. "I'll ride with you, with whoever's going."

"Ye'll do no such thing," Tavis snapped, turning on him with a frown. "This is Sinclair business, lad. It's nae concern of yours."

"She's missing, Tavis," Cole shot back, stepping closer to the table. "Your sister could be—" His throat tightened, and he couldn't bring himself to finish the thought. "Jesus, you are sending out a search party, right?"

Father Gilbert arrived at his side, laying a hand on his shoulder. "Calm yourself, lad."

Tank spoke up. "How the hell can anyone be calm? Let's go! Assemble the posse! All hands on deck!" When the priest turned toward Tank, presumably to calm him down as well, Tank jumped on him. "And before you say a damn thing about it, Padre, let me remind you that Cole and I know how to save lives." He faced Tavis then, his scowl dark. "Wouldn't you want all the help you can get?"

Tavis raised a hand to stop the argument, impatient and annoyed. His piercing gaze locked on Cole. "Aye, come along, Spaniards. But ken that we'll nae wait for ye, will nae give ye a second thought if ye fall behind."

"I won't fall behind," Cole vowed, his voice steady despite the storm raging inside him. He turned to Tank, who nodded solemnly.

They had faced plenty of danger before, Tank more so than he, but this was different. This was Ailsa.

"Ready the troops," Tavis ordered. "We leave at once."

Chapter Fifteen

At once evidently meant within the hour, much to Cole's dismay. He'd gone back to the rectory, but only to grab his own coat, putting on that underneath the wool cloak he'd been given, which he'd worn every day trying to fit in. After that, he'd gone directly to the stables, where several young kids and the stable-master, Angus, were already saddling horses. Cole jumped right in, saddling the horse he'd been using for lessons. Though speed was his goal, he did not forget either Ailsa's or Roibeart's constant harping about outfitting the horse properly, correctly.

He needn't have bothered to hurry. Aside from only a few soldiers idling, waiting in the courtyard, Tank included, by the time Cole joined them, neither Tavis nor the bulk of his army were ready to go.

"Feels like I'm back in the Marines," Tank decided impatiently after they'd been waiting a quarter hour. "Hurry up and wait."

It was another half hour before the party finally moved out from Torr Cinnteag, during which time Tank had twice persuaded Cole to hold back. Tank insisted they had no business venturing out alone— they had no clear destination and no idea what dangers lay ahead. Cole, however, was restless, frustrated by the delay. Tavis, when he finally emerged from the keep, made no apologies for the wait, and since no one else seemed eager to move any faster, Cole decided with mounting frustration that this must simply be how things worked in this time.

With no idea whether Ailsa's disappearance was due to a natural disaster—if it had anything to do with the snow that had fallen—or was the work of an enemy, Tavis had brought the entire army along. Only the house guards were left behind to protect Torr Cinnteag.

Shortly after they set out, news spread to Cole and Tank that it wasn't only Ailsa who was missing, but her maid, Anwen, as well. Six soldiers, including the carriage driver and footmen, had also vanished without a trace. The list of the lost only deepened Cole's sense of urgency, but at the same time, he was somewhat appeased that she wasn't alone, that she was accompanied by men whose sole job it was to protect her.

Though it wasn't yet something he was entirely comfortable with, Cole wanted desperately to gallop to where she'd last been seen. Instead, Tavis set a pace that was decidedly, maddeningly slower.

Snow began to fall again about an hour after they'd left Torr Cinnteag.

The young soldier, Rory, who sometimes rode beside Tank and Cole, advised when they left Sinclair property, and that they must now be more vigilant.

The snow kept falling and the cold bit through his coat and the wool plaid, his breath fogging the air as he glanced up at the gray sky. The snow was heavy, but not like any blizzard conditions Cole had lived through over the years in Buffalo, and yet it was enough to slow their progress to a crawl. Cole wondered what they had to be vigilant about—who else would be out in this?

He muttered a curse under his breath, knowing that in modern America—maybe anywhere in the world—a missing person could be tracked with helicopters, drones, thermal imaging, or at least a damn cell phone. Here, they had to rely on the scouts' memory, instinct, and luck—all of which seemed so much less valuable to him.

Cole exhaled hard, his gloved hand gripping the reins tightly. "We'd already be there if we had paved roads," he muttered to Tank.

"Or cars," Tank added. "Hell, even a four-wheeler."

Cole grimaced. He thought of Ailsa constantly—the idea of her out here, in the cold and danger, gnawed at him.

As the day stretched on, and they were forced to climb one hill after another, the snow began to fall heavier, the wind picking up. Cole asked Rory to ride ahead and inquire how much further.

Despite his concern for Ailsa and the others, the details of the march did not escape Cole. Rather, it fascinated him. The scene was unlike anything he had experienced: the army marched in double columns, creating an impressive line that stretched far into the snow-laden distance, the long procession winding like a dark ribbon through the white landscape. All of it was mostly silent, the sound of their movements shrouded by snow and wind.

The men were disciplined, their movements orderly despite the uneven terrain. Snow clung to their faces and cloaks, but they pressed on, after a while looking like more a white army. Certain riders, who Cole presumed to be messengers or officers, moved up and down the line on horseback, carrying orders or checking on the men. Their horses left tracks that were quickly blurred as fresh snow continued to fall.

Rory, a very helpful guide, explained that the scouts— other than those leading the party to where they'd left and lost Ailsa—would regularly venture out, up to two miles ahead to ensure the safety of the path.

Cole realized then that what he had perceived as a delay earlier might have been necessary preparations. The soldiers had packed their own food and supplies, ensuring they could march without stopping for meals. As they rode, they ate chunks of bread or gnawed on strips of dried meat as they marched and sipped from flasks of ale.

Cian and Colin, two younger soldiers who had taken a liking to Cole and Tank, generously shared bread with them. Cole accepted the gesture with a nod of thanks, chewing thoughtfully as he watched the snow swirl around the procession. Both Cole and Tank declined the offered ale, drinking from their water flasks instead, knowing hydration was more important.

By late afternoon, Cole's ass was sore and his feet were freezing and he was beginning to lose hope. He had no idea how much further they needed to go, but was struggling to imagine any way Ailsa and those lost could survive the elements for so long.

At one point while he rode somewhere near the front third of the group, they passed Tavis and Dersey, who'd pulled off to the side of the columns and watched them go by.

Dersey, his red cheeks all that wasn't white on him, was calling out something in Scots as they passed. Anxious, not understanding, but with renewed hope, Cole stood in the saddle to see the front of the column begin to angle toward the left. It looked as if they were aiming for a pass between two mountains.

At the same time, Tank asked Rory, "What's he saying? Are we close?"

"Nae close enough," Rory replied. "Cap'n says we'll stop for the night at Torr Dubh."

Cole sat back down, pinning Rory with a feral glare. "Stop? We can't stop. Aren't we getting close? We must be getting close."

"Torr Dubh?" Tank asked. "What's that?"

"The Black Tower," Rory said, ignoring Cole's concern. "The MacLae stronghold."

"Why are we stopping?" Cole persisted, thinking he should step out of formation and address this with Tavis.

With a grimace of sympathy, Rory explained, "We canna press on in the dark."

Momentarily distracted, Cole's brow knit, and he asked, "MacLae? The guy Ailsa's supposed to marry?"

Rory nodded, his expression revealing some confusion, either about how Cole knew that or why it seemed to upset him.

"Jesus Christ," Cole muttered. "But aren't we close?"

Rory shrugged a bit, burrowing into his breacan, possibly to escape the censure Cole leveled at him. "Nae close enough. 'Tis too dangerous. Torr Dubh land is harsh. Rocky. Laird willna risk the horses, nae in the snow—nae his men."

Cole was as angry at this weak explanation as he was stunned. *Not even for his sister?*

At his side, Tank tried to make him see reason. "Dude, he's right. It's a good call. We've been out all day—the guys and the horses need a rest."

Cole clenched his fists, his breath coming in quick bursts as he fought the urge to shout. "I can't just stop. Not when she's out there." Desperately, he suggested, "We don't need them. We can keep going."

Tank's mien softened slightly as he met Cole's gaze. His beard was completely white and his nose and cheeks were noticeably red. "I get it, Cole. But it's gonna be dark soon, and we don't know these lands. We'd be lost within an hour."

"Christ, Tank," he implored, hardly able to comprehend the fear that gripped him. "Would you be able to stop now, if someone you...?"

Tank lifted a brow, but Cole did not finish. Tank filled in the blanks. "If someone I cared about was out there, possibly in danger? It'd be tough, yeah. But there's no way we can move forward without them. And we're no good to her if we wind up dead."

The words hit home, though they did nothing to ease the frustration roiling in Cole's chest. He turned away, biting down on the urge to argue further.

As the group rode toward the castle, the snow continued to fall, blanketing the world around them in ominous silence. Cole's heart ached, fear clawing at him while he felt that he was abandoning Ailsa.

***

The toasty hall of Torr Dubh was a stark contrast to the biting cold outside. The fire in the massive hearth roared, sending waves of heat through the space, but even with the physical warmth, an undeniable chill hung in the air. Cole noticed it almost immediately, in the way the Sinclair soldiers sat together, huddled with each other in their dark tartans, speaking low among themselves but sparing little more than curt nods for their hosts.

The MacLaes seemed no more welcoming. They sat clustered at different tables, their expressions guarded, except for what glares they aimed at the Sinclairs. Even the servants, darting between the tables to deliver plates and refill cups, seemed a bit more thin-lipped as they approached the Sinclairs. Certainly, they delivered less food and drink to the visitors than they did to the home team.

Cole took it all in as he sat among the Sinclair men, chewing absently on a piece of cheese. He'd heard enough during his few weeks at Torr Cinnteag to understand that relations between the Sinclairs and MacLaes were as cold as the weather outside. The feuding, apparently, had been infrequent but long-standing—small slights and border disputes festering into grudges over the years. Ailsa's marriage to Alastair MacLae was supposed to warm those relations, to serve as a bridge between the clans. But looking around, Cole had his doubts.

The MacLaes on one side of the hall were an unremarkable group, at least in Cole's eyes. The men were clean and well-dressed, their tartans crisp and their tunics embroidered with subtle but deliberate details, but it wasn't their appearance that set his teeth on edge. It was the way they acted.

They leaned close to one another, speaking in low tones, their murmurs punctuated by the occasional smirk or quiet chuckle. After each burst of laughter, their gazes would flick toward the Sinclair tables, lingering just long enough to make their target feel the scrutiny before turning back to their own group.

One of the MacLaes—a broad man with a scar running from his temple to his jaw—caught Cole's eye and didn't look away. His expression wasn't hostile, but there was a cool detachment in the way he stared, as if weighing Cole and finding him lacking.

Cole tore his gaze away and glanced at the others. They, too, carried themselves with a sense of ease, leaning back in their seats and gesturing languidly as they spoke. They weren't careless, exactly, but their casual air felt deliberate, as though they wanted it known that they were entirely unimpressed by the presence of their Sinclair guests.

It reminded Cole of opposing teams in the lacrosse arena. Yeah, there were teams—and certain players—who exuded that arrogant indifference. Though he'd been conditioned to ignore posturing from other teams, it rubbed Cole the wrong way now. It felt dismissive. Superior. And he didn't like it.

Tank, seated beside Cole, leaned in slightly. "Damn, I feel like we're sitting on a powder keg," he muttered, obviously having noticed the strained tension as well.

Cole's gaze drifted back to Alastair MacLae, whom Rory had pointed out earlier. Alastair sat at the high table near his brother William, the laird of Torr Dubh, and despite his finely tailored tunic—its rich fabric catching the firelight—he looked every bit a man who'd long stopped caring about appearances.

Looking like he was nearly fifty, Alastair carried his weight poorly, his belly straining the fit of his clothing while his broad shoulders were rounded and drooped. His thinning hair had been combed in a desperate attempt to cover the bare crown of his head, but the sorry comb-over only highlighted the effort's futility.

Still, it wasn't his looks that made Cole's jaw tighten. It was the way Alastair's eyes roamed the hall, showing interest in only the female servants, and lingering far too long on one of them—a young woman balancing a tray of empty tankards, her full bosom straining against the fabric of her dress. Alastair's gaze followed her with a lewd intensity that made Cole grimace with disgust.

There was nothing subtle about it. Alastair didn't bother to hide his interest, his lips curling into a smug half-smile as the girl passed close to the high table. Cole watched with disdain the casual way Alastair tilted his head, leaning slightly to get a better view of her figure.

Cole exhaled sharply, forcing himself to look away before his expression betrayed him. He'd seen men like Alastair before—men who thought wealth or power gave them the right to take whatever they wanted. It didn't matter the century; that kind of arrogance was timeless, and it infuriated him.

"Shit, he's a piece of work," Tank commented, his attention seemingly on Alastair as well.

Cole murmured an angry assent.

He kind of understood the necessity of the match, but knowing didn't make it easier to accept.

How could Ailsa stand it? How could she possibly resign herself to spending the rest of her life with a man like that? Alastair wasn't just older; he was smug, crude, and entirely unworthy of her. Cole tried to imagine what it would feel like, to know your future had been decided for you, to see it coming like a slow-moving train you couldn't stop. His twenty-first century brain couldn't wrap around it.

For more than an hour they remained inside the hall. Cole's attention again and again on the high table, where Tavis and William MacLae were locked in quiet conversation. Whatever they were saying, it hardly seemed like any friendly conversation. Tavis wasn't known for his humor, but Cole had seen him smile here and there—certainly he liked to poke fun at Cole during drills. But not tonight. His jaw was set and each nod he gave to William MacLae appeared stiff.

"Tavis looks like he wants to haul off and punch him," Cole remarked to Tank.

"That's some workout, holding back," Tank agreed. He shook his head. "I'm not sure how a marriage is supposed to change that."

"One more thing about medieval life we don't understand," Cole suggested.

Around Cole, the Sinclair men carried on with their meal. The young ones, like Cian and Colin, shared quiet jokes, while the older soldiers cast wary glances toward the MacLaes at the opposite side of the hall.

When Tavis stood, indicating he was finished with his meal, the Sinclairs, almost as one, rose as well.

They were given accommodation in the stables, which left Cole and Tank wide-eyed with disbelief. The Sinclair soldiers crammed into the space like sardines in a can, barely any room between them as they unrolled thin blankets onto the packed dirt floor. The men didn't seem to mind the close quarters. They were used to this, clearly, settling in shoulder to shoulder as if it were just another night on the road.

The overflow of men spilled into the nearby barns, where the conditions weren't much better—no heat, just the faint warmth of the animals, whatever blankets they had brought along, and their comrades to keep them from freezing.

Though he suffered not at all from cold—the press of bodies was indeed helpful—Cole barely slept, tossing and turning with Tank snoring in his ear and the image of a freezing or injured Ailsa in his mind.

Still, when morning came, Cole felt a renewed sense of urgency, anxious to get going, being one of the first in the courtyard, which was much larger than that of Torr Cinnteag.

Alastair MacLae emerged from the keep as the Sinclair army gathered, and Cole guessed it made sense for the man to join the search for his fiancé. That was not the case, however; he was simply here to wave goodbye, apparently—though he did commit six of his men to the effort. Six.

Cole rolled his eyes and happened to catch Tavis's eye as the Sinclair laird walked his horse past Cole.

"That's the guy you want your sister to marry?" he challenged with disgust, earning him a ferocious scowl from Tavis.

***

Though the snow had stopped falling, the cold bit into Cole's skin almost more bitterly than it had yesterday. He felt more frantic, more anxious today, believing too much time had passed by now. He feared they'd come to find it was no longer a rescue mission but only the recovery of bodies. What snow had fallen yesterday amounted to about a foot in these parts, the horse's legs sinking up to their knees. The horses seemed sluggish to him, their trek ponderous, while the world seemed blanketed in an oppressive silence. The landscape stretched out before them, white and desolate, with jagged mountain peaks looming in the distance beneath dark clouds.

The group had been traveling for hours, scouts racing ahead and coming back—no news, no sightings— when they neared the largest mountain they'd seen yet. It came down through the ranks as they approached that this was where Ailsa, the carriage, and the others had last been seen.

"Oh, shit," Tank cursed, staring up at the mountain.

"What? *Oh shit* what?"

Tank, bundled in his parka and cloak, lifted his gloved hand, pointing toward the mountain—a football field away, but visible enough now that the pattern was undeniable. "See that stripe of snow cutting through the trees on the mountain? Right there? The one running from the top to the bottom?" Tank's voice was grim, his familiarity with the scene evident. "That's a clear indication of an avalanche. Look at the broken trees—limbs scattered like matchsticks—and the snow... it's not just fresh snow. That's snow that crashed down from the mountain. And look at the debris field—no way this happened just from a storm. This mountain's been pissed."

Cole didn't question Tank's observation. He knew the man had spent years skiing the Rockies in Colorado, and his expertise in avalanches, however indirect, was something to trust.

"Damn it," Cole muttered, urging his horse forward, wanting to reach the base of the mountain. As he passed Dersey and Tavis, who had turned to look at him when they heard him coming, Cole called out, "An avalanche—Tank says it looks like there was an avalanche."

The scene before them grew clearer as they neared the bottom of the mountain. The snow had settled in deep drifts, stretching out across the land in soft, undisturbed sheets. Yet the way it lay, the broad expanse of smooth snow interrupted by jagged edges and ridges, was unmistakable: this was no natural accumulation. The avalanche had carved a wide, jagged scar into the landscape. Snow had crashed down with such force that it had ripped apart trees, sending large branches and limbs flying, leaving only broken stumps behind. Rocks, large and small, lay strewn across the path as though the mountain had unleashed a great fury.

Tank caught up with Cole and both men dismounted at the same time at the edge of the debris field of snow, where it had come to rest at the base of the mountain. Tank turned and held up his hand to the approaching Sinclairs. "No horses beyond this point," he called out, his voice carrying easily. "Watch your step. This ground's unstable. The snow might look solid, but it's packed in layers—some areas could be pockets where it hasn't settled yet."

Cole faced Tavis, thinking to instruct, "Have some rope on hand. Bring up the strongest horses for pulling someone out if they disappear beneath the surface."

"What do we do? How do we search?" Dersey asked, swinging down from the saddle.

Cole looked to Tank for the answer.

"Slowly and carefully," was Tank's suggestion. "Maybe only a few men to any grid of"—he shrugged, possibly only making it up now— "ten square feet. We don't want to put too much weight on this snow."

This gave Cole pause. He stopped abruptly and looked down. *Christ.* Could Ailsa be somewhere beneath him?

Tavis, seeming to perfectly understand what might have happened, and what Tank had suggested, hollered for Stewart, who Cole knew to be the army's engineer.

"Map it out, lad," Tavis said, "by sight. All this area, all this snow that is taller than what we walked through to get here—Jesu, it's nearly ten feet higher. Dersey! Where are ye? Och, Dersey, assign three men to each grid as Stewart directs." He went on, calling for rope to be attached to several of their huge war horses, and to have them at the ready. And then Tavis himself began searching, awaiting Stewart's direction.

The first clue came before Stewart had assigned even twenty men—a crumpled shape just visible beneath the surface.

"There!" Colin alerted.

Hearts stopped as first one shape and then another were recognized beneath the snow. A booted foot was visible with very little digging from Colin, half-buried in the snow, the other leg twisted unnaturally beneath him. More joined in the digging, pushing aside the snow, revealing another man—this one more badly crushed, his body mangled, his expression of shock frozen forever on his young face.

Cole's blood ran cold. They were already too late.

They moved on, the grim discoveries continuing. Shattered wood and broken harnesses marked the remnants of the carriage. The horses lay buried in the snow, their massive forms still hitched to the splintered yolk. Soon after, the carriage was discovered. It took half a dozen men, on their bellies, digging down, trying to get to the door or window. Cole knew a surge of hope—the inside of the carriage might have a large enough pocket of air to survive in. Hope was quickly dashed, though, when they bared one of the windows and Cole realized they had no glass or none had survived, and that the interior of the cab was filled with snow. He kept digging though, alive with fright that at any moment, his hand might find hers.

It seemed to take forever, but eventually, they'd dug out almost to the bottom, the left side of the cab, encountering no bodies. Cole's heart pounded as he stepped back, his mind racing, struggling to keep up with the terror that slowly crept in. With every step, he felt the weight of time ticking away.

He paused to shout her name. "Ailsa!" He roared.

Others called out as well, their voices echoing across the empty expanse.

Then, near the edge of the debris field, one of the men held up a shoe—a woman's shoe, its delicate leather darkened by the damp.

Cole clambered through the snow, his heart hammering in his chest.

He didn't know the name of the man who held the shoe that he, Tavis, Tank, and others had come to investigate.

Tavis couldn't say whether or not it belonged to Ailsa, or even Anwen.

The man holding the shoe pointed to how close he was to the end of the avalanched snow pile. "Sure and someone might have escaped," he suggested.

The discovery renewed their efforts, and minutes later, a trail was found—a faint series of drag marks leading away from the wreckage. Drops of blood dotted the snow, sparse but unmistakable.

"This way," Rory said, already moving forward.

A large group followed the trail, eventually stepping onto solid ground, having only to walk through the snow that fell yesterday, making running easier. Ailsa and Anwen's names were shouted again.

The path led into a dense stand of trees up ahead, toward which at least fifty men ran.

Then, as if answering the desperate calls, two bedraggled figures emerged from the trees ahead of them.

Ailsa and Anwen.

Ailsa!

Relief washed over him in a tidal wave, so powerful that he almost lost his footing, stumbling in his haste to reach her.

Ailsa moved stiffly, looking frozen and bedraggled, her once-vibrant cloak tattered and coated with a crust of ice. Her hair was a tangled mass, strands stuck to her face with frost, and her skin was pale—almost ghostly—against the white backdrop. Her eyes, wide with shock and tinged with exhaustion, locked onto Cole's with a frantic, desperate recognition.

His heart pounded and his hands shook as he pulled her into his arms. He cupped her cold cheeks, checking for any signs of injury, his eyes searching hers for any trace of harm.

"Ailsa," he breathed, his voice low with relief. "Are you all right?"

She nodded, her eyes wide with shock but clear. Her legs buckled just as he wrapped his arms around her.

He kissed her—without thought, without hesitation. It was a kiss of relief, of yearning, of everything he felt for her, what his fright had shown him. The world seemed to pause, the wind stopped, voices faded beyond his awareness. Everything that mattered was right here, in this moment, with her in his arms.

"Thank God," he said over and over, kissing her brow and her cheeks, her lips and hands.

"Cole!"

The roar of his name startled Cole, his body tensing instinctively as his eyes found the source of the fury.

Tavis stood rigid, glaring, beside the mounted MacLaes—who Cole had forgotten all about, and who had not even bothered to dismount and aid in the search.

But Tavis's furious displeasure was then explained, as the MacLae men stared at Cole, still holding a weakened Ailsa to his chest.

A swift scan of others close by—Tank, Dersey, another dozen Sinclair faces, men he knew by now—all showed varying expressions. Each face was a mask of shock, some grimacing as if they'd tasted something bitter, others more solemn, but all were marked by the silent knowledge of what Cole had just revealed—what he had just destroyed—with his actions, by kissing Ailsa in front of so many witnesses.

"Shit," he hissed under his breath, hindsight coming as it did, too late.

"Seize him," Tavis growled, red-faced with rage, his command slicing through the cold air like a blade.

Chapter Sixteen

Time was cruel, stretching endlessly in the damp, airless dungeon. The only markers were the faint shifts in the shadows cast by the single sputtering torch and the occasional creak of the iron-bound door as guards came and went. Cole had tried to keep track of the changes in their keepers, but it didn't really matter. Most of them avoided speaking to him anyway, brushing off his questions with gruff indifference. Only Rory and Somerled, and less generously Davey, when their turns came, offered scraps of news.

Tank was amused by their short shifts, anywhere from two to four hours, but with no regularity that they could figure out a pattern.

"Must have a pretty good union here," he'd remarked.

In the beginning, when they'd first been thrown in here, Tank had talked quite a bit, trying to keep up their spirits. Cole wasn't sure if he should be worried now, as the hours dragged on, that Tank had become increasingly silent. Cole felt terrible for Tank—he hadn't done anything wrong. There was no reason for Tavis to have imprisoned him as well. Apparently, the Sinclairs employed a mindset of *guilt by association*.

The stink of the chamber was unbearable. The pot they'd been given for their needs was foul and humiliating, sitting in the corner, a nasty reminder of their indignity. Cole hated it. Hated that they were fed—better than he expected, to be fair—but treated like animals all the same, with metal plates being slid under the gate of the iron cage.

He paced when Tank didn't, muttering curses under his breath, his fists clenching and unclenching.

He thought the Sinclairs must not keep many prisoners, as there was only this one cell, which he and Tank shared. The generous size of it might suggest that many people could be jammed in here, Cole figured fifteen to twenty if the laird didn't care too much about a person's comfort. He might guess that was of little concern since there were chains on the wall, dangling to the ground, the end of them outfitted with thick iron cuffs just large enough for a man's wrist. He supposed he should be thankful that wasn't their circumstance, chained to the wall.

It was Somerled, many hours after they'd first been thrown in here, who finally brought the first news Cole had been clamoring for.

Ailsa was all right.

"The lass was carried straight away to her chamber when we returned," he'd whispered through the bars, "half the women in the household fussing over her. She's warm, safe. Sleeping off whatever draught they gave her."

Cole relaxed slightly, though he still kept his fingers curled tightly around the bars. "Good," he murmured, though his tension didn't fully ease. "And Anwen?" He thought to ask.

"She's fine too. They've been seen to, both of them. Luck, if you ask me, that they went into the woods when they did." He'd paused, awkwardly adding the reason they'd done that. "Seeing to personal business—what timing, eh? The maid said they felt it—the snow crumbling down the mountainside—heard a roar, and sadly, came to the tree line just in time to see the men being buried. Anwen said they were frozen, shocked. Then when it was done, Peile was the only one they saw. His hand was sticking out of the snow. They dug feverishly, she said—and I dinna ever see that maid do anything feverishly—and pulled him out. He wailed all the way, she said, as they dragged him into the trees—well, ye saw his leg, I'd be wailing, too."

The anger that had been constant since he'd been seized by the Sinclair soldiers gave way to a surge of relief. He let out a long breath, pressing his palms into his eyes. "Good," he muttered, the word heavy with exhaustion.

But even the knowledge that she was safe didn't erase the bitterness. It wasn't just the injustice of it—it was the sheer absurdity. Yeah, he'd overstepped boundaries, he was sure—but damn, you didn't put a guy in jail for kissing a woman! He had plenty of time to reflect on that, by the way, why he'd kissed her. He hadn't planned it, obviously. Hadn't thought to himself if we ever do find her I'm going to take her in my arms and kiss her. He'd just reacted, his relief—his joy!—at the moment possibly being the most overwhelming emotion he'd ever known. He hadn't thought, he'd just acted. And touching her, needing to feel her, to know that she was alive, had been his unconscious priority. The kissing part, well, that was just a furtherance of his joy, seemed natural at the time, in that moment.

Tavis didn't see it that way, obviously.

He got that part, too, how it must have looked to the MacLaes standing, open-mouthed, watching. It didn't look good, not for the woman who was expected to wed Alastair MacLae to be kissing another man.

Still, it didn't mean he needed to be locked up. Certainly, Tank shouldn't be made to pay for Cole's crimes.

"Will he hang us, you think?" Tanks' voice broke into Cole's thoughts. "He'd hang us, right? Or...what? Do they have medieval firing squads, stand us in front of those archers? The ones we trained with?"

Willing to be distracted, Cole suggested, "Maybe they'll pit you against me in an arena, a fight to the death—knowing damn well you'd be the likely winner."

"Hey, don't count yourself out so easily," Tank argued. Cole could plainly hear the smirk in his voice. "You're a scrappy little guy."

Cole chuckled despite himself. "That'll take me far in the 14th century."

Quiet for a moment, until Tank spoke again. "Disembowelment?"

"I think that's used with something else," Cole mused. "Like drawing and quartering."

"That sounds like a good time," Tank laughed.

"Flaying," Cole offered as another possibility.

Tank grimaced. "I'll take the hand-to-hand combat with you—sorry, dude."

Another minute of two of quiet while Tank stood at the gate, leaning against the bars, and Cole sat with his back against the wall, his knees drawn up, arms laid over them.

"You think he'll kill us?" Tank asked again. "Seriously."

Cole would like to think that Ailsa—if she had any sway at all with her brother—wouldn't let it come to that. But frankly, he just had no idea. He let out a bitter laugh. "If he does, I'll haunt him for the rest of his miserable life."

Tank cracked a faint smile at that, but the moment passed quickly, the silence resuming its oppressive weight. The hours stretched on, with the only upside being that Ailsa was safe and well. That was enough.

Tank resumed his pacing, the scrape of his boots filling the silence once more.

Above them, the muffled sounds of the keep carried faintly through the stone—footsteps, voices, the distant clatter of metal. Life went on, even as they waited in the cold, damp stillness.

***

The tension in the air was almost suffocating as Ailsa faced her brother in his private chamber at Torr Cinnteag. The cold stone walls seemed to amplify the weight of their words, every syllable echoing like a hammer blow. Though her pulse raced, she forced herself to stand tall, her composure fragile, but not broken yet.

Tavis, the brother who had once been her steadfast protector, now sat behind a heavy oak table, his fingers drumming a slow, deliberate rhythm that betrayed his barely restrained fury. His narrowed eyes pinned her where she stood, a scathing glare that made her feel like a trespasser in his domain.

Below them, three floors down in the keep's frigid dungeons, Cole and Tank were imprisoned under Tavis's orders. The laird had refused her an audience the previous day, and her attempt to visit the dungeon had been similarly denied. "Laird's orders," Colin had said, shifting uncomfortably beside Davey as they stood guard at the door. The younger lad hadn't met her eyes, wincing as he was compelled to rebuff her.

"Tavis, this is a gross overreaction," she said calmly, trying to reason with him, somehow managing to refrain from wincing herself as her brother leveled her with a scathing glare. "I dinna ken why you're making such a fuss about this," she said, her voice tight with frustration. "Cole's actions were naught but... he was worried for me, just as any decent man would be!"

Tavis's eyes flashed with fury. "Dinna insult my intelligence," he growled savagely. "I dinna see any other man—lads ye've ken all yer life— hurrying to ye! Kissing ye, for the love of St. Columba!"

Ailsa clenched her fists, but she fought to keep her voice steady. "It was a reaction. Tavis," she insisted again. "He was frightened. He was frightened for me, but nae because of any attraction—but because aye, we had become friendly...but nae close." The lie felt hollow even as she spoke it, and the flicker of doubt in Tavis's eyes told her it hadn't landed.

Tavis stared at her for a long moment, his jaw set. "Ye ken I'm an eejit, lass?" he finally asked, his voice low and dangerous. "Ye ken I dinna *now* see what goes on—beneath my bluidy nose!" He banged his fist on the table, rattling an ink pot and shivering papers. "The MacLae will have every right to back out! He willna wed ye! Nae with yer virtue in question. He dinna want spoilt guids."

Ailsa bristled at the vile insinuation, the heat of indignation rushing to her cheeks. "I am nae despoiled," she declared, her voice ringing with conviction. "And dinna speak to me of virtue in the same breath as ye mention Alastair MacLae's name. 'Tis nae secret what he is. How he hounds his servants, the mistresses he keeps—under the same roof as his sisters and nieces! Aye, I've heard it all. Everyone has. The man is depraved, Tavis, a spineless predator!" Her fists clenched, and her chest heaved as her words poured out, raw and unrestrained. "I said naught when ye sought to bind me to him for the rest of my days. Even as I kent the distasteful nature of the man, his repulsive ways, I made nae objection. I *kent* what was expected of me! But ye ken this—ye broke my heart, brother, sacrificing me to that man without so much as a second thought."

Tavis's face darkened, his eyes blazing. "Dinna ye question my—"

Ailsa stepped forward and banged her own small fist on the table, stunning her brother into silence. "I *will* question it!" she cried, her voice cracking with fury and heartbreak. "How could ye? How could ye have done what ye did to Orla? How could ye spare so little consideration for your own flesh and bluid?" Her voice rose to a crescendo, shaking the very rafters. "And God's bones, Tavis, dinna say the word *peace* to me even one more time!"

Tavis opened his mouth, but Ailsa pressed on, her voice breaking under the weight of her emotions. "Damn ye, Tavis, for your cold-hearted ignorance, for sacrificing your own sisters with so little care! Ye should have destroyed the MacLaes years ago, should never have suffered their ignorant tyranny and petty cruelty, their devious plots and their constant pecking at Torr Cinnteag and any Sinclair! *Ye* should have done that, Tavis." Her breath came in ragged gulps, her chest rising and falling as the torrent of her emotions finally began to ebb. "Have ye forgotten, Tavis, what they've done to us? How they snatched our wee brother—our bonny Callum—when he was just a bairn? How we wept, how mam near lost her mind until he was returned—sick and frightened—only after Da paid them half the fortune of Torr Cinnteag? Did ye forget the *creach* of a decade past, when they burned every home in the village, leaving naught but ash and two charred ruins? Did that slip yer mind, as well?" Her breath hitched, but her words poured out, unstoppable.

"And Uncle James—stabbed in the back like a common dog. Oh aye, highwaymen ye say, but everyone kent it was the MacLaes. They never paid for it, were never made to answer." Her voice dropped, raw with emotion. "And do ye forget the desecration? The MacLaes crept onto Sinclair land, to our ancestors' resting place, and shattered the stones of men and women who've been dead for centuries. Desecrated our family's bones, Tavis! And yet, here ye stand, pretending nae any of it ever happened, asking me to bind myself to the MacLaes with so much Sinclair bluid on their hands—however do ye sit there with a clear conscience and suggest that I have ruined the peace?"

Having spent her fury, she straightened her back and lifted her chin, her icy gaze boring into Tavis's stunned face. Never in her life had she unleashed such an unladylike, fiery tirade. And far from feeling ashamed, she was glad—no, *relieved*—to have finally unburdened herself. Swallowing thickly, she spoke again, her tone frosty and resolute.

"Aye," she said, her voice edged with steel. "I'll keep to your plan, Tavis. Your indolent, foul wish to secure peace in the most expedient manner—even by way of this abomination of a marriage. I'll wed the *predatory* bastard." Her words hit like hammer blows. "But nae unless and until ye release Cole Carter and Tank Morrison." She stepped back, her hands steady now despite the rawness in her heart. "And nae if you mean to hold Cole's actions against him in any way, shape, or form. If the man is more forgiving than I and decides to remain at Torr Cinnteag after what you've done, I'll nae stand for him to be punished further. Mayhap ye should try it, brother—forgiveness rather than punishment," she suggested smartly.

"That is nae how a laird governs—"

"Then you're doing it wrong, brother," she suggested somberly.

She drew a slow, shuddering breath, her defiance stark against the ensuing, oppressive silence of the room.

Tavis hadn't moved, save to clench his fist even more rigidly upon the table, since she'd begun speaking.

He didn't move now. Save for a muscle twitching in his cheek, pulsing with the heat of his wrath, he made no move, didn't even blink.

A cold shiver ran up Ailsa's spine.

"Begone from my sight," Tavis said, his whisper more dangerous than any roar, "ere I do something I will later regret."

After a small gasp, Ailsa left the chamber, pulling the door closed sharply behind her. She paused, her chest rising and falling as she struggled to steady her breath. The weight of the confrontation lingered, making her knees weak.

It was only when she caught the faintest shuffling in her peripheral vision that she realized she wasn't alone. Anwen was there, her presence as cautious as a shadow, tiptoeing forward as if afraid to break the tenuous quiet—or alert Tavis to her presence. Ailsa slowly turned her head, her watery eyes meeting the maid's.

They hadn't been the same, not as they once were. Not since Orla's house. There had been flickers of warmth, however, hesitant and fragile, in the aftermath of the avalanche, and all those harrowing hours spent together. Something like a tentative understanding—or ceasefire— had thawed them toward each other.

But now, there was no censure or judgment in Anwen's eyes, no priggishness in her demeanor. Her face was soft with compassion, her brow pinched as though she might cry for the pain she'd overheard. Quietly, Anwen slipped her arm around Ailsa's shoulders, her gesture hesitant but full of genuine care.

"Come, lass," she said gently, her voice low and soothing. "Still weak ye are, and that dinna help. Rest ye need, and let's see to it."

The simple kindness nearly undid Ailsa. Her chin trembled, and though she wanted to brush the offer aside, to steel herself with the same stubbornness that had carried her this far, she couldn't. The weight of it all, her own helplessness, pressed too heavily on her.

She let herself lean into Anwen's support, just for a moment. "I don't need rest," she said weakly, her voice lacking the conviction to make the lie believable. "I need—" She stopped herself, uncertain what to say.

"I ken what ye need," Anwen replied softly, leading her down the corridor with gentle insistence. "Sure and we'll figure it out, how to help the Spaniards. But that willna come tonight. Come now—rest your bones, and let your mind settle. The battle will wait for the morn."

***

The next morning, unable to stand the weight of guilt any longer, scarcely able to entertain a thought that was not about Cole locked up in Torr Cinnteag's dungeon, Ailsa went in search of Father Gilbert.

Cole was in the dungeon because he'd kissed her.

The memory of it flared to life in her mind, as vivid now as it had been in the moment. The warmth of his hands at her cheeks, the brush of his lips against hers, and the unrestrained relief in his eyes—it all surged back with a force that made her stop in her tracks, pressing a hand to her chest. That kiss hadn't been some calculated move, some selfish whim. Cole had simply been overcome with relief that she was alive and well—it was clear as day to her.

Thus, beneath the guilt, another feeling stirred. What did his joy at her safety say about his feelings for her? She wanted to believe it meant something, that it reflected more than just relief or gratitude. Could it mean he cared for her, truly cared for her? The possibility was... exhilarating.

Still, what good was hope in the face of her reality? She was expected to marry another, had only yesterday verified her pledge of duty to Tavis. To entertain even the smallest flicker of joy at the idea that Cole might feel something for her was folly. Worse, it was cruel—to herself and to him. No amount of hope could change what was required of her.

But hope was stubborn, and it nestled itself in the quiet corners of her heart despite everything. She tried to bury it, to smother it beneath the weight of her guilt, but it refused to die. And so, guilt and hope warred within her, each one sharpening her urgency to act. She owed Cole more than rueful longing. She owed him his freedom, his life.

Squaring her shoulders, Ailsa quickened her pace toward the chapel. Whatever it took, she would convince Father Gilbert to help. She couldn't change what had happened, nor could she alter the path she was bound to walk, but she would not let Cole suffer for merely expressing joy.

Ailsa pushed open the chapel door where the early morning light cast a pale glow through the high windows, passed through to the offices in the back. Inside, Father Gilbert sat at his desk, engrossed in his daily readings. He glanced up at her entrance, his expression softening briefly before tightening with concern.

"Ailsa," he greeted warmly but then frowned. "Lass, you should be abed, recovering still from—""

"I need ye to talk some sense into Tavis," she blurted out. Her throat tightened, but she forced herself to continue. "He's locked Cole in the dungeon, Father—and Tank as well. It's absurd. It's criminal what he's doing—Cole did nothing wrong."

The priest's wince gave her pause.

"Did he not, upon finding you safe from the tragedy, kiss you?"

Some of the things that had come to her after she'd met with Tavis—things she'd wished she said—came to her now. "Father, Cole believed me lost to the avalanche, perhaps even dead. His kiss was nae born of any improper intent but of relief so overwhelming it overtook him in the moment. Surely, ye understand how emotions can spill over in such dire circumstances."

Father Gilbert frowned, setting his book aside. "Lass, I am not in any position to—"

"It was a fleeting gesture, Father," she argued further, "nae some calculated or licentious act. If Cole had realized how it might be perceived, I'm certain he would have restrained himself."

The priest rose to his feet, his face a mixture of shock and unease. "And you believe I can and should speak with your brother?"

"Ye must," Ailsa urged, her voice trembling but resolute. "Cole dinna deserve this, Father. He risked his life for me. Whatever ye may think of him, he's a good man."

Father Gilbert hesitated, his gaze searching hers. "And what of his claims? This... other time he speaks of?"

"Whether it's true or nae dinna matter, nae in this moment," Ailsa replied, stepping closer. "He's nae threat. You ken him—ye must see that."

The priest sighed, rubbing his temples. "Tavis is not easily swayed, especially when it comes to the importance and necessity of this contract with the MacLaes."

She refused to go down that path with the priest—he certainly didn't deserve her censure, her thoughts on Tavis's poor handling of the feud with the MacLaes. "But if anyone can speak sense to him, it's ye. Please, Father. I'm asking ye to help Cole—if nae for him or nae for me, then simply because ye ken it's right. What Tavis is doing—God only kens what he plans to do!—is wrong."

Before Father Gilbert could respond, heavy footsteps echoed outside the doorway. Ailsa turned sharply as Tavis entered, his broad frame blocking the light.

"Hmph," Tavis grumbled, his tone cold as his gaze settled on her. "Here ye are."

Ailsa stiffened, refusing to meet his eyes. "I came to speak with Father Gilbert."

"Och, I dinna suppose I need to inquire about the content of yer discussion," he snarled, his voice laced with accusation. "It seems ye are nae all that's been ruined by Cole Carter."

Ailsa fisted her hands. "I am nae ruined!"

"What do you mean?" Father Gilbert interjected, the only calm one in the chamber.

Tavis pulled a folded missive from his belt, tossing it onto the priest's desk. "A message from the MacLaes. They've declined to proceed with the betrothal. Ruined or nae, sister," he said darkly, "ye are perceived as such."

Ailsa's breath caught, and a flush crept up her neck. "That's nae—"

"Enough," Tavis snapped, silencing her. "What's done is done."

Father Gilbert picked up the letter, scanning its contents with a frown. After a long moment, he set it down and met Tavis's glare with steady resolve. "This is unfortunate, but it is... not insurmountable."

"How is it nae?" Tavis demanded angrily. "Nae marriage, nae peace! And now, her reputation is in tatters. Nae man will take her now."

"Perhaps," the priest conceded, his tone thoughtful. "But it also presents an opportunity."

Ailsa and Tavis both turned to him, Ailsa's expression confused while Tavis only scowled more grimly.

"Speak plainly, man!" He commanded.

Father Gilbert clasped his hands, addressing them both. "Yes, it might be true, that Ailsa may find it difficult to secure another match, given the rumors and conjecture that will surely follow... the lad's demonstration near the mountain. But there he is, a man who has already proven his regard for her—and his commitment to her well-being."

Tavis's eyes narrowed. "Ye canna be serious."

"I am," the priest said calmly. "Untimely, ill-advised kiss aside, I believe Cole Carter *is* an honorable man—one you, yourself, laird, spoke in positive terms about only a few days before your sister's return," Father Gilbert reminded the laird, lifting a knowing brow.

Tavis growled, "I said he finally showed some improvement with the blade—something we kent we'd never see."

"No," Father Gilbert replied, shaking his head, ""you said, and I quote, 'He's a man who keeps to his duties, even when they appear to be fruitless.' Aye, laird, you recognized that his persistence and willingness to learn are marks of a man of some character."

Ailsa's mouth had fallen open with Father Gilbert's suggestion and still, moments later, her mind was reeling. "Ye want me to marry Cole?" Her heart stumbled over itself, caught somewhere between shock and a startling flutter of excitement. Marry Cole? Of all the things she'd expected as a result of her efforts to free Cole, that suggestion was nowhere among them. The shock of it thrilled her in a way she wasn't entirely prepared to admit, but the thrill was followed swiftly by worry. What would Cole think? Would he agree solely to be released from the dungeon and spared whatever Tavis's punishment would be? She'd never once worried about what Alastair MacLae thought of wedding her, if he would abhor his circumstance, same as she, forced to wed to promote peace, but Cole... she wasn't sure she could stomach the idea that Cole might not want to wed her, mayhap not even to save himself. And yet, the idea of it, bound to him for life, standing beside him, sharing the weight of her world with someone so steadfast, was not at all unappealing to Ailsa.

"It dinna solve our problem with the MacLaes, Father," Tavis declared in a low growl.

"There are ways to mend relations beyond the union of a marriage," the priest offered sagely. "Surely, a laird as wise as yourself can see that compromise need not mean surrender, and that strength comes not only from force but from unity within your own walls. Consider it well, laird." When neither Tavis nor Ailsa had a ready response available, Father Gilbert continued, "You have two problems, laird—the MacLaes and now Ailsa's reputation and future prospects. With the MacLaes bowing out, these are now separate issues. One can be addressed simply by wedding Ailsa to the lad." He tilted his head and offered a thin smile. "Cole Carter may not bring a banner or a title, but his devotion—and his resilience—are gifts no contract can guarantee."

Tavis looked equally stunned but far angrier. "Ye propose I hand my sister over to the very man who's caused this mess?"

"Neither of them caused this," Father Gilbert countered emphatically, his voice firm. "The embrace was innocent—a moment of relief after great peril. Surely you see that. You risk further scandal—and greater harm to Ailsa's future—if this is not handled smartly and, dare I say, speedily." The priest's gaze softened as he turned to her. "You may not have chosen this path, my child, but perhaps it is God's will...after all."

Ailsa swallowed hard, her heart pounding. She assumed Father Gilbert was trying to impress upon her some meaning in reference to their earlier discussion about Cole, and the possibility of him having traveled through time. She glanced at Tavis, but he refused to meet her eyes.

Instead, he addressed the priest with a scowl. "'Tis madness."

"Is it?" Father Gilbert asked. "Or is it the best solution for all involved?"

Silence fell, the weight of the proposed idea settling over them. Ailsa's mind raced with questions and doubts, trying to comprehend the magnitude of her relief that she wouldn't be compelled to marry Alastair MacLae, and of greater consequence, the wild and stunning proposal that she wed Cole Carter instead.

But only if Tavis allowed it.

Ailsa looked again at her brother, saw that he wore a pained expression as he considered the idea, his scowl dark and his lips curved downward. He turned a ferocious glare onto her, wordlessly pinning her with what looked to be an accusation, either for her part in the collapse of betrothal talks with the MacLaes or for having to now consider this, marriage to a man he might yet consider a stranger.

She held her breath.

Tavis turned to the priest once more. "See it done."

Ailsa's breath burst from her in a small whoosh of disbelief. She hadn't really believed Tavis would accept the idea.

"Bring him to me—"

"No," she argued suddenly, a bit frantically. More calmly, she continued. "No, Tavis. Let me be the one to present the...option to him." She needed to see his reaction, needed to know if he would wed her as she would him, with a quiet, hopeful thrill, or if he would do so only to escape his imprisonment. And if he refused, she needed to hear it from him. Clearing her throat, she said, "I need to know what his fate will be if he rejects the...proposal, as that option should be known and available to him."

"I've made nae decision yet about his fate," Tavis replied. He shifted a bit on his feet. "However, I dinna ken I was set to hang him," he admitted.

"Likely you were considering banishment as a wiser course," Father Gilbert said, quietly asserting his suggestion.

"Hm," was all Tavis said.

"I will go to him," Ailsa declared. "It should come from me."

***

Somewhere beyond his view, the door to the cellar groaned as it was opened, as it did every few hours when either guards came or prisoner food arrived. Cole froze as the sound of a soft, feminine voice could be heard exchanging words with whoever was currently on shift as guard.

Ailsa.

He was on his feet in an instant, a flood of relief and something sharper—joy—surging through him.

A moment later, the flicker of torchlight illuminated a familiar silhouette walking toward the cell.

"Ailsa," he breathed, equally as happy to see her up and about as he was sure this was a good sign regarding his fate and Tank's.

She approached carefully, the ground beneath her feet uneven earth with puddles of dampness. Briefly, she put her fingers beneath her nose as if to ward off the onslaught of unpleasant odors. Her soft features were lit in golden light, her presence banishing every shadow.

God help him, but he knew at the first sight of her that he'd been wrong. It wasn't just relief at seeing her safe. It was something far deeper. If she'd perished in that avalanche...well, he didn't want to finish the thought. Though he didn't quite understand the depth of it or even the why of it, he knew that he wouldn't have survived losing her.

But her expression as she neared gave him pause. Her smile was forced, tight. She might be happy to see him, but she wasn't bringing good news, he guessed.

Directly in front of him, she raised one small hand and curled her fingers around the bars between them. There was an unmistakable tension in her posture and Cole's jaw clenched.

"I cannot begin to express to ye," she began, her gaze on his neck, not meeting his eyes, "and ye, Tank," she added as he'd come to stand beside Cole, "how deeply sorry I am for my brother's treatment of ye."

"Shit," Tank responded, "but you're here to tell us there's nothing you can do about it."

She shook her head immediately, but it was a wobbly motion. "There is something...a resolution has been worked out."

It was everything she wasn't saying—or couldn't bring herself to announce directly—that worried Cole. "But...?" he prompted, tightening his own hands around the bars.

Finally, Ailsa lifted her eyes to his. He wasn't sure exactly what he saw but he decided she was trying to appear braver and more optimistic than she felt. She cleared her throat. "Mayhap a...kiss in your time is less...damaging. Here, however, well...it is nae. A missive arrived today—Alastair MacLae has decided nae to wed me."

"Having met the guy, I feel like that should be cause for celebration," Cole said, "but I'm guessing that's not the case."

"Tavis desperately wanted the peace," she reminded him quietly.

"And now we're to pay for it?" Tank speculated.

Ailsa kept her gaze on Cole. "Mayhap nae. Tavis has agreed to release ye. Tank as well."

Hope conflicted with caution inside him. There was a catch, he presumed, based on her hesitant demeanor.

"To tamp down any...scandal that will undoubtedly attach itself to me," she continued, lowering her gaze again, her lashes sweeping down over her cheeks, "and ultimately...inhibit any possibility of a respectable match, Tavis has decided that we—ye and I—should wed."

The words staggered him.

Marry her! His mind spun wildly, bombarded by the possibilities. Ailsa as his wife. Legally, undeniably his. The thought sent a rush of exhilaration through him, though it came as a vivid, yet complicated hope. To hold her, kiss her, make love to her without hesitation or fear. Her laughter, her fierce spirit, her everything—belonging to him. He realized in an instant he didn't *dislike* the idea. Not at all.

And yet... his gut twisted.

"Ailsa," he began, forcing the words through the chaos in his mind, "I... can't. I don't belong here. In this time."

Her brows drew together, confusion and hurt blooming in her expression.

"I might be pulled back at any moment," he continued. "I don't know how this works. What happens if I marry you and then...disappear?"

Tank groaned at his side. "Dude, you're overthinkin' it. Say yes and worry about the rest later."

If only if were that easy!

But then, what choice did he have? It wasn't just about him but about Tank as well. Apparently, he'd endangered not only his own life, but Tank's, with his heartfelt but ill-advised reaction to finding Ailsa alive two days ago.

Into the awkward silence, Ailsa announced in a stilted voice, "Ye should ken that Tavis was nae set to...execute ye. Father

Gilbert had impressed upon the laird that banishment from Torr Cinnteag was a more appropriate...punishment. Thus, I presume banishment would be yer fate if ye choose nae to wed."

Tank scoffed at this. "Send us out into the wilds of the Highlands? In the middle of winter? That's not a death sentence?"

Neither Cole nor Ailsa responded to this. For a long moment, silence fell between him and Ailsa. She didn't press him further, but her eyes stayed locked on his, filled with sorrow, determination—and maybe a cautious, indistinct hope?

Finally, Cole exhaled, running a hand through his hair. "Ailsa, I can't... promise you anything. Not anything lasting—I just don't know what might happen."

Her chin lifted, her jaw tightening ever so slightly. "I understand," she said, though her tone betrayed her pain. She gave him a small, brave smile, but the hurt lingered in her eyes. Still, she seemed resolved, willing even, to bind herself to him in order to save him, and that made his chest ache.

"But yeah," he said, "I'll do it. I'll marry you."

Chapter Seventeen

It was still several hours after Ailsa had left the underground dungeon with his agreement before anyone had come to release them. That had been Colin, who'd seemed surprised by the turn of events though he'd asked no questions, had merely unlocked the door to their cell and had delivered them to the hall. There, they were met by two women—Margaret and Mary, who had been the first to tend Cole inside the rectory when he'd first come to Torr Cinnteag—who directed them to a room upstairs. This, Margaret explained in her broken and thick English, was the keep's garderobe, a large open room that appeared to serve as both bathroom and washroom.

Cole found himself marveling at the room; it was his first time inside any chamber beyond the hall and dungeon. Tall walls of cold stone loomed over him, though their surface was smooth and gleaming with dampness from rising steam. The space was stark, with minimal furnishings, but the deep wooden tubs, already filled with steaming water, were inviting enough to distract from the otherwise austere setting.

The tubs themselves seemed almost comically small to Cole at first glance—round and shallow, looking more like oversized barrels than proper baths. He and Tank exchanged a quick, uncertain glance when the maids lingered expectantly, one near each tub, clearly prepared to assist with the bathing.

Cole cleared his throat awkwardly, glancing at Tank, who stepped back defensively. "We can manage, thanks," Cole said, trying to sound polite but firm.

The maids exchanged a confused look, until Tank said—speaking slowly, enunciating each word, as if they were deaf and not only struggled with the language—"We're fine. You can go." Possibly, waving his hand toward the door was what actually sent them scurrying from the room.

Cole shed his filthy clothing with no small amount of relief, grimacing at the stiff, dirt-encrusted fabric. The moment he lowered himself into the hot water, his skepticism about the size of the tub vanished. The heat soaked into his aching muscles, dissolving the tension he hadn't realized he carried. Even if he had to sit with his knees drawn up, the cramped position was a minor inconvenience. "Man, this beats those cold baths in the lake," he muttered, leaning his head back and closing his eyes as steam curled around him.

"Holy shit, that feels good," Tank groaned as he sat.

By the time the maids returned with fresh clothes—where they'd come from or who they belonged to, Cole couldn't begin to guess—he finally felt somewhat human again. The pale brown tunic was snug across his shoulders, just shy of restrictive. Tank's shirt, on the other hand, looked as though he'd been poured into it as liquid and then somehow expanded after the fabric had settled. Cole's pants, while clean, were laughably short, but tucking their hems into the oversized leather boots that had also arrived—a half-size too large—helped him feel at least moderately presentable.

Tank, standing there crammed into a tunic that pulled tight across his chest and arms, with sleeves so short they barely reached halfway to his wrists and wearing pants that stopped well above the boots that had been supplied to him, making him look like a child who'd outgrown his clothes overnight, had no business laughing at Cole.

But he did, swiping his hand down his beard while a grin overtook him. "Dude, that might be your wedding tux."

He had fully expected to be summoned to meet with Tavis beforehand, bracing himself for a stern lecture on how he'd single-handedly shattered the possibility of peace with the MacLaes. That would have undoubtedly been followed by another sermon on how he was expected to treat Ailsa, likely laced with thinly veiled threats about the consequences of stepping out of line—banishment, or worse. But to his surprise, there was no such meeting. Instead, the maid, Margaret, awaited them just outside the bathroom, and they were led directly from the soothing bath to the chapel, which, upon arrival, was empty and eerily silent.

The heavy smell of incense hung in the air, wafting up from a brazier near the altar. It was sharp, earthy, and strangely comforting—though Cole couldn't say why, unless because it reminded him of those Sunday masses he'd attended as a child or more recently, on holy days with Aunt Rosie. He suspected that going forward, the scent would forever be tied to this day, this moment.

Of course a shotgun wedding would not be celebrated with any great fanfare, but he kind of expected there would at least be some witnesses aside from Tank.

There would be, he realized a moment later as the door opened and Anwen strode inside. Like Ailsa, the maid seemed none the worse for wear despite having barely escaped an avalanche. Cole never could tell if she was actually smiling or not; it always looked as if she was, though her mood never quite matched her expression. Today, however, the quick glance she cast toward Cole as she walked toward the altar seemed genuinely pleased, the smile seeming to reach her eyes as she nodded a wordless greeting.

Cole flexed his fingers, his palms damp despite the cool air. He wasn't nervous though, or at least he didn't think he was. He wasn't already regretting his decision to marry Ailsa. He knew that he was attracted to her, not only her body and her kiss. But let's be real: this wasn't the wedding he'd imagined back in the twenty-first century. If someone could step up right now and give him a guarantee—some kind of cosmic confirmation that he was stuck here for good—maybe he'd embrace this moment with less resistance. Maybe he'd dive into this marriage with both feet.

But without that assurance, he kind of felt that it was wise to tread lightly. Even as he stood here, wrestling with caution and hope, he knew one thing for certain: his feelings for Ailsa were no joke. Being married to her might have him falling harder and faster than he had already. And that was the part that made him nervous, because there was no guarantee that they had any chance at a future together.

Tavis arrived then, accompanied unsurprisingly by Dersey. While the captain's expression seemed at worst annoyed to have this thrown into his schedule for the day, the laird's face was a mask of stony displeasure. Tavis's lips were pressed together so tightly, it appeared he snarled. Cole thought a baring of his teeth was soon to come as he walked forward.

He stopped directly in front of Cole.

"Ye dinna get to fail her, nae even once," he said, nearly eye to eye with Cole, "Nae Torr Cinnteag. I'll be watching for any opportunity to cast ye out—either walking or being carried in a pine box, makes nae difference to me."

Cole didn't blink as he nodded solemnly. *Good talk.*

Father Gilbert arrived then as Tavis stepped aside, entering from the door at the side of the altar. He positioned himself in front of the altar and signaled Cole to approach. He looked...on edge, which was not particularly reassuring. The priest's gaze darted between Cole and Tavis as though he expected he'd have to break up a fight at any moment.

And then came Ailsa...

Cole's breath caught as she entered the chapel. She moved toward him with a quiet grace, her steps judged as just slightly less than hesitant, her hands clasped tightly in front of her though she carried no bouquet. Her gown, though simple, was undeniably beautiful—a light blue wool embroidered with delicate vines of white and gold along the hem and neckline. The threads caught the faint light of the candles, glistening, giving her an almost ethereal glow. Her dark auburn hair, loose and cascading over her shoulders, framed her face, accentuating the gentle angle of her cheeks and the delicate curve of her jaw. Her face was pale, her expression tense, and her eyes—those striking blue eyes—flicked toward him only briefly before darting away. She was nervous, he could plainly see, but she was also radiant.

As she arrived at his side, he caught the faint scent of lavender, subtle but enough to momentarily cut through the incense. The combination of the two scents—earthy and floral—etched themselves into his memory.

If she had looked at him then, or at any point during her short procession, he knew he would have smiled at her. He wanted to offer her something—a silent assurance that everything would be all right. Whether or not it would prove true, he couldn't say. But in that moment, it felt like a small and meaningful gift he could give her, a sliver of peace amidst the uncertainty.

The ceremony began, Father Gilbert's voice low and steady as he spoke the necessary words. Cole barely heard them, his attention fixed on Ailsa. She didn't look at him directly, her gaze flickering between the priest and some point beyond him, but every now and then, her eyes darted his way.

Cole was pretty sure that Tank and Anwen were the only people smiling.

When Ailsa finally met his gaze, prompted by Father Gilbert's instruction to face each other and recite their vows, Cole seized the moment to look directly into her eyes. He didn't blink, his stare steady and intentional, trying to convey his resolve. This was his way of showing her that he'd made his peace with their union, as much as one could under such circumstances, and that he was stepping into it willingly.

As he repeated his vows, which the priest kindly recited in English, and while Cole had no illusions about this marriage, being born of necessity, not choice, he couldn't help but feel an odd, tiny surge of joy.

***

With little fanfare, they emerged from the chapel into the biting air of the courtyard. Ailsa flinched as icy rain began to fall, the cold droplets stinging her skin. To her surprise, Cole reached for her hand, taking it firmly in his own as they crossed the bailey. The strength of his grip and the warmth of his palm against hers, warding off the chill, offered a quiet reassurance she hadn't known she needed.

Inside the keep, Ailsa and Cole, Tavis and Tank took their seats at the family's table. The supper hour had arrived and the hall filled quickly, the chatter of the Sinclair folks carrying an air of normalcy that felt at odds with the monumental shift in Ailsa's life. Most of the attendees arrived blissfully unaware of the marriage that had just taken place, greeting one another with laughter and the occasional complaint about the cold or the day's work.

Once everyone was seated, Tavis rose, his expression composed but his jaw tight—a telltale sign to Ailsa of his frustration, though no one else would likely notice. He raised a hand for silence, and the room quieted. His tone was firm, yet laced with an unmistakable edge of forced goodwill as he announced, "Before we begin, I bring news. My sister, Ailsa, is now wed to Cole Carter, who has already proven himself a loyal and willing ally to Torr Cinnteag."

Ailsa felt the weight of every gaze turn to her and Cole, some only mildly curious while others appeared utterly stunned. Her heart quickened as murmurs spread through the hall, but she lifted her chin defiantly.

Tavis continued, his voice steady. "This marriage was conducted with my blessing, as is proper. We welcome Cole as one of us, as... our kin now."

Though his words were smooth, Ailsa detected the subtle undertone of tension, a barely veiled warning to anyone who might question the union. It was, she realized, an act for the sake of the clan, a show of unity and control. Though she believed her brother's amiability was feigned, it was clear he meant to leave no room for dissent.

Ailsa's gaze shifted to Cole, who sat quietly beside her, his posture relaxed but his eyes scanning the room, clearly aware of the scrutiny. For all the awkwardness of the day, he looked remarkably composed. She wondered what he was thinking, whether he felt as out of place as she suddenly did.

As the meal began and the hall returned to its usual hum of conversation, Ailsa tried to act as though this evening was no different from any other. Yet, a quiet ache gnawed at her—a nervous little voice whispering that Cole Carter didn't appear even remotely pleased about their marriage.

She wasn't blind to the circumstances. She knew he had married her to escape the dungeon and whatever grim fate awaited him, but still, she had allowed herself to hope. Surely, after that kiss—the one that had upended both their lives—and the one before it, there must have been some spark of feeling on his part.

Now, she wasn't so certain. Throughout the meal, his jaw remained clenched, his expression tight, as though the entire affair was an ordeal

Though this wasn't a proper wedding feast—there were no toasts, no speeches, no honored guests, and no music played in celebration of their union—Ailsa had tried to treat the supper as a normal evening, but in her heart, it felt monumental. Yet, seeing Cole's unchanged—or perhaps slightly darker—demeanor left her feeling small and disheartened by the end of the meal.

Finally, as courage and desperation warred within her, she summoned the nerve to speak. "Ye are nae pleased," she ventured softly, her voice careful, hesitant. "Despite having your freedom."

The words seemed to shift something in him. His gaze slid to hers, and though his expression softened slightly, his tone remained clipped.

"Ailsa, I'm not upset—certainly not with you," he said, though the frustration laced in his voice suggested otherwise. "I understand you're bound by the rules and conventions of this time. But I'm not, or at least I wasn't meant to be. Where I come from, something as...harmless as a kiss would've done little more than raise a few eyebrows. To end up imprisoned for it, forced into marriage..." He exhaled sharply. "It's a lot to accept."

Her heart sank, though she kept her voice steady. "Ye dinna want to be wed to me," she concluded quietly.

He ran a hand through his hair, shaking his head. "I didn't want to be *forced* to marry—you or anyone," he admitted, his voice strained. "Christ, Ailsa, don't you find it odd that your brother doesn't trust me, yet he allowed this to happen?"

"He is trying to protect me," she replied, though the words felt hollow as she said them.

Cole scoffed, his disbelief evident. "He's got a funny way of showing it."

Ailsa lowered her head, the flicker of hope she had been nurturing all evening snuffed out.

For a moment, silence stretched between them, heavy and uncomfortable. But then Cole's voice came again, quieter this time, more measured. "Ailsa..." He hesitated, as though weighing his words. "I don't know what's expected of me in this marriage. But I promise you this—I'll never hurt you. And I'll try my damnedest not to cause you any more trouble than I already have."

She looked up at him, warmed by the sincerity in his tone. Though his words weren't overflowing with affection, they held a kind of promise—small, but steady. And though it wasn't the declaration she had been hoping for—was scarcely a declaration at all—it was something. And for now, she decided, it would have to be enough.

She smiled with a wee bit of gratefulness at him.

Though Ailsa knew she and Cole were expected to retire to her bedchamber together—and feast or no, sooner rather than later—Ailsa still needed to be prodded by her brother.

"'Tis time ye took yer leave of the hall," Tavis said to her shortly after the platters had been cleared, when only tankards and crusts of bread remained on the table.

She nodded without meeting her brother's gaze, her cheeks warming instantly with heat.

She angled her face toward Cole but did not meet his eye. "We will retire now," she advised and waited for him to stand.

He hesitated but a moment before rising to his feet and pulling out her chair.

It wasn't often that she felt either put on display or deeply aware of scrutiny in her own home, but she felt it now. The weight of the hall's collective gaze settled heavily on her shoulders as she rose from the head table. The low murmur of conversation ceased almost instantly, replaced by a silence that seemed deafening in its intensity. Even the crackling of the fire in the great hearth seemed to fade to silence.

Though her cheeks burned, Ailsa kept her head high. She was acutely aware of Cole at her side, his presence solid and calm, his hand at her elbow, his stride steady and purposeful as he steered her away from the table.

She, on the other hand, felt as though she might stumble.

They were all watching her—of that, she was certain. Were they thinking of her wedding night, mayhap more than she was? Did they imagine her blushing beneath a veil of stoicism, or picture her submitting meekly to her new husband, a stranger to Torr Cinnteag? The thought made her stomach twist into knots. It wasn't that she hadn't thought of it—of course she had—though the idea of intimacy with a man she barely knew left her feeling more wary than wistful, despite what she was sure was some feeling for Cole Carter—despite even the tantalizing thrill she'd known from his kisses.

They strode through the corridor and climbed the stairs to the second floor, Cole's hand having dropped away from her arm as soon as they'd left the hall.

Lifting her chin, Ailsa pushed open the door to her chamber and stepped inside. Once there, however, she paused, not quite sure what to do, where to stand even. Nervously, she scratched her right arm with her left hand, turning near the bed to face her husband.

She watched as he surveyed the chamber, his eyes seeming to linger on the details—the tapestries, the low glow of the firelight on the stone walls, the carved bedposts. Did he find it strange? Dull? Did it lack the comforts he might be accustomed to, wherever—or whenever—he was from?

To her, the chamber was a sanctuary, familiar and comfortable. To him, she realized, it might seem a relic, an odd mix of austerity and charm, stripped of any modern convenience he might have known. Did he see the years of history in the stone? The care in the stitching of the coverlet? Or was it simply another reminder of how far from home he was?

"So, I'm not sure how this works," Cole confessed. He turned and slowly closed the door before facing her again. "Is this to be a real marriage, or am I here in your bedroom only to pretend that it is?"

Ailsa felt a sudden constriction in her chest. Any idea that this would not be a real marriage hadn't occurred to her, and she felt suddenly ridiculous for not having considered it. "I...dinna even think to imagine... what were ye expecting?"

"I think this comes back to: expectations regarding...the time-travel thing," he said, wiping a hand over his mouth and jaw.

She thought the answer was a wee bit evasive. She wondered if, rather as she'd just done, he'd simply tossed it back to her to answer.

Meaning to settle it here and now, Ailsa bravely asked, "If nae for the time-travel...event, if ye had nae expectation that ye might possibly be returned to your time, how would... ye like our marriage to proceed?" She swallowed nervously, waiting his reply.

Cole unclenched his fists and crossed the chamber toward her, his gaze locked on hers.

"I'm here and well, we're in this," he began, "and you are fully aware that I simply can't guarantee a future, but..." He stopped two feet away from her and ran a hand through his hair, his expression unreadable. "I don't mean that we need to rush into... anything. But then, I won't lie and say I'm not attracted to you or that I don't want to kiss you again or..."

His words hung in the air, heavy and uncertain, but oh, so invigorating.

And yet, Ailsa wasn't quite sure how to respond.

"I'd like to kiss you," he repeated with greater certainty, as if he knew this one thing for certain. His mesmerizing blue eyes imprisoned her, holding her gaze. "I've thought of little else all day."

Ailsa's responding smile, small and wobbly, one she'd have not been able to deny even if her life depended on it, likely served as permission granted, so that her new husband took two steps forward and did not stop, but kept coming until he'd taken her face in his hands and covered her mouth with his.

Her eyes drifted close, and she was jolted by wild, glorious sensations as his tongue explored her mouth until, wanting to give and not only receive, she touched her tongue to his. Cole groaned and he curved his hand around her nape. He moved his other hand to her waist, his fingers curling into the fabric of her léine, pulling her closer. He sucked her tongue deep into his mouth, twisting his against it with a muted sound of desire.

Anwen had repeatedly warned Ailsa that a man could be carried away by his ardor, and that he might begin to behave in an inappropriate—though unspecified—way. Presently, and despite her vast innocence, Ailsa had a theory that she desperately wanted Cole to behave inappropriately. Her insides were melting, like wax becoming liquid over a flame. She brought her hands up to his chest and shivered as his lips slid away from hers, moving along the column of her throat as she instinctively arched her neck. She felt his hand come between them and curve around the side of her breast. Heat bloomed within her and her nipples tightened.

He brought his mouth back to hers and pushed her backward, toward the bed. One hand skimmed down her back and pressed her hips against his. Ailsa gasped into his kiss, feeling the hard line of him pressing against her softness.

She nearly wept a moment later when he stopped. Completely. Took his mouth and his hands away and just stopped.

With a whimper of discontent, Ailsa opened her eyes, her fingers clutching at his tunic.

"Ailsa, I have to ask... have you done this before?" While she shook her head slowly in answer, he questioned, "Do you...know what we're about to do—what I very desperately want to do with you right now?"

She felt no shame confessing that she hadn't a clue, shaking her head once more. In truth, she had *some* idea, but as were Anwen's warnings about a man's possibly inappropriate behavior, Ailsa's knowledge was vague, lacking specifics.

He took her face in his hands again and kissed her forehead and then said, "Do you want me to lay it out for you? Well, wait—first, are you sure you want to do this?" With seeming regret he lowered his hands and put a bit more distance between them. "I have a feeling that you're going to—and not because you're a woman or anything, but just because of the time period, that gulf of centuries between us—that you're going to be looking at our marriage as a forever thing... even though I've said and I hope you understand that I just don't know what the future will bring."

It struck Ailsa that this was the most amount of words Cole had ever strung together all at once, and she sensed that he was nervous about something.

"I'm saying it wrong," he admitted when she failed to respond. "I just mean, once it's out of the bottle, so to speak, you can't put it back."

Ailsa narrowed her eyes at him, trying to understand exactly what he was saying.

He grimaced a bit and tried again. "Ailsa, I'm guessing you're a virgin," he continued bluntly, "but you won't be after tonight. And I'm wondering if you'd rather remain a virgin, maybe if... well, if something does happen and I somehow get back to my time, maybe you would marry for real and would want to be a virgin for your husband. Correct me if I'm wrong, but I think virginity is kind of prized in a bride in this time period."

The words, *for real*, stung. Sharply. But she didn't let on—she'd already been holding her breath so a gasp was impossible. She wanted his touch, wanted more of his kiss, wanted his hand on her breast again, felt as if she would die of hunger if she wasn't fed these things. So she focused on the one thing he'd said that would—or might—get her what she wanted.

"Ye are my husband."

He smiled. It came with a burst of a sigh, something like relief. "I was hoping you would feel that way."

If only you *did*, she thought with a bittersweet twinge.

In truth, she counted herself lucky, to have had as many moments as she had with this handsome, considerate, mysterious man from the future. But she was greedy and wanted more. She'd take whatever she could get before he was taken away as he supposed he might be.

"I trust ye," she told him.

"That's funny," he said. "When I first came here, I felt the same about you—I trusted you almost immediately. I still do."

They stared for a moment at each other. Cole brushed her hair back from her temple.

"This is desire, what I feel when ye kiss me?" She asked, wanting that clarified. "Passion, mayhap?"

"Um, yeah," he said, grinning playfully, "if I'm doing it right. And yes, if you're wondering, I feel the same."

"We have desire and trust, then," she told him. "That's a guid beginning, even if the beginning is all we have."

He liked this, she decided. One corner of his mouth lifted and he looked into her eyes, left and then right. "Sometimes I look at you and I can't believe you're real. But yeah—then we're good. Although I still need to know, do you want me to spell out what...making love is, or...do you want to feel?"

"Feel," she answered automatically, greedily. "I want to feel...everything."

"That's a good answer," he said. His white teeth flashed briefly. "I really don't think you want to hear me stumbling and fumbling through some lame explanation of all the moving parts and what they're going to be doing. It'll be so much better if I show you."

Once more he pulled her close and kissed her again. His mouth was like warm silk against her lips, infinitely persuasive, and soon he deepened the kiss, ravishing her, and Ailsa clung to him.

He lowered his head and claimed her lips with a scorching kiss. Her mouth opened instinctively, allowing his tongue to tease and torment with relentless skill until her knees threatened to give way. Was this to be her fate—to be undone again and again by him, by the relentless pull of the desire he stoked in her?

Somehow, they had gotten turned around—or Cole had turned them around without her realizing—so that the bed was behind him. He pulled her forward, his lips not leaving hers even as she felt him lower a bit. He leaned or sat against the side of the high bed and reached for her hips, easing her into the space between his thighs. She was happily trapped and greedily drank in his kiss while he raised his hands and stroked strong fingers down her back and then up until he found the laces of her léine. As if he were facing the ties with his eyes opened, he loosened them effortlessly. Next, he moved his hands to her arms, pushing them up, dragging his mouth from her so that he could raise her léine over her head. He did not kiss her again immediately though but stared at her chest for a moment, compelling Ailsa's gaze to drop as well.

Her breasts ached and her nipples stood hard against the thin fabric of her chemise.

Time, that funny thing that brought him to her, stood still when next he touched her breast.

With worshipful awareness he closed both hands around her breasts. Ailsa shivered but otherwise did not move. He kneaded her flesh through the fabric, his thumbs stroking over the peaks. Ailsa moaned and dropped her head to the side, closing her eyes, reveling in the sensation, the way her pulse pounded with delight. Her eyes jerked open, however, in the next moment, when he put his mouth to the fabric, pulling at her nipple with his teeth. The sensual shock of it weakened her knees but Cole moved his hands to her hips steadying her, bringing her more intimately between his legs, bringing more of her breast into his mouth.

"Christ," he murmured thickly and worked quickly, gathering the fabric of her chemise into his hands before lifting that up and over her head as well, until Ailsa stood before him in only her hose and short boots.

At first his gaze moved with the fabric, over all the parts of her revealed, but soon his eyes focused on her bared breasts. Ailsa watched him, marveling at the lean, severe contours of his face, how such austere lines could make for so handsome a man. Again there was a reverence in his touch, his hand moving with an aching slowness as he cupped the swollen mounds. He stared at them, his lips parted, his chest rising and falling.

Ailsa thought with a rare and kind self-appreciation that her skin looked like ivory in the soft light and that her breasts fit his large hands almost perfectly.

"Kiss me," she whispered, nearly incoherent, wanting him to take her nipple between his teeth again, "there."

Obligingly, he bent his head.

Ailsa sucked in a breath as his lips touched her nipple. But he did not tug at it again but first drew his tongue around it, creating an exquisite path of delicious torture to its peak. Her body reacted, blossoming at his touch. She was an instrument, and he merely plucked at strings, creating a melody in her pulse until she vibrated for him. "I like it," she confessed breathlessly. "I like this very much."

In response, he focused again on her nipple, holding it in his teeth, while inside his mouth, his tongue stroked the bud.

Ailsa gasped, her fingers tightening on his shoulders. Cole shifted her until her other breast was directly in front of him and repeated the beautiful torment. He was firm but gentle, clever, so easily eliciting a cry from her, begging for more.

"Please," she whimpered as heat pooled low in her pelvis.

His lips, teeth, and tongue abandoned her breast.

"Say my name," he instructed.

Chest heaving, Ailsa tipped her face down to him. "What?"

He laved his tongue over her nipple, his eyes locked on hers. "Say my name."

"Cole," she breathed.

He licked again and a muscle between her legs clenched involuntarily.

"When you beg, Ailsa, say my name," he said, his breath warm on her cool, wet nipple. He watched her and waited.

"Please, Cole," she managed, her voice suddenly unfamiliar, throaty. Desire soared even higher.

He gripped her tight and yanked her to him, plundering her nipple with renewed vigor.

"Cole," she heard herself whisper again.

A moment later, while her head was thrown back and her hands were threaded in his hair, he paused and put his hand at the back of her thigh, lifting her leg off the ground. A wee bit dazed, Ailsa moved her hands to his broad shoulders and glanced down as he removed her shoe and then glided his hand slowly up her leg to the top of her hose, slowly rolling it downward, his intense blue eyes worshipfully following his hand. Indifferently, he tossed the hose aside and repeated the process with her other leg.

And Ailsa stood completely naked before him.

Cole's hands returned to her hips, his strong fingers curling possessively but not painfully into her flesh. His smoldering gaze lingered on her as though she were something rare and precious, his eyes tracing her shape and curves with an intensity that made her heart flutter. In that moment, as never before, she felt truly beautiful.

"Christ, Ailsa, you are unreal." He met her gaze, his eyes softening, a subdued warmth flickering in the blue depths.

He stood then and pressed a brief kiss to her lips.

"Climb in bed," he directed, his hands moving to his waist as he began to unbuckle his belt.

Ailsa did as instructed, pulling back the bedlinens, distressed by a fleeting, disheartening thought that it was done. But they couldn't be, she reasoned. She was yet a maiden, she knew. God's teeth, but she didn't want to be!

Tucked under the blankets, she returned her attention to Cole.

Silhouetted by golden firelight, he doffed his tunic and then bent and removed his boots before peeling away his breeches and hose. Of course, his impressive chest she'd seen before, but still, she was not prepared for the thrill that nearly curled her toes at the sight of him fully naked, a masterwork of rugged beauty, corded muscles everywhere. As he returned to her, she took note—wordlessly, breathlessly— of his powerful thighs and then gulped, having her first glimpse of a fully aroused man.

And her thoughts became wildly inappropriate.

Cole might have caught sight of her wide-eyed gaze. "That's one of those moving parts I mentioned," he said, a hint of laughter in his tone.

Apparently at ease with his own nakedness, he walked slowly to the bed and sat down next to her. Gently, he tugged at the blanket, pushing all the layers down below her knees, leaving her—inexplicably at this moment—vulnerable. He pushed her arms and hands aside and leaned down to cover one nipple with his lips, while his fingers gently explored the triangle of silken hair between her legs. Ailsa was overcome, delirious with some notion that she was being attacked on several fronts.

Her eyes flew open wide. "Cole!" She struggled up on her elbows and stared down at him, at the muscled perfection of his body. Her objection, if it could be called that, lacked authority, sounded yet like another plea.

Unprepared for the sheer delight that tore through her, she moved her hips against his fingers. With his free hand, Cole slid his palm and fingers up over her belly and between her breasts, gently pushing her down until her arms went limp and she melted into the mattress. She stared at the ceiling and let herself feel. Somewhere inside her an emptiness burned, and instinct told her Cole knew how to fill that. His fingers stroked her, blatant promise in every caress.

An urgent look hardened his face when she lowered her gaze to him.

Slowly he slipped one finger inside her, the strange and exquisite sensation wringing a startled moan from her. He changed position, stretching out beside her, kissing her everywhere, wherever he pleased, nuzzling her neck and crashing down against her lips, then traveling back to her nipples to tease them gently. All the while, he worked magic with his fingers, discovering her while she discovered herself.

Ailsa moaned his name again, her voice low and wispy. She slid her hands into his hair, holding him to her, lest he stop or leave and deny her the mysterious, spiraling pleasure he brought her.

He ceased anyway, gently pulling his finger from within her hot channel a moment before he moved over her. His weight and warmth as he came over her was wonderful, sturdy, yet he took care that he didn't press too heavily upon her. She ran her hands over his arms, feeling the muscles tighten as they held his weight on his elbows. Her legs parted naturally to cradle him and she sighed at how perfectly they fit together. Her body opened to him as he moved against her, slowly nudging. His eyes held hers, a smile in them that Ailsa selfishly, hungrily decided held more promise.

The head of his cock met with the very center of her, and Ailsa somehow knew this would complete her and deliver to her what her untutored body craved right now. She moved her hips to draw him inside her, heard him growl, suggesting he liked this, and she shifted again. Cole went still, his lips returning to hers as he flexed his hips and answered her want of more, entering her slowly. With his elbows and forearms on either side of her head, pressing into the flat mattress, he watched her as he pushed further inside her. Ailsa stared back, her fingers digging into his sides with this new sensation and wished now for so much more light inside the chamber to see him, to see if he felt what she did, how beautiful and perfect and right this was. She saw only that his eyes were shiny and that he breathed through his mouth as he watched her.

In the next moment, he slid his hands down and gripped her hips, and his mouth tightened as he murmured, "I'm sorry, Ailsa," just before he thrusted firmly, tearing her maidenhead.

She cried out, shuddering against the burning pain, clutching at his shoulders.

Cole stopped moving. "Give it a minute," he advised huskily. "Kiss me, Ailsa." His arms returned to her sides, his hands pressing into the mattress near her shoulders. He lowered his mouth at the same time Ailsa obediently lifted hers, and their lips met in a slow, languid kiss.

"It feels...very full," she murmured when their lips parted. She shifted her hips, hoping to find ease from the aching pressure. Alas, it didn't particularly feel good anymore.

Cole groaned when she moved, however—in restrained pleasure, she thought—and she moved again, suddenly deliciously aware that she held some power. Expecting more pain, she stiffened as she lifted her hips again, but to her surprise there was little, and then less again when next he moved, withdrawing and then pressing forward again.

"Oh," was all she could manage as that odd, tantalizing heat began to build again within her. The feeling continued to build until she thought it would be the death of her. She tightened her hold on his shoulders, desperately seeking more, that promise he'd made with his fingers. Her breath came in short, rapid bursts.

He lifted himself and slid deeper inside her, into the narrow passage he'd claimed as his own.

She sighed when he withdrew again, nearly all the way, and then entered her with excruciating slowness. He did this over and over, kissing her further into senselessness. Ailsa felt the need to move and rocked her hips against his, mimicking his motion.

Her body was slick and wet. Mindlessly, Ailsa arched her back as the wave crested, until finally it broke. Sensation washed over her, hot liquid pleasure coursing through her veins. She moaned her disbelief, the "Oh," being drawn out, being breathed with startled delight. She opened her eyes.

Cole's neck was arched, his head tilted upward. His eyes were closed, and he wore a tortured expression as his own body was racked with what she imagined was the same shuddering ecstasy he had given her.

A moment later, he slumped against her. Breathless yet, Ailsa swirled her short nails around the top of his back.

She couldn't smile, could scarcely move, but she felt a smile inside.

She was his, and he was hers now.

Chapter Eighteen

Cole had officially moved into the keep. It felt strange to take up space in what still felt like Ailsa's world.

The chamber they now shared was modestly sized, yet warm and inviting, tucked at the far end of the corridor on the same floor as Tavis's quarters. Thick stone walls framed the space, their surfaces softened and warmed by colorful tapestries depicting hunting scenes, heraldic symbols, and one long and thin one with blooming vines. A single, narrow window let in faint light during the day but at night was shuttered against the chill, with a fur-lined curtain drawn to keep drafts at bay.

The centerpiece of the room was the large wooden bed with a tall canopy draped in rich, if slightly worn, fabrics dyed a deep crimson. The mattress, stuffed with straw and feathers—about half a foot taller than what Cole had been sleeping on for the past few weeks—was covered with a heavy woolen blanket and furs that promised warmth during the cold Highland nights. At the foot of the bed sat a sturdy trunk—kist, Ailsa called it—its dark wood carved with intricate knotwork. It was here that Cole had stowed his few belongings, and where he kept the clothes he'd arrived in.

A small table and two chairs occupied one corner near the hearth, where a fire burned at almost all hours of the day, its glow casting flickering shadows across the room. The mantel above the hearth bore a few personal touches: a brass candlestick, a neatly folded stack of small cloths, and an unassuming earthenware pitcher. Ailsa's comb and a few small porcelain jars rested atop a second chest of drawers, clearly her domain, while an iron wall hook nearby held her woolen shawl and a spare cloak.

Against the opposite wall, a modest washstand with a basin and pitcher provided for their daily needs. A wooden peg rack next to the door offered a place for Cole's cloak and his borrowed sword, which looked slightly out of place hanging among Ailsa's more delicate belongings. Despite the practical arrangement, the space felt lived-in, marked by the subtle contrast between her touches of refinement and the hints of his presence now woven into it.

The sword, by the way, had been given to him by Dersey. There'd been no ceremony to the gesture; instead, Dersey had called out Cole's name shortly after arriving on the training field two mornings after Cole had wed Ailsa, grumbling under his breath as he tossed the sword at him with a casual, almost careless flick of his wrist. It sailed awkwardly across the few feet between them, hilt-first, leaving Cole no time to think. Reacting on instinct, he'd managed to catch it—barely.

Dersey, unimpressed, had grunted, "Laird dinna want to be embarrassed by ye, having nae weapon. What kind of man is that, a weaponless one, I dinna ken."

Moments later, Tank had received a sword in much the same way, its handle as plain and unremarkable as Cole's, solid but bearing none of the personalization that might mark it as a warrior's own.

Anyway, for Cole, the interior of the castle—anywhere outside the hall—was still a strange and unfamiliar world, but in their bedroom, the space he shared privately with Ailsa, it began to feel a little like home.

He'd returned to their chamber last night to an unexpectedly exquisite sight: his new wife submerged in a wooden tub placed before the fire, her auburn hair damp and loose around her shoulders. Anwen stood at her side, a rough cloth in hand, turned to see who came though Ailsa had not. At first, he'd felt like an intruder, halting at the door with an apology on his lips for not having knocked, ready to retreat. But Ailsa's calm, unflustered invitation—"Stay"—stopped him mid-turn, and he'd entered the room. Within a minute, while he'd shed his cloak and boots, having caught glimpses of Ailsa's bare, dampened shoulder, just the hint of the curve of her breast, and marveling at the way the firelight worshipped her face and her flesh, he'd huskily dismissed Anwen, and had happily stepped in to help Ailsa finish her bath.

What shyness she'd exhibited on their wedding night had slowly given way to a boldness that both surprised and captivated him. Ailsa, it seemed, was learning to trust him in ways that went beyond words. Her initial hesitancy had melted into a quiet confidence, her tentative touches becoming increasingly assured, her laughter freer, her kisses more daring. With each passing night, her passion revealed itself not only in her touch but in the way she looked at him. Cole knew for certain that no man had ever touched her as he had, but she looked at him at times, he was convinced, like he was the only man who had ever mattered. He found himself utterly enchanted by her.

The days quickly settled into a new routine.

Cole made every effort to contribute to both his marriage and to Torr Cinnteag. He continued his training under Tavis and Dersey's scrutiny, and though the laird remained as gruff as ever, there were moments—a brief nod here, a begrudging word of approval there—that told Cole he was making progress. When Tavis remarked that Cole should sit in on his meeting with the castle's steward—"Ye need to ken what it takes, what is needed, to manage a demesne of this size"—Cole had sat with Tavis and the steward, a gray-haired man named Murchadh, listening to the steward's suggestions for rationing the wheat supply for what was already seeming to be a long and rough winter. He learned that the Sinclairs sometimes traded cured fish and furs for grain with neighboring clans, though some recent skirmishes—and the loss of the MacLaes' good will— had complicated such arrangements.

Murchadh also spoke at length about the livestock—how the cattle would need additional fodder if the snow kept coming and the fields were buried, and how the hens' dwindling egg production might necessitate the culling of older birds. They discussed the state of the castle's stores of salted meat, the dwindling supply of candles and lamp oil, and even the need for mending torn woolens before the colder months settled in.

At first Cole had remained silent, only listening, but with some expectation that he was supposed to learn, he began to ask questions, needing some words, phrases, and processes defined and explained to him.

Murchadh also reminded Tavis that a neighboring clan's annual tribute was overdue, and that a decision would need to be made about whether to send men to collect it or risk seeming weak in the face of the delay.

Tavis decided that he would confront the clan, announcing that Cole should accompany him.

That night, he'd had to confess to Ailsa that he didn't understand the tribute, what it was or why it was owed to them, and that he had no idea what, if anything, might be expected of him when he rode with Tavis to this neighboring clan.

Naked in his arms after he'd made love to her, she'd traced patterns over his chest and explained as much as she could to him.

"The Henshaws were granted nearly a thousand acres of fertile soil generations ago," Ailsa explained. "Originally, it was part of a planned marriage alliance between our families, but the Henshaw groom was killed before the wedding could take place. By that point, they'd already begun working the land. Out of respect for their loss, it was gifted to them as tribute to their fallen son, with the agreement that after five years, they would begin paying a lease. Since the land is much closer to their keep, more accessible to them than us, it wasn't much of a loss to Torr Cinnteag."

"But why does Tavis want me to go with him? Is this some kind of test?" Unexpectedly, but in truth, Cole thought he might actually be spending more time in Tavis's company than he did Ailsa's of late. This didn't bother him as much as he thought it might. Honestly, he'd rather prove himself to the laird now, quickly, showing that he wasn't a threat, rather than be walking around on eggshells for any length of time.

"It might be," she allowed with a tilt of her head. "Tavis needs to be assured nae only of yer loyalty but of yer usefulness—yer capabilities." A faint grin curved her lips as she added, "Or maybe he intends to bring someone intimidating along for effect. The Henshaws have grown lax in recent years, delaying their tribute longer and longer. Perhaps he means to remind them of their obligations. Ye are rather fierce looking when ye are cross."

As the days passed, he and Ailsa slowly learned more and more about each other. They shared stories from their pasts—childhood misadventures, cherished moments, and particularly fond memories of their mothers specifically. Ailsa's curiosity about his world in the future led to many late-night conversations, though he sometimes struggled to explain certain inventions, abstract concepts, and the complexities of modern life.

From nearly the beginning, though, there was an undeniable sense of ease between them, a comfort that seemed to transcend the stark differences in their worlds. It didn't surprise him, not really. He'd been drawn to Ailsa from day one.

It felt natural, even as so much uncertainty loomed in the background. Neither of them spoke of what their marriage meant in the long term, but for now, they seemed content to take it day by day.

For the first few mornings after their wedding, Cole woke up to an unfamiliar weight draped against him. It was a sensation that startled him at first initially—the warmth of Ailsa beside him, her soft breath tickling his shoulder—but one that quickly became something he found himself looking forward to.

This morning, he took some time to simply stare at her while the faint light streaming through the shuttered window illuminated her sleeping face. Her braid had come loose in the night and stray strands curled against her cheek. Cole didn't dare move at first, half out of fear of waking her and half because he wanted to savor the moment.

He liked to lay still, watching as she stirred, as her long lashes fluttered open.

"Good morning," he murmured, his voice low and a little rough from sleep.

She blinked at him, a soft smile tugging at her lips even before she'd fully opened her eyes and lifted her gaze to him.

"Good morning," she replied, her voice a gorgeous, groggy purr that sent a pleasant hum through his chest.

As she shifted to sit up, the blanket slipping from her shoulders, Cole reached for her hand, pulling her gently back down beside him. "Not yet," he said, a playful note in his voice.

She laughed softly, her cheeks flushing, but didn't resist. Their lips met in an unhurried kiss, one that quickly deepened, revealing a growing familiarity between them. The passion from their wedding night hadn't faded—in fact, it simmered just below the surface, ready to ignite at the smallest spark, as it had each night since. Cole shifted, turning her onto her back as he deepened the kiss.

When they finally broke apart, Cole rested her forehead against hers, his breath mingling with hers.

"We'll be late to break our fast," she murmured, though she made no move to leave.

"Let them wait," Cole replied with a grin, his fingers brushing a stray lock of hair from her face.

"Anwen will come knocking," his wife reminded him, since the maid arrived each morning to help Ailsa dress.

"I dropped the bolt in place last night," Cole announced—a practice he'd begun after the first morning, when Anwen's arrival had shocked the hell out of him. Apparently, he'd learned, he was expected not to feel awkward, to rise naked from the bed and go about his day as if there wasn't a third person in the room, another one of those medieval things that would take some getting used to.

Ailsa grinned and moved her hands around his back, and down over his butt. "Ye have all the best ideas."

***

"I was never interested in hunting for just this reason," Tank whispered. "This shit is for the birds."

Cole grunted softly in agreement. Crouched low behind a cluster of snow-dusted bushes, the cold had seeped into his bones hours ago, and his patience was wearing as thin as the layer of frost on the meadow they overlooked. He was having trouble sitting still for so long as well. He'd kept himself busy by thinking of a million things he'd rather be doing or should be doing.

Eventually, his mind had wandered to Ailsa.

He pictured her as she'd been this morning when they'd parted, the wondrous smile she'd given him when he'd said he'd see her later and he'd winked at her playfully, a suggestive gleam in his eye. Her cheeks had pinkened—God, he loved her blushes. There was something thrilling about coaxing them from her, knowing it was him who made her skin bloom with warmth.

A sharp, muted crack of a twig broke his reverie. One of the men in their party, stationed farther downwind, raised a cautious hand, signaling that the red deer were approaching.

Tank shifted beside him, brushing snow from his knees and squinting out into the clearing where the deer were expected to come. "I don't even know why we're here," he grumbled. "Unless they're hoping we stab the deer to death."

Cole agreed with this as well. The deer hunting involved the bow and arrow, a skill in which neither he nor Tank had shown any proficiency yet.

Dersey had snorted a laugh the other day when Tank bugged him for more instruction, had said, "Calm down there, mate. One middling skill at a time."

Cole proposed now, "Maybe if we *aren't* so quiet, we won't be allowed on these hunts in the future."

"I like where you're going with this," Tank said.

But neither of them made a sound, knowing how far a single stag would go toward feeding Torr Cinnteag.

A moment later, Tank said, "I'm wondering if they'll shoot me if do make noise and scare off dinner."

"I wouldn't put it past them," Cole answered, almost mechanically.

He didn't really believe that. Though he still felt that he and Tank were looked upon as outsiders—odd and inept outsiders—they'd made great strides fitting in with the Sinclair men. In a way, it wasn't so different from what he'd experienced as a firefighter or as a member of the Bandit's team. Sure, the stakes here were life-and-death in a way his old life couldn't quite match, but the camaraderie, the good-natured rivalry and ribbing, the way men built bonds by giving each other hell while sharing experiences and long hours together—that was the same.

Whether it was hauling hoses through smoke-filled buildings or taking hits on the field for your teammates, there was a mutual respect that grew from those shared experiences. The Sinclairs might wield swords instead of axes or lacrosse sticks, but the way they ribbed each other, the way they worked together when it mattered, that kind of thing was apparently timeless.

A few minutes later, when still not a single deer had yet to emerge into the clearing, Tank shifted again.

"I don't know how you sit so still for so long," he said, "but I guess you got something to keep yourself occupied. You were grinning a few minutes ago and I hadn't said a word, so I guess you're thinking about your new bride."

"Might be," was all Cole allowed, the grin returning, but mostly for how put-out Tank sounded.

"Yeah, I'd be dreaming of her, too, is she were mine. Christ, dude, can you believe it? You're friggin married," he whispered dramatically. "In the friggin' fourteenth century."

Funny, he didn't think of it like that. To Cole, he was simply married to Ailsa. And yeah, though the married part was still a shock, the fact that it was Ailsa somehow made it all right. More than all right, actually, since there wasn't one thing he didn't like about it. Not one damn thing.

"Pretty soon there'll be little Coles and tiny Ailsas running all over Torr Cinnteag," Tank went on, his tone light. "Bugging Uncle Tank for piggyback rides," he imagined. "Maybe I'll be able by then to teach *them* how to ride horses and shoot arrows."

Tank's words hit Cole hard, knocking the proverbial wind out of him.

"What?" Tank asked, his grin fading as he noticed Cole's reaction.

Cole shook his head but said nothing, his mind suddenly racing.

Children. Ailsa pregnant.

The thought should have filled him with joy—and a part of him did feel a sudden flash of that—but it also brought with it a tidal wave of dread.

What if she did get pregnant? What if they had a child, and then he... disappeared? Zapped back through time just as suddenly and inexplicably as he'd been brought here? How could he live with himself knowing he might abandon her, leave her to raise their child alone? Worse still, how could he live with not being there to see their child grow up, to guide them, to hold them? The idea clawed at him, tightening his chest.

Cole's mind flicked back to his mother, to her words in her final days when cancer had stolen everything but her fierce love for him. *I'm not afraid of dying*, she had said, her voice thin and weak but steady. *I'm afraid of not seeing you grow. I won't get to see the man you'll become, the life you'll live. That's the heartbreak of it.*

At the time, he hadn't truly understood. He'd been too young, too focused on the fear of losing her, being left alone with his indifferent father. Her words, in truth, had been little comfort to him. Only now, as the weight of the future and the possibility of fatherhood loomed over him, did he grasp the depth of his mother's sorrow. Now, he understood her heartbreak with a clarity that knocked the breath from his lungs. He imagined holding a child of his own, feeling their tiny fingers curl around his, watching their first steps, their first words—and then imagined losing it all in an instant. The pain of it was stark, brutal, as if it were reality already.

"Cole?" Tank pressed, concern creeping into his tone.

Cole forced a smile, though it didn't quite reach his eyes. "It's nothing. Just a lot to think about."

It wasn't nothing, though.

Ahead, the faintest rustle stirred the air as a cluster of deer began to emerge cautiously from the tree line. Their sharp ears twitched at every sound, their noses testing the cold for scents of danger. The Sinclair men held their positions, the tension thickening in the air.

The hunt was on.

***

Cole found Father Gilbert inside the chapel, kneeling on the stone step before the altar, exactly where Cole had stood to be wed to Ailsa. The priest's head was bowed in prayer, his hands clasped tightly, a picture of devotion and serenity. Cole lingered near the door, unwilling to disturb the moment. He shoved his hands into his pockets, having worn his jeans today as wash day was still another few days off and his breeches were—as Aunt Rosie would have said of clothes beyond dirty— *walking*.

For several long minutes, he waited, letting his gaze wander. His eyes were drawn to the tall, slim stained-glass window behind the altar, a cascade of vibrant reds, blues, and golds glowing faintly in the soft winter light. The image was of the Blessed Mother cradling the infant Jesus, her serene face tilted toward the child in her arms.

Cole stared at it, the simplicity of the scene striking something deep within him. He'd seen similar windows in churches as a boy, hundreds of them he was sure, back when his mother had taken him to Sunday Mass without fail. He'd barely paid attention back then, more interested in sneaking a piece of gum from her purse or counting the tiles on the ceiling.

Now, though, it hit differently. The tenderness in the mother's expression, the trust in the child's tiny grasp—it was no longer just an artistic depiction to him. It was a vision of everything he might lose, everything he might never get to experience.

After a few minutes, when Father Gilbert hadn't moved, Cole walked quietly forward and sat in the first pew, the seat narrow, the wood cold. His attention returned to the stained glass and it dawned on him that the image depicted only mother and child. No father. He frowned, the familiar ache of disappointment resurfacing. His father had been a hard worker, a good provider, dedicated to his job as a firefighter, a hero to everyone else—but often a stranger to his own son. He was the disciplinarian, often gruff—rarely did he smile—and hardly ever did he spend time with Cole. They didn't play catch, he hadn't taught Cole how to ride a bike, he hadn't gone to any of Cole's games. After his mom passed, his father had withdrawn even further, had become even colder.

Cole remembered watching his dad sit in the living room chair, staring blankly at the TV after long shifts, as if the weight of the world—and the grief they both shared—was too much to carry. And yet, they never spoke about it. Never shared the burden. The isolation Cole felt during those years had been suffocating.

He'd vowed then, as a kid trying to make sense of loss, that if he ever became a father, he'd be different. He wouldn't hold his children at arm's length. He'd be there—not just in the room, but *present.* He wouldn't let his kids wonder if they mattered, wouldn't let them feel unseen.

The knot of dread in his chest deepened as he thought about Ailsa, about the children they might have.

"Cole?" Father Gilbert's gentle voice broke through his thoughts, pulling him back to the present.

Startled to awareness, that the priest was no longer kneeling, but standing and facing him, Cole exhaled, taking his hands from his pockets.

"Something troubles you, lad," the priest observed, coming to sit beside Cole.

Cole hesitated, then sat back. "I need your advice, Father. About something... I don't even know how to categorize it."

Father Gilbert regarded him patiently, his weathered face calm and open.

Cole took a deep breath, searching for the right words. "Whether you believe it or not, it is true. I am not from this time. I was born in 1995—that's where I'm from. And I don't know how or why I ended up here. But what worries me is that I might not stay. I didn't choose to come here, and I'm afraid I won't have a choice if I'm taken back to the present...or, what I know as the present, two-thousand and twenty-four."

Father Gilbert's brows furrowed slightly, but he said nothing, letting Cole continue.

"Ailsa..." Cole said softly. He swallowed hard and started again. "If we have children... what if I...?" He shook his head, his hands clenching into fists. "What if we have children and I'm moved again through time? I don't...I'm not sure..." his voice trailed off, his thoughts jumbled beyond reason.

The priest stood quietly for a long moment, his expression thoughtful. "You seek certainty in a world that offers little of it," he said finally. "Whether you remain or are taken, whether Ailsa bears children or not, you must live as though each day is your last. Commit yourself fully to the life you have now, or you risk losing both the present and the future."

Cole nodded slowly, his mind still whirling but finding a small measure of clarity in the priest's words.

Father Gilbert continued, "We've lost hundreds of men in half a decade, men who had hopes and dreams before they became victims of another's greed and want of power. Even now, the war will resume, death will claim more of us, but lad, do not allow that to dampen hope. Live a life of good intention, that is all we can ever do. Do not refuse to commit because you don't know what tomorrow will bring. Not one of us does. You are strong, as is Ailsa. If, as you fear, you might be taken from here—and her—you will survive, as will she. Ailsa is loving and giving and if...if you were somehow taken away, you cannot fear that your child would not know love, not be cherished, cared for, protected. Live purposefully, lad. Any moment not lived intentionally is only wasted moments."

"But I've never..." Cole began, grimacing a bit.

"Loved another as you do Ailsa?" Father Gilbert guessed, a small, pleased smile curving his mouth.

Cole nodded tightly, with Father Gilbert having voiced what he, himself, had suspected.

"What would you do if you knew *this* was your only life?" Father Gilbert asked gently.

"I would...live it. Embrace it," he said, knowing the priest was right, already beginning to feel much less paralyzed by fear.

"There is your answer, lad. To do any less is a disservice to both yourself and Ailsa. And to any child that might be born of your union."

"You're right," Cole agreed. "I know you're right." He exhaled at length and faced the priest, grinning a bit now. "I'd like to think I'd have realized that, that I'd have come to the same conclusion myself eventually."

"I'd like to think that myself, but it's probably best you came to me," Father Gilbert deadpanned.

Cole stared at him, the normally stoic, reserved priest, and burst out laughing, so surprised by this show of humor.

"Fair enough," he allowed. He stood and extended his hand to the priest, still smiling. "Thank you, Father."

The priest clasped his hand and laid his other over the top of them. "Be well, lad. Be at peace here and now."

Nodding once more, Cole took his leave. Somewhat calmed, he made his way to the keep to wash up for supper, oblivious to the person ducking around the side of the chapel, into the shadows.

Chapter Nineteen

Ailsa moved quietly through the corridors of the keep, her steps soft against the stone floors as she searched for Tavis. The further she walked from the bustling kitchen and the hall, where preparations for supper were in full swing, the more the silence of the keep settled around her. This part of the castle, far from the noise and activity, felt distant, almost detached, as she made her way toward the steward's chamber.

She respected Tavis's authority—always had—but in this matter, she knew he was wrong. He had been for some time. Ailsa had caught Ceitidh, one of the kitchen servants, leaving the plate room months ago, with no reason to be there. She'd voiced her concerns to Tavis then, but he'd dismissed her suspicions as mere paranoia. Today, though, Ailsa had found Ceitidh near the treasury once more. While she hadn't searched the servant's person, she'd grown more certain of her suspicions since that first encounter.

Since then, Ailsa had kept a closer eye on the household's inventory—silver goblets, plates, utensils—and had recently noticed a troubling discrepancy. At least half a dozen goblets and plates had gone missing since her last count over a month ago. The theft was no longer a suspicion; it was fact. Now, Ailsa had to confront Tavis again, knowing that he might dismiss her once more, at which time she vowed she would take matters into her own hands.

Ailsa had always suspected that Tavis had dismissed her allegations about Ceitidh simply because he fancied her. While it was common knowledge that Tavis didn't usually involve himself with the servants, it was also no secret that he had an ongoing relationship with Lias, a widow from the village. Ailsa couldn't help but think that perhaps Tavis kept Ceitidh around as a back-up, in case his relationship with the widow soured. After all, everyone also knew that Lias expected to marry the laird, but Tavis had resisted, unable to bring himself to wed someone he considered beneath his station.

But now, as she neared the steward's office, she hesitated.

She could hear Tavis's voice—low, controlled, but edged with something sharper, something darker—coming from the open door. He was in the middle of a conversation, though she couldn't quite make out the words. Ailsa knew better than to barge in when his tone was like that, when his mood was already foul.

She lingered in the hallway, fingers tracing the stone of the wall as she debated. A small, quiet part of her urged her to turn back—to handle the matter with Ceitidh herself. As mistress of Torr Cinnteag, she had every right to do so. But the rest of her wanted to present her case, to advise Tavis that he was wrong about Ceitidh—the woman was not innocent.

Stick with the widow, she wanted to tell him.

A moment later, as she stood waiting, Domhnall came sprinting down the corridor toward her, flushed and out of breath, his expression tense with urgency.

"Domhnall," she gasped, an instinctive fear gripping her as she took in his agitated appearance. "What is amiss?"

He shot her a quick, dark look—one that struck her as unusually impolite—and, without missing a beat, said with a sharp edge to his voice, "I need to speak to the laird, nae ye."

The tone in his words hit her hard, especially after she'd always imagined him to be someone who held her in high regard, was mayhap even smitten with her. But there was no mistaking the condescension in his manner now, and it left her momentarily stunned.

Tavis, possibly having heard the small commotion, whipped the door open just as Domhnall went to open it.

"What's this?" Tavis barked, his fuse short today apparently.

In the face of the laird's displeasure, Domhnall shuffled his feet and stammered, "It's...," he paused and glanced at Ailsa and then said through lips that barely moved, "it's about Cole Carter, Laird. I need to speak with ye—privately." Another pointed look was thrown at Ailsa.

But Ailsa's heart flipped, suddenly unconcerned with Domhnall's odd manner. "Good heavens, Domhnall, is Cole all right? Has he been injured?"

Tavis's lips pressed into a thin line. "Out with it, lad. I've nae time for games—"

Stubbornly, Domhnall thinned his lips and shook his head. "I'll nae say it in front of the lass—"

"My sister's ears," Tavis growled impatiently, "are as guid as mine. Speak, lad," he commanded.

Still, Domhnall hesitated. Ailsa thought Tavis was about to go through the roof. The steward had come to the door as well, stood peeking over the laird's shoulder—even he seemed annoyed with Domhnall's tentativeness.

"I'm about three seconds away from relieving yer body of what seems to be a worthless head," Tavis warned.

Domhnall cast a nervous glance at Ailsa, who gave him a steady look. "Whatever it is, say it plainly, Domhnall," she urged, her voice firm but not unkind.

The soldier took a deep breath. "I overheard him speakin' with Father Gilbert, Laird," he said, addressing Tavis and not Ailsa. "He said—he said he's nae from this time. That he comes from... the future."

The words hung in the air. Ailsa froze, her heart hammering in her chest as she tried to process what she'd just heard.

Tavis, however, was less restrained.

"Have ye lost yer bluidy wits?" Tavis growled, stepping toward the young man, who shrank back under his glare. "The future? What nonsense is this?"

"It's the truth, Laird," Domhnall insisted, though his voice trembled. "I heard it with my own ears." He flicked his thumb toward Ailsa. "Her husband said he was born—I dinna recall the year but it's...in the future, hundreds of years. Father dinna seem so surprised, ye ken, so I figured he already kent this. And he said he dinna ken how he got here, and how he fears he might be er, taken back." Color crept up into his cheeks and his hands clenched and unclenched as he briefly stared at the ground. "He said he was worried about...about getting the lass with child and then being ripped away."

Alarmed by this, that anyone such as Domhnall knew Cole's truth—Domhnall with his loose tongue—Ailsa forced a laugh and placed her hand to her chest, trying to stave off disaster. "God's teeth, lad. Ye had me worried something terrible had befallen Cole. Quite obviously, ye misheard the conversation ye eavesdropped on."

From behind Tavis, the steward harrumphed, a sound of disapproval that seemed to echo her stance. Spying on a private conversation was an egregious breach of conduct, after all.

Domhnall, however, squared his shoulders, his earlier hesitation evaporating as he fixed Ailsa with a look that was startlingly self-assured—and contemptuous. "I ken what I heard, mistress," he said flatly, his tone devoid of any attempt at appeasement. "Ask him yerself if ye doubt me, Laird. But I'm telling ye, he's nae from here—he's fae, or immortal, or some such thing."

Tavis's jaw tightened, his irritation plain as his eyes flickered between Domhnall and Ailsa. Clearly, he was no more inclined to entertain such claims than she was, but the soldier's conviction demanded some response.

Ailsa again attempted to dismiss Domhnall's claims as nonsense. "Tavis, surely ye dinna believe that—

He held up his hand for silence. "All the more reason to put such rubbish to rest here and now. Go on then, soldier. Fetch Father Gilbert," he snapped. "And bring Carter here. Now." As an afterthought, he shouted down the corridor, "And bring the other one, Tank!"

***

As it was nearly the dinner hour, Tavis chose to have the meeting in his private office abovestairs. He signaled to the steward, Murchadh, to follow, knowing the man would dutifully record notes on any discussions concerning the happenings inside Torr Cinnteag. Tavis swept through the hall with a purposeful stride, his voice ringing out as he ordered Dersey to be summoned and brought to him at once.

Filled with dread, wishing she could somehow warn Cole of the impending inquisition, Ailsa trailed reluctantly behind her brother, her steps heavy with dread. Her brother had made it clear she was to accompany him and attend the conference as well.

"See what kind of man ye've wed," he grumbled over his shoulder, as if Cole might not merely deny that Domhnall had heard correctly, and the matter would be put to rest, Tavis having learned nothing.

Inside his private office, Ailsa again appealed to her brother. "Tavis, ye dinna really believe any of what Domhnall said. Please tell me ye dinna."

"Nae, I dinna believe in his fae folk nonsense—a man passing through the centuries. But something was said, I'm sure, something damning, and I mean to get to the bottom of it."

A bitter scowl twisted her lips, dismayed by her his words. "When will ye trust him? What has Cole ever—"

"I'll trust him when I ken the truth," Tavis snapped. "Do ye take me for a fool, sister? He's hiding something—come from Spain, he says—bah! He's nae more a Spaniard than I. Dinna ken how to ride, how to fight—dinna ken anything at all—"

"But ye allowed me to wed him?" Ailsa challenged.

"Necessary evil, that," Tavis declared hotly. "There was nae escaping the truth—the consequences—that there'd be nae match for ye with another clan. But I liked the idea of having him right here under my nose."

Ailsa harrumphed, her own wrath increasing. "And what have ye learned? That he's willing to learn, that he's able, that he will devote himself to Torr Cinnteag, to the Sinclairs. Tavis, I swear to God, I dinna ken who ye are anymore. I dinna ken—"

She stopped when she realized that Murchadh had arrived, being so much slower to climb several flights of stairs than Tavis and Ailsa.

Dersey entered the chamber next, his brow furrowed in confusion, followed almost immediately by Father Gilbert, whose expression mirrored the captain's. The unusual timing of the summons—just before the supper hour—and the presence of Ailsa seemed to have caught them both off guard.

"Laird?" Father Gilbert asked cautiously.

"Wait," Tavis said sharply, raising a hand as he settled behind his desk. The table before him was cluttered with vellum sheets, a stack of ledgers, ink pots, quills, and the stubs of candles, though he paid them no mind. His gaze fixed on the window, his brooding silence casting a shadow over the room.

The door opened again, and Domhnall strode in, flushed from his errand. "Here they come, laird," he announced, his chest heaving slightly. He stationed himself beside the door, hand resting on the hilt of his sword, his stance resolute as though prepared to defend both his claim and his laird.

Tavis thought to issue a warning to the young man. "Yer first closed-door conference, lad, and I'll warn ye now—what is said here dinna leave this chamber. If I hear any more talk of this madness, I'll assume it came from ye and the punishment will be severe, as befitting the crime, ignoring a direct order."

Domhnall gulped but nodded smartly.

Moments later, Cole appeared in the doorway, his steps measured as he entered. His brow lifted slightly, clearly surprised by the assembly awaiting him. His eyes flicked to Ailsa, who stood to the left of her brother's desk, and though she tried to convey a silent warning in her expression, their exchange was fleeting—too brief for him to glean much, especially under Tavis's watchful gaze.

Tank followed close behind, his casual demeanor a stark contrast to the tension thickening the air. Over the weeks, Ailsa had come to realize that Tank rarely allowed solemnity to linger unchallenged. True to form, he surveyed the room with a wide grin, then clapped his hands together. "A seat at the big boys' table. What's the occasion, chief?"

Ignoring Tank's flippant comment, Tavis motioned for Domhnall to close the door. Then, fixing Cole—not Tank—with an unrelenting stare, Tavis leaned back in his chair, deceptively at ease. Absently, he toyed with one of the quills on his desk, flipping it end over end, then tapping it on the wooden surface in a rhythm too slow to be casual.

"Domhnall claims ye've been tellin' tales," he began, his voice sharper than the edge of any blade, "about being from another time. Is it true?"

Cole's gaze flicked to Ailsa, his expression softening for the briefest moment before he straightened his shoulders. "It's true," he said simply, his voice steady but low.

Ailsa gasped, the sound escaping her lips before she could stop it. Quickly, she recovered, stepping closer to Cole, though she was uncertain if it was to shield him from her brother's ire or to steady herself.

"From another time, ye are," Tavis repeated, twirling the quill between his fingers as if the conversation were of no more consequence than the coming of winter snow. The calculated indifference in his tone sent a chill down Ailsa's spine.

Cole nodded grimly. "Yeah."

Dersey, standing rigid near the wall, seethed quietly and crossed himself. "Mother Mary save us."

Tavis's hand paused mid-flip, the quill now pointing directly at Cole. "Are ye daft then?" he asked, his calm voice a dangerous contradiction to the undercurrent of fury in his eyes.

"No," Cole answered, his breath controlled but his jaw tight.

"Are ye fae? A sorcerer?"

Cole shook his head, drawing in a large breath. "No," he said on his exhale.

The quill flipped again, tapping lightly against the desk. Tavis shifted his focus to Father Gilbert, who stood at attention with his hands clasped behind his back. "Ye ken this?"

Ailsa's heart clenched. Though she had been willing to lie for Cole, she doubted Father Gilbert would—or even could.

"Aye, laird," the priest admitted, his tone measured. "I have been aware of Cole's...story."

"Ye dinna ken *I* needed to be made aware as well?" Tavis asked, his voice still calm but the quill's sharp point now aimed squarely at the priest.

Father Gilbert met his gaze evenly. "If I'm to bring to you each and every improbable tale, laird," he replied, "I fear there would be little time for anything else in your day."

Tavis did not like his answer, and waved an angry, dismissive hand at him before returning his attention to the two men standing directly before his desk.

"And ye?" he asked Tank, flicking the quill once more before stilling it in his grip. "Ye move through time as well?"

Her brother's voice, calm and almost polite, was far more unsettling to Ailsa than his usual tirades. It was the clouds holding back the storm, and she could feel the thunder gathering beneath his controlled facade.

Tank, unshaken, crossed his arms. "Chief, *we* didn't move through time," he said, his tone matter-of-fact. "Someone—or some*thing*—moved us. We had nothing to do with it, had no idea it was going to happen, and...well, frankly, no idea it *had* happened until it became obvious we weren't in the twenty-first century anymore."

Tavis didn't move, didn't even blink as Tank spoke. Then, slowly, he chuckled, the sound low and devoid of humor. Ailsa's breath hitched as the sound settled in her chest like a stone.

"The twenty-first century," Tavis repeated, each syllable drawn out, as if tasting the words for the first time. He raised his familiar blue eyes to Ailsa. "Ye ken of this as well, I take it."

She swallowed hard and nodded.

"And yet ye married him—a man evidently devoid of sanity."

"I married a man who is warm and kind, who—"

"Rubbish that," he spat, throwing down the quill. "and soft ye are, believing he's nae up to nae guid." He stood then, opening his mouth as if to unleash a tirade, wearing a suddenly thunderous glower.

Father Gilbert raised a calming hand. "Peace, Laird," he urged. "This man has been nothing but forthright in his actions and his intentions since arriving here. Whatever brought him to us, it was no act of malice."

"And why should we believe that?" Dersey cut in, his tone sharp. "For all we ken, he's bringin' trouble down on us just by bein' here."

Ailsa leaned into the table, speaking before he did. "Enough!" She cried and faced her brother. "Ye ken that he's nae mad, ye ken that he—"

Cole shifted beside her, his hand pressing gently over her clenched fist. "Ailsa, it's fine," he said, his tone steady and calming, though his jaw tightened slightly. He met her gaze briefly, a silent reassurance, before turning his focus back to Tavis. "Listen," Cole began, his voice firm but measured, carrying no trace of hostility despite the tension in the room. "I don't know how this happened. We didn't ask for it, didn't seek it out, but we're not part of—or engaged in—some black magic or whatever you're imagining. We've done nothing to harm you or anyone at Torr Cinnteag." He paused briefly, gauging Tavis's unreadable expression before continuing. "You want the whole story?" he asked, his voice sharpening slightly, though still controlled. "Fine. Tank and I were living in the year 2024. Life looks a lot different in some ways—technology, the way people live day to day—but in other ways, it's not so different, especially when it comes to how people treat each other. We can talk about that sometime if you're interested," he added curtly, a flicker of dry humor in his tone. "Anyway, we were hiking on a mountain trail. Just walking, nothing unusual, when the air...changed. I can't even describe it, what happened. Then I blacked out. When I woke up, I was lying in snow—snow that hadn't been there when we started climbing—and Tank was nowhere in sight. I didn't know what had happened, where I was, or why—and I still don't. That's the same story I told Ailsa, the same one I told Father Gilbert—because it's the truth. I don't know what brought us here, but I searched for Tank for nearly a day before I stumbled into your domain. The first person I saw was Ailsa. I had to ask her what year it was because the reality of what seemed to have happened—it was too impossible to believe." Cole leaned forward slightly, his eyes narrowing. "You think you're struggling to believe? You think I'm crazy?" he asked, his voice dropping to a quieter, more intense tone. "Yeah, I've been there. I'm *still* there," he added, his words deliberate now, his frustration finally breaking through. "Because I don't know what happened or why."

The room fell into an uneasy silence, all eyes on Tavis as he weighed Cole's words. Finally, he turned to Father Gilbert. "And what say ye, priest? What counsel do ye give me on this madness?"

Father Gilbert folded his hands again. "I say that Cole Carter's origins matter less than his actions. And his actions, thus far, have shown him to be a man true to his word."

A knock sounded at the door, which Domhnall opened, revealing not any house servants possibly wondering if supper should be delayed, but a young man Ailsa had never seen before, wringing a silent gasp from her.

He stood tall and lean, with light brown hair falling just to his collar. His eyes darted around the room with a mixture of caution and curiosity, eventually settling on Tavis. He wore a practical tunic of deep green, well-fitted and free of excessive adornment, paired with a sturdy belt and boots scuffed from long travel. In his hand, he clutched a rolled parchment sealed with crimson wax, its edges slightly frayed from handling. The sight of it immediately dispelled Ailsa's fleeting and fanciful notion that he might have also stumbled through time—his attire and demeanor rooted him firmly in their current reality.

The young man stepped forward hesitantly, the scroll held out in offering. "A message for the laird," he announced, his voice steady but carrying the faint rasp of someone who had likely spent days on the road.

Tavis shouted, "For feck's sake, what now?"

Domhnall received the scroll and passed it to Tavis, who seized it with such force that the vellum crinkled under his grip. He snapped the wax seal without hesitation and unrolled the message. The furrow in his brow deepened as his eyes scanned the lines, and a vein throbbed faintly at his temple.

For a long moment, Tavis remained rigid, as though the words had gutted him. Then, with a sharp exhale, his shoulders sagged, and the tension in his jaw slackened into something more raw—weariness, perhaps even fear. His hand trembled slightly as he placed the scroll on the table, smoothing it flat as though the act might lessen the burden of what it contained.

Finally, he lowered himself into his chair, the motion deliberate but heavy, as if his legs could no longer bear the strain. He rested his forearms on the edge of the desk, his fingers lacing tightly together, and stared at the message for a heartbeat longer. The room remained silent, the gravity of his reaction more unsettling than any outburst could have been.

At length, Father Gilbert prompted, "Laird?"

Seeming only then to recall that he was not alone, Tavis startled briefly and glanced up, moving his gaze over all the watchful faces.

"Tavis, what is it?"

A sigh preceded his answer, but he seemed to recover himself. He straightened in the chair and announced, "The truce expired weeks ago. I'd received word then that Edward would hunker down for the winter, that nae campaign would be instigated until spring. Now this, saying John Segrave, on Edward's orders, is assembling at Berwick on Tweed. Heading toward Edinburgh, meaning to carry out a large-scale reconnaissance as far as Kirkintilloch. Reconnaissance...mayhap more than that." He lifted his gaze, passed it over the priest and Dersey, and even included Cole and Tank in his sweeping glance once again. "Essentially paving the way, if ye will, for Edward to follow when he's ready again to make war on us." He shook his head, a fleeting grimness overcoming his fury. "*Jesu*, it willna end."

"Laird," Father Gilbert said, stepping forward, "is this...only news being passed, or are you expected—"

"Aye, Simon Fraser summons the Sinclairs to Biggar, to assemble against Segrave." He perused the missive briefly. "Possibly against Minton, mayhap Robert Neville as well," he said, his gaze straying toward Dersey. "Christ, they'll have twenty thousand men."

Ailsa's breath caught.

Father Gilbert clasped his hands together, his palms and fingers rigid and straight.

"When?" Dersey wanted to know.

"Now," Tavis answered, and then chewed the inside of his cheek. "Simon Fraser wants to shadow them, see what they're about. He needs troops now."

Murchadh advised, "Laird, we dinna have the means to send ye off well-supplied, nae if we want to feed Torr Cinnteag o'er the winter."

"Damn," Dersey mused, "I kent we'd be home for Yule this year."

Tavis stared blankly for a moment, his mind likely whirring in chaos.

Tank fisted his hand. "Let's do it," he said fiercely. "Let's put all this training to work."

The laird reacted angrily to this, snapping a hard glare at Tank, as if to say he was the last person Tavis wanted fighting beside him.

"You need us," Tank reminded him. "You said yourself you didn't have the numbers for this war."

"Aye," Tavis reluctantly agreed through clenched lips, "and I'm sure as hell nae leaving ye two here while I'm gone," he barked, as if the very idea was preposterous. With greater good humor than he'd shown in the last hour, he supposed, "Mayhap ye'll meet yer fate upon a battlefield and thus dissolve the need for me to ken what to make of ye."

Ailsa's heart lurched at the thought of Cole fighting alongside her brother and all the Sinclairs—fighting at all.

"Go on then," Tavis grumbled, waving his hand, shooing them all toward the door. "Supper awaits, the last one at home. We leave with the morning light." He picked up the quill he'd been fiddling with earlier and reached for an unused sheet of vellum, preparing his response for the waiting messenger, dismissing them from his mind.

Cole took Ailsa's hand, squeezing it gently. "Come on," he prompted.

Ailsa forced herself to smile at him.

***

Cole wasn't afraid, not exactly. Fear would have been easier to define, maybe even easier to confront. Instead, he felt an unshakable sense of inadequacy, a gnawing doubt in his own ability to meet the expectations of what would be required of him. He was a man thrown into a world that demanded skills and knowledge he hadn't had the time to acquire. The weight of it pressed against him more than any tangible fear of death or injury.

In a quiet voice while they supped, he confessed to Ailsa, "I don't even know how to prepare, what to do."

"I will help ye," she said simply, calmly.

Later, they spent the night tangled in each other's arms, bodies speaking the words neither dared to say aloud. The heat between them was desperate, almost frantic, a silent acknowledgment of his imminent departure and the possibility that this might be their last night together.

Still, as she slept beside him, her head resting lightly against his chest, Cole stared at the ceiling, wrestling with the storm of emotions raging in his chest. He wanted to tell her how much she had come to mean to him. But what good would it do to burden her with his feelings now, on the eve of his departure? To confess the depth of his feelings when there was no promise he'd survive to see her again? He feared giving her hope that might turn to sorrow. And, if he was being honest with himself, he wasn't sure he could handle the rejection, should she not feel the same. Better to leave with her last memory of him unmarred by clumsy declarations.

Instead, he tightened his hold around her, pressing a kiss to her hair as he closed his eyes.

In the morning, amid the bustle of the courtyard, where hundreds of people readied to leave or prepared to say goodbye, Cole and Ailsa stood close, their parting overshadowed by an attempt to appear brave for one another, though both were terrified of what the day and following weeks might bring.

"Like as nae, it will come to naught," Ailsa said, her voice calm despite the tears threatening to spill. "Mayhap they're nae moving to make war, but only scouting."

Cole managed a weak smile, attempting to lighten the heavy atmosphere. "I'll try like hell not to embarrass you."

"Mayhap instead," she countered, a faint smile breaking through her sorrow, "try like hell to come back to me."

He kissed her, long enough to feel her tremble, brief enough to keep the moment from breaking them both. When he pulled back, her hands lingered on his arms, her fingers curled into his sleeve.

"You're strong, Cole," she told him, her voice steady. "You're capable, and fierce."

He grinned. "Okay, I get it. Positive affirmations."

"It's nae just words," she said firmly. "Truth is what it is."

"I wish I had as much faith in me as you do, Ailsa."

She searched his face. "Did ye find yerself frightened or anxious, mayhap even outright terrified, in your...in that other life?"

He shrugged, drawing the motion out as he considered. "Yeah, I mean, sure. I've known fear, anxiety, dread."

"And ye walked through it, did ye nae? You're still the same man, here in this time, are ye nae? Ye'll face this as steadfastly as ye did any obstacle in your own time."

He didn't have the heart to tell her that the fears he'd faced in the twenty-first century—raging fires, death, the loss of friends—seemed to pale in comparison to what lay ahead. This wasn't a simulated training exercise or a controlled disaster response. It was war, and he felt woefully unprepared. It was like sending men overseas, Marines or any US military, with barely a week of training.

Still, he nodded, unwilling to let her worry more than she already did. Her fear was there, just under the surface, waiting to break free once he was gone, he was sure. "I got this. I can do this," he said, pulling her closer. "But not without one more kiss goodbye."

Their lips met again, a bittersweet blend of hope and heartache, a silent promise to find their way back to each other, no matter the odds.

"When I get on that horse," he said softly, his breath brushing against her lips as they parted, "I won't be able to look back. Don't wait for a final wave or anything like that." He didn't want his last sight of Ailsa to be her sadness or the fear she tried so hard to hide. Gently, he added, "I packed away some images from last night. That's how I want to remember you."

He might have pulled away then, but Ailsa held him firm. She locked her gaze with his, her expression fierce. "I would rather have this with ye, all those small but glorious moments since we wed, than naught at all."

Her chest tightened and he fought back the maddening tingling of tears at the back of his throat and eyes. "Same. Absolutely." Glorious moments, indeed. He kissed her one more time.

Ten minutes later, as they rode with Tavis and the Sinclair army, Cole turned to Tank, his voice low but edged with uncertainty. "I'm not sure I can actually kill someone," he admitted.

Tank, ever the Marine, didn't hesitate. "You will if you have to. You've heard it before, maybe even seen it in some meme on social media—this isn't about fighting *them*, the English. It's about fighting for what's *behind* us. If the English prevail, Cole, Ailsa and everyone at Torr Cinnteag are in danger. We fight for what's behind us."

Cole frowned, his thoughts circling back to yesterday. "Maybe I should've stabbed that red deer," he muttered. "Might've felt better prepared if I'd at least swung a sword for real."

Tank laughed. "Seems you'll have plenty of opportunity for that." He leaned toward him between their horses, extending a hand. "Whatever happens, it's been an honor, my friend. You've been solid, through and through, for more than a decade. One of the good guys—always have been. We've been here a month, trapped in this crazy century, and not once have you blamed me for dragging you to Scotland in the first place."

Honestly, the idea of blame had never crossed his mind.

He pumped Tank's hand. "Same, Tank. I'm proud to call you friend. And frankly, I think I'd have gone crazy here if not for you."

"What a freakin' adventure, though—right?"

Cole laughed despite himself, as they marched toward what might be their end.

He thought of Ailsa. "Yeah, what an adventure."

Chapter Twenty

The march was grueling, a steady, punishing trudge, often through deep snow and in biting winds that stretched the Sinclair army thin. For all the snow he'd seen living in Western New York, Cole was sure he'd never hated it more. Here, there was no relief from it; they did not return to any nice, warm house, putting their feet up in front of a blazing winter fire at the end of the day. Here, the end of the day only meant giving the horses a rest while they attempted to keep warm out in the mean elements, not daring to light fires at all once they'd gone too far south. For a week, they advanced toward Biggar, the sharp cold cutting through even the thickest woolens. The weight of their gear and the unrelenting terrain tested even the hardiest among them.

As Christmas loomed on the horizon, both Tank and Cole found themselves sinking into bouts of melancholy. They thought about the people back home—those who, after so many months of silence, might now be grieving their absence or assuming the worst, that their lives had ended somewhere in Scotland.

For Cole, the thought of Aunt Rosie's sorrow was almost too much to bear. Same as she was to him, he was basically all the family she had left. Rosie had envisioned her later years surrounded by the sound of children's laughter—Cole's children—filling her home with life and joy. The weight of knowing she was facing this Christmas without him, likely mourning what she thought was an irretrievable loss, gnawed at him until he thought constantly, desperately, trying to imagine some way to get word to her.

There were several evenings where even hardy, optimistic Tank was quiet, reflective, his gaze lingering on the fire while his expression was either blank or troubled. They didn't talk about it, but Cole was pretty sure he was thinking along the same lines as Cole, of family and Christmas.

What little comfort they did know during the march could be credited to Ailsa.

He silently thanked her once again for her foresight and efficiency. Her knowhow and care were evident, for it was she who'd ensured that he was as well-prepared as possible for conditions far removed from Torr Cinnteag, and from his time. Somehow she'd managed to procure another thick, woolen cloak, clasped with a sturdy brooch, several tunics, and linen undergarments. A woolen cap and heavy leather gloves were given to him to protect him against the cold. Though she'd told him the army itself—specifically the quartermaster and the armorer—were responsible for supplying the army with food, weapons, and gear, she'd given him a shirt of chainmail and a padded gambeson for protection, and had surprised him with a small dagger, which she'd advised should be tucked into his boot. Though the army had its own cook, Ailsa had made sure Cole had his own pack containing dried provisions—salted meal, oatcakes, dried fruits—and a fire-starting kit, flint and steel. Above and beyond those generous necessities, she supplied him with a rolled-up blanket, which she'd shown him how to strap to the back of his saddle, and some basic medicinal supplies—linen bandages, a small jar of salve, and an herbs she said to brew if he found himself with a fever. She'd come to bed late the night before they'd departed, having managed to assemble all these things for him. Tank, too, had benefitted from Ailsa's preparations. She'd ensured both men carried the proper gear and provisions for the march and the fight that might come.

After seven days, the Sinclair army reached Biggar, where the sight of Simon Fraser's forces was a welcome relief. Thousands of Scots had gathered, their banners flapping defiantly in the icy wind. The combined armies set out the next morning, their destination clear: John Segrave's massive English contingent, reported to be marching toward Edinburgh.

They were joined in the next week by John Comyn, of Badenoch—who was sometimes referred to as *The Red* by Tavis. Tank had frowned and seethed when they'd joined with his army, "Jesus, we're living inside the pages of a history book."

Cole glanced at him, raising an eyebrow. "Comyn?" He asked, not recalling the name from any history he'd been introduced to while in Scotland visiting museums, ruins, and memorials.

Tank waved a hand toward the two men in discussion with Tavis and several other generals, as he and Tank had come to think of the many lairds combining forces in this army. "Fraser *and* Comyn, actually. Sir Simon Fraser and John Comyn III."

Cole shook his head, feeling a flicker of guilt. He knew Tank had spent hours poring over books before their trip to Scotland, while Cole had mostly coasted, assuming Tank's enthusiasm would fill in the gaps.

"They're major players, man," Tank continued, his voice low. "But they're complicated. Both of them waffled during this whole mess of a war. Fraser fought for Edward I in Flanders not that long ago. So did Comyn. Hell, they both wore English colors for years before switching back to the Scots' side. But

Comyn, he's one of the nobles who left Wallace high and dry at Falkirk."

Cole frowned, the name "Falkirk" sparking a memory. "Wait, what happened at Falkirk?"

"Disaster," Tank said, his tone bitter. "Wallace needed cavalry—desperately. The English had knights in heavy armor, longbows, the whole shebang. Wallace had infantry and hope. Comyn and his lot refused to provide cavalry support. Treachery, man, pure and simple. According to some of what I read, John and his clan hated Wallace. Showed up on the battlefield just to make it look like they were helping, but they had no intention of lifting a damn finger."

Cole digested this, his jaw tightening. "And now we're fighting alongside this guy?"

"Yeah, history's messy," Tank replied with a shrug. He leaned closer, and quieted his voice even more. "But hey, good news—Bruce takes care of Comyn in the end. Stabs him in a church, before he takes the throne. The ultimate power move."

Cole snorted at Tank's irreverence but couldn't shake the unease settling in his gut. He realized he needed to pay attention, not just to Tank's impromptu history lessons but to these men themselves. If he was going to be stuck here for any length of time, he'd need to know who the players were, who could be trusted, and more importantly, who could not.

Christmas came and went, hardly marked by the army, which had now swelled, by all estimates, to nearly 8,000 strong. A brief spell of fair weather, or at least something less frigid, gave the men a small reprieve. Daytime temperatures might have crept toward forty degrees, and those days weren't so bad. There was a bit of hunting, and venison roasted over roaring fires dotted the sprawling camp that stretched for miles. The camaraderie and temporary ease of the days felt like a reprieve before the storm, though the men rarely spoke of what lay ahead.

By the end of January, scouts reported that they had caught up with Segrave, and the real grind began.

The daily marches were relentless, each one blending into the next as they shadowed Segrave's movements. Soldiers' breaths hung heavy in the freezing air, their steps crunching through ice and frost. Even the thickest cloaks offered little defense against the cold that seeped into bones and lingered. The moments of camaraderie over campfires now felt like distant memories, replaced by the monotony of trudging mile after mile.

Cole tried not to dwell on the inevitable clash ahead, but the occasional pang of unease crept in. His muscles ached, his hands stiffened in the cold, and though he tried to focus on the rhythmic sound of boots and hooves, the looming thought of battle pressed against the edges of his mind.

One day, Tank said to Cole out of the blue, "If the fight comes, stay near me."

Cole turned his head sharply, scoffing at the suggestion. "I'm not hiding behind you, Tank."

Tank didn't laugh, his expression deadly serious. "I can't lose you, man."

Cole felt the weight of the words settle between them. "Nor I you, Tank. But let's fight side by side and keep an eye on each other's backs."

Tank nodded but added with a faint smirk, "Fine, but seriously, stay a half step behind me. It'll make it easier for you to watch my back."

Cole grinned and shook his head, but then briefly worried more about his own competence. If Tank was questioning it, Cole felt like maybe he didn't realize the exact depths of his own unpreparedness.

"Deal," Cole said but knew he wouldn't be hiding behind anyone. Able or not, it wasn't his style.

Tonight, as ever, the camp bustled with subdued activity. They remained several miles from the English, a safe distance. Small fires lit up the landscape for miles. Cole and Tank sat around the one they'd made. Cole sat near their modest blaze on a small log he'd found, a warm bowl of watery stew cradled in his hands. Tank leaned back against a tree, his breath misting in the chilly air. They talked more now than ever, had possibly exchanged more words in the last month on this march than in all their ten years of knowing each other. Sometimes, they revisited shared memories, sometimes they talked sports, wondering if they could introduce lacrosse or football to the fourteenth century. On other occasions, such as tonight, they talked of trivial things, merely to pass the time.

"Coffee wakes you up *and* makes you a better, kinder person," Cole declared with mock authority as they debated the merits of coffee versus tea.

"Tea doesn't make you jittery," Tank shot back. "Plus, you can drink it hot, cold, sweet, plain—it's versatile."

Cole rolled his eyes. "Coffee is life, man. Besides, tea tastes like wet grass."

"You've just been drinking the wrong tea."

"Right," Cole said with a smirk. "And now—along with cold-pressed juices—you're a tea connoisseur."

Tank chuckled but didn't respond, his attention shifting to a figure approaching from the shadows. Cole followed his gaze, instinctively tensing as the stranger walked with purpose directly toward them.

The man moved with a predator's ease, his steps soundless against the frozen ground. He was tall, broad-shouldered, and wrapped in a plaid cloak that had seen better days. Long, dark hair framed a rugged, angular face marked by scars—testaments to a life spent in battle, Cole might presume. His sharp eyes glinted in the firelight, their intensity almost unnerving. Cole recognized him vaguely as one of the lairds in this combined army, though he couldn't recall his name. The man's presence radiated authority, a quiet, unyielding power that made Cole instinctively straighten.

"Mind if I join ye?" the man asked, his voice a low rumble.

Cole glanced at Tank, who shrugged. "Sure," Cole said cautiously.

The man settled on his haunches near the fire, his gaze flicking between them. For a moment, he seemed to be weighing something, then he spoke. "I have a question, and I'd appreciate an honest answer."

Tank raised an eyebrow. "What's on your mind?"

"What year were ye born?" the man asked, his tone even but his gaze sharp.

Cole froze, the question striking him like a bolt out of the blue. Tank, too, looked caught off guard.

"Why do you ask?" Cole managed, his voice steady despite the jolt of nerves.

"Yer English sounds similar to that of my wife."

Cautiously, Cole wondered, "And what does that have to do with what year we were born?"

"My wife is from some place I'd never heard of—Florida?"

Cole somehow managed to prevent his eyes from widening. This man, whoever he was, shouldn't know about Florida, not unless medieval Europe had one that he didn't know about. "Is she?" He asked, his hackles raised a bit.

"Aye," said the man, his tone mild, conversational. He glanced around to ensure they weren't overheard, then leaned in slightly. "If I asked ye what an airplane was, would ye ken what I meant?" He asked cryptically even as Cole had some suspicion that he was trying to appear casual, didn't want to alarm them, or give too much away.

Cole was flabbergasted by what he guessed the man was trying to say, to impart. Never had it occurred to him that there might be others, people aside from him and Tank who'd been moved through time.

"Son of a..." Tank breathed. "Was your wife born in a year that begins with one and nine?"

Very subtle, Tank, Cole thought.

"Might've been," the man allowed, his mouth lifting in the barest grin. "Ye?"

"Maybe," Tank returned, equally as non-committal.

"Yer secret is safe with me," the man assured them. "My wife—she's nae from here either." He stood and leaned over toward Cole, extending his hand. "Reid Nicholson," he introduced himself. "Charlotte tells me this hand shake is how it's done...eventually." He said hand shake definitively as two words.

Cole rose to his feet. "Cole Carter," he introduced himself, his brain still reeling. The man's grip was firm and sure. But here was further proof, since he hadn't seen anyone use a modern-day handshake in this time. They embraced. They clasped forearms. They nodded politely as a greeting. No one shook hands, not that he'd seen.

Tank stood and introduced himself as the man shook his hand as well.

The tension in Cole's shoulders eased slightly, though his wariness didn't entirely fade. And a whole bunch of questions came to mind. "How did you know?"

Reid's shoulders shifted slightly, a bare shrug. "The way you speak. It reminded me of her."

Yeah, Cole might have guessed that modern day English all sounded the same to folks here in this century—the same, but very rare.

"Have ye been here long?" Reid asked. "In this time," he clarified, "nae here, tracking Segrave."

"No," Cole answered. "Or, what's a long time? We've been here about two months."

"How long's your wife been here?" Tank inquired. "Shit, sorry—is your wife still here?"

"Aye, she's here—more than a year now." Reid said, his voice tinged with affection. "It's nae been easy."

Tank leaned forward, his curiosity piqued. "Has she ever thought about... going back?"

Reid's jaw tightened briefly before he nodded. "She has—nae that she has any concept of how that might be accomplished. There's a part of her that misses what she left behind, but she's found her place here."

The fire crackled between them, the weight of Reid's words settling over the conversation.

"We don't..." Cole began hesitantly, "we don't tell too many people—"

"Aye, keep that close," the Nicholson laird agreed. "Ye dinna want that getting around." Reid frowned then, as if it just dawned on him, that they were with the army. "What the hell are ye doing here? In this fight?"

"We're with the Sinclairs," Tank answered simply.

The Nicholson laird's scowl darkened. "Ye've nae business dying for a fight that's nae yers," he asserted, his hands on his hips." He inclined his head toward Cole's sword. "Ye ever use that? Against another man?"

Cole shook his head.

Reid Nicholson did as well, seemingly perturbed by the answer. "Stay in the midst of the cavalry," he advised tersely. "Whatever ye do, dinna lose yer seat, yer horse. Better yet, take yerselves away—"

"We came to fight, to support the Sinclairs," Cole protested.

"Ye owe Tavis something?"

Cole wasn't surprised that this laird would know Tavis, imagining they were like mayors across counties in the same state. "I owe my wife, Tavis's sister, my support," he maintained.

"I see," he said, eyeing Cole with more awareness now. He nodded then, as if that was all—he'd learned what he'd set out to learn. "When this is done, when ye return to Torr Cinnteag, make plans to come round to Kingswood," he offered, rather as an afterthought, Cole guessed. "My wife will nae take kindly if I tell her I met...others of the same fate and did naught to get ye together."

"Are there...more?" Tank wondered.

"Aye, at least one other, another lass, come from... your time."

"No shit," Tank mused.

Reid Nicholson, who didn't look like he smiled too often, or at all, grinned. "Nae shite," he confirmed. He shook their hands again. "God speed, men," he offered before taking his leave.

As he melted back into the shadows, Cole felt a strange sense of connection—or at the very least, nearly a small sense of peace. For the first time since landing in this impossible situation, he realized they weren't entirely alone.

"I'll be a son of a bitch," Tank mused, staring into the darkness where Reid Nicholson had just disappeared. He glanced at Cole. "He was real, right? And that conversation? We didn't just imagine that, did we?"

"Nope," Cole replied thoughtfully.

"Holy shit," Tank exclaimed.

"Yep."

***

Tavis lingered in the shadows, his breath shallow as he strained to catch every fantastic word spoken in low murmurs between Reid Nicholson, Cole Carter, and Tank Morrison as they stood round a small wind-whipped fire. He hadn't intended to eavesdrop, but something about Reid Nicholson's tone had stopped him in his tracks. Now, he stood frozen, hidden in the creeping darkness behind a sturdy birch, his mind racing.

...my wife—she's nae from here either.

Have ye been here long? In this time?

The words hit Tavis like a blow to the chest. He gripped the rough bark of a tree for balance, his pulse thundering in his ears. He must have misheard. Surely, Reid—*Reid Nicholson*—had not just admitted to believing the same outrageous tale that Cole Carter and Tank Morrison had spun. Time travel? Tavis had dismissed it as lunacy, the ramblings of men driven mad by the strain of war or some strange ailment.

But Reid Nicholson wasn't mad. He was the steadiest man Tavis had ever known—grounded, deliberate, and sensible to a fault. If Reid said his wife was from another time... Tavis felt a tremor run through him.

He didn't want to believe it, couldn't quite bring himself to, and yet... there it was.

He pressed a hand to his forehead, as if trying to physically push away the revelation.

Ailsa. He'd allowed his sister to wed this man. Aye, he'd abhorred the idea, but had felt he'd little choice, knowing the damned kiss would indeed have ruined her. *Jesu.*

A new wave of unease crept over him. If Cole and Tank weren't lying, if their claims of coming from the future were true, then everything Tavis thought he understood about the world, about time itself, had just been upended.

He peered through the tangle of branches and brush, watching as Reid departed, leaving Cole and Tank by the fire. He, himself, shrank further into the shadows. He wasn't ready to confront them yet, wasn't sure he could trust himself to speak without betraying the storm raging in his brain.

Tavis let out a slow, shaky breath. He needed time to process this, to think. One thing was certain—he could no longer dismiss Cole as a madman. If Reid Nicholson believed him—not only believed but reinforced the fantastic tale by admitting his wife had suffered the same fate—then there was more to their story than Tavis had been willing to see.

***

Ailsa tightened her grip on the coarse cloth, her hands red and raw from scrubbing the stone floor of the keep's main hall. The air was sharp with the scent of lye soap, overcoming even the bone-deep chill of February. Beside her, Anwen knelt with equal determination, her sturdy arms moving with surprising efficiency as she wrung out a rag and attacked a stubborn stain. More shocking, this chore had been Anwen's idea—Anwen, who preferred quiet embroidery by the fire in Ailsa's solar, regularly suggested small tasks and even larger chores such as this, as if hard manual labor had suddenly become her life's mission.

"This would've been done twice over by the servants already," Ailsa muttered, brushing away a loose strand of hair that dangled in front of her eyes, glancing at the slow progress made.

"Aye," Anwen replied, not looking up, "but they're busy enough, what with keeping fires lit and the bread made, and three of them down with fevers."

Ailsa cast her a sideways glance. "I ken ye do this simply to keep me from worrying."

Anwen sat back on her heels, sighing wearily as she stared at Ailsa. "Is it working?" She asked simply, her dark eyes meeting Ailsa's with a clarity that spoke of her usual unflinching practicality. "Dinna tell me having the flesh worn from my fingers and my back broke by the end of every day isnae helping."

Ailsa grinned at her maid, a deep sense of affection engulfing her. She nodded. "Aye, it helps."

Both women returned to all-fours and continued their scouring.

It did help, but it could not completely keep her thoughts from turning—as they did nearly every hour of every day—to Cole. The silence between the women stretched, broken only by the rhythmic sound of cloth and occasionally a wire brush against stone.

The winter had not been kind to Torr Cinnteag. With Tavis and his men gone, the keep was quieter than ever, the usual hum of activity dampened by the harsh season and the strain of rationing. Supplies were thin, and though Ailsa knew they could manage until spring, the weight of survival bore down on her. It wasn't just the food—though every meal of porridge stretched thinner than the last—but the waiting.

Weeks had passed since they'd received Tavis's letter, reassuring them that the army was in good health and had yet to meet the enemy. Weeks of silence since then. No news of Cole. No way to know if he was safe, if he was hurt—or worse.

Ailsa sighed and sat back on her heels again, tossing the rag into the bucket of lukewarm water. She stared blindly up at the tall windows, where white winter light poured in.

Worry gnawed at her as she imagined Cole out on the battlefield, wondering if he had the instincts and resilience to handle the brutality of medieval warfare. She thought of the warriors she's known all her life—her brother, Dersey, any Sinclair, men who'd been molded by years of training and born into a society that prepared men for such harsh realities. For Tavis and men like him, war was second nature, not just a skill but a mindset that required shutting out fear and focusing on survival, even at the cost of compassion.

But Cole was different. Despite his physical prowess, by his own admission, he came from a time where violence was tempered by rules and largely left to controlled arenas, like sports, rather than mortal combat. She can't shake the fear that he might lack the cold determination needed in battle—a determination that came not just from strength but from a mental hardness, the ability to silence any empathy or hesitation and do what's necessary to survive.

While she prayed religiously and fervently for his return, Ailsa wrestled with the thought of what he might be or have become, forever changed or perhaps hardened beyond recognition, his spirit dulled by the violence and bloodshed that has scarred so many of her people.

"Ye ken it's impossible nae to worry," she ventured quietly to Anwen.

Anwen paused her scrubbing and turned to Ailsa, her expression softening. "About Cole."

Ailsa nodded and allowed her fears to spill out. "He's nae like Tavis, Anwen. He wasnae raised to this life, to war. He's strong, aye, but... I dinna ken if he has the kind of resolve it takes to survive out there." She gestured vaguely, as though the battlefield were just beyond the stone walls.

"Ye underestimate him," her maid testified without hesitation.

Ailsa's brow furrowed. "Do I?"

"More resolve than ye ken, is my guess," Anwen affirmed with a single, sharp nod.

Ailsa hoped so, but she simply wasn't sure, certainly not when it came to war. "I only long for him to be safe. I canna help but worry that the very traits I admire in him—his kindness, his warmth, his eagerness to earn a place among the Sinclairs—are what could make him vulnerable." She'd been impressed with his resilience, his ambition to prove himself, to conquer necessary skills, but for months she'd been anxious that same determination in him might bring him to his end.

She missed him terribly. There were days when the quiet loneliness that came with his absence was enough to hollow her out.

She ached to have his arms around her, the solid, reassuring strength of him pressing against her as if to ward off all these hardships and fears. She longed for the way his hands would cradle her face as though she were the most precious thing in his world. And she yearned for his laughter—the soft, unguarded chuckle that escaped when she said something that amused him, or the deep, booming laugh when she surprised him with her wit. That laugh could chase away even the darkest of days. She yearned for one more of those sweet, crooked grins he reserved just for her—those ones filled with joy, promise, and something deeper that made her breath catch every time. She'd convinced herself they meant something more, that their marriage was indeed *real* to him, though he'd never spoken the words aloud. She clung to that hope, fragile as it was, like a lifeline in the storm of her worry.

But most of all, she missed the quiet moments between them, the times when words weren't needed. She longed for him to be beside her in their bed, the weight of his body against hers, the feel of his skin under her fingertips, and the steady rhythm of his breathing in the dark. It was in those moments, when the world fell away, that she'd felt most at peace but now felt most vulnerable and afraid.

Anwen's soft, knowing voice cut through her thoughts. "Ye love him."

Ailsa blinked, startled by the bluntness of the statement. But as the truth of it had been known to her for some time, she found she couldn't deny it. "I do," she whispered.

"And that," Anwen said with quiet confidence, "is why he'll come back. For ye."

Chapter Twenty-One

Cole Carter gripped the hilt of his sword, his knuckles white against the leather-bound steel. The pre-dawn air was crisp, biting against his cheeks, but the warmth of his chainmail and gambeson smothered him. Around him, men moved into position, silent shadows against the gray light.

They'd been briefed on the layout of the enemy's encampments and the decision to move now. The English force, far too large to settle in one area, had divided into three separate camps, a strategic necessity for both space and foraging. This division made it easier for the Scots to finally target smaller, isolated groups, rather than confronting the full might of Segrave's army at once. The camp they meant to surprise now was the furthest out, distanced from Segrave's other contingents. Though he understood the advantage this provided, the enormity of the task ahead still settled heavily on Cole. This was just one piece of the enemy, one camp of three, and they were vastly outnumbered overall.

They'd marched through the night to enact this surprise attack. From their position on the hill, the enemy's tents looked like small, pale dots against the frozen earth—and still too many for the heavily outnumbered Scots. Tavis and other lairds moved among their men, their voices low but steady as they gave orders. Cole stayed close to Tank, whose anxious humor kept them both from unraveling.

"Would've been nice if they'd invented guns *just a little* sooner?" Tank murmured, hefting his axe onto his shoulder.

Cole forced a grin, though dread weighed him down. "You'd still find a way to miss."

"Not with my M4 Carbine," Tank boasted. "And damn, what I wouldn't give for a grenade launcher."

Their quiet exchange was interrupted by Tavis's sharp whisper. "Eyes forward. It's time."

It's time meant another fifteen minutes, waiting, worrying.

Without the customary horn blast to signal the advance, as Cole had been told would normally be expected, the Scots surged silently down the hill, a unified force intent on delivering a surprise attack on the sleeping enemy.

As they gathered speed, the sound of thousands of horses barreling down could neither hidden nor mistaken, and soon, war cries sounded out, ripping through the quiet valley, rousing the sleeping camp to life. With Tavis having advised that neither Cole nor Tank were ready to fight atop horses, they ran among the foot soldiers. Cole's heart thundered in his chest, louder than the clash of steel that soon engulfed the camp, coming from the mounted cavalry forerunners.

Chaos erupted as the Scots descended upon the unsuspecting English soldiers.

Just as Cole reached the encampment, wondering if any Englishman would still be standing by the time he got there, if he'd need to fight at all, he came upon his first opponent, a man groggy and barely armored but still wielding a blade, which already dripped with blood, aiming it at Cole. They locked swords, the jarring force of the impact rattling through Cole's arms. The Englishman swung again, but instinct took over; Cole sidestepped and slashed downward. The strike connected.

For a moment, everything froze. The man crumpled to the ground, blood pooling beneath him. Cole stared, his mind blank with shock. He felt the sudden urge to vomit as he saw the man's life extinguished at his feet and his own sword now red with blood.

The moment shattered as another enemy lunged at him. There was no time to process the horror of what he'd done. Cole blocked the coming blow, barely raising his shield in time to deflect the blow aimed at his head, saved by his lacrosse-honed reflexes kicking in. The force of it drove him to one knee, but he twisted and lashed out with his sword, catching the man's leg. The enemy stumbled, and Cole surged up, grimacing as he delivered a clumsy but effective blow that ended the fight.

His heart pounded in his ears, and his breath came in ragged gasps.

Christ, it was madness. He'd just killed a man. And then another.

The battlefield was a frenzy of sound and fury. It was like nothing he'd ever experienced, yet he found himself having no choice but to adapt, his focus narrowing to the immediate threats around him.

Turning, Cole spotted an Englishman crouching over a Sinclair soldier who lay on his back. He was too late to save the young man—the enemy's thin, lethal blade had already been driven into the boy's chest, piercing his heart. A cold clarity overtook Cole as he watched the murder unfold. Without hesitation, he drove his own blade into the Englishman's back. The man lurched forward, impaling his weapon further before he collapsed heavily onto the lifeless body beneath him.

Cole's gaze fell on the fallen Sinclair soldier and his breath caught—Domhnall. *Shit.*

"On yer left!" someone shouted, spinning Cole around, just in time to ward off another menacing swing of a blade. Just barely though, the enemy's blade slicing shallowly across the side of his neck before Cole could respond, lifting his shield to push off the blow, keeping it from becoming fatal. Again, he swung out wildly, with more a mind toward defense, keeping himself alive. Like a lightbulb going off, he realized in an instant that trying not to die meant, as had been proven already, that he would and did have to strike out against the aggressor. He did so now, not having any use for parts of Dersey's teaching, how to aim for vulnerable places in the thicker English chainmail, since this guy wore no armor. His blow was easily thwarted and so was the next. And while Cole managed to block the strikes aimed at him, he realized this guy was not going down easy. Despite his best efforts, Cole felt himself beginning to falter, his opponent's proficiency with the sword becoming overwhelming. Desperation clawed at him. For a moment, doubt crept into his mind—he was no match for this man.

He thought of Ailsa, being told he'd been killed in battle, that he hadn't lasted long. With every strike and parry, he thought of never seeing her again, never knowing another kiss, thought of Tank's words, how they should fight for what was behind them. He felt a surge of purpose and his grip tightened on the sword. With a roar of determination, Cole forced the momentum in his favor, his want of a life with Ailsa greater than even wanting only to survive. His next strike was cunning and swift, coming on a backhand, catching the enemy off-guard.

With a final, decisive blow, Cole dropped the man, emerging victorious.

He paused to catch his breath.

Nearby, Tank was locked in his own fight, his massive frame working to his advantage as he deflected blows with sheer brute force. He carried no shield, but a sword in one hand and an axe in the other. He was bleeding from a cut on his forearm but showed no signs of slowing. Cole caught a glimpse of him swinging his axe in a wide arc, taking down an opponent with grim determination.

And on it went, Cole progressing, meeting one combatant after another.

Just as in fighting the big, raging fires, where smoke, heat, and noise flood his senses, the battlefield churned with a storm of sounds and sights. Steel clanged, warriors shouted, grunted, and roared, and the raw smell of blood and earth overwhelmed him, much like the smell of burning materials or the roar of flames. In lacrosse, he was used to moving quickly through a crowded, noisy field, where every second mattered, and any distraction could mean getting hit, losing the ball, or failing to make a play. Cole drew on this ability to focus amidst the deafening sounds and chaotic movements surrounding him. Though he was used to body checks, fast hits, and falls on the field, and he'd learned to take hits and keep moving, this was different—these strikes were lethal, and he worked harder to avoid them.

The fighting field shifted, men moving forward after each kill—*gaining ground*, Cole reasoned, assuming the term must have originated in war—which put Cole and Tank somewhere in the middle of the decimated English camp by the time it stopped, slowly becoming quieter, clangs and groans growing fewer and farther between.

In the eerie quiet that followed, Cole stood amidst the wreckage of a conflict barely begun, his breath ragged, chest heaving as the first light of dawn began to spill over the hill. The bodies of fallen men—both Scots and English—lay scattered like broken toys, their twisted forms half-hidden by the morning mist that curled like ghostly fingers along blood-soaked earth that glistened where it caught the dull light.

Though there hadn't really been any doubt of the outcome, that the Scots would prevail over the sleepy enemy camp, Cole felt no sense of victory, only gladness that he'd survived.

He did not have long to savor the fact that he still lived while the English force retreated in disarray. Within minutes, calls to regroup shouted all around the scattered battlefield.

Nearby, Tavis repeated the call.

"Regroup! Regroup!" he shouted as he rode through the Sinclairs on his massive warhorse. Red life dripped from his sword, one drop splattering against Cole's boot as Tavis passed.

"More coming!" Tavis continued to shout. "Come to avenge these dead men, they do!"

Cole watched nearby Sinclairs rearm themselves with weapons confiscated from dead men before he and Tank exchanged startled glances.

"I just killed a man," Cole breathed raggedly, still not having come to grips with it. "A lot of men," he bemoaned. "Jesus, the one wasn't more than—"

Tank grabbed him by the shirt front, his fist taking hold of tunic, mail, and gambeson. He drew Cole close to him.

"Yeah, me too. And we're gonna talk about it—we're gonna deal with that, but right now, we've got to fight, man. We gotta get through this. Keep going, man. Don't leave me."

Cole nodded, grim but resolute, though his arms felt like lead and his legs threatened to buckle. He tightened his grip on his sword and the handle of his shield, the leather warm, nearly comforting.

"Close in!" Tavis barked, bringing the Sinclairs around him.

Tavis didn't wait to be met but charged forward, taking the offensive, his men following, once again with robust war cries.

The second clash was fiercer. These English soldiers were fresh while the Scots were still breathless from the first skirmish, and the fighting grew more brutal. Cole took a hard blow to the shoulder, the impact knocking him to the ground. His opponent loomed over him, sword raised for a killing strike. Panic surged through Cole, but he rolled to the side, onto his back again, driving his sword upward into the man's side. The English soldier fell with a guttural cry, and Cole scrambled to his feet, gasping.

Alarmingly—impossibly—they were not done, even as more English bodies and blood littered the cold earth. They hadn't yet gained a decisive victory when a third division of the enemy arrived, likely from the furthest of the three English camps.

Though exhaustion weighed on every Scot, they fought on, desperation fueling their strength. *Do or die*, Cole thought. His movements became automatic, his mind focused solely on survival, which meant putting down as many of the enemy as he could. His body ached—his heart ached for what he was doing, for what he was part of—but he kept going, the roar of battle drowning out everything else.

Hours later, when the final English force was routed and the battlefield fell eerily silent once more, Cole stood amid the carnage, his chest heaving. Blood smeared his face and arms, his sword hung heavy in his hand. Blood oozed from a glancing blow he'd taken to his shin, and more flowed from what he hoped was only a superficial hole in his side. A moment later, the surviving Scots raised triumphant cries, but Cole felt no victory, only a hollow exhaustion.

Tank, who had embraced the idea of fighting from the beginning, his hulking frame a natural advantage on the battlefield, now stood frozen, his eyes wide as he scanned the aftermath. His fists, still clenched from the previous moments of combat, trembled ever so slightly, betraying the shock that rattled him. He was good—damn good—at this. His years in the Marines had honed his physical strength, his reactions, had prepared him better for war than Cole had been. But this was different. This wasn't structured training or even the sharp—distant—conflict of war zones he was familiar with. The look in his eyes, glassy and remote, told Cole everything he needed to know. The fight was over, but the reality was settling in—this wasn't a movie, not a dream, this was real life.

"Hey," Cole called his attention.

Slowly, Tank turned, giving himself a shake as if to dispel whatever gripped him right now.

"You good?" Cole asked.

Tank swallowed, dropping one arm until the head of the axe rested on the ground. "Yeah, I'm good."

Cole managed a weary smile, though the weight of what he'd done—and survived—pressed heavily on him as well. He turned to find Tavis, twenty yards away, already being tended by the Sinclair surgeon, who sliced the fabric of Tavis's breeches to assess the damage done to his bloody thigh. The laird grimaced and lifted his gaze from his wound. His blue eyes met Cole's. He wore the look of a man in desperate pain but clenched his teeth, making appoint to nod solemnly at Cole.

Respect, Cole assumed, or at the very least, reluctant admiration that Cole was still standing.

Cole returned the nod across the distance.

The battlefield stretched all around him, a grim tableau of bodies and broken weapons. Cole swallowed hard, forcing himself to look, to take it in. His nose wrinkled as heat gathered behind it. He swallowed thickly and his mouth twisted against the rising tide of emotions. Tears welled in his eyes.

This was war, something he'd never thought he'd know, not in his wildest dreams. Or nightmares.

And he had, somehow—by the grace of God, he assumed—survived it.

***

A shout from the battlements pierced the stillness of the late afternoon, a sharp cry that sent Ailsa bolting from the storeroom where she'd been sorting linens. Gathering her skirts in her fist, she dashed through the keep and out into the bailey, just in time to hear the order given for the gate to be opened.

A familiar figure on horseback, the Sinclair scout, a lad named Anndra, galloped toward the gate, his plaid flaring behind him in the brisk wind.

Ailsa's breath came fast, not from exertion but from the tightening knot of worry in her chest.

The scout pulled his horse to a halt just inside the gates, the animal's flanks heaving with exertion. Dirt streaked his face and clothes, and the grim set of his mouth made her stomach churn.

"Speak!" Ailsa demanded as she stepped forward, barely waiting for the gate to close behind him. Her hand clenched over her chest. "What news?"

"The laird comes, lass, along with the wounded of our force," confirmed Anndra. "Many stayed behind with the Nicholsons, under Fraser and Comyn's banner, but the wounded Sinclairs come home, lass, battered but victorious."

"And my husband?" She asked desperately, her voice edged with panic. "Cole? Is he—"

"Aye, lass," the scout said quickly, eager to appease her distress. "He comes as well, injured but nae gravely."

Relief struck as if she'd been wobbled by a fierce gust of wind, so sudden and forceful that Ailsa staggered. Her knees knocked, but she steadied herself, reaching out to the horse's shoulder to remain on her feet. The burn of tears stung her eyes, and she knew no shame when they fell.

"Thank ye," she whispered, swallowing the lump in her throat. "Praise God." A hand touched her arm. She turned to find Anwen there. Ailsa's lips quivered as she tried to smile.

Anwen, always practical, attempted to steer Ailsa toward the keep, her voice calm and grounding. "Come now, lass. *Wounded, but nae gravely*, he said. We've plenty to do before they arrive."

Ailsa nodded, brushing a stray lock of hair from her face. Though her heart raced with relief and hope, she forced herself into action.

Straightening, she squared her shoulders and walked with strength into the hall, giving orders to the milling servants, those who'd come to see who the gate had been opened for. "Margaret, send a lad to fetch the healer from the Todrick keep, and then summon Father Gilbert. We must ready the hall to receive the wounded. Mary, we'll need boiled water, linens, salves. Bearnas, fetch the small tools, the pliers and scalpels, the irons for heating. Anwen, we'll need needle and thread, plenty of it, and pallets and blankets—move quickly, all of ye!"

As the women and girls scattered, Ailsa moved to the hearth and crouched, feeding the low flames until they leapt higher, casting warm light over the long tables. She lit candles around the room, illuminating every shadowed corner. The faint scent of tallow mingled with the rich aroma of the crackling fire.

She busied her hands with tasks, but her mind wandered, unbidden, to Cole—wounded, on his way home. Relief mingled with trepidation. He was alive. That alone was an answered prayer.

By the time the sound of hoofbeats echoed through Torr Cinnteag, rhythmic and steady, the hall was prepared. The gates were flung wide once more, and Ailsa gathered her skirts, striding outside.

She stood at the courtyard's edge, her heart hammering as the first figures came into view. It was not the triumphant return of a victorious army but the weary march of wounded survivors. Two dozen men, bloodied and battered, rode at a slow pace, some leaning heavily against their saddles.

Her eyes scanned the group frantically, searching, happily taking note of her brother's presence before she noticed Cole, a few paces behind the laird, coming into view as they drew closer.

Both men rode their horses, both upright despite the visible strain it cost them. Tavis would never allow himself the indignity of a litter, and it seemed Cole shared the same stubborn pride.

But Cole looked... changed. His skin was pale, his face leaner than when he'd left, his shoulders weighed down by exhaustion. To Ailsa's mind, it seemed a miracle that he hadn't slid out of the saddle altogether. His usual fire—his energy—was dimmed. Her chest tightened painfully.

Still, as his gaze met hers, something flickered in his eyes. He straightened in the saddle with visible effort, a faint smile pulling at his lips. It was for her. She knew it. Just as she would not falter in front of him, he would not allow himself to look weak before her.

The moment their eyes met, the weight of her worry lifted just slightly. The battered soldiers who trailed him seemed to blur at the edges of her vision as she stepped forward, her focus narrowing to the man she loved.

"Welcome home," she whispered, the words catching in her throat, though she knew he couldn't hear her over the shuffle of hooves and murmurs around them.

She ducked sideways near the gate, allowing room for the horses to pass. She reached up her hand to Tavis as he entered the yard. Her brother clasped her hand briefly and met her teary gaze. "Home we are, Ailsa. For a spell at any rate."

"And blessed we are to have ye," she smiled with genuine affection at him.

When he released her hand, she angled between the slow-moving horses, going next directly to Cole. A larger cry of greater relief burst from her as she touched him for the first time in months, her hands latching on to his boots and his cold breeches. In the next moment, he'd slid from the saddle, and Ailsa was in his arms.

"Oh, Cole," she wept with joy into his shoulder. Though his embrace was not fierce, Ailsa reveled in it, lost herself in it.

"Ailsa," he breathed into her hair, kissing her temple. "Thank God."

She lifted her face and stood on her toes, raining kisses over his cheeks and his mouth, her hands holding his face.

She felt his weakness and somehow restrained herself from leaping all over him. "Come now, directly inside, out of this cold." She slid her arm around him and walked with him toward the door to the keep. "Everyone," she called, "inside."

It was then she noticed that Cole was limping, and that he was far weaker than she'd assumed. He winced with each step and at the same time Ailsa pulled back to scan her gaze over her, he put his hand to his side.

"It's minor, I'm sure," he said, "but it sure does hurt."

"Sweet Jesus," she whimpered, "and here I am, throwing myself at ye—"

"Ailsa, it's fine," he insisted, though his voice was more weary than firm. "I wanted you to throw yourself at me, so thank you for that."

A strangled laugh erupted, and she shook her head to clear it, and again, she steered him toward the keep.

As soon as they stepped inside, Ailsa turned to Cole, her hands going to his arm. "We'll go straight to our chamber."

Cole shook his head, the movement slow but resolute. "This'll be a hospital ward now?" He asked, glancing around the hall, where straw-stuffed pallets were laid out on all the trestle tables and along one wall, and half a dozen maids, and Anwen assisted the soldiers as they entered, directing them to lie down and await the healer, or Father Gilbert's attendance.

"Aye," said Ailsa. "But this is nae for ye, husband. Ye'll heal better in peace, away from all this. It is expected that ye and Tavis will take to your chambers to recover."

"That's not right, Ailsa," Cole objected weakly. "I need to be here, with them."

"Cole, it is nae—"

"Lass, he speaks true," a voice interrupted.

Ailsa turned, finding Father Gilbert had come.

He smiled warmly at Cole. "Welcome home, lad. God has blessed you."

"He has," Cole agreed.

The priest then addressed Ailsa. "His place is here, lass, beside the men with whom he fought."

Ailsa's throat tightened, her frustration warring with the truth in the priest's words. She looked up at Cole, at the exhaustion etched into his features, the pale cast of his skin, and the stubborn set of his jaw. She had some suspicion that he wouldn't yield, not on this.

"I only want what's best for ye," she said quietly, her voice thick with emotion.

"I'll be fine, Ailsa. I promise," Cole replied, his tone softening. He reached out, brushing his fingers lightly over hers. "But I need to be here."

Father Gilbert offered Ailsa a reassuring nod before gesturing toward an empty pallet nearby. "Come along, lad. Let's see what we're dealing with."

Cole moved carefully, each step measured, as he approached the makeshift bed. He began to climb onto the pallet but paused, his sharp gaze cutting to Father Gilbert. "Check on Davey and Somerled first," he said firmly. "They're in worse shape than I am. I can wait."

The priest nodded and turned toward the other injured men, leaving Ailsa to guide Cole as he eased onto the board. She fussed over him as he lay back, her fingers hovering nervously above him, reluctant to touch. Her eyes caught on the blood-stained linen wrapped around his neck, and her stomach churned.

"God's bones, Cole," she whispered, her voice trembling. "What happened—"

"It's just a scratch," he interjected quickly, offering a crooked grin. "I swear to you."

"But there's more," she guessed, her voice growing sharper with worry. Her hands fluttered helplessly over his chest as though afraid to uncover the full extent of his injuries.

"There is," he admitted, the grin strengthening slightly, "but nothing that can't wait."

His easy confidence eased some of her panic, but another thought struck her suddenly, making her breath catch. She raised a hand to her lips and frantically scanned the hall, her heart tightening. "Where is—" She stopped mid-sentence and turned to him, dread darkening her eyes. "Where is Tank?"

Cole's hand closed over hers, his grip warm and comforting. "He's fine," he said gently. "He remained with the larger army. Dersey's looking after him. He promised me he'd keep him alive. Tank's fine, Ailsa. I promise that too. Hardly a scratch on him."

Relief flooded her, overwhelming and unstoppable. Tears welled in her eyes and spilled over, though this time they came from joy. She dropped her face into her hand, trying to regain control, but Cole gave her hand a squeeze.

"God, I love you," he said, his voice soft but certain.

Ailsa froze, her hand falling from her face as she gaped at him, utterly speechless. Her cheeks flushed, tears streaked her face, and her jaw hung open as she stared at him in disbelief. "What?" she managed to whisper.

"I'm in love with you," he repeated, his smile growing into a full, dazzling grin that made her heart skip. "I should've told you sooner, but I realized it too late."

Her shoulders sagged, the tension leaving her body. "But I wanted to tell you the same thing," she said, her tone almost petulant in its frustration.

Cole's laugh, warm and rich, filled the air just as a familiar voice piped up behind her.

"Ye still can, ye ken. It's nae proprietary."

Ailsa whipped around to see Anwen standing nearby, her hands on her hips and a pointed look on her face.

Cole chuckled again, his gaze flicking to Ailsa with amusement. "She's going to be our children's nurse, is she?"

Ailsa, her cheeks still pink, managed a nod, her lips curling into a smile despite herself.

"God help us," Cole muttered, the affection in his voice unmistakable.

Ailsa laughed then, leaning down to kiss his forehead.

"Ailsa I know I once hinted that this marriage wasn't real," he said, frowning. "I was an ass, or at least unprepared for how important and critical it is—you are—to me." His blue eyes held her, promises glistening in their depths. "I'm so in love with you. Don't hold that against me, what I—"

Ailsa silenced him with a kiss. "I love you, Cole Carter," she whispered against his lips.

***

Ailsa paused outside the laird's chamber, one hand resting lightly on the wooden doorframe. She had intended to knock but hesitated, listening to the quiet within. It was rare for her brother to be still, but then his wound had made him so in the three days since he'd been home.

She tapped lightly and pushed the door open.

Inside, the chamber was warm, the fire that crackled in the hearth casting long shadows across the room. Tavis sat in a sturdy upholstered chair, his head leaning back against the high backrest, his face lined with weariness. His injured leg was propped up on a low stool, bandaged tightly, but he seemed otherwise unharmed.

"Ye look like a soul in need of cheering," Ailsa teased gently, her voice soft. She stepped inside and closed the door behind her.

Tavis grunted in response, his lips quirking into the ghost of a smile. "Then send me a buxom woman bearing a dram of guid whisky."

She rolled her eyes as she moved to the small table nearby, pouring a goblet of wine instead. "Ye are stuck with me, brother. And I can fill your ears with tales from below or I can sit quietly in your company, so that ye ken that I care."

He accepted the goblet but didn't drink, staring into the fire instead. "We lost guid men, Ailsa," he said quietly, his voice heavy. "Too many—and this was but a skirmish. Nae even the war. That'll come again, and soon, I fear. Scotland needs us, everyone blessed one of us."

She rested a hand on the arm of his chair, leaning closer. "And ye will heed the call, same as ye have, same as ye always do. Ye are a fine man, Tavis. A guid leader of men, of all Torr Cinnteag. Father and Mother would be proud."

Tavis gave a small nod but said nothing, his gaze fixed on the flickering flames. Silence stretched between them, but it wasn't uncomfortable. It was the silence of shared grief, shared reflection. Finally, he lifted his head and looked at her, his expression thoughtful.

"He's a guid man," he said at last.

Ailsa blinked, caught off guard. Her heart swelled with pride, knowing he was speaking of Cole, and she smiled softly. "He is," she agreed.

Tavis snorted, a wry smile tugging at his lips. "His fight needs work—*Jesu,* does his fight need work—but he's a guid man."

Ailsa laughed lightly, the sound breaking through the somber mood.

Her brother's expression grew serious again, his eyes narrowing as he studied her. "Do ye believe it, Ailsa? That he comes from some other century?"

She drew in a deep breath, considering her answer carefully. "It's nearly impossible to believe, is it nae? But... *he* believes it. And who am I to say what is possible or nae? I ken his heart, Tavis, and that is all that matters to me."

Tavis leaned back in his chair, nodding slowly, his gaze returning to the fire. "Trial by combat, he just survived," he murmured. "Made himself a Sinclair out there in the field."

Ailsa's chest swelled with warmth and pride. She bent down and kissed her brother's cheek, wrapping her arms around him in a rare embrace. He stiffened for a moment before relaxing, patting her arm awkwardly.

"All is well, brother," she said softly. "Torr Cinnteag is safe in your hands."

He didn't respond, but as she straightened and turned to leave, she thought she caught the faintest flicker of a contented smile on his lips.

Epilogue

The following winter
Torr Cinnteag

Winter draped Torr Cinnteag in a shroud of frost, though thankfully much less snow had fallen as of yet. Still, the sharp chill of the season brought with it a slower pace, one that allowed the people of the keep to savor the rare peace. Cole stood atop the battlements, the wind whipping at his Sinclair plaid, having come to appreciate the rhythm of medieval life—hard work rewarded with small but profound satisfactions. A wolf pelt was draped across his shoulders, the fur provided by a kill he'd made himself. He was no archer and likely never would be, but he'd mastered the skill enough to hunt and to be of some use—if every other assigned Sinclair archer was somehow unavailable. The sword at his side—custom-made at Tavis's request—bore the Sinclair crest, its hilt well-worn from months of combat, from which the Sinclairs had only just returned a few weeks ago. He appreciated greatly the medieval practice of laying low over the winter, war mostly set aside in favor of warm beds, daily hot meals, and a few months to catch your breath. He'd learned well after the fact that his first battle last year, near some little burgh called Roslin, had been a rarity, fought in the midst of winter.

The echoes of men laughing and shouting drew his attention to the distant training field, where lacrosse had quickly become a favorite pastime. It had started as a way for him to share a piece of his former life with the men, but it had become much more. To his amazement, even Tavis had joined in, though with the gruff insistence that it was for the sake of conditioning his men. Cole smirked, squinting across the distance, watching now as the laird deftly intercepted a pass and slung the ball into the makeshift net. He high-fived Tank, another modern practice Tank had introduced to the Sinclairs and medieval Scotland, and which only yesterday Cole had caught two maids doing.

Cole and Tavis had come a long way. The laird had become more than a brother-in-law; he was a comrade, an ally, and perhaps even a friend. Cole thought that maybe his brave—if clumsy—fighting in that battle at Roslin had been what turned around Tavis's suspicions about him. Shortly after their return to Torr Cinnteag last winter, both injured but recovered pretty quickly, Tavis had summoned Cole to his study, where he'd proceeded to question him extensively about the still incomprehensible phenomena of time-travel. He'd wanted to know all about modern life, which had stretched their conversation into hours. But never on that day or since, had he expressed any more disbelief. For whatever reason, Tavis had become open to the possibility, hadn't again insisted that Cole was simply mad. It was revisited often, with Tank being included as well. They'd taken to drawing pictures for the laird. Neither one being an artist of any competence, Cole and Tank's charcoal sketches of airplanes, modern homes, thruway systems, and armored tanks among other things looked more like a collection of kid's scribblings. Tavis had saved them all, at which Cole raised a brow.

"Some archaeologist is going to find those one day," Cole had suggested wryly, "and the entire working theory of when things were invented will be thrown into turmoil."

One day, Tavis had point-blank asked Cole, "But if given the chance, to stay here or to return to your time, which would ye choose?"

"I want to be here," Cole had answered without hesitation. This was his life now, happier and far more fulfilling than he ever could have imagined. He struggled enough leaving Torr Cinteag to go to war, leaving Ailsa, but fought like hell each time to return to her. He didn't want to die, and he didn't want to imagine a life without her.

Rosie crossed his mind often. He worried for her, picturing her easy smile dimmed by his absence. He hoped she'd found comfort among her friends and his, and that the firehouse family had embraced her in his absence. Sometimes he'd send silent thoughts into the void, hoping they'd find her. If entire people could cross centuries, maybe thoughts could bridge that distance too. *I'm all right, Rosie. Be happy as I am.*

Cole and Tank had made the decision together, a private agreement decided after long and heated debates, that they would not reveal what they knew about the immediate future of Scotland. The stakes were simply too high. Not the outcome of the war, not the fates of its great leaders—none of it. Tank had argued passionately for intervention, his voice thick with frustration.

"We could save lives now," Tank insisted, pacing in front of the hearth. "Good lives, important lives. You can't tell me we should just sit back and let it happen."

Cole, seated with one arm draped over the chair in Ailsa's solar, watched Tank's fervor with a quiet resolve. "And what if saving one life today means losing a hundred tomorrow?" he replied. "Christ, Tank, we've got no business playing God with history."

Tank stopped mid-step and fixed Cole with a sharp look. "That's bullshit, Cole. If we have this knowledge, we've got a duty—"

"Our duty," Cole interrupted firmly, "is to Torr Cinnteag. To Ailsa, Tavis, and the people here. The future—this immediate future—has to play out as it's meant to. If we start tampering with what we know, there's no telling what we could ruin."

Tank had finally relented, muttering, "Fine. But I'm writing stuff down. Not about this war, maybe, but about other things—Hitler, Stalin, all the people who'll cause hell later. I'll write a book, something someone could find in the future."

Cole arched an eyebrow. "You're going to write a book about the 20th century in medieval Scotland? That'll go over well."

Tank's expression shifted into a sly grin. "Maybe they'll think I'm a prophet."

The gleam of satisfaction in his eyes made Cole laugh in spite of himself. "Tank the Prophet. God help us all."

As the day waned, Cole retreated to the chamber he shared with Ailsa. The hearth crackled warmly, its glow casting golden light over the chamber. She was already in bed, her hair spread like silk over the pillows. His heart clenched at the sight of her, more beautiful every day, more loved.

He undressed quickly and slid beneath the covers, resting his hand gently on her rounded belly, awed as always by the life growing within her. She stirred, her blue eyes fluttering open to meet his.

"Remember that one time? When I told you that I couldn't promise you anything?" He whispered. "Nothing lasting?"

It wasn't the first time he'd brought it up.

Ailsa grinned, recalling several previous conversations that had begun the same way. "Aye, I do recall," she said, remembering her previous response as well.

"I've changed my mind," he continued, as he had on more than one occasion.

"Have ye now?" She feigned surprise but kept to the script they'd made up months ago.

"Yeah, I think I like it here," he said. "In fact, I'm sure I'm in love with this time period."

"Only the time period?" She wondered.

"Well not only the time period," he admitted, rising above her on his elbows. "I love Torr Cinnteag. I love most of its people. I do not love war, but I do love those pork pies Cook makes."

"Hm," she murmured, her eyes gleaming, crinkled at the corner with her smile. "Ye are a lucky man. So much love."

"I know, right?" He kissed her nose. "Oh, also, there's this woman...." He kissed her lips.

"Mm."

"I really love her."

"She's a verra lucky woman."

Cole went still and met her gaze. "I'm the lucky one." He went off-script then. "I love you, Ailsa. Wherever—and whenever—I am, I will love you."

She laid her palm against his cheek, warm and steady. "Ditto," she whispered, using a phrase he'd taught her, her lips curving in a smile.

He bent his head and captured her lips in a slow and satisfying kiss.

Their child stirred against his hip, a gentle reminder of the future they were building together. Whatever trials lay ahead, Cole knew one thing with absolute certainty: this was his place, his time, and his love.

***

The fluorescent lights of the grocery store buzzed faintly, but Rosie paid them no mind. She pushed her cart down the aisle mechanically, her thoughts far away. She thought she might or should go back to Scotland again. Her daily phone calls to the Scottish investigator in charge of Cole and Tank's disappearance seemed to yield less results than when she was standing directly in front of him or sitting across from him with his desk between them. She'd been three times to Scotland in the last year, had pushed Detective Sargeant Butler to search more, to question more—to do more to find Cole. Not to say the man and his team weren't doing anything at all, but since Cole and Tank hadn't been found, clearly enough wasn't being done. Rosie refused to believe that Cole and Tank had simply vanished off the face of the earth. He was there, in Scotland, somewhere—she knew he was. They just needed to find him.

Life without Cole had become a hollow routine, her once-bright spirit dimmed by the weight of his absence. Sure, she had plenty of friends and commitments to keep her busy, and her church and those sweet guys at the firehouse had helped her to keep her sanity—and to keep fighting to find Cole—but she lived with constant, gnawing worry over Cole. Not a day went by that she didn't think of him, worrying about his fate.

She was reaching for a box of cereal when it hit her—a sudden, inexplicable warmth that radiated from her chest outward. It stopped her in her tracks, her arm arrested in motion. It wasn't a memory or a ghostly echo; it was *him.* She knew it as surely as she knew her own name. *Cole is at peace.*

Tears sprang to her eyes, not of sorrow but of release.

Cole?

She jerked her hand back and looked around. The cereal aisle was empty except for her.

Had she just imagined that? That sweeping warmth that had so profoundly filled her with peace.

She stood still again, waiting for it to pass.

But it did not.

I'm all right, Rosie.

Dropping her face to her chest, Rosie let the tears fall. They heated her nose and cheeks and shook her shoulders, the weight of her relief so intense.

I'm all right, Rosie.

She felt it again. Again and again until she knew—believed without question—that Cole was reaching out to her.

It was a long time until she lifted her face and drew a deep, soothing breath.

She didn't notice the woman approaching her until she spoke.

"Ma'am, are you all right?" Asked a young woman, pushing her grocery cart, an infant strapped to her chest.

Rosie swiped at her tears, nodding at the same time. "Yes, thank you. I'm fine."

She looked at the woman, who then opened her mouth as if she recognized her.

"You're Rosie, aren't you? From the news?" The woman's tone was hesitant, kind. "I always thought you were so brave, speaking for your nephew like that, keeping it alive, the search. I'm so sorry for your loss."

Rosie smiled, the warmth of Cole's presence still holding her. "Thank you," she said, her voice steady, serene even as happy tears continued to fall. "But he's not lost. He's at peace."

The woman nodded, awkward now, probably wondering if Rosie had finally lost her mind, and then gave a wobbly smile before she moved away.

Rosie stood in the aisle, her heart lighter than it had been in a year. For the first time since Cole's disappearance, she allowed herself to smile—a real, genuine smile. Wherever he was, he was happy. She just knew it.

"Good for you, Cole," she said as she began to push her cart again.

The End

Other Books by Rebecca Ruger

Highlander: The Legends

The Beast of Lismore Abbey
The Lion of Blacklaw Tower
The Scoundrel of Beauly Glen
The Wolf of Carnoch Cross
The Blackguard of Windless Woods
The Devil of Helburn by the Sea
The Rebel of Lochaber Forest
The Avenger of Castle Wick
The Dragon of Lochlan Hall

Heart of a Highlander Series

Heart of Shadows
Heart of Stone
Heart of Fire
Heart of Iron
Heart of Winter
Heart of Ice

Far From Home: A Scottish Time-Travel Romance

And Be My Love
Eternal Summer
Crazy In Love
Beyond Dreams

Only The Brave
When & Where
Beloved Enemy
Winter Longing
Stand in the Fire
Here in Your Arms

The Highlander Heroes Series
The Touch of Her Hand
The Memory of Her Kiss
The Shadow of Her Smile
The Depths of Her Soul
The Truth of Her Heart
The Love of Her Life

Sign-Up for My Newsletter and hear about all the upcoming books.
Stay Up To Date!
www.rebeccaruger.com

Printed in Great Britain
by Amazon